HIGHLAND PASSION

Feeling Gytha tremble as he traced her collarbone with kisses, Thayer said, "I will be gentle with you. Trust me, Gytha."

"I do," she whispered, her voice as husky as his.

Glancing up at her, he could read no guile in her look. "Then why do you tremble with fear, little one?"

"'Tis not fear." It was hard to speak when he still fondled her breasts, his touch stealing all clear thought from her mind. "I am not really sure what ails me."

"What do you feel, sweeting?" He slowly moved his hand over her abdomen feeling her shudder faintly beneath his touch.

"Afire. 'Tis as if my blood runs hot. That does afright me some."

Choked with elation that his touch could affect her so, he found it hard to speak, and his voice became little more than a raspy whisper. "There is naught to fear in that."

Beauty and the Beast

Hannah Howell

LEISURE BOOKS **NEW YORK CITY**

A LEISURE BOOK®

September 1992

Published by

Dorchester Publishing Co., Inc.
276 Fifth Avenue
New York, NY 10001

The name "Leisure Books" and the stylized "L" with design are
trademarks of Dorchester Publishing Co., Inc.

Printed in the United States of America.

Chapter One

England, 1365.

"Dead?"

"Quite dead."

"But how?"

"Fell off his mount. Snapped his neck."

Gytha blinked, then stared closely at her father. She saw no sign of lying in his round, plain face, although he did look strangely uncomfortable. She waited to feel grief for the loss of her betrothed, the handsome and gallant baron, William Saitun. A pang came and went. She had seen little of him, after all. What puzzled her now was why the wedding preparations continued. If William was dead, then surely the wedding could not go on? A moment later her mother revealed that her thoughts had followed the same path.

"But what of the wedding? The feast is being prepared even now." Bertha's ever-rounding figure trembled as she grew increasingly upset. "The guests are arriving. Should I turn them away?"

"No need to do that, Bertha, loving."

"Papa, I cannot marry a dead man."

"Of course you cannot, dearling." John Raouille briefly covered his daughter's delicate hand with his thick, calloused one.

"Then the preparations must be halted." Gytha frowned in confusion when her father still did nothing.

"Now, my sweet child, the agreement made with my good friend, Baron Saitun, God bless his soul, was that you would marry the heir to Saitun Manor."

"And that was William."

"True, true, but there are other heirs. The one following William was Thayer."

"Then, are you saying I am now to marry Thayer?" She was not sure she understood the arrangement her father spoke of.

"Alas, nay. He died in France."

Either she was cursed or the Saituns were an ill-fated lot, she mused. "Am I to be wed or not, Papa?"

"You are. The third heir is Robert. He is the one you will wed on the morrow. I believe you have met the fellow."

Her memory was something many admired

her for. It was quick and very exact, even the smallest details clear and precise. She put it to good use now, but what was called forth left her feeling little joy. If she had not been gifted with such an acute memory, she knew Robert Saitun would not have lingered in her mind. He had been William's shadow and had spent most of his time trying to avoid being kicked or cuffed by William or his own uncle, a rather unpleasant man who had exerted complete control over Robert.

"Aye, I did. Is it not—well, disrespectful to William to wed another man so soon?"

"Er—William died a while back. He was far afield, so you could not be called to his side."

Or told, she mused. "As was the second heir? This Thayer I have never met?"

"I told you, daughter, he died in France. I do not mean to be unkind, but mayhaps 'tis just as well. He was not the man for you, Gytha."

Removing the woman's hand from where it rested in the mat of flame red curls adorning his broad chest, Thayer Saitun sat up. "Morning is here, woman. Time for you to be on your way."

Taking his purse out from beneath his pillow, he extracted a few coins and tossed them at her. She caught them with ease. His smile was tainted with cynicism as he watched her weigh them in her hand before smiling at him.

It had ever been so. He was weighted with honor, his name respected—even feared—by men, but women needed to see the glint of his coin before they showed any interest.

Flopping onto his back and crossing his arms beneath his head, he idly watched her dress. He grew weary of nameless whores, but at least there was an honesty about them, and they could not afford to show any displeasure with his size, his plain looks, or—he grimaced as he glanced down at himself—his redness. While his skin had none of the ruddy hue that often cursed redheads, he knew few people really noticed that. Flame-red hair and freckles too often hid the color of his skin. Even his large size worked against him, for it simply provided a greater area for the wretched flame color to display itself. The sound of the door opening pulled him from his self-denigration.

"Do you mean to spend the day abed?" drawled Roger, his right-hand man, as he let Thayer's night's entertainment slip out of the room before shutting the door.

"Nay." Thayer sprang to his feet, then moved to wash up. "A revel awaits us."

Roger settled his slender frame on the rumpled bed. "Your position as heir will soon end."

"Aye. William will soon breed an heir. I have no doubt of that. He has proven his skill at that many times over."

"You sound little concerned that you will remain a landless knight or become some lordling's castellean."

"It troubles me little. Only a fool would think a man like William would never wed or sire an heir. Far better that the chore falls to him than to me. 'Tis a duty I would be hard set to fulfill."

"You belittle your worth. I have never seen you lack for a wench to warm your bed."

"They check the value of my coin first."

Thayer ignored Roger's cluck of disapproval over the bitterness he had been unable to fully hide. Roger did not see him as a woman did. He saw a valued fighting companion, a friend and someone who was like a brother to him. Roger found nothing wrong with the wealth of flame-red hair. In a man's eyes, the mat on his broad chest, the healthy tangle of curls around his loins, and the furring on his strong forearms and long, muscular legs were merely signs of manliness. Men also saw his large, robust frame as something to envy. Many a man would like to stand head and shoulders over other men. They did not understand that dwarfing many a pretty young lady inspired more fear than admiration.

Neither would Roger see what was wrong with his face, a visage as strongly hewn as his body. Years of living by the sword had begun to turn Thayer's lack of beauty towards ugliness. When Roger saw how several breakings had left his strongly angled nose faintly crooked, the man simply recalled the battles that had caused it. Thayer knew that possessing all his own teeth was something to take

11

pride in, yet that pride was dimmed by the knowledge that his thin-lipped mouth was beginning to show scarring from all the times it had been split. Idly he fingered the ragged scar that marred his high-boned cheek. Here too Roger would see little fault, recalling only the glorious battle that had caused it.

He tried to put some order into his hair, which had the unfortunate tendency to curl. Even if Roger was right—that he could capture a woman's heart—it did not matter. He had no place to house it. If he found love, he would only see the woman given over to another. Few men wanted to give their daughters to a landless knight.

"Come, Roger, help me truss my points. We must soon be away. I am eager to see the one William calls an angel."

Gytha slammed the door behind her as she strode into her room. Flinging herself upon her bed, she began to curse, colorfully and continuously. Her full red mouth, so often praised by her suitors, spat out every foul oath she knew. When she ran out of ones she knew she made up new ones. As always when she indulged in such a venting of her temper, she finally mouthed one that struck her as funny. Chuckling softly, she watched her door open and grinned when her cousin Margaret cautiously peeked inside.

"Are you done?" Margaret slowly entered the room, easing the door shut behind her.

"Aye. I just put a curse on every man in the kingdom. Then I thought on what could happen if it took hold." She giggled again.

"There are times when I feel you ought to be doing a great penance." Smiling faintly, Margaret placed an elaborately embroidered gown on the bed. "Your bride's dress. 'Tis finally done. Let us see how it fits."

Sitting up, Gytha gently touched the gown, recognizing and appreciating its beauty but not very pleased to see it. "You must be the best seamstress in the land. You could be dressmaker to the queen." She smiled faintly when her cousin's pretty face turned pink.

In fact, she mused, Margaret was not only pretty, with her wide hazel eyes and light brown hair, but nearly eighteen. She too ought to be wed. While it was true that Margaret could not reach too high, it did not mean the girl lacked all prospects. Her uncle had endowed Margaret, his only bastard child, with an admirable sum as a dowry. Perhaps, Gytha thought, there would be a suitable man for Margaret amongst her husband's entourage. She would have to look into the matter.

"Nay, Gytha, you will cease making plans for me. Right now."

Attempting to look innocent and knowing she failed, Gytha murmured, "I would never be so impertinent."

"Humph. Cursing and now lying. Your sins grow. Shall we try on this gown?"

"I suppose we must. The wedding is tomorrow, after all." Gytha did not move but continued to stare blindly at the gown.

Sighing, Margaret collected a hairbrush, sat behind her cousin, and began to brush out Gytha's thick, honey-gold hair. Even pouting, Gytha was beautiful, yet the girl was never vain. Margaret felt her cousin deserved better. In truth, she really believed that a girl like Gytha should be allowed to choose her own mate, to marry for love.

Gytha's beauty ran to her soul. While her wide, brilliantly blue eyes, perfection of face, and lithe yet sensuous figure could leave men gaping, Gytha's loving spirit softened even the most cynical. Along with her stunningly handsome brothers, Gytha saw her beauty as a gift from God, something to be briefly appreciated then set aside as something of no great importance. Quite often, after escaping the arduous pursuit of some lovestruck swain, Gytha saw her looks as more a curse than a blessing. What Gytha needed was a man who could see beyond her lovely face to the real treasure. Margaret felt certain Robert Saitun was not that man.

Shaking free of her sulk, Gytha murmured, "Somehow it seems wrong to wed William's heir so speedily."

"I am not sure 'tis so speedily. I think William died some time past. Even so, to halt all the preparations now would cripple your father's purse." Helping Gytha stand to remove her gown, Margaret asked, "Do you know Robert at all?"

"Nay. Why do you think I spent so long here cursing all and sundry? I am unprepared for this."

"Many would have said Lord William needed little preparing for."

"True, he was fair to look upon, strong and steeped in honor. Howbeit, marriage is a large step. Some time to think on it is best. In but a day's time, I must wed a man I know not at all. I know nothing of Robert's character."

"You were lucky to know William as well as you did. Few women have such an advantage."

"True enough, but it seems a monstrous way in which to conduct the business. A woman is kept sheltered and pure all her growing years. One day she is set before a man, marched up before a priest, and told, 'Off you go to do all we have told you naught of with this stranger who is now your husband, your lord and master.' I fear I shall do something very silly due to nerves. Mayhap I shall even swoon."

A soft laugh escaped Margaret. "You never swoon. I daresay you never will."

"Pity. It would relieve me of a great deal of awkwardness."

"Surely Aunt Bertha spoke to you. You must know what to expect."

"Aye—I think. She did talk to me. Howbeit, t'was monstrous difficult to understand her. All those blushes, hesitations, and flutterings."

15

Again Margaret laughed. "I can just see it. Poor Aunt Bertha."

"Poor me. Still, the matter that most occupies my mind is that I must disrobe. I cannot like the sound of that."

Concentrating on doing up the laces on Gytha's wedding dress, Margaret hid a grimace. She did not like the sound of it either. Gytha's figure was of a style to set a man's lusts raging. Although Gytha was apparently unaware of it, that was one of the reasons she had been so fiercely sheltered. Somehow Gytha managed to be lithe and slender as well as voluptuous and sensual. More times than she cared to count, Margaret had seen a man's eyes grow hot at the mere sight of her cousin. So too had there been incidents, despite careful watching, when Gytha had had to make a hasty retreat to preserve her virtue. Placing a naked Gytha before any man was highly dangerous, let alone before one who knew he had all right to her. Poor Gytha could find her wedding night a violent and painful experience.

"He must disrobe as well," Margaret finally muttered. "There." She stepped back from Gytha. "Ah, you will make such a lovely bride."

" 'Tis a lovely dress." Gytha turned around slowly before the mirror. "It needs no adjusting. The girdle sits perfectly. Have you ever seen Sir Robert?" She smiled a little at Margaret's startled look, knowing she had changed subject without warning, a habit she found hard to break.

"Aye, and so have you. The young man acting as squire to Lord William on his last visit?"

"Aye, I but sought your opinion."

"Well, he is slim and fair. Quiet."

"Mmmm. Very. As unobtrusive as possible. I cannot help but wonder when he was knighted and why. I cannot say he gives much honor to the title now. Most of his time was spent being cuffed by William or by his own uncle or desperately trying to avoid both." She sighed. "Ah, well. At least I need not fear he will be a brute."

"There is a lot to be said in favor of that." Margaret helped Gytha get out of the gown.

"Mayhap without his cousin or uncle about he will show a better side to his character."

"There is a very good chance he will."

It was not long after Robert arrived that Gytha began to think there was no chance at all. Robert's uncle, Charles Pickney, stayed close by at all times. All she did discover was that she could not like Charles Pickney, not in the slightest, no matter how hard she tried. As soon as she had the opportunity she slipped free of her husband-to-be and his shadow to seek out Margaret, dragging her cousin off in search of flowers.

The day was sunny and warm, the fields beyond the manor covered with blooms. Gytha's mood was swiftly improved. She loved the springtime, loved its promise of life and bounty. Laughing and dashing about with Margaret helped her forget her worries. In no time at all, she looked more like a rough, un-mannered girl than a lady on the eve of her marriage, but she did not care. For just a little while she intended to forget Robert, his uncle, and the wedding.

Thayer spotted the two maids romping in the field and reined in a few yards away from them. He quickly signaled his men to do the same, knowing that the more impulsive of them would charge towards the maids like bucks in rutting season if he let them. Despite the girl's tossled state, he knew they approached no peasant wenches. The gowns were too fine. Not wishing to frighten the maids, he started towards them carefully, his men following suit. Their approach was soon spotted. As he reined in near them, Thayer felt himself struck hard by the beauty of the little blond.

"Hallo, mistress." The smile she gave him took his breath away. "Do you gather these pretties for the bride?"

"Aye. Do you ride to the wedding, sir?" Gytha found it easy to smile at the big red man, even though he towered above her as he sat atop his massive black destrier.

"That we do. 'Tis my cousin who weds on the morrow."

Openly flirting with the two maids, Roger asked, "Does it promise to be a revel worth the journey?"

"It most assuredly does, sir." Gytha held sway over the conversation, for Margaret was apparantly struck dumb. "The wine and ale promise to flow like a flood-swollen river. The food is plentiful and unsurpassed in flavor. There are minstrels who play as sweet as any lark might sing." She could not fully restrain a laugh over her elaborations.

" 'Tis fitting, as my cousin claims he weds the angel of the west." Thayer caught his breath over her sweet, open laugh.

"An angel is it?" Gytha glanced at Margaret, who had emerged from her stupor enough to grin. "I could not really say." She gasped Margaret by the hand. "We will see you at the manor," she called as she raced off, towing a laughing Margaret after her.

" 'Tis a shame we cannot follow their path." Roger glanced at Thayer. "This fête becomes more promising by the moment."

Thayer felt the heavy weight of depression settle over him. Every part of him had been drawn to the delicate maid with the thick hair the color of sunlight. Her response to him had been more than he had gained from a gently bred maid in many a year. He knew she would go no further, however. Not with him. He began to dread the festivities ahead. It was a struggle, but he conquered the sudden urge to bolt. William was his favorite amongst what few kin he had, and he would not allow a tiny maid with wide blue eyes to keep him from attending William's wedding.

"The little blond had many a smile for you," Roger said as they started on their way again.

"She was polite, nothing more." He urged

his mount ahead of Roger's, curtly ending the conversation.

Roger inwardly cursed. Thayer had great confidence in his wit and skill, almost to the point of arrogance. When it came to women, however, Thayer had no confidence at all. The blame for that Roger set squarely at the feet of Lady Elizabeth Sevielliers. One could argue that Thayer had been a fool to love such a woman. However, the damage that witch had done was indisputable. Even if he could get Thayer to believe the little blond had shown an interest, it would only make the man take to his heels. Thayer was the scourge of any battlefield, but a pretty, well-born maid put the fear of God into the man. Elizabeth had been a pretty, well-born maid.

Deciding not to waste his breath arguing, Roger muttered, "Aye, mayhap. Let's go and see William's angel. 'Tis clear that a fair crop grows in this land."

Gytha halted her mad dash within sight of her home. It took her and Margaret a moment or two to catch their breath. In silent accord they struggled to put some order into their tossled appearance. Gytha noted idly that Margaret needed far less tidying up than she did, and by the time she had cleaned herself up as much as she could, she was able to watch the arrival of the knights they had briefly met.

"He looks nothing like William or Robert." Gytha sighed as she watched the large redhead dismount with an easy grace. "Such lovely eyes."

"I know." Margaret sighed as she watched the knight who rode beside the big red-headed man. "Like grass, fresh and newly freed of the earth."

Frowning at her cousin, Gytha muttered, "Green? How could you think his eyes green?" As she realized whom Margaret meant, her eyes widened and she started to giggle. "Oh ho! So that is where your gaze rested."

"Hush. They could hear us. Who had lovely eyes then?"

"Why, the large red man of course."

"The large red man? You jest."

Gytha felt a real need to defend the man against Margaret's open-mouthed astonishment, yet she was not sure why. "Nay. He had lovely eyes. A beautiful color. Such a soft, sweet brown."

"Sweet? You cannot call a color sweet."

Margaret felt sunk in confusion touched with not just a little amazement. Some of the fairest knights in the land had wooed Gytha but never moved her. One brief meeting with a large, very red, and somewhat battered knight, and the girl raved about the man's eyes.

"I am not quite sure, really," Gytha answered. "Still, sweet is the word that comes to mind." With a sigh Gytha started towards the rear of the manor. "Ah, well, back to Robert."

Quickly following her cousin, Margaret

asked, "What did you think of the young knight with the green eyes then?"

It took Gytha a moment to recall the man Margaret referred to. "He was well-favored."

The words echoed in Margaret's mind again and again as she had what she decided was a revelation. Since she and Gytha had to creep through the back ways of the manor to get to their chambers unseen, her startled silence went unnoticed, much to her relief. When Gytha said a man was well-favored, she was merely being polite. It meant nothing. To pick out a feature and praise it was Gytha's true form of accolade. After being surrounded by some of the fairest men in England, Gytha chose to give that rare accolade to a large red-headed man with a battle-hardened face. As they stepped into Gytha's room and Margaret shut the door, she stared at her lovely cousin in bemusement.

"Ah," Gytha sat on her bed, "safe and—best of all—unseen. Mama would be upset if I were caught out in this state."

"We are not in too disreputable a state."

"I have mud upon the hem of my gown."

"Oh. Aye, that would set aunt in a twirl. What do we do with the flowers?" Margaret set her flowers next to Gytha's on the bed. "A circlet for our hair?"

"What a good idea. I will wear mine tonight while they are still fresh and sweet. If there are any left, we can have the maid set them in the bridal chamber. They will sweeten the air in there very nicely." Gytha began to chose the flowers she wanted.

Sitting down on the bed and doing likewise, Margaret asked, "What do you like about that huge red knight?"

"What does it matter? I marry Robert on the morrow." Gytha was unable to keep her sudden sadness from tainting her voice.

"It puzzles me, if you must know. You have had many fair young men lay their hearts at your feet...."

"I doubt they truly did, although they would beleaguer me with bad poetry."

"Let us say they flirted with you then. All you ever said about them, if you said anything at all, was that they were well-favored. Then, up rides a man who is not well-favored at all. In truth, next to William that red knight is near to ugly."

"Depending on when poor William died, he could be beautiful next to him by now."

"Gytha." Margaret could not fully suppress her amusement nor the twinge of annoyance over Gytha's evasive replies.

"Have you never looked at someone and felt like smiling for what seems to be little or no reason?"

"Aye, babes mostly. There is something about a babe that brings out a happy tenderness in me."

"That is how I felt when I looked upon that man. I wanted to take care of him, to make him smile."

"Men take care of women," Margaret mumbled, feeling somewhat stunned. "Women cannot take care of men."

"Oh, aye—men fight, protect, lead, and such. I know that. I once asked Papa if women were truly put upon this earth only to bear children. He said nay. He said we were made to keep men from forgetting the soft and pretty things in life, to keep alive the gentler emotions. He told me we were here to ease a man's way, to comfort him and give him refuge from the world when it grows too harsh to bear."

"And all that is what you wished to do for that man?"

"Aye. I wanted to wipe the lines of care from his face, to make that rich voice tumble out in a laugh." She sighed. "But 'tis not my place. I wed Robert in less than a day's time."

"You feel none of those things for him?"

"I fear not. Mayhap later. Now I mostly wish to cuff him as he allows so many others to do."

"That does not bode well for your marriage."

"Well, a marriage is often what you make of it." Gytha moved to view her crown of flowers in the mirror. "There, what do you think of it?"

Accepting the change of subject as she moved to answer the rap at the door and let the maid in, Margaret nodded. "Very lovely. Do you wear it this eve?"

"Aye. Ah, Edna." She smiled at the young, pretty maid. "Have you gained any news of our latest guests?"

"That I have, mistress. The Red Devil they call that big one. The Red Devil and his band of bastards."

Gytha frowned slightly. "That seems a rather cruel appelation."

" 'Tis true though. More true than not, leastwise. The man is indeed very red and 'tis said he is the very devil upon the battlefield. Most of his men are bastards, the natural sons of highborn men. They were given skill and knowledge, but no coin or land. So, they ride with the Red Devil and sell their swords with his. Why, 'tis said the very sight of them is enough to end a battle. The enemy flees before him or surrenders at once."

"A pleasant thought, but I doubt the Red Devil gained his scars from mass surrenders," Gytha drawled. "What of him?"

"He is a Saitun, I think. Unwed, landless, but rich in honor. Not too poor in pocket, so rumor has it."

Margaret shook her head. "You should not encourage her in this prying and spying."

"T'will be done anyway. No encouragement is needed. Why should I not gain from it? What of the man who rides at the Red Devil's right, Edna?"

"Gytha," groaned Margaret, unable to fully suppress a blush.

Seeing it, Gytha winked at her cousin. "Come now, admit you are curious. Well, Edna? Any news of him?"

Her dark eyes growing wide with a dreamy

look, Edna sighed. "Ah, such a man. Such a beautiful smile."

"Heed that," grumbled Margaret. "Here but a few moments only and already he eyes the maids."

It was not easy, but Gytha smothered a giggle. "Is that all you know of him, Edna?"

"Nay. He too is unwed. In truth, I think the lot of them are. His name is Roger. Sir Roger. So, 'tis a knight he is."

"Thank you, Edna. We will be needing some bathing water, please." After Edna left, Gytha turned to grin at her cousin. "There you are, Margaret. The man is unwed."

"Aye, and a flirt. Most like a lecherous rogue as well."

"Tsk, tsk." Gytha pulled a mournful face. "To so brand the poor man for but smiling at a pretty maid. I fear you are possessed of a hard heart, cousin."

"Bah, wretched girl. Cease trying to goad me. It will not work this time. Aye, he is handsome. True, my heart acts strangely when I look upon him. Howbeit, 'tis best if I cease to think of him. He is landless, mayhap poor as well. If he ever seeks a bride, t'will not be one in near the same state as he."

Gytha felt her spirits immediately sink. There was no argument she could make against that sad truth. Even if she could think of one, it was best if she kept it to herself. She realized she would do Margaret no good at all by raising hopes that would turn out to be false ones. If name rich, a knight could gain the land and coin he lacked through marriage, obtaining all his bastardry had denied him. That would take precedence over any emotional tie. Purse and property would always rule over love. It was a fact of life she would not deny, deplore it all she might.

Her spirits sank even lower when she was forced to admit that it was the deciding factor in her own marriage. She was secure in her father's love, yet when it came to marriage, he gave not a moment's thought to the state of her heart. He looked at her husband's bloodline, his property, and his purse. His interest was in ensuring that she was well placed and well provided for, not in the vagaries of love. If she ever attempted to suggest some other arrangement, he would undoubtedly think her mad. That opinion would be shared by many another as well.

While she did worry about her emotional future, it was not the greatest of her concerns. Her parents had found love. She had to believe that she had every chance to do likewise. If love did elude her, she could at least find contentment. She sternly told herself that that would be enough.

Pulled from her darkening inner thoughts by Edna's return, Gytha started to prepare for the evening's festivities. With most of the guests having already arrived for the wedding, it promised to be a lively time. Gytha fought to regain her usually high spirits. The guests would expect a smiling bride.

"Are you at all afraid of what is to come?" Margaret voiced the slightly timid question as they helped each other dress.

"A little. My greatest fear is that I shall loathe warming my husband's bed."

"A lady is not supposed to enjoy that."

"So 'tis often said. Howbeit, if that is true, why is so much of it done? Why do women take lovers? I think we are told such things to keep us chaste." She shrugged. "It matters little. Enjoyment is not necessarily what I seek. I simply do not want to be repulsed. If God grants me a long life, I will spend a great deal of it in my husband's bed. Think of what a torture life would be if I found I could not abide it."

"Exactly what do you think you might find repulsive?"

"I am not certain. I told you, Mama was not very precise."

"Surely you gleaned some knowledge from her talk."

"It has something to do with what rests between a man's legs. He will do something to me with that. It also has to do with what lies between my legs. It was how the two are connected that I was unable to discern." Gytha frowned, then stared at her maid when Edna burst into a poorly muffled fit of the giggles. "Mayhaps Edna can clear away the fog."

Choking slightly as her laughter abruptly

ended, Edna inched towards the door. "Oh, nay, mistress. 'Tis not my place."

Moving quickly, Gytha barred the exit with her body. "Edna, would you send me to my marriage bed in ignorance? I will never tell that you spoke about it. Everyone will think Mother was more coherent than she was."

"I fear I know only coarse words, not fit for your ears."

"My ears will survive. Edna, it is best you speak. You will not leave this room until you do. Can you deny that 'tis best if I know, best for all concerned?"

After a moment Edna nodded. Despite a great deal of stuttering and blushing, she told Gytha exactly what would happen on her wedding night. When she was done, it was a moment before Gytha could find her voice. Finally, murmuring a quiet thanks, she let the little maid flee the room. After shutting the door behind Edna, Gytha slouched against the heavy wood.

"Well, I am ignorant no longer."

"Do you fear it now?"

"I am not sure, Margaret. Mayhap that is for the best." She sighed and shook her head. "I do feel better now that I know. There is one thing I do fear, now that I think on it."

"And what is that?"

"That I will begin to think too much on how it will be with Robert."

Chapter Two

"By the blood of Christ! I told you the Red Devil was too good a knight to have been taken down by a Frenchman."

Brought to such an abrupt halt that she stumbled, Gytha softly cursed. She told herself it was her own fault. If she had not been staring so hard at the Red Devil, who had entered the hall but steps ahead of her, Robert, and Margaret, she would have noticed that her escort had halted. She winced as Robert's grip tightened on her arm. She looked down, frowning at the white-knuckled hand on her arm. As she tried to loosen Robert's pinching grip, she finally looked at him and frowned even more.

Robert had no color in his thin face. His hazel eyes were open so wide they bulged slightly. Small droplets of sweat began to bead on his forehead. Following his horrified gaze she realized that he was staring at the Red Devil. Since there was no threat coming from that quarter, she was puzzled as to why Robert looked ready to collapse from fear.

Thayer looked to the man who had spoken. He recognized him as one he had met a few times and fought beside once. Intent upon finding out what had prompted such a strange remark, he strode over to the man.

"You heard I was slain in France?" The man nodded. "Where did you hear such a tale?"

"Why, from our host—my cousin, Sir John Raouille."

Looking to his host, who stared at him in evident shock, Thayer demanded, "Who told you of my death?"

"Your own kin."

"William?"

"Nay, Sir Robert and his uncle." John pointed towards Gytha and Robert, who lingered in the doorway.

Turning, Thayer eyed his trembling cousin with little affection. "You were premature. Why?"

Giving a strangled cry, Robert released Gytha. He turned to flee but was not quick enough. Thayer caught him up by the front of his bright cotehardie. Robert's feet dangled several inches above the floor and he began to make choking noises as his slender, soft hands plucked uselessly at the large hand Thayer held him with.

Noting Robert's difficulty, Gytha murmured, "I should think t'would be somewhat difficult for him to answer whilst held so." She smiled faintly when the Red Devil briefly glanced her way.

Easing his choking hold on his cousin, Thayer snapped, "Answer. Why?"

"Uncle told me," Robert gasped. "He was the one who said you were slain in France."

Releasing Robert, who squealed softly as he tumbled ungracefully to the floor, Thayer rubbed his chin as he frowned in thought. "But of what use is such a lie? Neither you nor Charles could gain from my death."

With Gytha's and Margaret's help, Robert unsteadily got to his feet. "Of course I gain. Are you not William's heir and I yours?" He gave a soft, high-pitched scream as he was yet again grabbed by the front of the cotehardie.

His face but inches from Robert's pale one, Thayer bellowed, "Where is William?"

"Dead," squeaked Robert and was tossed aside, striking his head on the floor hard enough to render him unconscious.

Whirling to glare at Gytha's father, Thayer snarled, "As dead as I?"

"Nay, William is truly dead."

"Claims who? That lying adder Robert claims as kin?"

"William's own squire brought us the news."

"How did William meet his death?"

"He fell from his mount or was thrown. His neck was broken. I am sorry." Despite the

Hannah Howell

many clues tossed out in the brief, loud confrontation, John was still uncertain of who the
angry man was. "You are Sir Thayer Saitun?"

"Aye." His thoughts centered on the loss of
William, Thayer absently endured a round of
introductions. "William is dead, yet the wedding goes forward?"

Pausing in helping Margaret try to revive
Robert, Gytha answered, "I was to marry your
cousin here."

Seeing the dark frown that continued to mar
Thayer's face, John rushed to explain. "It ad-
heres to the agreement."

"What agreement?"

"The one between myself and William's father—foster-father and uncle to yourself and
Robert. We arranged the marriage while Gytha was still but a babe. The plague had just
left its first scar upon the land, so the agreement was drawn up a little—er, strangely." He
paused to send his wife to fetch his copy. "Gytha's name was used, but not William's. His
father wanted the houses joined. As I did.
There were three of you who could reach ma-
turity to achieve that. William, yourself and
Robert. All of you were in his care at the time.
The agreement was made that Gytha would be
wedded to the heir of Saitun Manor—the sur-
viving heir, be it William, yourself, or Robert."

Hurt pricked at Gytha when Thayer turned
to stare at her. His eyes widened as the color
seeped from his face. He looked horrified. It
was the one reaction she had never received

34

from a man. She knew it would not have pained her if it had been from any other man. She had never cared what a man thought of her. It struck her as decidedly unfair that she should care now with the one man who seemed to see her as a curse.

Lady Raouille thrusting a document into his hand yanked Thayer from his shocked stupor. For a moment he stared at it blankly, his mind plagued by scattered thoughts. He was a man of property now, of property and title. That largesse he would find no hardship in accepting. It was the price he had to pay to gain it that nearly stopped his heart. He had to take a wife. And what a wife! For a man like him to wed such a beauty was nothing less than a curse.

Finally he forced himself to read the document he held, but he found no release there. In his foster-father's bold script, it stated that the holder of Saitun Manor would wed Gytha Odel Raouille when she reached the age of seventeen. It was no longer William's wedding he attended, but his own. His gaze settled briefly on Gytha as she and another young woman helped a still groggy Robert to a seat. Then he looked at John Raouille.

"This is legal?"

"Legal and binding. Surely you must see that the king himself affixed his seal, approving the joining of our houses."

Thayer saw that all too clearly. He was bound by his foster-father's word to wed Gytha. The king's approval added even more weight to that which duty set upon him. In truth, that approval was much akin to a royal command. The title of Lord, baron of Saitun Manor, was now his, as was Saitun Manor. So too was the wealth it held. So too was Gytha Raouille whether he wanted her or not. He was there. The bride was there. The wedding was prepared. There was no escape.

Still stunned by the turn of events, Thayer allowed himself to be set at the table between John and Gytha. He only vaguely took notice of a concerned Roger sitting down next to Gytha or an equally concerned Margaret sitting next to Roger. He needed more than concern at the moment. Robert sat next to Lady Raouille looking as if he would burst into tears at any moment. Thayer had a fleeting urge to do the same. He barely acknowledged the high quality of the food and wine he partook of as he struggled to find a way out, only to fail again and again.

Gytha took one look at her morose bridegroom, emptied her wine goblet, and had it immediately refilled. She saw that it stayed full as the meal dragged on, hoping to wash away her hurt with wine. She knew it was not stung vanity that caused her pain, not fully. It was true enough that men had always reacted to her favorably. It was also true that she had never particularly cared whether they had or not. This time she cared. For the first time in her life she had felt an honest stirring of interest in a man, real feeling for him. This time the man took little interest in her smiles. This man reacted to the news of their impending marriage as if just told he had contracted the plague. She decided that soaking herself in wine was exactly what she needed. Holding her goblet out for yet another refill, she ignored Margaret's attempts to catch her attention.

Margaret finally grew so concerned for Gytha she forgot her manners. Leaning back, she reached around an amused Roger to poke at Gytha, drawing her cousin's attention at last. The brightness of Gytha's eyes when she turned to look at her did nothing to ease Margaret's concern.

"Will you cease swilling wine like some—"

"Reveler?" Gytha smiled brightly and took a deep drink of her wine. " 'Tis a revel, is it not? My very own revel in fact. So, I am reveling."

"You are wallowing."

Gytha looked at a grinning Roger. "Tell me, sir, what does one do at a revel?"

"Eat, drink, and be merry," he replied, laughter filling his voice.

"Aha! I have eaten. Now I drink. And now I am merry. See, Margaret? There is naught to fret about."

When Gytha turned away, Margaret tried to reach for her again, only to have Roger stop her. "Leave the child be, mistress. She does no more than all the rest."

"Which is far more than she has ever done.

Gytha drinks but a little wine with her meal. Never like this. I have no idea how such an indulgence will take her."

"Straight to her bed, no doubt."

Even as Margaret opened her mouth to reply, a familiar male voice cried, "Pardee! Have you left me naught to eat then?"

"Bayard," screeched Gytha as she leapt from her seat to greet her brother, Margaret quickly doing likewise.

She raced towards the slender young man in the doorway, who easily caught her and Margaret up in his arms. They all laughed as she and Margaret peppered his face with kisses even as they belabored him with questions. She took a minute to smile over her brother's broad shoulder at her burly uncle, Lord Edgar, who stood behind Bayard. Soon her mother and father joined them and, after a more restrained welcome, urged them all to sit down. Glancing around at the merry group momentarily gathered in the doorway, Gytha realized there was one thing about her wedding she could truly be thankful for. Her family would be together again.

Watching the happy reunion, Roger murmured, " 'Tis a fine looking young man. John Raouille produces a fair crop, it seems."

Thayer grunted his agreement. He could not help but wonder how two such nearly plain people as John and Bertha could have produced such stunning offspring. When he found himself wondering what his children would look like with such a beauty as Gytha for a mother, he inwardly cursed. To ponder future children was a sign of acceptance of his fate, nearly a hint of hope for the future. He had no real qualms about marriage itself. It was a natural step now that he was a man of property. However, he did not want such a beauty for a wife. The only future in that was one of trouble, deception, and pain.

"You have sorely bruised the girl's feelings," continued Roger.

"How so?" Thayer found that a little hard to believe.

"How so?" Roger shook his head in a gesture of amazement. "You can ask that when you have sat there acting as if you have been asked to clasp an adder to your bosom?"

" 'Tis much the same when a man like me takes such a beautiful wife." Thayer easily envisioned a future spent kicking men out of her bed.

"My friend, for once in your life you judge without knowledge, make assumptions without fact. Aye, the girl is lovely and fair sets a man's blood afire. Yet, here I have sat, ready to exchange smiles and flirt. She has not made one effort to do so. I cannot feel the girl is the fickle sort."

"She does not need to be. I shall still be tripping o'er lovesick men all my life. Ere she grows too old, she will succumb to one or more of a wooing throng."

"Then harden your heart and merely let your

body revel in the possession of such a comely wife."

There was a sharpness to Roger's tone that startled Thayer. However, he was not given the time to find out the reason for it. He was immediately caught up in a round of introductions to Bayard Raouille and Lord Edgar Raouille, his bride's brother and uncle. A few subtle comments which passed amongst the family told him exactly who Margaret was. It also told him that she was the reason neither Edgar's wife nor his children would attend the wedding. What few qualms were expressed over the situation concerned only the absence of Edgar's children.

"Have John and Fulke not arrived yet?" Bayard asked.

"Nay," replied his father. "They sent messages explaining their tardiness. We can only hope they arrive in time to attend the wedding."

"I am sure they will." Bayard grinned at Gytha. "Another change of grooms, I see."

"It appears so. Robert was somewhat premature in placing himself as heir. The report of Sir Thayer's demise was exaggerated."

As Bayard chuckled, Thayer stared at his delicate bride. He was certain he detected sarcasm behind her words. Yet, she looked too sweet of face to possess a sharp tongue. The bland innocence in her gaze, however, made him decidedly suspicious. Inwardly shaking his head, he decided he would ponder that matter at some later time.

He let the conversation whirl around him, only half-listening as he again pondered the situation he found himself in and struggled to come to terms with what faced him. It was a moment, therefore, before he caught the import of Gytha's response to Margaret's mention of the wedding on the morrow.

"We shall see," grumbled Gytha. "We may wake on the morrow to find the groom has taken to his heels."

Turning to face her, Thayer gave her a stern look. "I will be here. 'Tis not my way to break a bond."

"Pardee!" She placed a hand over her heart in an overly dramatic gesture. "Romance lies heavy in the air tonight."

Roger choked on his drink. A giggling Margaret slapped him on the back. Thayer felt little amusement, however. He eyed the goblet of wine Gytha held. Her too-bright eyes and the high color in her cheeks told him she had imbibed too heavily. He reached out to retrieve her goblet only to discover that, along with a tendency to employ sarcasm, his bride could be obstinate.

Gytha clung tightly to her goblet when Thayer tried to take it away. She eyed him and his large hand alternately. A voice in her head told her she had indeed had more than enough wine, but a louder voice cried out for more. She had no intention of giving up her wine. It made her feel good, easing the sting of her bridegroom's insulting attitude.

Seeing the way Gytha eyed Thayer's hand, Margaret quickly handed Roger a sweetmeat. "When she opens her mouth, stuff this into it."

"But why?" Roger was not sure he ought to obey the strange request.

"There is no time to explain. There she goes. Do it—quickly."

Just as Gytha was about to give into the urge to sink her teeth into Thayer's hand she found her mouth full of sweetmeat. She crossed her eyes in her attempt to look at the unrequested food resting half in, half out of her mouth. When she heard Margaret's gentle laughter mix with Roger's more hearty guffaw, she knew her cousin was behind her inability to inflict any damage upon Thayer. Watching Thayer closely, she slowly ate the sweetmeat.

It was hard, but Thayer swallowed his amusement. He felt it best to hide the grin threatening to turn up the corners of his mouth. The one thing he ought to ask of his wife was obediance. He felt it necessary to let his bride know that from the very beginning. Gytha's father, however, stole the opportunity.

"Gytha, my child, why not show Sir Thayer the gardens?" John Raouille looked at Thayer, thinking the man too grim for his daughter but hoping that, if the pair had some time alone, matters would improve. "My wife insisted upon them. Their only purpose is to please the eye. I thought it foolish at first, but I have grown quite fond of them."

Sensing the man's intentions, Thayer murmured, "It might be better done in the daytime."

"No need to wait. The gardens are well lit by both torch and moonlight."

Even in her wine-fogged state, Gytha had no difficulty in guessing what her father intended. She was just about to tell him that she felt no immediate need to get to know her sulking bridegroom when she saw Thayer send Roger a pleading glance. Roger sighed but stood up as Thayer did. As Thayer helped her stand, Gytha signaled Margaret. If Thayer insisted upon company, so would she. With a reluctance equal to Roger's, Margaret stood up.

"I thought t'would be but the two of you," muttered John, frowning at his daughter.

"But, Papa," Gytha said, "my betrothed chose to bring a chaperon, so I thought it best to do the same."

Feeling himself flush, Thayer grasped his bride by the arm and hurried her away. He noted a little crossly that she had her goblet of wine as well as a good supply to keep it filled. A brief glance over his shoulder told him that Roger and Margaret followed. That helped him regain some of his lost calm.

Once outside he understood what Gytha's father had been saying. Bushes, trees, and flowers were arranged so that one could stroll amongst their beauty in peace and privacy. It must have seemed a frivolous waste of space to the man at first. Although Thayer had seen such gardens in several European manors, he knew the style was still new to England. Here gardens were simply wild tangles or utilitarian vegetable patches. John was also right in thinking it an excellent place for romance.

Thayer grimaced as he thought on the last word—romance. The girl did deserve a little wooing. He could not bring himself to deny the truth of that. She was not to blame for the situation nor for the beauty which unsettled him so. Unfortunately, the art of wooing was a lost one to him. Watching her stroll ahead of him and a silent Roger, he searched his mind for something, anything, to say.

Ignoring Margaret's murmured disapproval, Gytha refilled her and Margaret's goblets. She then handed Roger the wine. Anger gnawed at her no matter how she tried to shake its hold. Come the new day, she would be married to the man who stomped along behind her. In a place conducive to romance, he kept his distance, scowling at her back. Suddenly she had an urge to speak directly, with full honesty. She needed to discover exactly why he seemed so loathe to marry her. Stopping abruptly, she whirled about to face him.

Still deep in thought, groping for words with an increasing desperation, Thayer did not see her stop and walked right into her, sending her sprawling in the grass at his feet. Roger moved at the same time he did to help her stand and they almost bumped heads. Margaret hurried to lend a hand as well.

"You should have told me you were stopping," he snapped as he watched Gytha and Margaret brush off the skirts of her gown.

"I was intending to have a word with you, sir," she snapped back, glaring at him.

"Aye? So what do you have to say?"

Staring up at him, Gytha decided it was an extremely awkward position. With all that whirled in her head, all that demanded saying, she felt she could get a severe crick in her neck before she was done. Glancing around, she espied a low bench. Grabbing his hand, she towed her startled bridegroom over to it. She then stood upon the bench and stared at him.

"Just what is it that you so abhor about our coming wedding?" she demanded.

"Gytha," Margaret began in soft protest.

" 'Tis a reasonable question, cousin. Well, sir? Do you perchance prefer darker ladies?"

"Nay." He could not tell her of his fears, of how he dreaded a future filled with pain and the shame of being cuckolded.

"Then mayhap I am too short for your tastes?"

"Well, 'tis true that if you were much smaller, I might have trouble finding you."

"Ah, I see. You wish me to be taller?" She frowned when he shook his head. "Thinner? Fatter?"

Despite his efforts to resist, his gaze moved over her figure. He could find no fault there.

High, full breasts, a tiny waist and gently rounded hips stirred only intense interest. His body quickly revealed its eagerness to begin married life with Gytha.

"None of those. Child, I had a shock. I came here expecting to attend William's wedding. Instead, I find that William is dead and myself proclaimed so. I came intending to meet William's bride. Instead, I meet my own. 'Tis a situation that would set any man reeling."

She found that easy enough to believe. Nevertheless, she felt sure he was not telling her the full truth. Despite the wine that fogged her senses, however, she knew it would be useless to press for more. Even as she decided to drop the matter, voices from the other side of the hedge behind her drew all her attention.

"We should not," gasped a husky female voice. "My husband—"

"Is soaked senseless with wine."

"Your wife?"

"Abed. She cares little how I entertain myself. Ah, so lovely. Breasts as full and sweet as ripe melons."

Gytha gasped and looked at Margaret, who hastily covered her reddened face with her hands. Although she had often heard gossip of lovers and trysts, infidelity and adultery, Gytha had dismissed most of it as just that—gossip. Her parents were deeply in love, and she had seen their faithful marriage as the true way of things. It was now clear to her that the gossip had held a few grains of truth.

In the heat of righteous indignation, she decided that such things would not be allowed in her home. After glaring at the amused men, she leapt off the bench and started around the hedge. Hearing her three companions come after her, she hurried to elude them. The sight of the entwined couple on the ground enraged her. Even as the man saw her and hastened to stand up, she gave him a good kick in the backside. She glared at the couple as they scrambled to pull together their tangled clothing. Then she began to lecture them, punctuating certain statements with an occasional swat at one or the other miscreant. Although she felt she understood human frailties and could be tolerant of mistakes, this was too much. That someone would commit flagrant adultery in her father's newly constructed gardens, her mother's pride and joy, was more than she could bear.

Fully dressed, the woman finally grew angry with Gytha. "What do you know of love?"

"You love this faithless rogue?" Although she thought the woman a fool if she did, Gytha was willing to temper her condemnation if love was involved.

The woman hesitated and, when she did speak, her voice lacked the ring of conviction. "Well, of course I do."

"Fie! You add lying to your sins. Go back to your lawful husband where you belong."

"Have you ever set eyes upon my husband?" the woman snapped.

47

After a moment of concentration, Gytha nodded. " 'Tis true that he is not as fair of face and figure as this swine. Howbeit, he is clean, healthy, possessed of all his own teeth and hair. He also appears to be cheerful of disposition. You could have done far worse. Begone, dam, you grow tedious." She was a little surprised when the couple hastily obeyed her imperious command.

"Oh, Gytha," Margaret murmured when the couple was gone, loving amusement in her voice, "you should have let be."

"But, Margaret, my mother often strolls here with my father."

Although his sides ached from all the smothered laughter he had already indulged in, Thayer started again. He joined Roger in whooping with unrestrained laughter. Gytha was staring at the ground as if the trysters had left some bold stain, forever tainting the area. She still looked beautifully indignant.

Slowly, Gytha turned to look at Thayer, drawn by the sound of his laughter. It was deep, hearty, yet with an open boyish quality, and very contagious. She half-noticed that Roger's was like it and that it left Margaret bemused. Fleetingly, she wondered if Roger's laughter caused Margaret's insides to warm as Thayer's caused hers to.

"I suppose it was silly of me to interfere," she murmured, walking over to him where he sat upon the ground, his back against a tree.

As she sat next to Thayer she noticed Roger

carefully get up. The man grabbed Margaret's hand and the pair slipped away. Her father was obviously not the only one who felt she and Thayer ought to have some time alone. Although she made no effort to stop their desertion, she was torn in her feelings. His bout of laughter had softened Thayer, making him less aloof. However, she was not sure of what to say, what to do. For the first time in her memory she felt nervous, almost shy.

She knew that aloofness of his could return. There were many reasons behind it. The shock over finding himself betrothed to her was not, however, the real cause. She simply did not know how to discover the true one.

Trying to think of some way to start a conversation made her head ache. She had never had a problem before. The only difficulty in the past had been in keeping the conversation idle, so that no words of love or desire escaped the lips of any man other than her betrothed. She sighed as sadness crept over her. That would be no problem here. It was hard not to dwell upon the rather cruel twists of fate. For once she felt an honest desire to hear sweet words, but she was certain the man at her side would give her few.

Thayer studied the girl at his side. When she looked up at him, he read no guile in her wide-eyed, upturned face. No pinching vanity marred her loveliness. There was the aura of a sheltered child about her. Despite that he clung to his wariness, almost afraid to let it go. Once he had done so, and no wound he had ever suffered in battle had equaled the pain that had resulted.

"They will only go elsewhere." He kept his tone gentle, not wishing her to think he ridiculed her in any way. "You may have made it more difficult, but you have not stopped them."

"That did occur to me. They are surely doomed to Hell."

"Gytha, 'tis a thing often done. Women take lovers, men have lemans...."

"My parents do not commit such sins. They hold to vows given before God. Now I know that it aids fidelity that their marriage has love to strengthen it."

"Aye. Any who meet them can see it. In that they are fortunate. Not all are, thus they take lovers."

"Lovers—bah. Partners in lust. That pair held no love for each other. That is where the sin truly lies." She suddenly had a thought that struck her cold to the bone. "Will you have lemans?"

For a moment he was tempted to give her a strong lecture on impertinence. The subject was one a wife dutifully ignored. Gytha was endearingly unworldy. She still believed in the sanctity of marriage. He decided it was not the time for a lecture. He also knew that, as long as she remained faithful, he would have no difficulty in doing likewise. His sexual appetite was a hearty one, but it did not demand variety. If Gytha brought some warmth to their bed, he would feel no need to stray.

"Not unless you take a lover to your bed." He caught his breath at the beauty of her smile.

"Then you had best write farewell missives to all your lovers and lemans."

"I have none." The disbelief in her face was dangerously flattering. "The women I have known tested the worth of my coin first." He laughed softly over her continued look of doubt, then grew serious. "Did you know William very well?"

"Nay, not well. We spent only a few hours together. Do you wonder if I grieve?" He nodded slowly. "I did not know him well enough for that. What I felt was but a passing sorrow at the loss of a young, healthy man."

"Aye, and in such ignominious circumstances."

He spoke absently, his thoughts centering upon their proximity and their seclusion from all the others. Hers was a beauty the minstrels often sang of. The knowledge that she would soon be his by the laws of both king and God was a heady one. He reached out to touch her bright hair. His gaze became fixed upon her upturned face, upon her full, inviting mouth.

Although she recognized the look upon his face, she did not feel the usual urge to retreat. "Are you going to kiss me?"

"Are you always so bold with your questions?"

" 'Tis said I am. Howbeit, I think the wine

makes my tongue looser than usual. Are you?'' she whispered.

"The thought sits comfortably in my head.'' He brushed her cheek with the knuckles of one hand. "Did William kiss you?''

"Aye, and I had to box his ears a time or two. He held some bold ideas about the art of wooing.''

Thayer could easily picture how his cousin would behave towards such a beauty and smiled slightly. "And Robert?''

"I had barely become betrothed to him when you arrived. If you must have a listing,'' she drawled, "I must admit to a paucity of kisses. I have, however, suffered a deluge of stomach-churning poetry.''

Her tartness made him grin. "The wine makes you impertinent as well.''

"I fear 'tis not the wine that prompts that fault.'' She watched him with an expectant, eager expression, curious as to how his kiss would feel.

Seeing that look, Thayer shook his head in wonder. A slightly foolish grin ghosted over his face as he took her into his arms. It was intoxicating to be the object of her attention. He firmly told himself it would be a fleeting pleasure, leaving as she grew more wordly, but the thought did little to subdue that intoxication.

He brushed his lips over hers, savoring the trembling warmth of her mouth. When she encircled his neck with her slim arms, shyly burrowing her soft hands into his hair, he increased the pressure of his mouth upon hers. It was not until he tried to slip his tongue into her mouth that she pulled away, if only slightly. She eyed him with curiosity and a hint of annoyance, but a warmth still lingered in her gaze.

"At such a moment I boxed William's ears." The slow movement of his hands over her back stirred a strange, fierce heat within her.

"Did you warn him as you now warn me?" He traced the delicate lines of her face with soft, gentle kisses.

"Nay." She was briefly surprised at how breathless, how husky, her voice was.

" 'Tis but a part of the kiss, dearling. Come, part your lips for me." When she did, he gave a soft growl of delight. "Ah, now there is a lovely sight."

When his mouth covered hers again, she mused that, although she did not know how it looked, it certainly felt lovely. His tongue eased into her mouth, each stroke adding to the heat seeping through her. She tightened her grip upon his neck when he neatly moved her onto his lap. When the kiss ended, she slumped against his arm as she stared at him. Passion clouded her mind, amazement nudging through its haze. He made her insides feel very strange indeed.

Thayer felt a little dazed. Never had a mere kiss stirred him so. He tried to blame the half-light or imagination stirred by an errant hope for what he thought he read in her face. Nothing he told himself could change the soft, heated look in her eyes. Women had been stirred by him before, but none like Gytha. Women like her did not get close enough to test his skill or the lack of it.

"Did I do it well?" she whispered.

He grinned. "Aye. Very well indeed. So well," he set her away from him, "that I think we had best rejoin the fête." He winked at her as they stood up. "I have no wish to have my ears boxed."

Exchanging idle bits of information about each other, they made their way back to the manor, rejoining Margaret and Roger there. Although he participated in their conversation, Thayer was sunk deep into his own thoughts. He found himself weighted down with doubts and fears. Gytha had been betrothed to William, an exceedingly handsome man, then to Robert, who was fair enough to look at. Now she faced marriage to him. She warmed to his kisses now, but he felt sure she would soon resent being bound to the plainest of the cousins. Try as he would to dispel the thought, he looked at his lovely bride and all he saw ahead was trouble.

Chapter Three

Despite a heavy dose of wine, Thayer continued to feel knotted with tension. He stood with Gytha's three brothers while he waited for his bride. They were as handsome as she was beautiful. Cheerful and witty, they did their best to keep him relaxed with their repartee. It was failing, much to his dismay. Even their camaraderie could not dispel the whispers around him, nor could it blind him to the look in people's eyes. Pity was what the wedding guests felt for the bride. They felt her beauty was wasted on a man like him and he could not stop himself from agreeing with them.

"I feel 'tis our duty to tell you of our sister's character." Fulke Raouille winked at Thayer, his aquamarine eyes alight with laughter.

Thayer managed a smile for the younger

man. "Do you mean to list her faults?"

John, the eldest brother, assumed a false air of outrage. "Our sister has no faults. Merely a bend or two to her perfection."

"Well said," Thayer murmured.

His indigo gaze fixed earnestly upon Thayer, Bayard said, "She has not been pampered, yet she has been cherished. As has Margaret, who will go with her. Both have been as sheltered as two maids could be."

"That is clear to see in their manner. Aye, and that of their kin. Still your fears. I intend to be a good husband to Gytha."

"You will find times when your patience runs short."

"John has the right of it," Fulke continued, grinning faintly. "Our sister has been allowed to be free with her opinions."

Nodding, John added, "And her sense of humor can oft seem strange."

Joining the foursome, Gytha's father said, "And she insists that you listen to what she has to say. Do not mistake us. We do not bind you to a purely disagreeable wench. 'Tis just that she will take few orders in meek silence. She will insist upon an explanation. Aye, and a chance to air her own views on the matter. She can prove most stubborn about it."

"Aye," Fulke nodded, "she has been known to cling to things until she has been heard."

Briefly diverted from his worries, Thayer started to grin. "Cling to things?"

Gytha's father sighed. "Chairs, tables, even

people. Clings like ivy. 'Tis nigh on impossible to unhitch the wench."

Unable to hold it back, Thayer laughed aloud. "What have you set upon me?"

Lord John grinned slowly. "She will not be a dull wife. There is much to be said in favor of that."

Before Thayer could respond, Roger walked up to ask, "Has anyone seen Robert or that uncle of his?"

"Aye," replied Lord John, "the pair left ere the sun had even begun to rise."

Frowning, Thayer rubbed his chin as he thought on that information. He had assumed his lack of immediate retribution would make it clear that he was willing to give the pair the benefit of the doubt. They had had no reason to flee. The act seemed to confirm their guilt. A moment later, he shrugged aside all thought of them. They had gained nothing from their duplicity. The pair would make themselves scarce now.

What few thoughts he did have were fully scattered when Gytha arrived. Her loveliness took his breath away. It was a beauty enhanced by her unconsciousness of it. She made her way to his side slowly, her progress interrupted by those guests greeting her and relaying their good wishes. Despite that, she kept sending him shy smiles. He saw no sign of reluctance in her yet that only eased his tension a little.

Gytha felt no hesitation as she went to

Thayer. Although she felt some nervousness, she also felt eager. Neither William nor Robert had given her such a feeling of rightness. Thayer Saitun did. Neither William nor Robert had caused her dreams to grow sensual. Thayer Saitun did. Those dreams had stirred a curiosity within her. As she placed her hand in Thayer's, she found herself looking forward to her wedding night despite fears bred of inexperience.

The ceremony took less time than she had anticipated. She suspected her bemusement had robbed her of any real sense of time. All her attention had been on the priest, the words she spoke, and the sound of Thayer's deep, rich voice as he repeated his vows. She had knelt at his side filled with the knowledge that, whatever trouble lay ahead of them, it was her rightful place. When the celebration separated her from Thayer, she found herself annoyed with it.

The celebrations were well under way before Roger managed to grasp a moment alone with Thayer. "A lovely bride, Thayer."

"There lives none who will argue that."

"But you wish she were plainer."

"Aye, though many would call me mad. Even you, I think. Look you there. We have been wed but hours, and she is already surrounded by moonlings."

"True, but note her eyes, my friend. That sweet gaze often rests upon you, not those boys gathered around her. Do not be unjust. Do not condemn her with neither proof nor trial."

Thayer breathed a heavy sigh. "I know that would be best. Howbeit, it will be a battle hard won. Too many seek to feed my fears. Too many tell me that I wed beyond myself, that I now possess something of greater worth than I. They remind me that there will be many who seek to steal that prize away."

"So stop up yours ears."

"Not such an easy thing to do, as you well know."

"If the girl seeks naught but a pretty face, then she is worth neither your worry nor your pain."

"I know," Thayer murmured, his gaze fixed upon Gytha as he prayed he could heed those words of wisdom.

The face Gytha constantly sought in the crowd was judged far from pretty by many, a fact too many felt obliged to tell her. She smiled and was always polite to the young men besieging her, but her gaze followed Thayer. Try as she would to let him know she wished to be rescued from her court, she continuously failed. Finally, she looked to her father for aid. He proved not so obtuse, soon extricating her.

To her dismay, he did not take her to Thayer but left her with a group of young women. Margaret was there, which pleased her, but this soon proved to be the only thing that did. Margaret was the only one who held her tongue. The others plagued her with expressions of sympathy over the ill choice of a groom for her. Despite her efforts to remain calm, to ignore them, Gytha felt herself grow angrier and angrier.

A plain young girl named Anne sighed heavily. "Oh, you are so brave. How well you bear up beneath misfortune's weight."

"I have suffered no misfortune." Gytha spat the words out between gritted teeth, yet none of them heeded her anger.

Her cousin Isobel spoke up in a too sweet, falsely soothing voice. "There is no need to hide how you feel. He is such a lubber. So horribly red."

Gytha hissed softly over hearing Thayer referred to as a hulking oaf. "He is a good, strong man. His bravery has been proven ten times over."

"Oh, there are no doubts raised about that," said a pert blonde named Edwina. "Ah, but after sweet William? How it must pain you to find yourself wed to a man so lacking in beauty and grace. But, keep heart, fair Gytha. A man so wedded to his sword rarely lives a long life."

Just as Gytha raised her goblet, intending to pour her wine over the fair Edwina, her wrist was grasped. She was not pleased by her brother Fulke's intervention, glaring at him as he took her goblet away. The knowing grin he wore only added to her temper. She did not protest, however, when Fulke started to lead her away from the group.

Having kept a close, if covert, watch on his new bride, Thayer saw the brief contretemps.

He followed when Fulke led his sister away from the group, Margaret hurrying after them. Gytha turned to look at him when he reached her side, and he was a little taken aback by the fury darkening her eyes. He grew curious about its cause.

Fulke shook his head even as he started to laugh, the sound destroying his meager attempts to sound stern. "Tsk, sister love, t'will ne'er do to douse our guests in wine."

"T'was that or scratch the strumpet's eyes out." Gytha snatched back her goblet of wine.

"Language." Fulke rolled his eyes in an exaggerated expression of false dismay.

Margaret patted Gytha's arm in a soothing gesture. "They are merely jealous. They wish this was their celebration."

"Ah," Thayer murmured and slowly lifted Gytha's hand to his lips, "they sharpened their tongues on you, did they?"

Calming herself slightly, Gytha stared up at the large man she now called husband. His strong hand easily enclosed hers, yet his touch was gentle. That gentleness was reflected in his fine eyes, the deep brown alluringly soft. She noted idly how long and thick his dark auburn lashes were.

"Aye, but I should know by this time that such foolishness should be ignored. I fear I have a slight temper." She gave Fulke a mock glare when he hooted with laughter. "Ignore this fool," she told Thayer, then took a drink of her wine.

They began to banter amongst themselves, Roger soon joining them. Thayer decided that, whatever other worries he had, he had none about the family he had married into. There was a closeness there which easily spread to include new members. It was an important benefit. A troublesome family, one beset with infighting and grasping natures, could become a lifelong plague to a man. After but a few moments in their company, he knew he could trust the Raouilles. He wished he had the confidence to trust Gytha as well.

Soon the dancing began. Thayer quickly realized that Gytha loved to dance. Unfortunately, he indulged in it so rarely that he was not confident of his skill. He obliged her a few times, however, loathe to hand her over to the many young men who eyed her so covetously. To prevent those anxious courtiers from moving in, he turned to his men. They proved more than willing to partner her. Trusting them implicitly, he was able to allow her the pleasure of dancing as well as enjoy watching her.

He was relieved, however, when the time came for the bedding ceremony. It was conducted by a small, select group. Their stay was short and their teasing remarks only slightly ribald. As soon as the door shut behind the group, Thayer turned onto his side to look at his new bride.

Although she had only briefly been revealed to the group, Gytha felt embarrassed. She clutched the sheet around herself and fought to stop herself from blushing. When Thayer held out a goblet of wine, she managed only a fleeting shy glance his way as she accepted it.

"Are you afraid, Gytha?" he murmured, reaching his hand out to gently stroke the thick mass of her hair.

"Nay. Aye. Ah me, I am not sure. I am not accustomed to being looked at," she whispered. "I did not like it much."

Silently, he admitted that he had not liked it much either. He had chosen Roger, Merlion, Reve and Torr as his witnesses. They had stared at Gytha in wide-eyed, silent wonder. It had pleased him no end when she had been allowed to scramble beneath the bedcovers within an instant after dropping her robe. Although he resented its presence, he knew his sense of possession was already strong.

"T'was but your kin. The men I chose are the nearest I have to kin aside from that fool, Robert. They have been with me from the beginning, fighting at my side for many a year. I cannot count the times we have saved each other's skins. 'Tis something only done the once, sweeting, and 'tis over now."

She nodded, relaxing a little, then looked at him as Edwina's words flashed through her mind. "Will you continue to live by your sword?"

"Nay. I am a man of property now. There is no longer the need. I now hold the bed and board I fought to supply myself with. Howbeit, a man must fight from time to time, little one, be it for king or his own reasons. Living where we do, I doubt my sword shall rust from disuse. Aye, and the property you bring me lies even closer to the troublesome Welsh than mine. I have asked my men to stay on as my retainers."

The relieved smile she gave him was nearly enough to make him swear to never lift his sword again. He moved his hand over her bared shoulder. Her skin was warm and as soft as the finest silk. Her lashes were long, thick, and light brown, tipped with gold. When, as she lowered her gaze, those lashes brushed her newly flushed cheeks, he bent to kiss her small, straight nose.

Briefly, guilt pinched at him as he thought of the woman he had bought so recently. He shook the guilt aside. At that time he had not been betrothed or even anticipated such a thing. It was possibly for the best as well. His blood ran too hot for Gytha as it was. He wanted to make her introduction to the mysteries of the marriage bed slow and gentle. If he been long without a woman that could have proven even more difficult than it was going to be.

Taking her empty goblet from her hand, he set it aside. "I will try not to hurt you, Gytha."

"I know it must hurt a bit. My maid, Edna, was most exact in what she told me."

"Your maid?" He laughed softly as he gently urged her to lie down. "Did your mother never speak to you?"

"Aye." There was a tremor in her laughter

that revealed her nervousness. "But with all her hesitations, mumblings, and talk of duty and modesty, I learned very little. I was telling Margaret about it when Edna started laughing. So I knew she knew, and I made her tell me."

"A maid," he muttered. "Aye, you will have need of one. Would this Edna wish to join our household?"

"I cannot see why not. She has neither kin nor lover here to hold her back. 'Tis very bright," she squeaked when he started to tug aside her covers.

Thayer preferred it bright but knew it was best to cater to her modesty for now. He rose to douse all the lights save for two candles by the bed. As he returned to bed he smiled crookedly at the wide-eyed look upon her face. Inwardly he shrugged. They were married. She would have to get accustomed to his looks. There was nothing he could do to improve them.

Despite the heat of her blushes, Gytha watched Thayer. She knew her opinion was biased, but she found him lovely. The bright hair and battle scars did not repulse her. Her gaze lingered on broad shoulders, a trim waist, slim hips and long, muscular legs. He had a lean, strong body which held an animal's grace. He was also fully aroused. She could not stop herself from wondering if her small frame could accommodate him. Despite her efforts not to, she eyed him a little fearfully when he

65

rejoined her. Reluctantly, she eased her hold on her cover as he reached for it.

Seeing her fear, Thayer ached to vanquish it, yet felt his need would be hard to control. That feeling was confirmed when he threw back the covers to view his new bride in the faint candlelight. A flush of modesty tinted her creamy skin, and she fluttered her hands in an attempt to cover herself. Gently, but firmly, he grasped her by the wrists and held her hands to her sides, his gaze roaming freely over her delicate beauty.

The rosy tips of her full, high breasts hardened beneath his gaze. He judged her waist small enough to be encircled by his hands. Her gently curved hips tapered into slim, well-formed legs that looked long despite her lack of height. His gaze briefly rested upon the nest of golden curls at the juncture of her lovely thighs. Drawing a shaking breath, he lifted his gaze back to her face.

"Ah, Gytha, my wife, you are indeed beautiful," he murmured in a thick voice, then bent his head to kiss her.

She quickly slipped her arms around his neck and parted her lips for him with no hesitation. When he partially covered her body with his, she shuddered. The feel of their flesh meeting sent shivers through her from head to toe.

Slowly, he began to move his hands over her lithe curves as she lay in his arms. She began to feel drugged by his kisses. A soft noise akin to a purr escaped her when he slipped his hand over her breast. His calloused palm and long fingers teased her nipple until it ached. It felt as if liquid fire was being poured through her veins. When his mouth left hers, she gave a soft cry of protest, which changed swiftly to a cry of delight as his warm lips touched the frantic pulse point at her throat, caressing the life-giving vein with his tongue.

Feeling her tremble as he traced her collarbone with kisses, he said, "I will be gentle with you. Trust me, Gytha."

"I do," she whispered, her voice as husky as his.

Glancing up at her, he could read no guile in her look. "Then why do you tremble with fear, little one?"

" 'Tis not fear." It was hard to speak when he still fondled her breasts, his touch stealing all clear thought from her mind. "I am not really sure what ails me."

"What do you feel, sweeting?" He slowly moved his hand over her abdomen feeling her shudder faintly beneath his touch.

"Afire. 'Tis as if my blood runs hot. That does afright me some."

Choked with elation that his touch could affect her so, he found it hard to speak, and his voice became little more than a raspy whisper. "There is naught to fear in that."

"I do not wish to fail you. Ah, Thayer." She clenched her hands in his thick bright hair when he flicked his tongue over the tip of her breast.

"You will not fail me, dearling. B'Gad, how could you?" he murmured before covering her hard, pink nipple with his mouth.

She squirmed beneath him as he lathed and suckled her full, taut breasts. What fear she did have was soon swamped by passion. Shyly at first, she moved her hands over his broad back and strong arms. The feel of his warm, smooth skin stretched tautly over hard muscle added to her rising desire.

The way he caressed her thighs produced a strange heaviness in her legs. Her passion was checked slightly when he touched the curls that lay between them. She jerked away from his touch. Her eyes wide with shock, she met his gaze.

"Hush, love." He brushed kisses over her face, soothing her. "Open for me, sweeting, give me your secrets."

Gytha found she had no choice. Her body ruled her. He trailed hot, moist kisses from her lips to her breasts and back again. The intimate stroking of his hand restoked the inner fire her modesty had briefly tamped down. The caresses she gave him grew somewhat frantic. She was so caught up in the sensations conquering her body that she was hardly aware of his shift in position. When she felt the solid proof of his arousal press against her, she moaned, rubbing her body against his in mindless urgency. It was not until he began to ease into her that any further check occurred in her passion. The tension of anticipation crept over her.

Thayer grasped her slim hips to hold her steady. Deciding a pain was easiest to endure when it came quickly, he possessed her with all the speed he could. He winced when she softly cried out. He met the barrier of her innocence and ploughed through it. Trembling with the effort, he kept still, holding her close as he tried to restir her desires.

Lying still, Gytha stared up at him. His eyes were nearly black. Something had tautened the lines of his face and he looked slightly flushed. The brief, sharp pain he had inflicted was a fleeting one. She grew fiercely aware of how their bodies were joined, of how they were now one. The strange heat he could invoke was again racing through her, resurrected by his feverish yet gentle kisses.

"I feared you would not fit," she blurted out in an unsteady voice, then blinked in surprise at her own outspokenness.

Tracing the delicate lines of her ear with his tongue, he laughed softly. "Aye, I fit. And a sweet haven it is. Wrap your pretty legs around me, sweeting."

"Like so?" She firmly encircled his hips with her strong legs.

"Aye." He moved slowly within her and heard her gasp. "Did I pain you?"

"Nay." She clutched at his shoulders as pleasure forced her to close her eyes.

Resting on his forearms, he watched her as he fought to maintain a slow, gentle rhythm. "Parry my thrust, dearling. Aye, aye."

She clung to him, soon matching his rhythm. His movements quickly grew more fierce, but so did her own. A tautness grew within her that drove her on. Moving her hands to his hips, she clutched him as she tightened her legs around him. She tried to take him deeper within herself. A small part of her was aware of how she lightly scored his skin with her nails, but she was unable to stop it. Suddenly, something within her snapped. She heard herself cry out his name, then lost all sense of consciousness. Only faintly was she aware of his arm slipping beneath her hips to hold her tightly against him.

A sudden wildness in her movements warned Thayer of Gytha's impending release. When it tore through her, Thayer found himself dragged along. He bellowed her name as his passion peaked. Collapsing upon her, he was blurrily aware of how their bodies trembled, of how their breath came in hoarse, unsteady gasps. He pressed his face to the curve of her neck, savoring the scent of her as he struggled to regain his composure.

With the return of her sanity, Gytha was too shy to speak. She barely glanced at Thayer when he left the bed to fetch a cloth to wash them with. She hid her face in her hands when he gently cleaned her of the stain of her lost innocence. When he rejoined her in their bed, she burrowed into his hold, hiding her face against the thick pelt on his broad chest.

As the silence dragged on, Thayer began to grow anxious, fearful of having left her revolted. "Did your maid, Edna, tell you true then?"

"Aye, but . . ." she bit off her words, suddenly afraid of disgusting him by saying too much, by speaking too boldly of things a woman should not.

Having braced himself for her words, he was a little piqued when none came. "But what?" He had no real desire to hear her voice her disgust, yet he needed to know her true feelings.

"I do not think I should speak on it."

"Gytha, tell me—but what?"

Taking a deep breath, she hoped she would not be penalized for the truth. "Edna told me true about what would happen. Mama told me about how it was my duty, a necessary part of marriage needed to beget heirs. Neither told me I should like it—which I rather did." Fear of how he would react to her bold words began to steal the strength from her voice. "I should not speak of it, for mayhap 'tis unladylike for me to like it or say that I do."

She felt tension creep through his frame. Her heart sank. Time and again she had been warned about speaking too openly, told again and again that it did not become a woman. When she mustered the courage to sit up and look at him, she found him staring at her in amusement.

"You liked it?" His voice was a little strained as he fought to smother an urge to laugh, knowing she would never understand it as joy.

Flushing, she stared at her hands. "Aye, but we need not speak of it again."

A wide grin brightening his expression, he pulled her back into his arms. "Oh, I think we might. Daft wench."

Hearing the amused affection in his voice she peered up at him from beneath her lashes. "You do not mind that I like it?"

" 'Tis a burden I am willing to bear."

A mock scowl shaped her mouth as she saw the laughter on his face. "You tease me. Wretched man."

"Aye. Our thoughts ran against each other. I thought you disgusted by the act. You thought to like it would disgust me." He shook his head. "I know not what other men might think, but a wife who likes it suits me just fine."

"Did"—she nervously cleared her throat— "did you like it?"

Hoisting her up his body until they were nose to nose, he cupped her small face in his hands. "I have ne'er liked it so well." He kissed her gently. "In truth, I liked it so well I believe I shall have me another taste."

Her passion reawakening, she arched into his touch. "Right now?"

"Are you sore, little one?"

"Nay, not truly."

" 'Tis all I need to know."

Yet again he carried her to passion's heights. With knowledge came an easing of her fears, allowing her greater freedom to enjoy it all the more. She reveled in the feelings he stirred in her.

Thayer made love to her with less restraint, allowing his passion full reign. The signs he had questioned before he now knew to be indicative of her desire. He luxuriated in that knowledge, finding it nearly as intoxicating as the woman herself.

Dawn's light was swiftly growing into daylight when Thayer awoke. He stared at the small woman sprawled so comfortably across his chest. Soon the wedding breakfast would be brought to their chamber. The stained bed linen would be duly witnessed as proof of his bride's innocence and the consummation of the marriage. Not eager to have Gytha stared at again, he slid out from beneath her. A faint smile curved his mouth when she frowned in her sleep, then murmured his name. He hurried to fetch their robes. After donning his own, he brought Gytha hers only to discover that his new bride could be difficult to wake up.

" 'Tis morning already?" she muttered as he prodded her into a sitting position then began to put her into her robe.

"Aye, and soon there will be people arriving. They need no second view of your charms."

"Thoughtful of you." She yawned, letting

her head droop forward to rest upon his chest as, finally, he got her adequately covered.

He laughed softly as he lay back down. "Ah, well, 'tis true that I allowed you little sleep."

"Mmmm. Very little." She curled up in his arms feeling warm and contented. "We can sleep now."

With a yawn and a sleepy rub of her cheek against the fiery curls adorning his chest, she proceeded to let sleep reclaim her. Although she had never been a lazy person, waking in the morning had never been one of her favorite chores. She had never found it quite so difficult before, however. But then, she mused with sleepy amusement, her sleep had never been as broken before. Sleep and wedding nights were not really compatible. The pleasure of snuggling up to Thayer made her even more loathe to leave the haven of a warm bed.

Thayer had almost joined her in sleep when the same group that had attended the bedding ceremony arrived. A maid followed, carrying a tray laden with a hearty meal. When he was unable to wake Gytha, Thayer had to endure many a subtle ribald remark. The ceremony was carried out while they were still abed. To his consternation, he blushed when, roused by the disturbance, Gytha murmured his name, then moved within his hold in a blatantly sensual manner. The women fled the room blushing and giggling. To Thayer's annoyance and consternation, the men were slower to leave and far less reticent.

When they were gone at last, he struggled for a while to eat while still holding the sleeping Gytha. His movements as well as the smell of the food worked as he had hoped. Gytha began to wake up. She sat up slowly, blinking a few times and rubbing the sleep from her eyes. He thought her adorable.

"You had best eat," he said, setting the tray on his lap, "ere I down it all."

Smiling sleepily, she helped herself to some food. Shyness engulfed her, tying her tongue, and even his occasional soft smiles did little to ease it. When he set the emptied tray aside, she huddled down beneath the covers.

Lying on his side, Thayer lightly traced the color that stained her cheeks with his fingers. "So quiet this morn. No kiss for your husband?"

Tentatively, she slid her arms round his neck, then tugged his face down to hers. For a moment he was satisfied with the shy, sweet, yet untrained kiss she gave him. Then he deepened it, dipping his tongue into the honied recesses of her mouth. By the time he lifted his head he was breathless. He was glad to see that she suffered the same condition.

" 'Tis morning," she murmured as he shed his robe, a little disgusted at how timid she sounded.

Grinning, he tugged her robe off of her. "Aye, little one, and I know just the way to celebrate the sun's rising."

Despite her shyness, as well as a soreness

she was increasingly aware of, she did not push him away when he lay down in her arms. "You do not prefer the dark?"

Resting on his forearms, he looked her lithe body over with ill-concealed hunger. "Nay, not when it hides such loveliness from my eyes."

He traced and teased the rosy tip of one breast with his finger, savoring the way it tautened beneath his touch. One reason he was eager to possess her in the stark, revealing light of day was to reassure himself that her passion was no dream. He wanted to see her response to him, to see it without the deceiving half-light of candles distorting his assumptions.

After the hell Elizabeth had dragged him through, he had sworn never again to get involved with a woman both lovely and gentle-bred. Now he found himself wed to one. Worse, there was a treacherous softening within him, a response to her every smile. When he touched his lips to her breast, he felt a fire seize him. He greatly feared he was going to make a fool of himself again.

Gytha shuddered with delight when he drew the hard apex of her breast into his mouth, drawing on it slowly. His tongue curled around and stroked the tip. She moved her hands over his large muscular frame with a greater surety. With an increasingly eager abandonment, she began to squirm beneath him and edged her hand upwards along the inside of his thighs.

A hoarse cry broke from Thayer when her hand reached his aching maleness. His body shook with the force of his pleasure. She gave a gasp of surprise, then withdrew her hand. He quickly grasped that retreating hand, tugging it back to his groin.

"Aye, sweet Gytha, touch me." Desire tautened his voice, put a ferocity behind his caresses. " 'Tis a pleasure near to pain. Aye, loving, aye. Stroke me. Curl those pretty fingers round me."

Despite his efforts at restraint, his passion grew wild. Her touch stirred him past all caution. To his delight, she caught his fever.

Gytha found only pleasure in his increasing ferocity, even though his lovemaking bordered on assault. His possession of her was nearly painful, but she reveled in it. When her release came, she knew he was with her.

It was a while before Thayer retrieved his senses. Propping himself up on his forearms, he gazed down at the woman he was still intimately entwined with. He winced when he saw the red marks left by his rough loving. Yet, her touch as she moved her hands over his chest and the smile she gave him revealed no anger or fear—only sated lethargy.

Idly, Gytha flattened some of the flame curls on his chest with her hand, watching as they curled back up again. She moved her legs up and down his, enjoying the feel of their hair-roughened strength. The unity of their bodies was something she savored.

" 'Tis wondrous, is it not?"

"Wondrous?" He was not sure what "it" she referred to.

"We are so different, yet we fit together so perfectly."

"Aye, we do." Tracing the remnants of his love-making upon her breasts, he asked, "Did I hurt you?"

"Nay." She gave him an impish look. "I begin to wonder if t'was not the men you fight in battle who dubbed you the Red Devil. Mayhaps t'was the women whose beds you have shared."

"Witch." He gave her a soft kiss. "You set me aflame, sweet Gytha. I fear I lose control."

"I can understand that."

"Can you now."

"Aye, 'tis no lady I am at such a time."

"Ah, well, a lady does not often please a man in his bed." He eased the intimacy of their embrace. "A little wantonness in a wife is a fine thing," he teased as he rolled onto his back, pulling her into his arms.

She gave a sleepy chuckle. "Wretched man. We should rise soon."

"Rest a while, dearling."

"It seems a sin to lie abed so late."

"We will not be missed. I must also lay plans for the next few days."

"More reason to get started."

"Rest, wife. It can wait awhile."

"As you command, husband."

"A very proper attitude for a wife."

Laughing softly, she snuggled up to him.

Here were the arms she was meant to curl up in. Their lovemaking had only increased her sense of rightness. Only one thing troubled her. Despite his passion, she sensed a reticence in Thayer, as if he tried to keep a distance between them. He would obviously need time. She would do all she could to show him how perfectly matched they were. As sleep crept over her, her thoughts were filled with visions of the children they would have and the peaceful future that stretched out before them. She was sure he would soon share those dreams.

Gazing down at the woman resting so comfortably in his arms, Thayer felt a twinge of amazement. Despite the fever of need that had gripped him, he had watched her. Her passion was no trick of the light. She truly burned to his touch. It was exhilarating, but it was also a source of consternation. Now that he had introduced her to the joys of passion, she might not be so quick to box the ears of opportuning gallants. That morality she displayed could stem mostly from ignorance. She would no longer view men and women through a child's eyes but a woman's. He feared he had set the seal on his own fate—that of an unhappy cuckold.

Chapter Four

Excitement and sadness gripped Gytha. It had taken a full week, but she and Thayer were now ready to leave. She was starting on a new life. Unfortunately, it meant leaving behind all she had ever known or loved. She knew her family would always be there for her, but things would be forever changed. They had to be. Her husband was now her world.

When her father bade her farewell, hugging her tightly, she saw the bright sheen of tears in his eyes. She had seen it in her brother's eyes as well, and her mother now stood away from her, weeping loudly. Afraid she would give in to tears, Gytha quickly joined Margaret and an excited Edna in the cart. As they started on their way, she found it impossible to watch her home fade from sight without tears. She did her best to halt them.

Their first destination would be Saitun Manor. Gytha was eager to see it, having heard nothing but good about it. Once all had been set to order there, they would journey to the small holding she had brought to the marriage. It was hard not to be excited about the trip. She had traveled very little in her life and never too far. It was also hard not to feel just a little afraid.

Glancing at the twenty men who rode with them, she told herself that such fears were silly. Thayer and Roger, along with the dozen men in their service, were all hardened fighters, most of them knighted upon the field of battle. Her father had contributed six men to their number, each a strong, willing fighter. They had been hard put to hide their delight at a chance to ride with the famed Red Devil. She knew she had no need to fear.

What little she had been able to discover had confirmed all Edna had said of Thayer and his men. Most were indeed the illegitimate sons of nobles, as were many of the small knot of pages and squires attending them. In fact, many of the pages were half-brothers to the men they served.

One page in particular interested her. He had flame-colored hair, and she was determined to ask Thayer about the boy. Jealousy had tightly gripped her the first time she had seen the boy, but she had shaken its hold. The boy had to be eight or nine years of age. She would have been only a child herself when he was born. Even so, she would find out the truth. She just wished she knew what she should do if her suspicions were right.

Roger caught Gytha watching the boy again. "You had best tell her," he murmured to Thayer.

Glancing towards his wife, Thayer sighed. "Aye. Knowing that she is not reticent, I have been taking the coward's way out. I but awaited her asking about Bek. 'Tis a sordid tale. I have little stomach for repeating it. Especially not to her."

"She is one of the few who can claim a right to know. I understand your reluctance, however. The innocence she holds is a wonder. Even the maid and Margaret hold that sweetness. 'Tis as if they have lived in a world apart from ours."

"Lord John has kept his home a world apart. Who can blame him? There is much darkness in the world. His people follow his lead. They are good, God-fearing folk who feel rules are made to be obeyed. He treats his people with kindness and understanding, and they repay him with an unswerving loyalty. 'Tis a shining example of what can be."

"But rarely is."

"Sadly so."

"I could have wished for a little less godliness, however. I sorely missed the light maids found at other keeps. Why, his own sons must journey to town to bed a woman." He shared a soft laugh with Thayer. "Ah, well, I can see how it can be a good thing."

"How so?"

"There is no chance of some maid setting herself above the wife, thinking herself better than she is. There is none of that strife for the lady of the keep to bear."

"Aye." Thayer frowned. "I may have to clean out my own keep."

"The ladies will see to that. Have no fear."

By the time they stopped for the night, Gytha felt far less excitement about traveling. It was tedious and dirty. As soon as Thayer's tent was set up, she called for some water. It was the boy, Bek, who delivered it, reminding her of something she had struggled to forget. She watched the young flame-haired boy walk away, then stepped inside the tent.

Margaret shook her head. "Why have you hesitated to ask him about the boy?"

" 'Tis a difficult question."

"I have ne'er known you to suffer such reticence before."

"Ah, Margaret, mayhap I fear the tale I will be told."

"Best if you know it, m'lady," Edna said as she took the water from Gytha.

"Why do you say that? 'Tis often said a wife is happiest when kept ignorant."

"Pox and piles. What if the woman still lives? What if she is some fine lady? You could meet her at some time. What if you are told

by others? Aye, and by those who would poison
the tale and your heart as well. Nay, 'tis best
to know it all, m'lady, not to be surprised later.
And—" Edna took a deep, steadying breath before adding, "best to know if 'tis a past love or
one you may have to fight."

Gytha winced, afraid of just that. "All you
say is true, Edna. I but need to gain the courage
to ask him."

"Come," Margaret patted Gytha's arm in a
gesture of sympathetic understanding, "we
shall walk to the edge of the camp. I saw flowers scattered in the wood. We shall gather a
few to ease the scent of horses and hard-
worked men. It may keep you from fretting too
much on the matter."

Before Gytha could protest the idea, Edna
shooed them out of the tent. The men paid little
heed to her and Margaret as they walked
across the camp. Idly, they strolled through
the surrounding forest, yet kept close enough
to the camp to hear the men working. Gytha
was quickly soothed by the quiet of the wood.
She smiled her gratitude to Margaret as they
gathered some flowers.

Just as they prepared to return to camp, Gytha spotted a particularly lovely wildflower.
Falling several paces behind Margaret she bent
to pick it. When she straightened up, she came
face to face with a well-armed man.

For one brief instant she was shocked into
stillness. Then she looked around her. Other
men began to appear. They crept through the

surrounding trees leading their horses. An attack was in the making. She ducked when the man she faced reached for her, neatly eluding him.

"Run, Margaret," she cried and, eluding the man a second time, raced towards camp.

Margaret hesitated only long enough to glance over her shoulder to see what was happening. Hiking up her skirts, she too bolted towards camp.

"Alarm them, Margaret," Gytha shouted as she ran a losing race with the man cursing heartily behind her.

"To arms! Attack! To arms!"

Even as Margaret used precious breath to scream, the men in the wood were mounting. She could only pray that she had robbed them of the element of surprise.

Thayer tensed as Margaret's screams pierced the air. Her words were unclear, but their meaning was not. Although his men were already racing to arm themselves, Thayer bellowed his orders. He glared at a frantic Edna, who rushed to his side.

"They were in the forest alone?"

"Aye." Edna backed away from his fury. "They went to pick flowers."

He began loping towards the trees even as Margaret broke free of the concealing depths of the forest. "Where is Gytha?"

"Right behind me," she replied, then kept running towards the tent, easily understanding his curt gesture.

Standing near the edge of the wood, Thayer fought the panic suring through him. "Gytha!"

"Here, Thayer," she cried as she broke clear of the trees.

One look at Thayer's face was enough for Gytha. She made a slight detour around him. When he jerked a finger towards the tent, she obeyed without a word. His fury was a nearly tangible thing. She winced when she heard her pursuer scream. Gytha raced on to the tent where Edna and Margaret awaited her. Together they watched the battle with a mixture of horror and fascination.

Gytha suffered little fear. She could not believe her large, skillful husband was going to be cut down. At least, not this time. She tried to soothe her companions' fear that all that stood between them and a fate unknown and horrifying was the small knot of young pages standing firm before the tent. It was a concern she could sympathize with. Stalwart though the boys were, they could be easily disposed of if the enemy broke through to them. She simply did not believe this particular enemy would get past Thayer and his men.

A slight draft ruffled Gytha's skirts from the rear. Glancing over her shoulder in absent-minded curiosity, Gytha froze. A man had cut his way into the tent and was stepping towards her. She shoved Margaret and Edna out of the tent, out of immediate danger. The startled young women were momentarily entangled with the boys. Before anyone looked her way

again, Gytha found herself firmly in the grasp
of the intruder.

Despite her desperate struggles, he kept her
held before him as he started out of the tent.
Even in the midst of her fear, she was touched
by the action of the pages. They quickly encircled the women. Swords held at the ready they
made no move for fear of what would happen
to her as a result.

It quickly became clear to Gytha that she
was not going to be murdered but taken as a
hostage. Her fear was swiftly overtaken by
fury. She struggled with renewed vigor. It did
not free her but did work to make her captor's
retreat awkward. Even as she heard him curse,
she felt a blinding pain in her head. Then she
slipped into blackness.

Pulling his sword free of yet another body,
Thayer paused to look towards the tent. A loud
wailing was coming from the women's refuge.
At first he attributed it to panic, but it troubled
him. Even as he looked, the man holding Gytha
struck her on the head with the flat of his
sword. A bellow of rage escaped Thayer when
he saw her go limp in the man's grasp. Without
thought to his back, he raced towards Gytha.
A small part of his fury-choked mind was cog-
nizent of Roger rushing to protect him even
though the battle was nearing an end.

Making sure that none of the retreating attackers took lethal advantage of Thayer's in-
attention, Roger kept pace with him. He
noticed that it was not only Gytha's captor

who paled as Thayer hurtled towards him. Margaret, Edna, and the pages did as well. Any sane person, Roger mused, would be frightened by the advance of so much fury. He was relieved when Thayer finally checked his murderous charge.

Thayer grasped enough sanity to halt before he ran into the man holding Gytha. The way her captor had shifted her limp form to shield himself completely had cut through rage's blinding force. Thayer stood glaring at the man, his sword held at the ready, and ached to bury that finely honed blade deep into the one who had struck his wife.

"Careful," Bek murmured, acquainted with the rage, though rare, that twisted his father's face. "The mistress is his shield."

"Aye," snapped Thayer. "The dog cowers behind her skirts. Come out, you craven slug, and deal with me as a man."

"I wish to yield." The man looked towards the calmer Roger. "I wish to yield."

Gripping Thayer's arm to halt any rash moves, Roger ordered, "Toss your sword aside then."

After a brief hesitation, and still clinging to Gytha, the man threw his sword at Thayer's feet. Thayer shook with the urge to kill, but he let Roger pick up the sword and move to the man's side. Without a word, Thayer sheathed his sword, then took Gytha from the trembling man. Picking her up in his arms, he went to his tent. Even as he gently placed Gytha on her cot, Margaret and Edna hurried into the tent.

Looking down at Gytha, Edna ordered, "See to your wounded, m'lord. 'Tis but a knock on the head."

"Are you certain?"

"Aye, m'lord. See? She already stirs. We can tend to her."

Thayer stared at Gytha for a moment. He had to fight his panic over how still, how wan, she looked. Edna was right. Gytha was already stirring, her brow creasing as her thoughts awoke. Turning sharply on his heel, he strode out of the tent and almost knocked down a waiting Roger.

"How many have we lost?" he snapped, heading straight towards their only prisoner.

"Two are dead. Three were hurt, but not badly. It was foolish of the women to wander off like that, but their warning saved us." As they halted before the prisoner, Roger murmured, "You will learn naught if you kill him."

"Nay, I will not kill him." Thayer glared at the cowering man. "Your name."

"John Black, m'lord."

"Who sent you here, John Black?" When the man hesitated in answering, Thayer cursed. "I shall have the skin from your bones—strip by strip."

"We were in your cousin's hire, m'lord."

"Robert Saitun?"

"Aye, though t'was his uncle who ordered us."

Grabbing the man by the front of his heavily

quilted jupon, Thayer snarled, "You will return to my dear cousin Robert and that slinking dog who leads him. You will advise them to fade from my sight. I have no stomach for killing my own kin but, by God's bones, I will find it if I catch sight or scent of them." He tossed the man aside. "Cut three fingers from his sword hand," he ordered the men guarding the prisoner, "then send him on his way." He started towards the water barrels, closing his mind to the man's pleas and his screams as the order was carried out.

"The mistress?" Bek hurried to fill a bucket of water for his father.

"Edna assures me 'tis but a mild knock on the head."

Roger smiled his thanks when Bek fetched water for him as well. "Is that why your punishment was so mild?"

"Nay." Thayer sighed as Bek helped him shed his upper clothing. "The man only did as commanded. 'Tis plain he checked his blow when he struck Gytha. He but wished to still her thrashing. I saw that, once the blazing red of fury had cleared."

With Bek's help, Roger also bared his torso. "Was it wise to warn Robert or his cur of an uncle?"

Shrugging, Thayer began to wash. "Who can say? It was in my head that this was but a blind, unthought lunge. Robert wanted Gytha. I saw the look in his eyes when I was named bridegroom. Then too, he is my only kin aside from Bek here. I have no real wish to cut him down. That uncle of his was the one behind this. I know it. He wishes Robert to hold all, and he may be willing to try any means to see to that. We must keep a closer guard. I have no wish for the tale of my death to be true next time 'tis told."

"Especially when there is so much to live for," Roger murmured, flicking a glance towards Thayer's tent.

"Aye." Thayer could not stop himself from looking that way as well as he dried himself off.

"She was the one to see the man enter the tent," explained Bek. "She pushed the other two ladies to safety."

"And got herself taken," grumbled Thayer.

"When you bellow at her, mayhap you could do it softly."

"What say you?"

"Well, her head will surely ache for a time."

After staring at his son for a moment, Thayer laughed. "A gentleman does not bellow at a lady."

Bek briefly returned Thayer's grin before exclaiming with boyish enthusiasm, "Did you see them run?"

"Aye, the dogs were easily routed," Roger said.

"I did not mean the men, Sir Roger. I spoke of the ladies." He smiled when the two men laughed. "I did not know that ladies could run so well. Why, I would wager they could outrun a few here. Aye, more than a few."

"Aye, they were swift. There's a thought. Mayhap," Thayer drawled, "we could set them to race and earn ourselves some coin." He burst out laughing at the look of shock upon his son's face. "I jest, lad. Go now and fetch us a meal. I shall eat ere I see Gytha. I just saw Edna fetch some food. Gytha must have roused by now."

While Bek hurried to obey, Thayer went to see to a chore of his own. He aided in the shrouding of the two dead men. At the first churchyard they reached, he would see to their internment. He felt sorry about their deaths, yet glad that neither of them had been with him a long while or were close to him. After a brief word with the wounded, assuring himself that none was too badly hurt, he sat with Roger to eat his meal.

There was a lengthy silence before Roger murmured, "You are sunk deep in thought, my friend."

" 'Tis but the lull after the storm." He could see the doubt upon Roger's face and grimaced. "How does a man stop himself from softening towards a beautiful woman?"

"He does not. Cannot if it is meant to be."

"What was meant to be was Gytha wed to William."

"Mayhap not. Who knows how God and fate work?"

"None of we poor mortals, to be sure."

"I should not let it gnaw at me. Enjoy her.

For all the trouble and pain such feeling can bring, there is still none to equal it."

"You sound as if you speak from experience." Thayer could not recall Roger ever mentioning such a problem before.

"Aye, I do, though it has been many a year. There was no hope for it. I was a landless knight and as poor as I am now. Short lived though it was, t'was glorious."

"And from that you learned naught of how to hold back such feelings?"

"I have no wish to. What I did learn was to see where it might be stirred. Then I might avoid a like happenstance." He took a deep breath, knowing he would touch upon a sore spot with his next words. "I knew my love to be a fruitless thing ere I gave it. Aye, and as I gave it. The lady made no false promises, but always spoke true. When what little we had was ended, the pain was shared. She dealt out no scorn. Her heart may not have been as enslaved as mine, but she gave me no sign of it. She never found my feelings a source of amusement and play."

"And therein lies the difference," Thayer murmured and Roger nodded.

"Aye, therein lies the difference. Mayhap you could ponder that a little."

Promising himself he would, Thayer retired to his tent and quickly ushered out Margaret and Edna. For a while he thought Gytha asleep. Then he caught her peeking at him. Like a child, she sought to hide behind closed eyes to avoid his wrath, a wrath he no longer felt. Snuffing the candle, he shed his clothes, slid into bed, and tugged her slightly tensed body into his arms.

"How fares your head?" he asked, brushing a kiss over her forehead as he felt her relax a little in his hold.

Gytha knew he was no longer furious. She had felt like a coward feigning sleep to avoid the anger he had every right to. However, she had dreaded hearing it. She had known, deep down, that if any of his words were cutting she would bleed freely.

"It aches a little but not overly much." She slipped her arms about his waist.

"You were foolish to rush off alone."

"I did not rush." She felt his broad chest tremble faintly with his soft laughter.

"Gytha, I am lecturing you. Be silent and heed me closely."

"Aye, my husband."

He ignored that touch of impertinence. "It was foolish to leave the safety of the camp. You must never wander off unless you tell me where and why first. I know you expected fury from me. You would have received it save that I stayed away until my blood cooled. Neither were you badly hurt. And the warning you gave saved my men. A surprise attack like that would have been a slaughter—ours. Instead, I lost but two men. But why did you wander away?"

"I wanted some flowers to scent these quarters."

"Next time you wish to gather some, tell me. I will send a well-armed man with you. Mayhap two."

"They will not like it much."

"They will do it all the same. Heed me?"

She nodded her acquiesence. "What happened to the man who seized me?"

"He lost three fingers on his sword hand. I then sent him back to his master with a warning."

She trembled faintly but knew the punishment was quite merciful compared to what many another would have meted out. "And who was his master?"

"My cousin—Robert."

"Robert?" She shook her head in surprise. "Are you certain?"

"Aye. That is the name the attack was carried out under. Howbeit, t'was his uncle who plotted and commanded. I think you know that as well as I."

"Aye. And Robert, no matter how he felt, would allow it. Yet, why? Why do such a thing?"

"He wants it all—my estates, my fortune. They would rest in Robert's name, but the uncle would rule. Then too, Robert wanted you. Nay," he murmured when she began to protest. "He did and he does. I think now that it would not have been a very safe marriage for you."

"How so?"

"Because you might well have made Robert a man."

She slowly nodded her understanding. "If Robert grew stronger, took more responsibility, then he could become a threat to his uncle. That man would not long tolerate a threat."

"Nay, he would be quick to see to the permanent removal of a threat like that."

"What do you mean to do about him?"

"I sent that man back to Robert and his uncle. Now they will know their plot has failed, know I am aware of their schemes. I told them it would be wise to make themselves scarce—very scarce indeed. It will be my only warning."

"Do you really think it will be heeded?"

" 'Tis my hope that it will be. I have no stomach for killing my own kin."

"How sad it is when families battle amongst themselves. My father came from such a family."

"That is hard to believe. Your own family is a close one, a loving one. 'Tis clear for all to see."

"Papa learned from mistakes he saw made as he grew, Thayer. He saw a husband turn his own wife against him. He saw how, in her hurt, she then turned his own children against him. He saw how bastards, bred and recognized yet unloved, turned bitter, greedy eyes on what was denied them. As he grew he saw those who should have stayed together and been a haven of trust and love for each other, pull away from each other. They schemed and murdered until none but my father and his brother were left. He and my uncle vowed they would never let that poison touch them." She shook her head. "My aunt does try, though."

"Because of Margaret?"

"Aye. My aunt is jealous of a bachelor's one error, though I hate to consider Margaret so. Because of that jealousy, my aunt tries to poison the family against him. She tries, but she will fail."

"Are you sure of that?"

"Very sure. Soon the boys will go for fostering, the girls as well. Uncle will send his children to my parents. Margaret is now with me, as was always planned. The two houses will mix more. Whatever poison has been planted will be drawn out."

As Thayer listened to her tale he realized that now was the perfect time to speak of Bek. Margaret's plight was fresh in Gytha's mind, softening her attitude. Still, he found it hard to begin. He was not overly concerned about her acceptance of Bek. That could be worked on. It was the tale he had to relate that troubled him. It was sordid and, he feared, left him looking the greatest of idiots. Neither would any wife be glad to hear a tale of her husband's love for another, long dead though it was. Nevertheless, he struggled to swallow those qualms and begin his story.

"Speaking of bachelor follies," he began, still hesitant.

Gytha fought against tensing. She wanted nothing to halt the tale he was about to tell. As she waited for him to continue, she prayed she would not hear anything that would hurt too badly.

"I must spit this out now," he muttered, mostly to himself. " 'Tis easier to speak of such follies in the dark."

"One feels less bared to view."

"Aye. Bek is my son."

"I had suspected that." She slid her fingers through his thick hair. "This color is somewhat rare."

"This is a confidence."

"I will tell no one," she said, adding to herself, "except, mayhap, Margaret. Mayhap Edna too."

"His mother is Lady Elizabeth Sevilliers. Her birth name was Darnelle."

"Neither family is familiar to me."

"You will come to know of both if we are summoned to court. Where the court is, there is Lady Elizabeth."

"She is very beautiful, is she?" Gytha grimaced over the insecurity that prompted the question.

"Aye, very. Ebony hair, ivory skin, green eyes, and soft, full curves. I was very young, but one-and-twenty, when I met her. At sixteen, she was already well trained in the flirtatious ways of the court, her virtue already naught but a memory. But I was not only young, I was foolish. I thought her an innocent, overwhelmed and misused by the corrupt, sinful ways of court. I became her lover."

A flash of pain made Gytha inwardly wince. She sternly reminded herself that she had been but a child of eight at the time. It was enough to push aside her hurt.

"How blithely she returned all my vows of love." Thayer shook his head. "She let me believe there was a chance for us to wed, though I was but a landless knight. I sold my sword to an earl in the hope of a reward which would alleviate that. She carried on mightily when it was time for me to leave. It made me feel sure of her avowed love."

"So you returned to her?"

"I did. Six months later, with no land but a heavy purse. It was heavy enough to purchase some small manor. She, however, was no longer at court. It took me over a fortnight to find her."

"Where had she gone?"

"To a nunnery to bear my child. Bek was several days old when I found Elizabeth. She sat, listening calmly, as I told her of my gains and spoke of love and marriage. Then she began to laugh."

Hearing the pain of humiliation in his voice, Gytha tightened her hold on him. She wished she could wash it from his heart, from his memory.

It was hard, but Thayer pressed on with his

tale. "She said she had not thought me such a fool. Did I truly believe all she had vowed? I reminded her of the son she had just borne me. Surely that proved her love. Again she laughed. All that showed, she said, was that the tricks she used to stop my seed from rooting were not perfect. Neither were the methods she had used to rid her body of the child."

"She tried to kill the child she carried?" Gytha whispered in deep shock.

"Aye, but Bek was strong. I found out later that his first breath could well have been his last. When left alone with the babe, she tried to smother him. One of the nuns caught her, and they took the child away. They excused her actions by saying she had been driven to near madness by the living proof of her sins. I knew she planned to leave no proof of her lack of chastity. You see, a wedding was arranged.

"I could not believe it, did not want to. Yet again I pressed her to wed me. She called me a fool to ever think she would choose a landless knight, one who must sell his sword for his livelihood, over the rich, titled Sevilliers. Over a man with many a rich holding. I told her he would lose his love for her quickly when he found her unchaste. She laughed off that warning. There would be blood spilt at the bedding, and the Sevilliers would be made to believe her virginal."

"And so you left her, taking Bek."

"I took Bek, aye. But I could not quit Elizabeth, and therein lies my shame. Not long after her marriage to Sevilliers, I became her lover again. God's tears, but she could play upon the blindness of my heart. I thought myself her only lover. There were whispers of her wanton ways, but I stoutly ignored them."

"But the whispers were true, were they not?"

"Aye, very true. I discovered that truth in a garden one night. She was frolicking with some courtier there, much like some hedgerow whore. Do you know, I think I was stupid enough to forgive her even that? It was what was said that finally broke her grip upon me. The man spoke as if he had gained some great victory over me by lying with her, one he could never have gained with a sword. She laughed, saying I was but the longest enduring of all her lovers. She said my besotted state amused her. The man confessed surprise at her bedding of one so large, so red, and so lacking in looks. She agreed that I was an ugly brute, well deserving of all the taunts, but I was handsomely endowed. I have not been near her since that day."

He sighed. "Well, there is the whole ugly tale. Now, I must ask you—what of Bek?"

Hurt settled into a corner of her heart when she realized he had not said he had ceased to love the woman. She set that trouble aside. Right now, he needed her answer concerning his son. He needed to know that she would not scorn him or the boy because of the past.

"Bek is your son. He is a very good boy from what little I have seen. I would never turn him away because of some mischance about his birth."

"I thank you for that."

"There is no need to. And ... you are not an ugly brute."

"I am not handsome, Gytha," he muttered, thinking she would now try to gull him with empty flattery. "I am no William. Nay, nor a Robert or a Roger."

"I did not say you were handsome." She sent him an impish grin. "S'truth, if you continue to allow your face to be knocked about so, you could well become ugly." She grew serious again. "Aye, you are large and very red. But you are also strong and healthy. You hold all the grace that fate can bestow. Your build is large but you are well proportioned. Nothing is too large, too long, or too short. Your face may not be fair, but it holds strength and inspires trust. Your voice and the way you laugh are more than passingly fine. When you smile, 'tis not to gull one or to hide a lie. 'Tis lovely." She reached up to touch the corners of his eyes. "You have lovely eyes. That deep, soft brown brings to mind gentle things."

"Lovely eyes?"

"Aye. I have thought so from the first."

He held her close to him. Instinct told him she spoke the truth, said exactly what she felt. She had seen and praised what few favorable points he had. Suddenly he was desperate to make love to her, but he fought that need. After the events of the day, she was in need of her rest.

"Enough, woman. You shall put me to the blush and I am red enough." He smiled when she giggled. "Go to sleep, wife. 'Tis the surest cure for an aching head."

As she snuggled up against him, the evidence of his arousal pressed impudently against her belly. "What aching head?" she inquired pertly.

Laughing, he rolled so that she was sprawled beneath him, then set about heartily accepting her implied invitation.

Chapter Five

"My cousin and that swine who rules him cared little for this place."

Struggling to keep up with her husband's swift strides, Gytha made no reply. She shared Thayer's fury as they walked through Saitun Manor. What beauty it might have had was well hidden by neglect—neglect and filth. The rich, beautiful Saitun Manor she had heard so much about was barely fit for the swine that ran so freely through its halls.

She fought to subdue her anger. It served no purpose. The damage was done. Work and lots of it was needed now, not a fruitless raging at the absent perpetrators.

"I cannot believe William let it get like this," Thayer muttered.

"Nay." Gytha was so out of breath that she

found it very difficult to speak. "He appeared to appreciate cleanliness."

Hearing her breathlessness, Thayer paused to scoop her up into his arms. He idly noted that she was a dainty, light bundle. Not so idly he also noted the way her full breasts rose and fell as she strove to catch her breath. It was an effort to turn his gaze to her flushed face. Anger still gripped him, however. He began to walk again. Fury made it necessary to move. Stepping outside the manor did nothing to ease his fury. Things were as bad outside as in.

"So much work to do," he mumbled.

"Cleaning mostly." She settled herself more comfortably in his arms.

"Aye, of every stone, every corner. Are there enough hands to do the work?"

Slipping an arm around his neck, she kissed his cheek. "If not, we can bring in more from the village."

After a quick check to be sure the ground beneath a tree was clean, Thayer sat down. He smiled faintly when Gytha made no move to leave his arms. She simply arranged herself more comfortably. He had quickly seen that she was very open with her affection. It gave him a pleasant feeling, one he knew could prove dangerous. It could weaken his resolve to stay aloof, to protect his much-abused heart. He had to return her smile, however. That was something he was not strong enough to resist.

"You are taking this very well, Gytha."

"Well, I must admit to being less than pleased to find so much work awaiting me. Still, 'tis work that can be easily done if enough hands are set to the doing of it. There will be reward for the work as well. Beneath the neglect and filth lies a worthy place."

In the days that followed, Gytha found it hard work to prove her words—hard work for both men and women. She hired a few more helpers but did so cautiously, recalling all her training to be careful with her coin. Since the plague had devastated the population, she knew she could no longer count on the unpaid, plentiful labor of serfs. Her father had quickly learned the arts of wage-paying and hiring, and she was soon very glad he had taken the time to teach her the skills. Thayer left it all in her hands, having never had to concern himself with such matters before.

Her first decision was to clean everything. She was certain that, once that was done, she could more easily see what needed replacing or mending. For one solid week, she pushed herself to work alongside the others. By the time she deemed the place clean enough, she was exhausted.

Looking around at week's end, Gytha realized she was simply too tired to appreciate the hard-won cleanliness just yet. Dismissing the hired workers, she dined, then collapsed into her bed. She stirred, roused only slightly from her sleep, when Thayer joined her. For once she was too tired to even wish him a good sleep.

Smiling a little, Thayer tugged his groggy wife into his arms, hungering for the passion they could share. He knew how exhausted Gytha was, however. She murmured his name but barely moved, her slim body limp. He would have to set his needs aside this time. It was clear that no amount of skill would stir her interest now. As she drowsily curled up closer to him, he twitched his nose, his thoughts abruptly veering from his frustration.

"What is that smell?"

"I fear 'tis me, Thayer." Gytha yawned as she spoke, her words slightly slurred.

"Aye, I thought it wafted up from you. What is it?"

"Something I was using to clean with."

" 'Tis rather foul. What was in it?"

"It might be best if you do not know." She dragged herself out of his arms. "I know I should have bathed, but I could not. I am simply too weary. I will sleep on the far side of the bed."

"That helps little," he grumbled as he got out of bed.

She called him back but half-heartedly, then settled down to return to sleep. She knew she would feel bad in the morning about driving him from their bed, but at the moment she was too tired to care. Just as she was taking the last step into the recuperative oblivion of sleep, Thayer yanked the bedcovers off of her.

"What are you doing?" She tried to yank the covers back up, but he picked her up into his arms. "I want to sleep."

"You are going to have a bath."

"I should—I know—but I am too weary. I should likely fall asleep and drown myself."

"Nay, there is little chance of that, for I intend to see to the chore myself." He set her down next to the tub he had had brought in and filled.

Suddenly, she was awake enough to realize what was happening. "I smell that bad?"

"I fear you do, loving." He laughed softly as he tugged her shift off.

Gytha was too tired to be embarrassed. Although she was still not quite comfortable when naked before him, her exhaustion subdued her usual modesty. Feeling as weak as some small, ailing child, she gave herself over completely to his care.

Thayer found the chore of bathing her a frustrating delight. It was a great pleasure to be allowed such freedom to look at her, to touch her. Yet, because of her weariness, he would not be able to ease the hunger such freedom stirred. At times he found the ease with which she could rouse his passion unsettling. For all its glory, it could only be called a weakness.

He watched as he moved his hand over her full breasts. Sighing, he decided she could produce that weakness in any man. It was hard for him to accept that he possessed such beauty. Each morning that he awoke to find her in his arms, he was surprised anew. That did little to ease the wariness that gripped him. He began to think he would never fully subdue it.

As he dried her off and slipped a clean shift on her, he had to smile. She was as good as blind drunk with weariness. Gently, he tucked her back into bed. Dousing the lights, he climbed in beside her, then tugged her into his arms.

"Ah, much better," he murmured as he nuzzled her hair.

"I was that foul, was I?"

"Aye, you were. You are sweet of scent again."

"Thank you, Thayer, and"—despite her state, she was aware of his arousal, of the need she was too tired to ease for him—"I am sorry. I am just too tired."

He smiled crookedly. "You will be rested come the morn."

"Well, aye, I will. So?"

"So, I can wait."

"Oh."

She fell asleep even as she laughed softly, surprising Thayer into an echoing laugh. However, he decided that she would not be allowed to exhaust herself so again. Not only his body's needs prompted his decision. She risked her health. That was too precious a price to pay for cleanliness despite how good that cleanliness felt. Only half-jesting, he deemed his frustration too high a price as well. Closing his eyes, he reached out for sleep to deaden his unsatisfied needs.

Stretching langorously, Gytha watched her husband wash up. She decided that it was nice to wake to passion, to gently stroking hands and soft, heated kisses. The glow his lovemaking gave her could not even be dimmed by thinking of the work ahead.

"Now, Gytha," Thayer sent her a stern look as he began to dress, "you are not to work so hard again."

"Nay?"

"Nay. I understand the need to clean this sty. 'Tis clean now. What work remains need not be done as swiftly. Your good health is more important than any added comfort. S'truth, if you fall ill, you will only lose time."

"Aye, you are right. I thought on that as I staggered to bed last night. T'was the filth. I could not bear it."

Moving to the side of the bed, he bent to kiss her. "I know. 'Tis gone now and can be kept away with, for the most part, simple supervision. Take care now. That is a command," he added with a warning shake of his finger before leaving.

She made no protest. It was a command she could easily obey. There were many things she could live without, but not cleanliness. She had been unable to endure the filth that had inhabited every corner of the place. That was gone now. She would be perfectly content to go more slowly. There would be plenty of time to make the keep as lovely as she knew it could be. She would take it one step at a time. It was not long before she began to wonder if even one step at a time would prove to be too much.

Glaring at the garden, Gytha muttered, " 'Tis hard to see the herbs for the weeds."

"Aye." Margaret sighed. " 'Tis clear those fools cared naught for medicines."

"Nor for pleasing scents."

"That was easily seen."

Pulling up her sleeves, Gytha knelt in the dirt. "Well, we have sore need of both. We will seek out what useful plants still thrive amongst this tangle. They may have been weakened by neglect. Howbeit, I think there is still time in the season for them to recover."

"Aye. And thrive." Kneeling beside Gytha as she also tugged up her sleeves, Margaret looked over the garden. "I believe I can see a few good things peeping out."

A companionable silence fell as Gytha worked side by side with Margaret. She liked to work in the garden. Work in either the utilitarian kind or a garden planted solely for its beauty pleased her. Hard though the work was, it gave her a sense of contentment.

"Gytha? Are you happy?"

Startled by the abrupt question, Gytha stared at her cousin for a moment before answering. "Aye. Did you fear I was not?"

"Well, nay. Yet you have said little about it."

"There is little to say. I think one finds words far easier to come by when things go wrong."

"Aye, sometimes. Do you love Thayer then?"

"Ah me, that question."

"Aye. That one. Do you?"

"I fear I am not sure. 'Tis not as easy to know as I thought it would be. There is but one thing I am sure of—I care. But is that caring—aye, and the passion—what makes love? I believe you can care deeply for someone yet not love them. Well, not as we mean. 'Tis a puzzle." She shook her head.

"Does he love you?"

"Who can know? We ne'er speak of it. 'Tis likely that silence that keeps me uncertain."

"Oh. He cares for you. I know it."

"Cares for me—aye. But is it a caring that will lead to love or simply the caring a man might have for the one who shares his bed and will bear his children? See what I mean? There are too many answers to each question. Too many questions. It could be love. It could be so much else with him and with me. Mayhap if we would talk about it, such confusions would be cleared away. But we never touch upon the subject."

"You must give him time."

"Mayhap, but I am not certain Thayer is a man who could speak of such things. Some men cannot."

"True. Then, there are some who speak of it freely, too freely, and lie."

"I believe I prefer silence to lies."

" 'Tis much better. Mayhap there is one thing that adds to the confusion—something that, if cleared away, would reveal the answers to many questions?"

"Well, there is one thing." She shrugged. "I am not certain clearing it away would settle anything. Thayer does not trust me."

"Nay, Gytha. You imagine things."

"I fear not. I am everything he has learned to be wary of. There is definitely a wariness in him. I can sense it, although I am not certain how deep it runs. Sadly, I am not sure of how I can rid him of it. 'Tis a barrier to all we might feel towards each other."

"It certainly is. Gytha, I think all you can do is exactly what you have been doing. If any woman can be trusted, you can. He must soon see that, see that his wariness is foolishness. Time only is needed. After all, though wed, you are still veritable strangers. You each have so much to learn about the other. While this learning takes place, there is bound to be some wariness."

"Mayhap. Simply muttering vows before a priest, despite how one might honor those vows, does not mean one must immediately give another trust and love. I am most fortunate. My trust has never been abused. His has—badly so. I can give trust with more ease than he can." She smiled at Margaret. "So, what have *you* decided about my husband?"

"I have not really decided anything. Not completely. S'truth, he can make me very uncertain at times."

"Aye, when he roars his anger." Gytha laughed softly when a light flush colored Margaret's face. "There is naught to fear in that, cousin."

"You sound very sure of that."

"I am. Trust me. There is naught to fear in Thayer's anger save that he might deafen you. Look to those fists he waves about, cousin. Aye, they might smash things such as that stable door last week. Rarely do they touch a person's flesh. He knows his own strength well—knows his hot temper too. Oh, aye, he bellows, he curses, he flails—but I have yet to see him hurt anyone while seized so."

"The stablemaster should have liked to know that. He feared for his life."

"And well he should have. His carelessness nearly maimed Thayer's finest stallion. Many another would have cut him down on the spot. Instead the man still lives. The fool may still hold the position of stablemaster if he does not err so badly again."

"Of course. I will try to recall such things next time Thayer sets the walls to trembling," Margaret drawled, causing them both to laugh.

"Is this basil?" Gytha frowned at the cluster of stunted plants before her.

Margaret carefully studied them. "Well, I

think the three in the middle are."

After pausing to vigorously scratch her nose, Gytha began to thin out the growth around the herbs. "I shall probably pull the basil and leave the weeds."

Margaret giggled, then grew serious again. "I feel torn two ways about your confusion. I understand, yet I had hoped for some answers, some knowledge. Mayhap some revelations."

"Revelations? About what?"

"Love," Margaret murmured, then blushed.

"Oh ho—Roger."

"Aye, Roger. I think. 'Tis hard to be certain, not only of my own feelings but his. He has a flirtatious manner. I often fear I see more in his pretty words and soft smiles than may be there. I thought you could help me sort out my own confusion. Mayhap make me see more clearly, understand such matters better."

"Yet you find me as confused as you." Gytha edged along to the next snarled pocket of green. "I am sorry, Margaret. There is this. I have never seen Roger try to beguile any of the maids hereabouts. Neither does he travel to the village as the other men sometimes do."

"I can see that as well. Yet, then I fear I see only what I wish to. If you say you have noted it as well, then it must be true. And, if it is true, mayhap he is sincere."

"Do you wish to know what I would do?"

"Aye. It might help." After tossing a weed on the growing pile, Margaret edged up next to Gytha.

"I should trust Roger until he gives me cause not to. I should believe he is sincere and act accordingly. My thinking is that, if I were too wary, I might lose all I truly want. True, I would be risking hurt if he proved insincere, but the prize that could be gained is well worth the risk.

"Thayer is my husband, so I must endure his wariness. Roger need not tolerate yours. He is free to look elsewhere, to seek one who will not weigh his every word or act for its sincerity."

Margaret nodded slowly. "You are right. I hope I can heed your advice and be brave enough to take the risk."

Returning their full attention to putting some order into the herb garden, they fell silent again. The afternoon sun warmed Gytha's back so that she was quickly aware of the moment that warmth left her. Next, she got the distinct feeling that someone was watching her—closely.

"Oh my, have the clouds come up then?" Margaret shivered faintly, then frowned up at the clear sky.

Glancing over her shoulder, Gytha murmured, "Just one. A big red one." She smiled faintly at her frowning husband. "Is there something wrong, Thayer?"

"I thought we had agreed that you would not work too hard."

Thayer found it hard to maintain his stern expression. Gytha was very dirty. She looked more like some urchin than the lady of the

117

manor. He found it oddly endearing to see her so.

"This is the only chore I have set for myself today."

" 'Tis no easy chore by the looks of it."

"True but, as you can see, I do not work alone."

"And this is all, is it?"

"Aye, this and ensuring there is food aplenty for the men at day's end. 'Tis not so much, Thayer. Truly. And I enjoy it."

"Just be certain you do not enjoy it to the depth of weariness you suffered last night."

"I promise. Oh, and Thayer?" she called as he started to move away. "Could you ask someone to bring us a load of manure?"

"Manure?" He paused to stare at her in slight disbelief. "What for?"

"To spread upon the garden. These poor neglected plants have a great need of it."

"Spread it, hmmmm? I will send someone to do that for you," he added in a tone of command as he strode away.

Gytha openly admired his form as he walked away. He was as enjoyable to watch, she mused, as the finest stallion, holding that same grace and strength. The beauty lacking in his face was more than compensated for in his form. Glancing at Margaret, she caught her cousin eyeing her strangely, a deep blush upon her face.

"Is something wrong, Margaret?"

"Oh, nay. Well—'tis the way you look at him,

Gytha. Why, 'tis a—a hungry look. Aye, hungry."

"And wanton, no doubt. Well, so I feel when I watch him."

"Truly?"

"Truly. Ah, cousin—I know he is not fair of face despite having a very fine pair of eyes. Yet, in form he nears perfection. 'Tis true, some would claim him too hirsute or too red for their liking. But he holds the power, the grace, of a prize stallion. I saw that from the beginning. Of course, now that I know what occurs within the marriage bed . . ." Gytha shrugged as she yanked a weed and tossed it aside.

"He is a good lover as well, cousin. Aye, I know I have naught to compare him with. Howbeit, I cannot believe any other could delight me so in the night." Her brief grin was impish. "Or the morning."

Shocked, Margaret stared at Gytha, the weed she had just pulled still dangling from her hand. "Morning?"

Taking the weed from Margaret, Gytha tossed it aside. "Aye—morning. A maid is told so little. I expected only an acceptable duty, mayhap pain or at best a simple pleasure, the latter found mostly in the knowledge that he enjoyed himself. Well, I found far, far more than that. More than words can ever describe."

" 'Tis fine, is it?" Margaret's voice was soft, revealing her shyness with the topic.

"Aye, which may be why we are told so little." She exchanged a brief grin with Margaret.

"With Thayer 'tis so fine I think I must love the man. Indeed, how could it be otherwise? Yet, then I recall that he also thinks it fine. Does that mean that he loves me?" She shook her head. "I think not. A man's passion need not come from his heart. So, mayhap neither does a woman's."

"And such thinking brings you full circle—back to confusion."

"Aye. I know so little about passion. What can it signify or not signify? How deep can it run? Yet, I do have a deep sense of rightness about this marriage. Neither doubt nor confusion changes that. I am content to muddle along."

" 'Tis all you can do, really."

Gytha nodded. "You have it easier. Passion does not cloud your thoughts or hide your feelings." She smiled at Margaret. "I think 'tis there." She laughed softly when Margaret blushed. "So I thought. Howbeit, though Roger courts you, woos you, plays all the games lovers do—he is not your lover.

"Thayer was a stranger to me and I to him. Then suddenly, we are man and wife. 'Tis the way of things, but I begin to think it wrong. I do not really know this man who holds me in the night. There are so many duties we must tend to during the day. When is there time for us to learn about each other? At night we talk some as we hold each other in the dark. Yet, the passion that flares between us often makes those talks short, little really being learned.

Sometimes I fear the passion will wane. Then all I shall be left with is the stranger. We will know each other's bodies, mayhap share a child, yet not truly know each other."

"Oh, nay, Gytha." Margaret briefly clasped Gytha's arm in a gesture of comfort then tried vainly to brush away the dirt her touch left behind. "Nay. I cannot see that happening. I think that, if you really thought on it, you would find you know a great deal about Thayer. True, you may not know his deepest feelings—his fears, his hopes or all that lies in his past. Howbeit, you do know something, and that will increase as you live and work together, for you do indeed talk to each other. I have seen it."

For a moment, Gytha thought on that, then nodded. "You are right, Margaret. We do talk to each other, not merely indulge in polite conversation and empty courtesies. In those talks lies the knowledge I seek about Thayer. I need to look for it, to think more on all that is said and done and that I have already seen. I will take the time to think hard on what I do know, what I feel sure about. Mayhap the rest will come easier. At least I will gain some idea of what I still need to discover."

The conversation was ended by the arrival of a man with the manure Gytha had asked for. She promised herself not to forget what she and Margaret had talked about. Much of it was worthy of note. She also promised herself she would really think on all she had or had not learned about Thayer and on what she needed to know.

It was not until she was preparing for bed that she found the time needed to fulfill that promise to herself. As soon as Edna left, Gytha made herself comfortable in bed. It would be several minutes before Thayer joined her. She intended to make full use of the time. Lying on her back she crossed her arms beneath her head. First she would look at the obvious, all that was directly before her eyes and which she was sure of.

Thayer was strong, a skilled fighter who had won many an accolade. She could be glad that Thayer was skilled in the art. It meant that she and their children could feel certain of protection.

Honor, she mused, was a large part of his character. Thayer was honorable and fair. Coin had never been his only consideration when pledging his sword to a man. The cause had to be honorable, had to be a just one.

He had a gentleness in him too, despite the way he had lived. She had seen it in the way he dealt with others, in the way he treated her. God had gifted Thayer with a large, strong body, yet Thayer never abused the power that gave him.

Thayer's abrupt entrance into their chambers ended her musings. However, she faintly resented the intrusion, for she felt she was getting somewhere, was finally nearing an understanding of her own feelings. Inwardly promising herself she would return to those contemplations, she sat up in bed to watch Thayer prepare to join her.

Glancing at her, Thayer stripped to his braies and then began to wash up. "You look as if you kept your promise to go more carefully today," he murmured.

"Aye, I did."

"Glad to hear it."

"I was most dutiful and obedient."

"And pert," he drawled, smiling faintly.

"How fares your work?"

Another good trait, she mused, a sense of humor. He also liked to gently tease her. She could appreciate both of those aspects of his character.

"Well enough," Thayer replied. "In truth, good enough to plan our next move. Soon, I believe, we can travel to your bridal lands."

"I have heard that the Western Marches can be a dangerous, trouble-laden place."

"So have I." He snuffed all the candles save the only one by the bed.

"Do you think it true?"

Shedding his braies, he slid into bed, then gently tugged her into his arms. "Sometimes the tales are not quite true. I cannot be certain of what awaits us there until we are there. I need to look about the place for myself. Often the troubles are caused by the very men who decry them, who complain about them the loudest." He frowned down at her. "Mayhap I should leave you here until I am more certain of what awaits us at Riverfall."

"I should rather go with you."

"Oh? Do you mean to argue with your husband then?" he teased.

"Well . . . not exactly."

"Not exactly? What do you mean to call it then?"

"Simply talking over the matter?"

He laughed softly, then brushed a kiss over her forehead. "Save your rhetoric, little one. I should rather you go with me as well. If naught else, I will be more at ease knowing exactly how your journey fares. I may see to your comfort and protection myself, not just sit at Riverfall awaiting your arrival."

"I have never heard my father speak of any great troubles at Riverfall. Mayhap all will be well."

"Mmmmm. Mayhap."

Gytha did not really need his distracted reply to tell her his interest was no longer on conversation. The way he stroked her with his hands as he removed her nightrail told her that. She smiled as she slid her arms around his neck. A faint shiver of delight rippled through her when he pressed her naked body against his.

"Weary of chatter, Thayer?" she murmured even as he teased her lips with soft nibbling kisses.

"Aye. How clever of you to notice."

"A good wife should know when to cease belaboring her husband with conversation." She tried to look righteous when he grinned at her and failed miserably.

"We can talk later." He gently rubbed his loins against hers, her soft sounds of pleasure increasing the need he always had for her. "My interest lies elsewhere."

"Indeed. And where is that?"

Pushing her onto her back, Thayer growled, "I mean to show you, wife."

Her soft laugh was ended by his hungry kiss. As always, she was quickly lost to passion. It was not until she lay sated and recovering from that passion, Thayer sprawled on top of her, that she wondered why she even bothered to try and sort out her feelings. Whatever they signified, they were good ones, not ones that needed fretting about.

She looked down at the man half-asleep in her arms. Idly stroking his thick, bright hair, she wondered just what was in his mind and heart. He gave few clues to his inner thoughts and feelings. She knew she would never be completely certain of her judgments if she based them solely on his actions.

Nevertheless, the look upon his face when she had been presented as his bride was seared into her mind. It was a large part of the worry that nibbled at her, of the doubts that could rise up to plague her at times. She could almost wish she had not seen it. There was something about marriage to her that bothered Thayer despite the passion he showed, despite how well he treated her. Somehow she would have to root out the problem. She prayed the discovery would not be too painful, nor the problem prove too hard to solve.

Chapter Six

"Riverfall is beyond the next rise."

Gytha breathed a sigh of relief at Thayer's announcement. She was more than ready to end the journey. It was too hot if they rolled the hide siding of their cart down and too dusty when they left it up. They endured the latter at the moment, and she felt as if she carried her own weight in road dust. Frowning in the direction of Riverfall, she could barely make out the rise Thayer had to be referring to. She turned her frown on Thayer, who rode beside the cart.

"That rise looms a fair distance away, Thayer."

"A day's ride, no more. We will camp up ahead. There is a small clearing and water for the horses."

As she watched him ride back to the front of the group she wished she had something to hurl at his broad back. His announcement had hinted that their journey was near an end. She did not consider a full day more near enough. Sighing, she tried to make herself more comfortable, praying there would be enough water at their campsite for a bath.

Dusk was well advanced before they halted. Gytha spoke as little as possible until Thayer's tent was up. Then, with Bek's help and making use of one of the empty water barrels, she indulged in the much needed luxury of a bath. As she washed the sweat and dust from her body, she felt her mood improve. It did not surprise her when, the moment she climbed out, Margaret hastened to take her place. Dressing quickly in the clean gown Edna set out for her and loosely tying back her still damp hair, she went in search of Thayer. She found him seated around a fire with Roger, Merlion, Torr, and Reve.

Thayer watched Gytha a little warily as she sat beside him. He had watched her usual cheerful mood fade with each dusty mile they covered. The sensible part of him said anyone's mood would sour on such a journey. No matter how he tried to scorn it, another part of him wondered if her silent, dark mood stemmed from other causes, perhaps from a weariness with him. They had been married long enough for the newness to wane some. Now that she had traveled, now that she had tasted passion, she could be finding that there was little else to hold her interest. Struggling to shake away the worries he saw as a dangerous weakness, he told himself he had more important things to worry about than a woman's fickle moods. When he saw her smile pleasantly as Torr served her some stew, he felt a wave of relief that her mood had improved.

"I would never have thought there was that much dust in all of England." Gytha shook her head. "And I think nearly every grain landed on me." After a few hearty spoonfuls of the stew, she murmured her approval.

" 'Tis dry," Thayer agreed. "Even some of the men less inclined towards cleanliness felt a need for a wash this time."

"Aye." Roger briefly grinned. "The stream is naught but a mudhole now."

"Some of us," Thayer drawled as he accepted the wineskin being passed around, "are not so soft we must heat our bathing water first." He hid his smile by taking a drink.

"There are those who might say 'tis slightly mad to leap into icy water when there is a way to heat it first." Gytha met her husband's look with a sweet smile, took a brief sip from the wineskin he handed her, then passed it along. "I, of course, would never malign my husband so."

"Nay, of course not." He laughed and ran a hand through his still damp hair. "T'was brisk."

"So I gathered from the howls that followed

129

each splash.'' She grinned when the men laughed.

"By day's end tomorrow we will be at Riverfall,'' Thayer promised when the laughter stilled.

"Have any of those who rode ahead caught a glimpse of the place?'' she asked.

"One. He said it looked a fine, sturdy place. Set well for defense.''

"That is good, but''—she smiled faintly— "t'was not the sort of knowledge I was seeking.''

"I know but he did not think to look for much else. Nor did he draw close enough to see anything else.''

"Oh? He did not tell them of our impending arrival?''

"Nay. I sent another ahead yesterday to tend to that. He stays there to be sure all is readied for us.''

"I wish I had taken the time to ask Papa more about the place.''

"It cannot be worse than Saitun Manor.''

"Please, God, I hope not.''

As the ensuing, rather idle conversation hummed around him, Thayer found his thoughts wandering. Since the first night of their tedious journey, he had done little more than sleep at Gytha's side. Weariness had forced her into a deep sleep each night before he could join her in their bed. Her bath had obviously refreshed her. He suspected the news that they were near the end of their travels also

130

helped revive her. His thoughts began to center on getting her to his cot before her renewed spirits were lost to weariness again.

Just as he grasped her arm, thinking to get her back to their tent as quickly as possible, a cry of alarm sounded from the surrounding wood. Even as he leapt to his feet, dragging Gytha up with him and shoving her towards shelter, one of the guards he had stationed in the forest staggered into the camp. Bloodied and weak, the man barely managed to cry out a warning of attack before collapsing.

Gytha stumbled along for a few steps before fully regaining her balance. She understood what was happening, yet hesitated to run and cower in the tent. She ached to help, to be active in fighting off the attackers, yet could think of nothing she could do. Then Thayer glanced her way. Despite bellowing orders to his scrambling men, he managed to command her as well. With one jab of his finger towards the tent, he made clear his wishes. She decided to obey and raced for that shelter.

Even as she reached its opening, the tent was surrounded by a mixture of pages and grown men-at-arms. This time Thayer was taking no chances. There would be no place for one of the attackers to creep up to the tent unawares. She stumbled inside and a man-at-arms quickly yanked the door flap closed behind her.

"What is happening?" cried Edna as she clung to Gytha.

Moving to hold on to her cousin, Margaret whispered, "Is it another attack?"

Despite the fear gripping the two women, Gytha found comfort in their closeness. "Aye. Another. There was some warning."

"So the men were not caught by surprise?" Margaret asked.

"Not fully. I saw them bracing for battle just before I saw armed men rush at them from the shadows."

"Thieves? Have we landed in a nest of robbers?"

"I would say nay, Edna. Too many men and too well armed."

"Robert and his uncle again?" Margaret finally eased her grip on Gytha but stayed close to her cousin's side.

"Mayhap. I dare not say. We are, after all, in a trouble-plagued area."

They fell silent, the sounds of the fierce battle outside the tent consuming all their attention. Gytha found herself afraid for Thayer. It seemed strange that she had felt little the first time he had fought for their lives. Briefly, she worried if she was having some kind of premonition, then quickly shook the thought away. Her lack of real concern the first time had been due to a lack of knowledge of the cost of battle, to a lack of any real depth of feeling for her new husband. She told herself that again and again in an attempt to make herself believe it as, hands painfully clenched, she prayed for the battle to end.

Thayer fought and cursed with equal ferocity. His usual cool-headed acceptance of the violence was lacking. He knew it was because Gytha was close at hand, because she could suffer if he failed to turn back the attackers.

It was as the battle waned, the attackers edging into full retreat, that Thayer found himself in the greatest danger. Jerking his sword free of a slain man, he turned slightly to find himself facing two large foes. They looked fresh, untouched by the battle raging around them. He knew he was hot and sweaty, weariness close at hand.

"Look about you, dogs. Your pack begins to tuck its tail between its legs. Best you join them." Thayer quickly drew his dagger, adding its lethal if limited strength to that of his sword.

"Then we shall have to send you to hell a little quicker than we planned," one of the men yelled even as he swung at Thayer.

He easily blocked that swing, but Thayer found it less easy to elude the second man at the same time. The skill of the men was average yet, by combining in their attack, it strained his own skills to the limit. Roger, who would customarily be at his back, had been cleverly separated from him. He would need luck to escape unscathed.

His major concern was in preventing either man from circling around behind him. He needed to keep both men in sight. That was going to require a great deal more tiring concentration than they would need to exert. Their grim smiles told him they were well aware of each of the disadvantages he suffered.

For a while he held them off without too much trouble. They tested his reputed strength, his rumored skill. They also studied his manner of fighting. Thayer knew that, if they had any wit at all, they would soon decide on the best method of attack. He needed to strike a telling blow before they could reach such a consensus.

At last a chance came for him to even the odds. He blocked a lunge from one man and turned to find the other open, unprepared to defend himself. Thayer swiftly lunged, his sword cutting deep into the man. As he pulled back, his victim crumbling to the ground, the second man struck again. Although he acted quickly enough to stop the strike from being a fatal one, Thayer felt his opponent's weapon cut a deep furrow in his sword arm. Staggering back a little, Thayer tried to prepare himself for a further assault, but the strength was already leaving his sword arm, seeping out along with the blood from his wound. He fought a sense of inevitability. In his mind, accepting defeat was the surest way to bring it on.

A cold smile seeped across his enemy's face. Thayer knew his weakness had been seen. Gritting his teeth against the pain he raised his sword to deflect the man's blow. Agony tore through him with the shock of that blow. He stumbled backwards in an awkward retreat, fighting the encroaching blackness of unconciousness. In what he knew was a vain, somewhat pitiful, attempt at defense, he raised his dagger to check his assailant's next sword thrust.

Instead of cutting through his flesh, the assassin's sword was checked in the midst of its downswing by another sword. When Roger came into view, fiercely driving the enemy back with his artfully wielded sword, Thayer allowed himself to give in to his weakness. Cursing softly, he sank to his knees and watched Roger end the life of his assailant. It was not until the man's death scream had gurgled into silence that Thayer realized what noise he could hear was that of the waning of the battle. The attackers were routed, running for their lives.

Crouching by Thayer, Roger half-smiled, but the look in his eyes revealed his concern. " 'Tis bad?"

"Nay. It but bleeds freely enough to sap my strength. We have won?"

"So it appears. I have no quick guess as to how much the victory cost us, however."

"I pray 'tis not too high."

"Not too high, but high enough," said Merlion as he stepped up to them. "Two dead, one who will surely die from his wounds, and four wounded enough to need a great deal of tending to before they can lift a sword again." He looked at Thayer's wound. "Mayhap five?"

"Nay. Weakening though it is for the moment, 'tis not serious."

"Your wife will be pleased to hear that, though she might question your judgment." Merlion nodded towards the tent.

Following Merlion's gaze as Roger helped him to his feet, Thayer saw Gytha, Margaret, and Edna cautiously emerging from the tent. "Gytha is a sensible woman."

The waning din of battle having drawn her outside, Gytha looked around the campsite. Yet again a warning had come in time to save them from the worst of it, although she saw enough to realize that this attack had cost them more than the earlier one. She did not ponder that long, however. Her main concern was finding Thayer. When she finally espied him, she cried out softly. He was covered in blood and needed Roger's help to stand. Hiking up her skirts, she raced over to him, Margaret and Edna at her heels. She did not stop in her frantic advance until she was directly before him, then clutched at his torn, bloody tunic.

"You have been wounded." She knew she stated the obvious and could hear the high pitch of fear in her voice.

" 'Tis but a scratch."

"A scratch?! You are soaked in blood."

"Not all of it is mine." Concerned over how white she looked, he said soothingly, "We won the battle. 'Tis over now. There is no more to fear."

"No more to fear? You stand before me bleeding like a stuck pig and say there is no more to fear?" She struggled to gain control of herself, to concentrate on the strength in his voice, not the gory sight of him. "Roger, Merlion, bring him to the tent. Water. I need water. And bandages," she muttered in distraction, then raced back to the tent to get ready.

Margaret caught Edna by the arm, stopping the maid from following Gytha, then looked at the three men. "If your wound is truly not life-threatening, m'lord," she said to Thayer, "mayhap Edna and I can help others in need of some care."

"Indeed you can," Thayer replied. "Merlion, Roger can see me to my tent. Take the women to the wounded."

Once that order was obeyed and Roger was helping him on his way to the tent, Thayer muttered, "What ails Gytha? She did not carry on so after the last battle, yet in that one she was nearly abducted."

"In that one her husband was not wounded."

"Mayhap it was but one battle too many. She might fear being continuously caught up in them."

Roger sighed in ill-concealed exasperation. "Of course. It could not be that she found you soaked in blood."

"My wound is not so serious," Thayer murmured, but Roger made no reply as they entered the tent.

Gytha felt she had gained control over herself until Roger brought Thayer into the tent. Seeing her blood-drenched husband again revived the terror that threatened to choke her. She barely collected her senses enough to hastily spread a cloth over the cot before Thayer lay down on it. Shaking with the fear she battled, she helped Roger strip Thayer to his braies. As she began to wash the blood away, Merlion entered. She knew they would discuss the battle now and bit back the urge to tell Roger and Merlion to leave. Instead, she concentrated on tending Thayer's wound, fighting the urge to weep over the sight of the gash in his arm as she half-listened to what they said.

"The women are going to see to the wounded?" Thayer asked Merlion, fighting to ignore his pain.

"Aye. They may even save the man I marked as near death. 'Tis the man who sounded the alarm."

"Thus saving most of us. I pray he does not pay for that with his own life. Any prisoners?"

"Nay. Do not scowl so. The dead told me what we needed to know."

"How so?"

"I fought one of them in the last attack."

"You are very certain of this?"

"One does not forget a face as ugly as his."

"So," Roger murmured, "Robert and his uncle did not heed your warning."

"It would seem so, curse their thieving hides. That first attack was no burst of rage."

"Nay." Roger sighed, knowing how this battle with his kin would trouble Thayer. " 'Tis war. Robert—or more likely his uncle—means to see this fight through to the end."

It was news that only added to Gytha's upset. She knew she was losing her battle to overcome the churning emotions afflicting her. Giving a last check to assure herself she had properly tended Thayer's wound, she bandaged it as she listened to the plans made to stop Robert and his uncle. The grim talk only exacerbated her feelings. She was relieved when Roger and Merlion left.

As she moved to wash up, she stared at her hands when she held them over the basin of water. The sight of Thayer's blood staining her hands severed what little control she had. Plunging her hands into the water, she furiously scrubbed them as she began to weep. Knowing it was impossible to stop her tears at the moment, she struggled to keep her distress silent. She did not want him to think her some weak-hearted, useless female who could not even tend his wounds as was her duty.

"Gytha," Thayer murmured after watching her viciously scrub her hands for several moments, "they must be clean by now."

A jerky nod was her only answer. He frowned as he watched her dry her hands, then dither about putting away what she had used to tend his injury. Her movements lacked their usual grace. He became certain she was weeping, yet he heard little more than an occasional sniff.

The way she was acting confused him. It appeared she was deeply upset because he had been hurt.

"Gytha."

She chanced a look his way, then gasped. He was almost on his feet. Forgetting that she wished to hide her tears, she rushed to his side.

"What are you doing?" She tried to urge him back into bed but only succeeded in keeping him from standing up.

He reached up to cup her face in his hands, ignoring the sharp twinge in his wound. "You have been weeping." Hot tears slid from her eyes, dampening his hands. "Wrong. You are weeping."

"I am not. Lie down—or do you forget you are wounded?"

Slowly he let her push him back down, but he kept his gaze fixed upon her tear-soaked face. "It appears you have more concern about this scratch than I."

"Scratch? Scratch you call it? Scratches do not need stitching. Scratches do not soak a tunic with blood." She could hear the frantic note in her voice, but could not seem to shut herself up. "Scratches do not sap the strength from a man so that he must be helped to his bed."

"It weakened me for but a moment." He fought back a smile.

"And in that moment you could have had your head taken off your shoulders." The mere thought made her shudder.

"Gytha, snuff the candles save for the one by my head."

"What?"

"Snuff the candles." He watched as she somewhat distractedly obeyed the command. "Now, shed your clothes and come to bed."

Giving an exasperated sniff, she did as he said, laying her clothes carefully over a chest and sliding into bed with as much care as possible. When his uninjured arm slipped around her, she nearly flung herself at him. Clinging tightly to him, she sought comfort in his warmth, in the strength of his body, in the steady beat of his heart. She promised herself that she would learn to control such emotion in the future. This time she had been caught unawares, shock stripping away all defense. She huddled even closer to him as he moved his big, calloused hand over her back in a soothing gesture.

"You have seen my scars and know I can take a blow now and then," he murmured.

"Aye. I know." She realized she had never thought on the blood, the pain, or the danger that had produced those scars.

"Though it bled freely and caused some weakness, 'tis not a serious wound."

"I know that too." And she did, knew the stitches were really only needed to lessen the scarring.

He kissed her forehead. "So you may still your fears."

"Nay. My tears and this foolish, weak

carrying-on—aye. My fears—nay. Robert and that stinking cur he calls uncle mean to see you dead. As Roger said, 'tis war. They will try again."

"I am ready for that." He frowned, reliving the battle in his mind. "We saw an attack, but now I see t'was more than that. Murder was planned."

"Your murder."

"Aye. They neatly kept Roger from his place at my back, leaving me with two foes and no aid at hand. That shall not happen again. We will be ready for such a ploy next time. I have survived battles with better men."

"I know. Forgive me my weakness. I shall not fail you so again." As she slowly regained control of herself, embarrassment crept in.

"You did not fail me. Despite your tears and all, you tended my wound as well as any could." He loosened her lightly bound hair, running his fingers through its thick silken length. "I will strive to shield you from such violence in the future."

"T'was not the violence," she snapped, then sighed, knowing she would have to try and explain or be treated as if she were weak, too delicate to endure life's harsher side. "T'was not the battle."

"Well, 'tis true you held firm through the first attack."

He felt the tickle of hopeful excitement. If it was not the battle itself, then it had to be because he was wounded. That she could be so

142

distraught over that had to indicate some depth of feeling for him.

"Aye, I did. 'Tis most odd. I felt no concern, no fear at all that you might be struck down then. This time I had no such confidence. The moment the attack came, I was afraid for you. I sought reasons for that change. I want no skill at—well, at foretelling what is to happen. The reasons I grasped at had no strength. I think seeing that what I had feared—what I had felt—had come to pass added to my foolishness."

"Such feelings are not as uncommon as you may think. Men facing battle often have a sense of their fate, or that of those close to them."

"Please God that I am not so accursed. 'Tis bad enough that you must fight at all."

"A man—"

"I know. I know 'tis the way of the world. I can learn to bear with it. I know I must. In truth, I learned it long ago, for my father and brothers have often ridden off to battle. But to sense how you will fare each time? Nay, that I pray I will not suffer."

"Mayhap you sensed the attack came from Robert, from his wish to murder me," he murmured.

"I do not truly think Robert wants to murder you. His uncle . . ."

"They are one and the same."

"Aye. Mayhap I did sense it. I did hold a few doubts that your warning would be enough. When the attack came, it may have confirmed

those doubts I thought I had shrugged aside."
She briefly pressed her lips against his chest.
"I have no wish to be a widow," she whispered.

"I have no wish to make you one."

A weak laugh escaped her. It was a perfect
time to speak what was in her heart, yet she
held back. The knowledge was still too fresh,
too frighteningly new. That final clarity about
her feelings had come when she had seen
Thayer weak and bloodied. For just a little
while she wanted to keep it to herself, wanted
to privately savor how it felt to be deeply,
wholely in love with Thayer. So too did she
wish to keep it untarnished by a lack of or an
unsatisfactory response from him.

She murmured with pleasure as he slid his
hand down to stroke her backside. "Your
wound..."

"Has not crippled me." He felt the hunger
for a woman he often suffered after a battle, a
hunger increased tenfold because the woman
he held was Gytha.

Wondering how her passion could be so
quickly, so fiercely, aroused when she had just
been so distraught, she began to squirm beneath his caresses. "You should rest."

"The battle has stirred my blood and you,
sweet little Gytha, have set it afire."

"Are you sure you have enough blood left to
be stirred?"

Easily setting her on top of himself, he
cupped her derriere in his hands, pressing her

loins against his. "More than enough. But are you too weary to test my claim?"

The way he slowly, erotically rubbed her body against his had her gasping slightly. "I believe I can be persuaded."

Sliding his hands up her slim body he cupped them around her face, tugging her mouth close to his. He teased her lips with swift, nibbling kisses until she burrowed her fingers in his hair, holding his mouth against hers and silently demanding a fuller kiss. Holding her close, he answered her demand, growling in soft delight when she matched his increasing ferocity. What little control he had over his hot need was lost when she continued to rub her body against his. Easing his hand down her soft midriff and between her restless legs, he did not need her husky purr to tell him she was ready.

"Mount your man, little one." Grasping her by the hips he edged her into position for what he wanted.

Blushing, although she was not sure whether the heated color came from embarrassment over his blunt words or the rush of desire his husky command invoked, she glanced at him through the tangled curtain of her hair. "I am not sure I know what you want."

"I want you to lead the dance. Set yourself on me, dearling."

Slowly she did as he asked, easing their bodies together. What passion had been stolen by uncertainty and some awkwardness came back in a rush and grew rapidly as she felt him fill her. Carefully, she sat up straighter. The deep groan Thayer gave told her he found this position as exciting as she did. She was not sure how it was possible, yet it was as if they were more thoroughly joined than they had ever been before.

Tentatively she moved. It was only a gentle motion, yet it left her gasping, the sensation so exquisite it stole her breath away. She did not need Thayer's grip tightening upon her hips to urge her to do it again. Her body demanded it of her.

Although pleasure struggled to close his eyes, Thayer forced them to remain open. The sight of her astride him, of the pleasure so clearly displayed upon her lovely face, gave him a delight no words could describe. He reached out to cup her breasts in his hands and her pace increased. Despite wanting it to last as long as possible, Thayer knew neither of them had the strength or will to tame their need.

When he sensed her release at hand he pulled her down into his arms, covering her mouth with his own. The way she mimicked the movement of her body with the thrusts of her tongue drove him wild. He clutched her hips, holding her tightly against him as her cry of release filled his mouth. Lifting her slightly, he sought to delve deeper within her even as he joined her in the blinding culmination of their desires.

It was several minutes before he found the wit or strength to do more than hold her close. Carefully, he eased the intimacy of their embrace, settling her sleep-weighted body more comfortably against him. The warmth of satisfaction could be heard in her every breath, felt in her cuddling movements. As always, it both pleased and amazed him. He could not stop wondering how such a delicate beauty could find such obvious delight with a man like him. Ashamed though he was to admit it, he knew that was one reason, however small, that he fought to watch her as they made love. Some part of him feared to see that it was all an act, that her pleasure in his arms was but a sham.

"How fares your wound?" Gytha asked, then hastily smothered a yawn.

"Nary a twinge," he lied, for it did ache, but he deemed it a small price to pay for what he had just enjoyed.

She laughed softly and sleepily shook her head. He was not telling the truth, but she did not challenge him on it. If it did hurt, she doubted the pain was very great. She felt no weakness in his hold nor heard any hint of pain in his voice. Giving into desire had evidently caused him little real damage.

That brought her thoughts back to what they had just enjoyed. She had firmly grasped the reins of the lovemaking, acting wanton and wild. Memory brought hot color into her cheeks. It also made her frown.

147

"About what we just did, Thayer—does the church sanction it?"

He could not help himself; he laughed. "I doubt it, sweeting. I do not think it carries a very large penance, though."

"Nay, you are probably right. Even if you are wrong, I doubt I will confess the sin. I should never get the words out," she murmured, then smiled as Thayer laughed.

"T'would no doubt disturb the poor priest to hear them." Reaching behind his head he neatly pinched out the candle. "Time for rest, wife. The morrow will be a long day, even if it will bring an end to this journey."

"Are you sure you should attempt it? Mayhap you should rest a day."

"I can rest when we reach Riverfall."

Opening her mouth to argue, she then closed it, recognizing the unswervable steel behind his words. "Will you at least take the journey carefully?"

"What? Ride in the cart like some fine, soft lady? Well, mayhap I will if the choice comes to that or halting before we reach Riverfall. Now, do not frown. I know this battered body well, know to what lengths I can take it. I am not such a fool as to push myself past return. Even now, with the title and land I fought for in my hands, I have need of this sword arm. You need not worry I would risk sapping its strength forever. So"—he brushed a kiss over her forehead—"get your rest."

Poorly smothering a large yawn, she murmured, "That is an order I shall find easy to obey." She rubbed her cheek against his chest. "And we will reach Riverfall at day's end?"

"Aye, we will." Silently he prayed they would find Riverfall in far better condition than they had Saitun Manor.

Chapter Seven

"Ah, I see you are still hale and hearty, Janet."
Gytha bit back a grin as she greeted the hefty
woman by the wash house.

" 'Tis early yet, m'lady. I might still take a
bad chill."

Gytha rolled her eyes in a gesture of mild
exasperation even as she laughed. Riverfall
had been a pleasant surprise. It had needed
little work to make it livable, although it was
plain. She did not really mind that plainness.
It would be enjoyable to add her own touches.

However, the workers and people around
Riverfall had been in sore need of a good scrubbing. She had ignored the howls, waved aside
the fears of taking a fatal chill from a bath,
and set about seeing to it that her people held
to the same rules of cleanliness she did. Most

of the complaints and fears had stilled as time passed and no one died from losing his thick coat of dirt. Some, like Janet, even felt free enough to jest and tease. Gytha hoped she would not have as great a struggle in two days' time when she enforced the rule of scrubbing body and home once a week.

"Well, in two days' time we shall try again," she teased Janet back as she briefly inspected the washing. "I see young Bek has been leaping on his bedlinen with muddied feet."

Laughing as she continued to scrub away at the heavily begrimed linen, Janet agreed. "Aye, he seems a quick, lively lad."

"That may be, but I shall speak to him about this. He must learn not to heedlessly make extra work for others. If a talk fails to teach him, I daresay having to scrub his own linens will work." She smiled faintly at Janet's hearty laugh, then continued on her rounds.

In the short time she had been at Riverfall, she had found little that needed correcting. The people may have been lax in their personal cleanliness, but they shirked little else. All worked hard and competently. She wondered if that contributed to the deep sense of belonging she experienced at Riverfall. If she were to have a choice of residence, she would prefer Riverfall, but she was not sure how she could convey that to Thayer. Saitun Manor was, after all, his family seat.

Espying Bek, she moved towards him. He watched the men practice their skills as he stood by his father. Thayer's presence at the boy's side made her pause briefly. Bek was his son—not hers. Shaking her head, she continued on. They were to be a family. If that was to work, she had to treat Bek as if he were her own. She just prayed that Thayer would understand and agree. Matters could become painfully complicated if he did not.

Thayer smiled at Gytha as she joined him and Bek. "We have found some skilled fighters here. Your father manned the place well."

"He sent those men here who seemed—well, bored with the relative peace at home."

"A good choice. They found enough to keep them busy here, yet not as much as rumor would have us believe."

"That is a great comfort." She exchanged a brief smile with Thayer.

"Can I do something for you?" Thayer asked when he noticed the seriousness of her expression.

"Actually, I came to have a word with Bek." She looked at the boy, who gave her a wary smile.

"You want me to help you with something?" The boy forced his attention away from the men.

"In a way, Bek. It appears you neglect to clean your feet before you climb into your bed. In truth, your linen looks as if you run and jump the length of the bed with very muddy feet."

Frowning, Bek shrugged. "The linen is washed. The women do it."

"Therein lies the problem. You dirty them so badly it takes the women much longer to clean yours than any of the others."

"It is their place to clean things."

"I know, but that does not mean we can be so careless as to make their work even harder." She watched a scowl blacken the boy's beautiful face and inwardly sighed. "I would like you to be sure you are clean before you crawl into bed, to think a little more about those who must clean up after you. Bek?" she pressed when he simply glared at her.

"Aye." He walked away.

Grimacing, Gytha looked at Thayer. "I did not mean to make him angry."

Chuckling softly, Thayer slipped his arm about her shoulders and brushed a kiss over her forehead. "I fear he has his father's temper, but being so young, he has not learned control."

She briefly grinned at him, then watched him thoughtfully for a moment. "You agree that I had to scold him?"

"Aye. He has to learn to think of others—all others. And if I did not agree, I would never say so in front of the boy. We would discuss it later." He frowned in the direction Bek had gone. "He must learn to heed you as he does me."

She quickly, fiercely hugged him. "Thank you, Thayer."

Smiling crookedly, he looked at her as she stepped away. "Well, you are most welcome, though I am not sure what I did."

Laughing softly, she patted his cheek before heading back to the keep. He accepted her authority over Bek. She doubted he would really understand what that meant to her. All she had to worry about now was Bek's accepting it. As the day wore on and the only expression she caught on Bek's face was a sullen one, she began to think a battle was brewing.

That opinion was confirmed, to her weary disappointment, the very next morning. As she left the hall where she had shared the morning meal with Thayer, she espied Janet descending the stairs, her plump arms full of linen. Even rolled up as it was Gytha could see the heavy dirt marks upon it.

"Bek dancing upon the linen again?" She moved closer to meet Janet as the woman finished descending the stairs.

"Aye, m'lady." Janet grimaced as Gytha looked over the sheets.

"God's toenails," Gytha muttered after a good, long look. "You are not to wash these. Prepare the washing tub but wait for me to bring Bek. How did you know they would need washing again?"

"The lad called me to do it."

"What arrogance."

Waving Janet on her way, Gytha sighed. She supposed she ought to be glad he was doing battle openly, even brazenly, rather than be-

155

hind her back. Turning to go in search of Bek, she came face to face with Thayer, who lounged gracefully in the doorway to the great hall.

"Trouble?" he asked.

"Only a little one. Have you seen Bek?"

Reaching behind him, Thayer tugged his son forward. "He was lurking in the hall. I begin to see why he was so careful to stay out of sight."

Placing her hands upon her hips Gytha gave Bek the sternest look she could muster. "What did you do? Find the worst muck heap at Riverfall to march through, then race to your bedchamber to smear it all over your bed? I should not be surprised to discover you took it up in buckets so that you could freshen the mire upon your feet and dance about on your bed again and again. I do not know how you could sleep with such filth."

The way he hastily averted his gaze told her he had not slept in his bed. She almost laughed. That, she knew, would be a serious error, so she quickly stifled the urge, keeping her expression stern.

"And then to command poor Janet to come and wash them again."

" 'Tis what she is supposed to do," Bek snapped.

"Aye, but not because some naughty boy feels inclined to misbehave. Well, mayhap a taste of the work you so freely burden others with is what you need."

"What?" Bek squawked in protest when she grasped him firmly by the ear.

"You will wash your own muddied linen, sir."

"Nay! 'Tis woman's work. 'Tis Janet's work, not mine. 'Tis her place. Papa!"

Thayer met his son's outraged, pleading look with a bland expression. "Sounds fair to me."

"Fair? I am to be a knight, a warrior."

"Aye," said Gytha, "a knight. And there are rules a knight follows. He has consideration for those who toil for his comfort, for those who must look to him for their protection. 'Tis time you learn what consideration is."

The grip she had on the boy's ear forced him to keep step as she marched him off to the laundry shed. At first Janet and the other women were hesitant. Bek was, after all, their leige's son. They soon fell into step with her, however, much to Gytha's relief. Bek was proving very obstinate.

It was nearly an hour before Gytha felt she could leave Bek with only the other women to watch over him. Sullen though he was, he seemed resigned to his fate. She hurried through her rounds, then sought her bed. Flopping down on it, she closed her eyes and felt a new sympathy for her parents. Disciplining a stubborn child was not easy. For several moments she contemplated how hard it was for a grown woman to impose her will on a small boy. Then she sensed she was no longer alone.

Even as she opened her eyes Thayer, sat down on the bed at her side.

"He can be stubborn," Thayer murmured.

"Aye, he can."

"And hot-tempered."

"Oh, aye, that is certainly true."

Thayer laughed softly at the heartiness of her reply. "Gave you some trouble, did he?"

"A bit, but he settled to the chore. I am hoping he will see how hard the work is and feel a little sympathy with those who must do it. At least enough to see they need no added work."

"Aye. 'Tis a lesson he should learn. He has not had much to do with—well, with life like this."

"I know." She sat up and settled herself comfortably in his ready hold. "That is why I did no more than gently scold him for making such a mess of his bedding the first time. He must learn, though. And learn from the start."

"Aye, and you must take time away from all this." He stood up and tugged her up after him.

"I must, must I?"

"You must. You have been hard at work since we arrived. First you tended me until my wound was healed, then you worked hard to see all ran smoothly here. And now"—he grinned—"you wrestle with a stubborn boy. Aye, you are in need of fleeing it all for a while." He led her out of their chambers.

"And where am I fleeing to?" She hurried

along, needing to trot in order to keep apace with his long strides.

"A quiet spot I found on one of my rides over the property."

She asked no more questions as they made their way to the stables. Thayer had only one horse saddled. He set her up before him as they rode out of the keep. She only partially noticed how he curtly waved away offers of a guard. Her attention was on the land around her. Tired from the journey, she had noticed little as they arrived and she had not yet done much exploring outside the keep's thick, protective walls.

The spot he brought her to struck her momentarily speechless with its beauty. Well watered by the same stream that curled by Riverfall, the area was lush and green. Wildflowers bloomed in abundance. The stream tumbled musically over a rocky bed. Walking to the edge of the swiftly flowing water, she dabbled her fingers in its clear depths.

" 'Tis just as cold as it looks," she murmured as she dried her fingers on her skirts.

Sitting down, his back against a gnarled, vine-cloaked tree, Thayer nodded. "It takes little warmth from the sun."

"A shame. It looks inviting." She moved to sit beside him, laughing softly when he picked her up and set her on his lap. " 'Tis peaceful here. When did you find it?"

"When I was riding the borders of the demesne."

"Is it good land?"

"Some. T'will not make us so wealthy that we need never count our coins, but t'will not leave us poor either."

"Good enough then."

"Aye." Wrapping his arms around her, he idly nuzzled her hair, enjoying the sweet, clean smell of it. "I will intercede with Bek if you like."

"Nay. I think it best if I do it on my own."

"Aye, so I thought, but I wished to make the offer. I think things have changed too quickly for the boy. His temper flares more often than it used to."

She placed her hands over his. "He will settle. There may be some fear that you will set him aside. He will soon see that his place with you will not change. I suspect he is also unused to a woman having any say over him."

"True enough. His has been the world of men and battle." He frowned when his mount began to act nervously.

Feeling the sudden tension in him, Gytha asked, "Is something wrong?"

"Not sure." Setting her aside, he stood up, his hand on his sword. "Something has made the horse restless."

As she began cautiously to stand, an arrow cut through the air. She cried out softly in utter horror as it pinned Thayer to the tree. When she scrambled to her feet, intending to help him, he used his free hand to shove her back down.

Cursing softly and viciously, Thayer drew his dagger to cut himself free. The arrow had not pierced his flesh but had pinned him by his tunic. He was a dangerously easy target. Even as he hacked himself free, another arrow thudded into the tree, ruffling his hair.

Once he was free, he caught Gytha up under one arm and raced for his mount. He skidded to a halt, bellowing a curse, as an arrow felled the horse. Turning quickly, he bolted into the wood, seeking the protection of the trees and shadows.

Spotting a good hiding place, he set Gytha down, then crouched down beside her. His enemy would have to hunt him now, expose himself as he searched for his prey. It gave Thayer a small advantage that he grasped tightly. He spared a brief glance to see how Gytha fared, then, assured that she was breathless but hale, he fixed his gaze on the area surrounding them.

Gytha sought to be as quiet as possible as she struggled to regain her breath. She looked Thayer over carefully to assure herself that he was unhurt. Her husband, she decided, had more luck than anyone else she knew. She prayed it would hold. She was sure they would need a wagonload of luck to escape unscathed.

She heard someone approach even as Thayer tensed, his gaze centered upon the direction of the sound. The brief touch of his fingers against her lips was not really needed to keep her quiet. She knew well the value of silence at such a time. Moving as little as possible, she looked in the direction Thayer did and saw three men cautiously making their way towards them. She knew instinctively that they were sent by Robert's uncle to murder Thayer.

"I think this is unwise," grumbled one man. "Too many places for him to hide."

"Hush, you whining dog. He is only one man and hindered by the woman. We will separate here." The taller of the three nudged one of his men to his left, then looked at the hesitant one. "You go straight ahead. I will search to the right. We will flush this bird."

"I think..."

"You are not paid to think. Find him and find that cursed woman." The leader strode off to the right.

A cold smile eased over Thayer's face, and Gytha shivered faintly when she saw it. Here was the man who had earned the name Red Devil. Hurried to safety during the other attacks, she had not really seen him. She knew she would see death strike soon, but she quickly hardened her heart. These men meant to kill Thayer. Mercy could prove fatal.

Despite knowing it was necessary, Gytha was still shocked when Thayer did what he had to do. For such a big man, he moved with a speed and stealth that left her gaping. As the man came abreast of them, Thayer struck. Leaping up, he clapped his hand over the man's mouth, yanking backwards to hold him through surprise and a greater bulk. The man was just reaching upwards to claw at Thayer's smothering hand when Thayer buried a dagger in his heart. Gytha faintly echoed the spasm that tore through the man's dying body.

Thayer gave her no time to fully react to what she had seen. He dropped the body and caught her up beneath his arm again. Struggling to breathe somewhat normally as he trotted towards another place to hide left Gytha unable to protest the undignified handling. She smothered her cry, forcefully reminding herself they fought for their lives, when he set her down somewhat abruptly amongst some bushes, then hunkered down beside her. When the rushing in her ears eased, she heard someone approaching and knew Thayer had moved to intercept another of their pursuers.

She did not watch, keeping her eyes firmly diverted as Thayer swiftly ended any threat the man may have offered. With numb resignation, she felt herself yet again lifted like some lump of baggage and toted to a new place. To her dismay, the last of their enemies did not die so quickly nor as quietly. Thayer needed some answers and faced the man squarely, sword, against sword. He got what little information he needed before being forced to end the man's life.

The man had carelessly revealed that there were only three attackers, so she knew she and Thayer were now safe. Therefore, she was a little surprised when she was yet again picked up and toted off. This time he set her down gently on a thick bed of grass, the area only slightly shaded from view by a few shrubs. She watched as he yanked off his jerkin and used it to clean himself, then his sword before carelessly tossing the garment aside.

Recovered somewhat from all they had just been through, she was ready with a few complaints when he turned towards her. The words struck in her throat when she saw the look upon his face. A hunger she well recognized darkened his eyes to black and tautened the lines of his face. She felt an immediate response, his hunger reaching within her to stir her own. Deciding she would make her complaints later, she opened her arms, laughing softly when he nearly fell into her hold.

Their lovemaking was swift, rough, tumultuous. Gytha lost herself completely to the blind ferocity of it. It was not until they sprawled sated in each other's arms that she realized she had been tumbled upon the grass like some coarse, roundheeled maid. A quick glance affirmed that they had not even bothered to undress. Her skirts were shoved up to her waist, and his clothes were tangled around his ankles. A flicker of embarrassment came and went, then she grinned. When Thayer showed strong signs of embarrassment as he moved to straighten out his twisted braies and hose, she started to giggle.

Smiling faintly with relief, Thayer watched her adjust her clothing. "Then I did not hurt you?"

"Nay, though I may well find a bruise or two come morning."

He tugged her into his arms, giving her a brief kiss. "Having you near when my blood still ran hot and fierce from battle was more temptation than I could resist."

Recalling what had happened to stir his blood, she leaned heavily against him. "Do you think we sin to carry on so after such a thing?"

"Nay. They sought to kill us, Gytha."

"I know. I know you had to do it. To show mercy would only have brought you death. Yet, to want to tumble so carelessly when three men are newly dead? I do not feel I did wrong, yet it seems so heartless."

Breathing an inner sigh of relief to hear her say she had welcomed the lovemaking, Thayer then sought to explain feelings he was all too familiar with. "Mayhap. I have often wondered the same. The lusting does not come upon me in the midst of battle. I am not so black of heart that spilling a man's blood stirs me so. Nay, 'tis after the fighting is done."

"As you stand amongst the dead and dying, yet still live."

"Aye." He looked at her in a appreciation of her insight. " 'Tis then that the need comes. I look about and know that I have lived to see another day—" He shrugged, unable to clearly describe how that felt.

"You seek more proof of your continued well-being," she murmured, half-smiling. " 'Tis a celebration, then?"

"Mayhap. You did not fight this battle, yet you were caught up in it. Mayhap the same happened to you."

"Could be. I think it had a lot to do with how you looked at me, actually."

"Did it now." He told himself firmly not to let her admission go to his head.

"Aye. It did. Such heat." She shook her head. "I felt it reach out and set my insides to burning."

"I will keep that in mind."

"Oh? So that you will be more careful?"

"Nay, so that I may discover exactly what look you mean, then practice it well."

She laughed. "It could be most awkward at times."

His responsive laughter stopped abruptly and he tensed, listening intently. "Horsemen."

"God forbid, not more hired murderers." She quickly backed more securely into the surrounding shrubbery.

Hastily gathering up his sword and tunic, Thayer crouched in front of her, staring in the direction of the sound. "If Robert had more men about, I would have thought they would come at me all at once. The chance of killing me would be greater. But best we tread carefully. There are others in this land we should take care with."

It seemed like hours to Gytha before the horsemen came into view. She felt her whole body sag with relief when she recognized Roger at the front of the small group. The tense fear she had suffered while waiting to see what new threat faced them had cramped her stomach so, she was a little slower than Thayer to rise and greet the men.

"Did I not say I wished to be alone?" Thayer drawled, even though he grinned a welcome to his men.

"Aye, I do recall something of the like," Roger replied, returning Thayer's grin before growing serious. "Something came to our attention, however, that made us think you might appreciate a little well-armed company."

"Which was?" Thayer draped his arm around Gytha's shoulders when she stepped up next to him.

"Merlion returned from town with some interesting news. Strangers have been seen in the last few days."

"How many?"

"Six was the count we got."

"Well, 'tis three now if the count was right."

Roger's eyes widened slightly even as he quickly looked Gytha and Thayer over. "Three are no longer a concern for us?"

Thayer nodded curtly. "They are in the wood if you feel reluctant to leave them to the carrion."

"It troubles me very little. Where is your mount?"

"Dead. We are in need of a horse. You have saved us a long walk."

Laughing softly, Roger neatly moved from

his mount to sit behind Merlion on his. "Mount up then. There is another reason we sought you. A messenger awaits you at Riverfall."

Mounting Roger's horse, Thayer tugged Gytha up and set her before him. "A messenger?"

"Aye. From the king."

Sighing with slight exasperation at this possible intrusion, Thayer ordered, "While I see to that, I want the other three strangers found."

"And killed?"

"Only if you feel it is necessary. I have no wish to fill Riverfall with dead," he grumbled, then abruptly started riding towards Riverfall.

Gytha held on and said nothing. She could feel the anger in Thayer, an anger she shared. Robert and his uncle were making life a constant battle. Most of her attention was centered on the messenger awaiting Thayer, however. She could only guess at what the king wanted, but she greatly feared it would be Thayer himself.

Once back at Riverfall, Gytha found herself neatly if cordially set aside as Thayer went to meet with the king's messenger. It was clearly something considered to be men's business, she mused a little crossly. Smothering the urge to march right into the hall where they met, she went to her chambers to clean up. She was sure she would find out what happened later.

Bathed, dressed in a clean gown, and brushing out her partially dried hair, Gytha frowned as a rap came at the door. She hoped it was not some domestic difficulty she would have to sort out, for she wanted some quiet time to get over the turmoil of the afternoon. It surprised her slightly when Bek answered her call to enter.

"I finished the washing." Bek stood next to her, watching intently as she returned to brushing her hair.

"It was hard work, was it not?" Gytha idly mused that when he reached manhood, Bek would set many a maid's heart to fluttering with those rich green eyes.

"Very hard."

Setting her brush down upon the small dressing table she sat before, she turned to look directly at him. "Yet you made Janet do it a second time in two days."

"I know." He stared down at his feet for a moment before meeting her gaze again. "That was wrong."

"Being able to see that is the first step to being the best knight in all of England." She met his grin with one of her own, then grew serious again. " 'Tis not as it was in my father's time. It was still right to treat your people well, of course, but now, since the plague took so many, it is even more important. We are fortunate that there are enough people at Riverfall to do the work needed." She frowned. "I may not be explaining this well. I do not want you thinking that you should be considerate simply to keep people working."

"I know. It should be done because it is right.

Hannah Howell

I was mean to Janet, making her do so much work, and being mean is not good. But I was angry."

"So I saw. Everyone gets angry, Bek. You have seen your father get into a rage."

"But he never does anything mean."

"Not that I have seen, and that is one thing that has gained him so much respect. And you, Bek, have just shown me that you hold the same quality." She hid a smile at the way he brightened, his thin chest expanding with pride.

"I am going to be as great a knight as Papa."

"Oh, I have no doubt of that. You will probably be as big as he is as well." When he straightened to his full height, she did smile, for he actually was tall for his age.

"Do you really think so?"

"Well," she drawled, "you will certainly be taller than me."

She was relieved when he recognized her teasing and laughed with her. To her delighted surprise, he sat down next to her on the little bench. Perhaps the battle was already over.

He began to pummel her with questions. Why was her hair so long? Did she like it that way? Did she always brush it so much? Gytha unhesitatingly answered every question to the best of her ability. She suddenly realized that Bek had had little association with women. There had undoubtedly been camp followers or the like, but Thayer had obviously kept the

170

boy away from them. She also took it as a good sign that the child showed some interest in her. And, she mused, if anything could keep her from worrying over what the king's messenger wanted, it was the chance to come to know Thayer's son better.

Thayer scowled and took a deep drink of ale, glancing darkly towards the king's messenger, who sat at the far end of the hall with several men-at-arms. The king was in the Western Marches ready to bring to heel all trouble-makers and rebels. To Thayer's annoyance the king requested his presence at court. And, Thayer thought crossly, at any battlefield that was formed. He still owed the king his forty days of service. It was clear that the debt was being called due.

"Come," urged Roger, "no need to look so dark."

"I have my own troubles to sort out. 'Tis a poor time to be called to sort out our liege's difficulties."

"Mayhaps not."

"Oh? And what are you thinking?"

"Well, I doubt Robert and his uncle would dare strike at you while you are at court."

"But he could make good use of my time away to strike at Gytha."

Roger frowned. "You do not intend to take her with you? Would it not be safest to keep her by you?"

Sighing, Thayer ran a hand through his hair.

"Would it? You know what the king's court is like, wherever it is set."

"Aha—Elizabeth would be there."

"There is that to consider, although she was not what I referred to. I meant all those courtiers, all those finely dressed, pretty peacocks that flit from bed to bed."

Swearing softly, Roger shook his head. "And of course they will flit into your bed. And of a certain, Gytha will allow it. Indeed, you being the petty obstacle you are, why should she not?"

"Roger," Thayer growled, stung by his friend's sarcasm.

"You continue to blacken her name without cause. Well, mark my words, my friend. Gytha is no fool. She will soon guess your thoughts, if she has not done so already. When she realizes how little you think of her, how little you trust her, she may well do exactly what you fear. Since you condemn her with no cause, she may see fit to give you one."

"Oh, I see. It will be my own fault? I shall plant the cuckold's horns on my own brow?"

"Aye, Thayer, if you keep waiting for it, it will come." Roger gulped the rest of his ale and abruptly left the hall.

After scowling in the direction Roger had gone for a moment, Thayer finished his ale. What annoyed him most was that he could see the truth in Roger's words. If one continually expected the worst, one usually got it. He had seen it happen far too often to doubt it. Unfortunately, he had also seen too many women like Gytha do exactly as he expected her to do. It seemed he was doomed no matter which way he turned. He courted disaster both by continually anticipating a shameful cuckolding and by having a wife as beautiful as Gytha.

Feeling thoroughly discouraged, he headed to his bedchamber. He would take his wife to court with him. It might be inviting trouble, but it was without doubt the safest place for her to be. At least, he thought darkly, safe from Robert and his grasping uncle. Elizabeth and the various loose-moraled courtiers would not be trying to murder her. Whatever else they tried he would deal with it as it presented itself.

When he entered their bedchamber, he found Gytha laughing with Bek. Seeing her happy, watching her form a bond with his son, he could almost believe that the idyll he had found in the months with Gytha would continue. He wanted to believe it, yet a part of him refused to release the fear of being fooled for a second time, of hearing that mocking laughter all over again.

Seeing the serious expression Thayer wore, Gytha asked, "Did the messenger bring bad news?"

"More inconvenient than bad. We have been summoned to court."

"We? You *and* me?"

"Aye, you *and* me. We leave in three days."

Chapter Eight

"Margaret, how could you do this to me?"

Gasping from the effects of a hearty bout of sneezing, Margaret struggled to sit up in bed and watched Gytha pace the bedchamber. "You think I suffer like this by choice?" She weakly lifted the goblet of mead from the table at her bedside and took a sip to ease the soreness in her throat.

Gytha sighed, then grimaced as she moved to sit on the edge of Margaret's bed. Poor Margaret looked horrible, her eyes and nose red and damp. The three women who shared the chamber with her had fled the room, terrified of catching what ailed Margaret. It was selfish to feel put-upon because Margaret would not go to the king's court with her. Gytha knew that but could not fully stem her disappointment at not having Margaret for support during what she foresaw as an ordeal.

"I am being a heartless fool."

"Nay, Gytha, I understand. I truly wish I could go, although I am not quite sure what troubles you so about the journey."

"*That woman* will be there."

"Lady Elizabeth? Bek's mother?"

"Aye. Her."

"Are you sure of that?"

"From what little Thayer told me of the woman—aye. That she frequents the court was the only reason he told me as much as he did about her."

"But Thayer also said he has naught to do with the woman now."

Waiting for Margaret to stop sneezing so she could be heard, Gytha said, "Aye, but he never said he no longer loves her. He avoids her. That is his answer to the matter. To me that hints that whatever hold she had on him might well still linger. If it did not, then he would feel no real need to stay away from her, would he?"

Rubbing her temples, Margaret smiled weakly. "I know there are a lot of things I could say to severely weaken that argument but I am unable to think clearly at the moment. My mood is also so sour that I feel inclined to say that if he wants such a cold, cruel woman, then leave the fool to his misery."

Laughing in surprise at Margaret's unaccustomed tartness, Gytha rose and kissed her cousin's cheek. "Rest. I have to take Edna with me, but do not fear I will leave you untended. Janet has offered to serve you, since Riverfall seems overrun with cowardly women. She may not be trained as a maid, but she is strong and able."

"Thank you. And I hope all your fears are groundless."

"So do I." Gytha was only mildly surprised to meet Roger coming in as she left, for she had seen his interest in her cousin grow keener with each passing day. "Where is Thayer?"

"With the armourer, so I thought to visit with Margaret before I spoke to him about what Merlion and I have discovered. Is Margaret's ailment serious?" he whispered.

"Nay, I think not. I have seen it before. 'Tis a misery, but I have rarely seen it be fatal."

"But the sneezing? 'Tis said it foreshadows the plague."

"Sneezing also comes with road dust. The signs of plague would have appeared by now, Roger."

"Aye, of course. I listen to the talk of foolish maids," he grumbled as he strode towards Margaret's bed.

Shaking her head, yet understanding his fears, Gytha went in search of her husband. Since the first deadly appearance of the plague, any illness was viewed with heightened terror. The fear creeping through Riverfall would ease soon. Even the most dim-witted would soon realize Margaret could not have the plague. She had been sick for two days already. If she had the plague, they would be burying her by now, with others already preparing to follow her.

As she approached the armourer, Thayer left the man. She met his smile of greeting with one of her own, although she suspected it was somewhat weak. It was proving impossible to still her fears. Going to the king's court should have felt exciting, like an adventure. Instead, she could only view it as a threat to her marriage and her happiness.

Briefly, she wondered if she should confess her love for Thayer. It could give him reason to stay at her side, strength to continue to avoid Lady Elizabeth. Then she shook the thought away. It was no good if she sought to bind him. If he did not return her love, the bonds would be those of guilt and obligation. That was not what she wanted. Pride was there as well. If he did not know how much he meant to her, he could not know how deeply he hurt her if he went to Elizabeth.

"All is ready for us to leave," Thayer said as he draped his arm around her shoulders and started towards the keep.

"All?" She tried to act as if that was welcome news and suspected she failed.

"Aye—all. We will leave to join the king's court at dawn's first light."

"How long will the journey take?"

"A few days. No more. It will not be as arduous as the others."

"How long will we stay there?" she asked as

they entered the hall, pausing to instruct a maid to bring drink, bread, and cheese for a light repast.

"I fear it might be the full forty days," Thayer replied as they sat at the table at the head of the hall.

"All of it? You did not say a war was in the making."

"Well, war has not been declared. 'Tis thieves and rebels the king seeks. He wants to end the constant nipping and snarling. To hunt down such as those takes time. They do not gracefully come to an open fight but flit through the hills and woods, strike, then melt away into the shadows again."

"Do you really think he can put an end to all such trouble?"

"Nay, but the king is determined. A strong, continued offense will quiet matters for a while. The king will think he has won, then return to the south. Once he is gone, the troubles will start again."

"A dismal picture."

Thayer shrugged. "We are the strangers here, taking land by might of sword. Keeping the conquered docile is never easy." He smiled faintly. "The Welsh do not take kindly to watching the English squat on their lands. I can only respect them for that. I should prefer compromise, but for now the king wishes to display strength and I am honor-bound to obey."

She nodded, then turned to serving him the

drink and food the maid brought. Just as she was about to broach the subject of fighting for the king again, Roger and Merlion arrived. Since they had been hunting down Robert's mercenaries, her interest quickly turned towards them. After seeing they were supplied with drink and food, she waited a little impatiently for their report.

In a way, she could not help but feel sorry for Robert. He was a weak man, controlled by Charles Pickney. Robert had probably been pushed and dragged into many a plot, yet gained nothing from any success. This time, however, Robert's uncle was putting Robert at the pointed end of a sword. By threatening Thayer's life, Charles had signed his and Robert's death warrant. A part of her hoped that Charles would die first, allowing Robert to make amends. Robert's only real crime was his spinelessness, and she wanted Thayer spared the pain of having to cut down his own blood kin.

"We found the other three," Roger announced after a few moments.

"And?" Thayer signaled a page to refill the men's goblets.

"They chose to fight us. Howbeit, we were able to gain some knowledge of Pickney's plans before they died."

When Roger paused to eat something, Merlion continued, "He wants you dead."

"That much we had guessed," Thayer drawled.

Merlion briefly grinned. "Something they said leads us to believe Pickney had something to do with William's death. And that he has been seeking yours for far longer than we may have thought."

"That too occurred to me. Thinking back, I could recall a few incidents that had the mark of being a murder attempt rather than accident or simple fight."

"Aye." Roger nodded. "I could think of some too."

"You mean"—Gytha's shock made her voice weak—"Charles Pickney has plotted to make Robert lord of Saitun Manor from the very start? He did not just come upon the plan because Robert was so close, then lost it?"

"Nay," Thayer replied, then shrugged. "We cannot be sure, however. And does it really matter? We know for certain he acts to murder me now. Puzzling over past crimes is a waste of time."

"I suppose it is. Still, if he murdered William..."

"He will pay."

There was a cold finality in his voice that made her inwardly shudder. She knew it was deserved, however. There could be no mercy for a man who plotted Thayer's murder. If a little cold-bloodedness was needed to keep Thayer alive, she fully supported it. She knew in her heart that if it came to it—if Thayer's life was at stake—she could kill the man herself.

"Did you discover any of his plans for Gytha?" Thayer asked, briefly considering sending Gytha away, then deciding it was better if she knew what she faced, whatever threat was in the wind.

"Oh, that was plain enough," Roger answered. "Pickney intends the thwarted marriage between your lady and Robert to go on. That would secure his grip on Saitun Manor and gain him this holding as well."

"And he expects her family to say nothing, to do nothing?"

"He will hold Gytha. It should prove protection enough."

"Aye—aye, it would. The Raouilles would feel their hands tied. No matter what suspicions they held, they would dare not act for fear of bringing harm to her. Do I judge that right?" he asked Gytha.

"Fully. There would at least be a great deal of time before, driven by desperation mayhap, they acted."

"True, there could come a time when they felt they had no more to lose." Thayer shook his head. "I cannot see how the man expects to get away with all this. At first, aye. No questions were raised as to William's death or mine. But now he boldly attacks me. He will have to take Gytha by force. There will be an outcry."

"I think," Roger said, "he has been made captive by his own plots. It will be played through to the end. I see no way to stop it now.

If naught else, you would forever need to watch your back. Pickney has shown he cannot be trusted. You must treat him as an enemy."

"True. But are you certain he means no harm to Gytha? That he does not plan her murder as well?"

"Not now." Roger shrugged. "This does not mean she will not be harmed. She has been at hand in every attack. Pickney may wish her alive, but he takes little care."

"Aye. Well, I must serve the king for now. I think you are right, Roger, in feeling Pickney will back off while we are at court. We shall use the time to try and hobble the man."

"How can you do that?" Gytha asked.

"That, I fear, will take a great deal of thought." Thayer took a slow drink of ale. "Still, we will be safe at court."

When Gytha finally left the men, she thought about Thayer's words. She did not really picture the king's court as a safe haven. While it was true that she had never attended court, she had heard enough gossip and rumor to suspect that court could provide a great many dangers of its own making. Intrigue and treachery were said to be rampant. She wondered if it was not the perfect place for Charles Pickney to play out his plots and schemes. But then she shook that thought away. Thayer knew far more of the world than she did. If he felt Charles Pickney would balk at pursuing them in the king's own court, she would value that judgment.

Rapping softly at Margaret's bedchamber door, Gytha obeyed the raspy command to enter. The bright, welcoming look on Margaret's face faded a little when she stepped inside, quietly shutting the door after herself. It took Gytha a moment to realize why that should be. She grinned as she went to sit on the edge of Margaret's bed.

"Roger is busy plotting plots to bedevil Pickney's plots. He will, no doubt, visit you again soon."

Although she blushed faintly at the mention of Roger, Margaret frowned. "What is this of plots?"

As succinctly as she could, Gytha told her all she had just learned. " 'Tis so hard to believe."

"Pickney suffers the sickness of blind greed. 'Tis not such a rare disease, sad to say. Thayer is right. 'Tis hard to see how the man thinks he can do all this yet suffer no penalty. He must be just a little bit mad." Margaret began to cough.

As she helped Margaret sip some mead to ease the scratch in her throat, Gytha sighed. "At the moment, I would prefer it if he was just a little bit dead, may God forgive me."

"I am sure He will." Margaret sagged against the pillows as Gytha set the goblet of mead back on the table and sat down again. "The man seeks to kill your husband and, no doubt, you in time. 'Tis good Thayer is such a skilled fighter."

"Aye, he is that, but if the man continues to send two or three or more men against him every time, even that great skill may not be enough. I am eaten alive with fear for Thayer."

"You love the man."

"Aye, I do."

"So, no more confusion. And I think I know when the confusion ended. When he was wounded."

"You look so smug, I should say nay just to spite you." She laughed briefly with Margaret. "Aye, that was when I knew. Revelation can be most uncomfortable," she drawled and Margaret grinned. "I acted as if he had lost a limb." Grimacing as she recalled how she had acted, she shook her head. "At least I did not fail in tending to his wound for all I drowned him in weak, foolish tears."

"And what did he say when you told him how you feel?" Seeing the look that fleetingly passed over Gytha's face, Margaret sighed. "Just why have you said nothing to the man?"

"I would like to keep it to myself for a while," Gytha muttered. Then, seeing Margaret's look of unreserved disbelief, she rose to pace the room. "I feel certain he will not respond in kind, and I know how deeply that will cut me. For a while, I seek to avoid that pain. You can hardly fault me for that."

"Nay, but you should be wary. Do not let that fear settle too deeply, or you may hold your tongue when it is time to speak out."

"I know, and I will not be cautious to the

point of stupidity. Also, there is Elizabeth."

"What does Lady Elizabeth have to do with your speaking your heart to your husband?"

Stopping at the foot of the bed, Gytha looked at Margaret. "A lot. I did think to tell him before we go to court, before he faces that woman again."

"It would seem a good time. You could give him the strength, if he needs it, to avoid the woman."

"I could. It could make him stay at my side no matter what lures she throws out. But for what reasons? Because he feels the same or some emotion close to it? Or for guilt and obligation?" She nodded when Margaret grimaced. "And what if he still went to her? There I would stand, heart bared and bleeding, and he would know it. He may even let Lady Elizabeth know."

"Ah, pride."

"Aye—pride. Not the most noble of emotions, but we all have some. Mine tells me that I should wait. Telling Thayer will not necessarily gain me anything. Not telling him can save me added pain—the pain of his knowing just how badly he can hurt me if he turns to his old love. Not telling can give me the chance to maintain at least some dignity in the face of defeat. I can pretend I do not care, and he will never be sure if it is otherwise."

"Gytha, I cannot believe the man would turn to Lady Elizabeth, to a woman who treated him so poorly. Not when he has you. He does not seem to be such a fool."

"Men can be appalling fools about women, and we both know it. She is not only his old love, recall, but the mother of his son. That has to be a bond of some sort. I know you seek to soothe my fears, but I think I might be wiser to cling to some of them. It will keep me alert for trouble."

"Aye, you may be right. Has Bek said anything about his mother? He must know she will be there."

"Oh, he knows. He says little about it though, and I have not pressed him on the matter. 'Tis something I feel he must tell me of his own free will. He does not seem upset. Nor does he seem happy or excited about it. Mayhap he has felt both at times and learned that neither is welcomed." She shrugged. "If Lady Elizabeth purposely causes him distress in any way, then I shall step in. Otherwise I think it best to stay out of it."

When Margaret only nodded in reply, Gytha smiled. She could see that Margaret was tiring. After helping her cousin to have another drink of mead, she left Margaret to get some rest. Resisting the urge to find Thayer and learn if any further plans had been made against Pickney, she went to her chambers to check that everything she needed for her time at court was being packed. If there was anything she could do to help fight Pickney, she was sure Thayer would tell her. After colorfully cursing

Pickney as viciously as she was able, she turned her full attention on the trip to the king's court.

"Six more men dead." Robert glanced nervously at his scowling uncle, who shared the rough table with him. "I think this campaign of yours grows too costly."

"No one asked you to think." Charles Pickney glared around the cottage they had taken as their hiding place. "Do you wish to live like this all your life?"

"We could make amends with my cousin. Then we could return to Saitun Manor."

"Are you fully witless? We have spent months trying to kill the man. Do you truly think he would just shrug that aside and clasp us to his bosom as kin and friends? He will have our heads from our shoulders if we get within sword reach."

"Well, we cannot reach him at court. It now grows difficult to get more men to go after him. The dead mount up and our coin dwindles. We should never have begun this." Robert cried out when his uncle struck him full across the face, cutting his lip.

"Stop your whining. We have not lost yet."

Robert opened his mouth to argue, then quickly shut it. With each failure his uncle had grown more vicious. Pickney's rages were more frequent and wilder. Even when Robert did not argue or speak up, he could suffer the brunt of that fury. Robert began to think he had tied his fate to that of a madman.

Inwardly he sighed, cursing the weakness that kept him tied to his mother's brother, kept him participating in plots he really wanted no part of. Although he had always been jealous of William and Thayer, he had never wished them harm. He certainly wished none to Gytha, yet he began to suspect his uncle had plans beyond letting him marry Gytha. It sickened him that even that did not give him the strength to combat his uncle.

"Thayer and his whore . . ." Pickney began.

"Gytha is not a whore." That earned him another blow, but Robert sullenly accepted it, refusing to take back his words.

"They will be kept busy at court. That could benefit us. We can take back Saitun Manor."

"Take it back? How can we hold it? That requires more men than we have."

"Then we will get more. As for holding the place, we need but one person to aid us in that. Little Gytha. Aye, she will be shield enough against an attack."

"If we can get her. She is well protected."

"I have already set that plan in motion. Aye, it will not be easy, but if we draw back for a while, her guard may grow lax. We have time. If we are careful in taking Saitun Manor, we can even make sure that Red Devil is unaware of the loss for a while. Why, we could even use his lady to gain the manor."

"He will come after her."

"Of course he will. I want him to. We will

use his lady to bring him to us, then we will kill him." Pickney smiled at the thought, his mind crowded with plans to bring about that satisfactory conclusion.

"And then I shall marry Gytha?" Robert watched his uncle closely as the man answered him.

"What? Oh, of course. You must, to strengthen our hold on the lands. You will have your pretty little wife."

For a while. Robert heard the words as clearly as if his uncle had said them aloud. He tried to tell himself he was being foolish. There was no gain in killing Gytha. Yet, he could not shake the feeling that Pickney did not intend Gytha to live a very long life.

There were a great many holes in Pickney's plans that he could see no way of closing. Did the man think Thayer's men would tuck tail and run when Thayer was killed? Did he really think Gytha's family would raise no cry? They would be surrounded by enemies, powerful enemies. His uncle did not seem to be thinking very far ahead.

Swept by a feeling of heavy defeat, Robert refilled his tankard and drank heavily of the ale. Getting drunk would solve nothing, but it would free his mind of doubts, fears, and confusion. For just a little while he would find peace and not have to face the weakling he was.

Sitting up in bed, Gytha hugged her knees to her chest and watched Thayer get ready for bed. In the morning they would leave to join the king's court. She firmly told herself it did not mean she would lose Thayer or see her marriage become a sham, but the fear lingered. Trying to set it aside, she turned her thoughts to the problems Robert and his uncle presented.

"Did you make any plans about Robert and Pickney?" she asked Thayer.

"Nothing firm. We talked over a great many, but there are a lot of possibilities. We have to choose carefully."

"Of course. Will you speak to the king about it?"

He smiled crookedly at her before drying off. "Another thing we talked over but could not decide upon."

"Why would you not want to tell him? Pickney commits a crime. Should the king not be told about that? If naught else, you can gain his seal upon whatever action you are forced to take."

"There is that to consider. It would save me having to explain matters later. Howbeit, 'tis a family matter. 'Tis a battle between blood relations. I feel reluctant to reveal all that. It seems it ought to remain a private battle. Can you understand that?"

"Oh, aye. But they are not my blood relations, so I can also see benefits and problems that you may not."

"So can Roger and Merlion." He sighed as he moved to douse all the lights save the one

Hannah Howell

by their bed. "They push for telling all to the king." Wearily, he climbed into bed, then gently tugged Gytha into his arms.

"You cannot care what ill might befall Pickney. So is it Robert you think about?"

"Aye. I find it hard to believe he is fully behind all this. He was always weak, easily led, but never cruel. Murder was not in his blood. God's beard, he dreaded even training for battle. He had no stomach for it."

"But he is not wielding the sword himself. He and Pickney send others to do their killing."

"True." He moved his hand up and down her arm in an idle caress. "I may confuse the child I remember with the man Robert has become. A man molded and honed by Charles Pickney."

"Poor Robert."

"Poor Robert?" He chuckled. "I am the one with all the sword points aimed at me."

"I know." She hugged him and kissed his chin. "Still, I cannot help but feel sorry for Robert."

"Sorry for him?"

"Aye. I did not know him really, yet I have this feeling he is caught up in something he neither wants nor can stop. This is so wrong, yet I never sensed any—well, evil in Robert. Try as I might I cannot envision him behind all this."

"Which is what I feel. But part of me warns I am just being weak, letting blood ties blind me to the truth. It leaves me doubting and that is not a welcome feeling for any man facing battle."

"And you do not wish to have Robert's blood on your hands."

He released a heavy sigh. "Nay, I do not."

"Is there no way you can be spared that? If he still lives when Pickney is gone, must you kill him?"

"Mayhap not. Still, would I be leaving a dagger poised at my back? I know Robert would never face me directly, sword to sword. I cannot be sure, however, that he has not gained the stomach to creep up behind me. That is a doubt I have no wish to live with." He did not add that that dagger could be aimed at her as well, although he knew she suspected it.

"Would it not be wonderful if Robert gained the strength to leave his uncle's hold, to come to your side?"

"Aye. If he did, I might feel he could then be trusted."

When he fell silent she held on to him, trying to silently convey her sympathy. She wished she could find a solution that would leave them both safe and happy with the results. Thayer had so few kin. It seemed unfair that he would have to lessen that meager number even more by his own hand. She prayed God would grant Robert the strength to turn his back on his uncle, to make his peace with Thayer and stop tearing apart what little family they had.

Thayer stared at the ceiling lost in his thoughts. He could see Robert as a child—a

pale, constantly frightened child. Despite all
his and William's efforts they had never been
able to take the fear from Robert's eyes. He
realized now that Charles Pickney had already
begun to tighten his grip on Robert. Few
chains were as strong as those forged by fear.
Thayer doubted Robert had ever known anything else.

Pity stirred inside of him for that child, but
he struggled against it. Pity could weaken him
at a dangerous moment. He would be fair. He
would not refuse Robert any chance to make
amends. What he would not do, could not do,
was let emotion of any sort interfere with what
had to be done.

Gytha shifted slightly in his hold, breaking
into his dark thoughts, and he looked down at
her. "I have just thought—I have told your
family none of this."

"Do you think it is necessary?"

He shrugged. "At the moment I have no need
of whatever added strength they might offer."

"Then it might be best not to say anything.
It would only worry them." Rubbing her hand
over the tightly curled hair on his chest, she
added in a quiet voice, "Keep your trouble to
yourself a while longer if you wish."

"I do wish. Pride makes me reluctant to tell
them my own kin seeks my death. Aye, and
yours."

After kissing him slowly, she murmured,
"You need to set aside these troubling
thoughts."

"That would please me." He smiled faintly as he tightened his hold on her, tugging her on top of him.

"As your wife, 'tis my place to see that you are ever and always pleased." She traced the life-giving vein in his throat with her tongue.

"Aye, it is." Cupping her face in his hands, he tugged her mouth back to his.

Teasing his mouth with short, nibbling kisses, she said, "So I shall make you forget all about Robert."

"Robert who?" he muttered as, his hand on the back of her head, he pressed her mouth more firmly against his.

Staggering into the cottage, Robert spared barely a glance for his uncle before collapsing on his rough bed. He had drunk ale until he felt ill, yet the peace he sought eluded him. Images and thoughts still plagued him, but now they swirled through his head in a drunken, discordant manner. It was enough to make him dizzy, to add to his queasiness. He lay on his back, eyes closed, hoping his uncle and his two men would soon climb to the loft, leaving him alone.

"Why do you keep the drunken fool around?"

"Because, Thomas, he is the rightful heir to all I seek." Charles cast a disgusted look at his drunken nephew. "It has always been his sole use to me. Do you think I would keep such a weight chained to me if there was any choice?"

"Is there no way you could gain hold without him?" Bertrand asked as he leaned back a little to scratch at his softening belly.

"Not that I have found as yet. I held all through him after his parents died. When he weds the fair Gytha and begets a child, I will then hold all through that child. Then I will have no use for this cursed nephew of mine."

Thomas shook his head. " 'Tis hard to believe such a weak sop came from the same family as you."

"My sister was weak. And I made sure the boy never gained the spirit to defy me. You need to start them young, to bend them to your will from the time they are suckling babes. That is why he still grovels to my command when, in truth, he has full right to all I rule. I will rear his seedling in the same manner."

"And hold all until you die."

"Exactly." Charles rose and started towards the loft. "Time to seek our beds. There is a lot we must begin on the morrow."

After their footsteps had faded, after all sounds of movement in the loft ended, Robert opened his eyes and stared into the darkness. All he had just overheard, all they had said as they thought him deaf with drunkedness, repeated itself over and over in his mind. For one brief moment, he felt the thrill of strength, a strength born of fury. He wanted to kill Charles Pickney. He almost wept at the knowledge that he was too drunk to take advantage of his sudden will.

With a return of his weakness came doubt. He was very drunk. It was possible he had not heard what he thought he had. Then he thought of Gytha—sweet, beautiful Gytha. She was the one thing he had ever truly wanted in his life. She was why he followed his uncle's plans. Wrong as they were, they would give him Gytha. She would keep the nightmares away. She would give him strength, make him a man. He would wait until he held Gytha before he looked too closely at his uncle, thought too much on what had been said. As the blackness he sought flooded over him, he smiled. Gytha would help him break free of Charles Pickney.

Chapter Nine

Sighing, Gytha made a final adjustment to her headdress. They had been at court for one week. She felt it was a week too long. The court was little more than a nest of immoral vipers. The sole pastime of the courtiers appeared to be the theft of each other's wives, husbands, or lovers. Only one thing diverted them from that sport—a chance to lessen another's position at the court, thus raising their own. She found it impossible to untangle all the plots and schemes. It was, she mused, surprising that more people were not tripped up by their own knot of lies.

And then, she thought, scowling at her image in the looking-glass, *there was Lady Elizabeth*. Her hands curled up slightly as she savored the thought of scratching the woman's eyes out. Thayer's first reaction to the woman had been a cold one, but the delight she had felt over that had soon faded. She feared he now warmed to his old lover. Courtesy required him not to rebuff such a highly placed lady too brutally—but was that all it was? Despite all her efforts not to, she feared the woman's wiles and beauty. She feared Lady Elizabeth was again working her charm on Thayer's heart, a heart that may never have ceased to love her.

"You look beautiful, wife." Thayer moved to stand behind her. "No need to frown so."

"Are you certain I look presentable?"

"Much more than presentable. Ready?"

"Aye." She grimaced faintly, then turned to face him.

He lightly kissed her then tucked her arm through his. "You must not fret so."

"I am unused to such high company and so consistantly," she murmured as they made their way out of their chambers towards the great hall. "I have never had to display such fine manners for so long before." She smiled when Thayer laughed.

" 'Tis not for much longer. Soon the plans for me will be made clear. Then I will see you back to Riverfall if you wish, do what the king requires of me, and return to you." He smiled down at her. "Court life sore tries my temper as well. 'Tis all subterfuge, treachery, and idleness."

"Mmmmm." She frowned. "I thought you wished me to stay here?" Suspicion crept into her mind, but she forced it aside. "You said it would be safer."

"And so it is. Still, I cannot like to see you wearied and unhappy. I know you find little to interest you here."

"True. At times—at many times actually—I find myself staring empty-eyed at the jongleurs while thinking of all that could be done at Riverfall."

Thayer laughed softly and nodded. "My thoughts often wander too. I find I rather like being a landholder. There is far more to do than I ever thought. Aye, and at Riverfall the Welsh make just enough trouble to keep me from growing restless and battle hungry."

"Kind of them," she drawled, her gaze revealing her laughter as she glanced up at him.

At that moment he led her into the great hall. It was all that kept him from heartily kissing her impishly curved lips. Then the fears came. They swept over him as he watched the way the men looked at Gytha. Too many wanted her, coveted her beauty. All of them were far more handsome and glib than he could ever be. Thayer ached to steal Gytha away from all the temptation laid out before her.

Gytha sighed as she glanced around. There were those looks again. Nothing she did seemed to halt them. It made her not only uncomfortable but angry. She was unmoved by the flattery and flirtatious manners of the young courtiers, yet they continued to plague her. She began to think her aloof air challenged them. However, she had little idea of what to do about it.

Her thoughts quickly changed direction as Lady Elizabeth sidled over to them. Gytha felt a growing tension in Thayer as the woman approached. What concerned her was what caused that tension.

She quickly reminded herself that he spent every night in their bed. He held her close, warm, and secure, even when they did not make love. Surely a man whose heart was elsewhere would not do so. Would a man who contemplated adultery hold his wife so gently through the night? She wanted to believe he would not, but uncertainty stole her confidence. Such reminders did, however, aid her in replying coolly when Lady Elizabeth purred that she had come to escort Thayer to the king.

As if he could not find the king on his own, she mused crossly as she sought a quiet place to wait for Thayer's return. To her dismay, Lady Elizabeth hurried back to her. Gytha knew this was to be the confrontation she had hoped to avoid. Inwardly, she sighed with resignation and prayed Thayer would return quickly to end it.

"You feel quite secure, do you not, Lady Gytha."

"And should I not, m'lady?"

"He loved me once."

"Once." The woman's confident chuckle made Gytha eager to slap her face.

"He will again. Have you not seen how he

softens towards me? Why, even now, I could snatch him from your hold with ease."

That was exactly what Gytha feared the most, but she struggled to act unconcerned, drawling, "To what purpose? I know you seek a husband. Thayer is wed already."

" 'Tis true I seek a husband, but while I do so, I must live. Thayer is no longer a poor knight. As a lover, I feel sure he would be most generous. Aye, very generous indeed."

"I do not believe you will have the opportunity to find out." Gytha hoped she sounded as confident as she wished to appear.

"Nay? He is such a big, healthy man. Healthy and so lustfully greedy. Ah, how well I recall just how greedy he can be. And how filling. One woman could never satisfy such a man's needs."

"One woman has been doing well enough so far."

"Has she? Mayhap there has simply been no choice offered him. We shall see."

"Thayer is a man who honors his vows." Gytha wished to God that she felt the same conviction she weighted her words with.

"Marriage vows?" Lady Elizabeth laughed. "Foolish girl. No man honors those. You reveal your naivete. I will show you, my innocent child, just how easily a man can forget those words muttered before some priest."

Gytha watched Lady Elizabeth walk away, invitation in the woman's every step. Elizabeth went straight to where Thayer consulted with the king and began to flirt with a young courtier Gytha recognized, a rather handsome youth named Dennis. But Gytha saw whom Elizabeth's fine green eyes were directed towards—Thayer. She too watched her husband closely despite wishing she had the strength to walk away, to completely ignore the taunting game Elizabeth played.

Although she loathed the doubts that plagued her, she could do little to halt them. She could not shake the memory of Thayer's saying he had loved Elizabeth, nor stop remembering that he had never told her that he had ceased to love the woman. Lady Elizabeth was very determined. Gytha feared there was a very real chance that Thayer would succumb to the woman's lures yet again. She knew that, where the heart was involved, even the wisest of men could be a fool. One of her fears was that her own heart was about to make her one.

When Thayer escorted Lady Elizabeth out of the hall, Gytha felt something within her freeze. Not once did Thayer even glance her way. His gaze was fixed upon the lady's lovely upturned face. Elizabeth leaned into Thayer and he put his arm about her. They looked like two lovers slipping away for a moment alone. Gytha did not want to believe Thayer would treat her so before so many people. She felt certain every gaze was turned her way.

"Ah, m'lady, come along. Allow me to take you to the gardens," murmured a soft male voice.

A little blankly, Gytha stared up at the young man who had gently tucked her arm through his. "The garden?" She slowly recognized him as Dennis. "To the garden, you say?"

"Aye." He inexorably led her towards it. "You look so stricken. 'Tis not wise to reveal a weakness in this pit of vipers. Ah me, these things will happen, sad to say. One must learn to maintain one's dignity."

Dignity was the last thing Gytha thought about. Her mind was choked with images of Thayer and Elizabeth in a myriad of torrid embraces. She struggled and failed to expel those agonizing pictures. They sliced at her heart. They also made her feel alarmingly violent. She frightened herself with the path her thoughts took. Side by side with the picture of Thayer breaking his vows was the image of herself swooping down upon the lovers like some avenging angel—an angel who would leave the pair with very little worth embracing. She nursed the urge to kill, to maim, and that horrified her. It was so foreign to her nature.

"What things?" she snapped at Dennis, struggling to grasp some calm, to hide the hurt twisting her insides.

"Lovers, sweeting." He stopped at a spot secluded from the other strollers in the garden.

Leaning against a tree, Gytha suddenly felt bone-weary and rather sick. "Give the sin its true name, sir. 'Tis adultery." She wished she could creep away to her chambers unseen, yet dreaded acting like a whipped dog.

" 'Tis common. Marriage is for the begetting of legitimate heirs. No more." He placed a hand upon the tree by her head and edged closer to her.

"Marriage is a union of a man and a woman sanctified by God." She wondered sadly why people found that so hard to understand.

"So that children may be legitimate and inherit without difficulty." Placing his other hand against the tree on the other side of her head, he lightly cornered her. "Everyone understands that."

"Everyone understands nothing."

"Come, sweet, let me ease the hurt." Cupping her chin in his hand, he kissed her.

It took Gytha a moment to overcome her shock. Then she swung at him. She put every ounce of the anger churning inside her behind the blow, and the sound of her hand connecting with his cheek echoed in the quiet garden. Dennis staggered back a little. One look into his eyes told her she had erred. A hasty retreat would have been far wiser. Dennis clearly took refusal as an insult. Fury narrowed his eyes and tightened his handsome features. She could not fully restrain a soft cry of panic when he roughly yanked her into his arms then slammed her up against the tree.

"Curse you, woman. Your husband is off merrily rutting with another, yet you play the nun."

She struggled to escape the hard, somewhat

feverish kisses he forced upon her face and neck, making her skin crawl. "I will not commit a sin to repay a sin. Leave me be. There are others who would welcome this. I do not."

"I will have you begging it of me, my little nun."

When he threw her to the ground, she was momentarily stunned. The breath was driven from her body by the force of the fall and she gasped to replace it, but by the time she regained enough to scream it was too late. He covered her mouth with his and kept her mouth covered with his brutal kisses or his hand. She tried biting him, but he gave her a cuff on the side of the head that had her reeling with dizziness. That was a state that could easily prove her downfall, so she discarded that ploy.

He kept her pinned to the ground as he struggled to undo her gown. She used his distraction with that to insinuate her leg between his. Her brothers had taught her of the vulnerability of a man's groin, thinking it knowledge she might need. Now she concentrated on remembering all they had taught her as she fought to free her arms from where Dennis had them pinned to the ground. She felt herself near success when, out of the corner of her eye, she saw Thayer, Lady Elizabeth, and Roger step into view.

Thayer had been smothering a laugh over Roger's obvious guard, over the glares Roger and Lady Elizabeth had exchanged. He also found Lady Elizabeth's shallow ploys to seduce him amusing. From the moment she had claimed faintness, he had known it for a lie, but he had been curious as to what game she played.

He felt nothing for the woman. He was finally, totally, free of her destructive hold. Thayer realized that Gytha had invaded every part of him, and there was nothing of his crippling fascination with Elizabeth left. He admitted to himself that Gytha had also restored his confidence. Elizabeth had none of that weakness in him to play upon. He found the woman amusing, somewhat irritating, but little else.

The heady delight that knowledge brought him vanished with a painful abruptness as they rounded a corner in the little-used path. Gytha was sprawled beneath a handsome young courtier. Her beautiful hair was loose, splayed out beneath her. Her fine clothes were in a revealing disarray. He halted in mid-step, stunned by the sight.

Suddenly, he was seeing another garden, seeing another time when all his illusions were shattered. Only this time the pain was much worse. He waited to hear the mocking laughter, waited for the stinging ridicule. Sensing Roger's move to interfere, he held his friend back. Thayer meant to see just how big a fool he had been. Here was where the truth would be revealed. He meant to face it squarely. This time he would not continue to play the fool for a woman.

Slowly, the truth he saw revealed was that Gytha was not willing. Her movements were struggles, not ecstatic thrashings. He had been seeing what was not really there, confusing the past with the present.

Then her gaze met his. He saw the plea there, but was held still by his continued confusion. Her look became one of shock, of deep pain, when he made no move to come to her aid. He knew she saw his hesitancy as nothing less than utter betrayal, yet he did not move.

Gytha felt stunned when Thayer made no move to help her. He simply watched, even held Roger back when the man stepped forward to aid her. Her husband, who was honor-bound to defend her, was leaving her to her fate.

A cool breeze over her thighs pulled her out of her shocked stupor. She would have to secure herself and time was no longer on her side. Later she would deal with the added wound Thayer had inflicted through his indifference to her plight.

Moving her leg that final inch, she brought it directly between Dennis' legs. Putting all her strength behind the blow, she brought her knee up into Dennis' groin. He screamed, clutched himself, and tumbled off of her. Stumbling to her feet, Gytha used the tree to support herself.

With no effort to hide the hurt she felt over his betrayal, Gytha looked at Thayer as she fought to catch her breath. Then, suddenly, she knew she was going to be ill. She waved Thayer away when he finally stepped towards her. Even as she hurried towards some bushes, she saw Lady Elizabeth help a pale Dennis to his feet, Roger nearby watching them closely. The couple exchanged a few angry words before taking advantage of Thayer's and Roger's distraction to flee. Gytha began to suspect that a great deal of what had happened had been planned, but her illness consumed all her thoughts.

Falling to her knees, she saw Thayer reach out to help her. "Do not touch me," she choked out before she succumbed to nausea.

Thayer jerked back, feeling slapped. He watched as Roger moved to Gytha's side. Needing to do something, he went to dampen his handkerchief, a gift from Gytha which he had thought a little frivolous, in a small fountain. Crouching by her side, he began to wipe her face. Frantically he tried to think of an explanation even as, with a chilling certainty, he knew there was little he could say.

As her head cleared of the dizziness induced by her illness, Gytha realized who gently bathed her face. With a cry of fury, she swatted Thayer's hands away. Nearly upsetting a concerned Roger, she struggled to her feet. A small part of her noticed that Bek now stood with them. Elizabeth and Dennis were nowhere to be seen. She knew it all meant something, but she was too distracted, too furious, to think straight. Her attention centered on the cause of the agony that ate at her.

"I told you not to touch me," she snapped.

"Gytha, let me try to explain...." Thayer began, faltering as no words came to mind.

"Explain! Explain what? Do you mean to tell me you lack the wit to see the difference between lovemaking and rape? I thought you so well versed in the ways of the world. Or mayhap this is some decadent court custom you neglected to tell me of. But what does that matter? You are my husband," she screamed, then struggled against the frenzied emotions threatening to overwhelm her.

"Gytha." Thayer reached towards her only to have his hand slapped away yet again.

"My husband." She sneered the words, making them sound an insult. "Whether I was willing or not, you should have run a sword through the man." She suddenly stared at him, an answer to it all growing clearer and clearer in her mind. " 'Tis what you wanted to see."

"Nay!" Thayer immediately knew he had protested too hastily and with a lack of conviction even he could hear.

" 'Tis. All this time you have but waited for me to step wrong. You did not see rape because it was not what you expected to see. I told myself so many times not to be so fearful, but I was right. You have never trusted me. Never."

"Gytha," he ventured with clear desperation, "come with me to our chambers. You need to clean up. Then we can talk about this."

"I will go nowhere with you. Nowhere." Her voice was flat as she was swept by a desolation so powerful it choked her.

"You cannot wander about court on your own."

"Nay? And why not? I have as much protection on my own as I do with you." She almost enjoyed his wince, the way he went slightly gray. "Why, an assassin could leap upon me, cut my throat from ear to ear, and be long gone ere you decided if t'was a ploy or real."

She sighed. "I believe I will go to our chambers—alone. It has been a very long evening. First your former lover whispers her poison in my ears. Then I must watch the two of you stroll away into the shadows like lovers. While I tell myself not to allow jealousy to cloud my reason, I find myself dragged out here by a courtier who goes slightly mad when I find his advances offensive. And then, the coup de grace—I discover my husband has always believed me naught but a whore. I fear that is too much entertainment for me." She felt someone take her hand and looked to see Bek at her side. "Bek?"

"I will go with you," the boy said.

She found the sympathy in the boy's eyes a balm for her tortured emotions. He could not possibly understand all that was being said. However, he knew she was hurt, a hurt she had every right to. Briefly, she squeezed his hand in a gesture of gratitude.

Afraid to let her leave before he could speak to her, Thayer reached for her. Gytha spat a curse that widened his eyes as well as Roger's and Bek's. Then she struck him forcefully in the stomach. Surprise more than anything else caused him to release her to clutch at his belly. He stood, crouched over, watching her walk away with Bek at her side, the boy casting nervous looks over his shoulder. When he finally moved to follow her, Roger halted him.

"Nay, Thayer. Leave her be."

"I must speak to her."

"About what? To say what? That she is right?"

Thayer abruptly turned away from Roger's gaze, staring blindly in the direction Gytha had gone. "Aye, that. Or lies. Or apologies. Anything."

"I think it would be wisest to just leave her alone for a little while."

"So her hate can harden?"

Roger grimaced. "I do not believe hate is what she feels. Hurt, anger, disappointment—aye. What in God's good name were you thinking of?" he demanded in exasperation. "How could you but stand there while some low cur mauled your wife?"

"I was doing exactly what she accused me of," Thayer replied in a voice weighted with guilt.

Moving to a rough log bench, Thayer sat down and buried his face in his hands. He heard Roger join him a moment later. Whatever Roger thought of his actions did not really matter now. He needed a way to right the wrong he had done Gytha, but he was not very confident that he could make amends. Whatever peace he made with his wife would be hard-wrung. Glancing at Roger, he found little hope in that man's face.

"Mayhap groveling would help," Roger murmured after several moments.

" 'Tis likely my only hope of even gaining an audience with her."

"To say what?"

"Well, I certainly cannot deny her charges. She would see that for the lie it is. It would only make matters worse—if they can get any worse. I have been waiting for her to cuckold me. You saw it." He shook his head. "You called me on it time and again. I should have heeded your words. I truly thought I was beginning to."

" 'Tis plain you heeded not a word or did so too late. Pearls cast before swine," Roger grumbled.

"Heaping insults upon me solves nothing."

"Well, do not look here for any ideas."

"Give me an army to face and I know where I stand, know exactly what to do and what not to do."

" 'Tis a shame Gytha is not an army."

Thayer ignored that. "Give me a woman and I stumble like an ignorant, untried boy. I treat the whore like a lady and the lady like a whore. The one thing above all others a husband should, indeed must, provide his wife is protection. In Gytha's eyes, I have failed dismally."

"Give her some time for her anger to ease."

"But will it ease?"

"Gytha's nature is not of the sort to cling to anger."

"Nay, I do not think it is, yet I have never tested it so strongly before."

"Look, spend this night in my quarters. Speak to her in the morning. T'will give her time to calm down and you time to think."

"That might be best. If I crawl into her bed this night, she may well cut my throat."

Gytha savored some very bloodthirsty thoughts all the way to her quarters. Edna watched her warily as she bathed her face and rinsed out her mouth, but Gytha did not feel inclined to soothe the maid. Once freshened slightly, she sat on the bed—then burst into tears.

Even in her despair, she realized that neither Edna nor Bek knew what to do with her. Bek finally fetched her brush, sat behind her, and began to brush the tangles out of her hair. Gytha felt deeply touched. She meekly sipped at the soothing herbal drink Edna pressed upon her, then sat docilely, still weeping, as Edna dressed her in her nightrail. All the while Bek told Edna what had happened. Gytha tried to help explain, but her crying made her nearly incoherent. She finally lay down, murmuring a thank-you as Edna placed a cool compress on her forehead. Staring up at the ceiling, she tried to still the hiccoughs and tremors that wracked her body.

"Poor Bek," she murmured, glancing at the boy, "you do not know what to do with me, do you."

"Stay with you." Bek sat by her side, taking her hand in his. "I will stay with you."

"I should like that."

"She planned it all."

"Pardon?"

"My mother, Lady Elizabeth. She planned it all. I heard her and that man say so. She wanted Papa to catch you with that man. Papa was supposed to go to her then."

"Well, she is welcome to him."

"Oh, nay, m'lady." Edna shook her head, twisting her hands nervously as she stood by the bed. "You do not mean that. Not truly. Lord Thayer would not go with that woman."

"Nay, he would not," Bek agreed.

" 'Tis not really Lady Elizabeth that is the trouble." Gytha sighed, then sipped a little more of Edna's herbal potion. "He just stood there doing naught. He has never had any trust in me. He has but waited for me to act as the whore he thinks I am."

"Nay," cried Bek and Edna as one.

"Aye. I wish to go home, to return to Riverfall."

"Papa will soon be here. I know it. Why, he will soon be able to leave court."

"I want to go home now, Bek. Edna, you will begin to pack my things."

"I will go tell Papa," Bek said, but halted quickly when Gytha spoke.

"No need. I will leave him a message. Do you wish to go with me, Bek?" While she had no intention of coming between Thayer and his son, she felt a need to take the boy with her.

"Aye, but Papa . . ."

"Papa will not be angry with you. Edna, you have not begun the packing."

Both Edna and Bek tried to talk her out of leaving, but Gytha refused to be swayed. She knew they both hoped for Thayer to appear and put a stop to her flight, but to Gytha's great relief, that hope was never realized. Rumor reached her that Thayer was in Roger's chambers drinking heavily and feeling very sorry for himself. She hoped he would continue to do so until she was well on her way to Riverfall, out of his reach.

Gytha did not allow herself the luxury of self-pity. She simply felt very tired. Court life had been a trial, but she had thought Thayer stood by her. Now she just wanted to go home, to turn her back on all of it.

Inside of her rested a hurt so great she knew of no way to ease it. She loved Thayer, yet wished she did not. That love caused her to be completely devastated by his mistrust, crushed by the discovery of what he truly thought of her. What had seemed so beautiful, so promising, now felt like the greatest of curses.

Dawn was barely tinting the sky rose when she started for Riverfall. Four of the men her father had sent when she left home rode with her as protection. Bek and Edna shared the cart with her. She briefly wondered if she was taking the coward's way out, then shrugged the thought away. Her sanity required her to retreat, to seek someplace to lick her wounds. She needed to think long and hard about what to do about her marriage, if she even had a marriage left to worry about.

Thayer greeted the new day with an aching head, a sour, dry mouth, and the knowledge that he had done something there might be no forgiveness for. Adding to his misery was an immediate summons from the king. Reluctantly he answered it, praying the man would be quick. He needed to see Gytha. To his great annoyance, the king held him captive for hours.

"Have you seen Gytha?" he demanded of Roger as he strode into the man's quarters late that afternoon.

"Nay, not a hair. Come to think of it, I have not seen Bek either."

"He is most likely with her," Thayer muttered as he washed up. "Who can that be?" he grumbled when a rap came at the door several moments later.

When he answered the knock, Roger scowled

at the woman standing there. "What do you want?"

Lady Elizabeth pushed by Roger to go to Thayer, ignoring his less than welcoming look. "You look well, Thayer."

"May I do something for you?" Thayer quickly moved away from her to tug on a clean jupon.

"Well, since your little wife has left, I thought you would want to escort me to the festivities this evening."

"Gytha has left?" Thayer felt as if his heart had abruptly sunk into his boots.

"Aye. I heard she left before dawn had fully broken. Where are you going?" she demanded, but Thayer did not bother to reply as he raced from the room, Roger close at his heels.

A moment later, Thayer strode about the chambers he had been sharing with Gytha, seeing all the proof of her abrupt departure. "Wait until morning, you said," he roared. "Leave her be for a while, you told me."

"I never would have thought she would leave you," Roger mumbled.

"Well, 'tis clear she has. What is this?" He snatched up the parchment left on their bed, sitting down heavily as he read it.

"Husband: I have returned to Riverfall. Bek is with me. So are my father's men-at-arms. You need not rush to join me. Gytha."

Thayer handed the message to Roger, who winced as he read it. It was chillingly blunt. Thayer wondered just how deep that chill went. He knew Gytha had been aware of Lady Elizabeth's pursuit of him; the woman was hardly subtle. Yet, Gytha had left him to the woman's ploys without a second thought. That said a great deal more than her terse note did. She was swiftly slipping away from him, turning her back on him.

"I have to go after her."

"You cannot leave, Thayer. Not until the king gives you permission."

"But that could mean weeks of delay."

"Gytha knows you cannot simply walk away from here. If this business drags on too long, speak to Edward. Tell him you have a personal matter you must tend to. At least she has gone to Riverfall, not to her own people."

"Aye, yet she makes it all too clear that my presence at Riverfall will be less than welcome."

"She was still hurt when she wrote this, Thayer." Roger sighed. "Mayhap this is for the best. Time will ease the hurt."

Thayer was not sure he agreed, but Roger was right in saying he could do nothing about it now. "Time will also allow me to find that cur who slinked away from me last night."

"He is most likely halfway to London by now."

"He merely steals a few more days of life."

Time quickly weighed heavily on Thayer's hands. The king sent him and his men on forays against small nests of rebels and thieves who plagued the Marches. Thayer swore to fulfill his forty days but give not one hour more.

A newly recovered Margaret met Gytha's arrival at Riverfall with ill-concealed surprise. Gytha told her cousin all that had happened as soon as she had refreshed herself from the journey. To her annoyance, Margaret was dismayed but expressed some understanding for Thayer. It quickly became clear to Gytha that Margaret hoped to imbue her with a little of it before Thayer returned.

Despite Margaret's subtle but persistent efforts, it was days before Gytha began to really think about what she needed to do concerning her marriage. She was stuck with it, but—she reluctantly admitted to herself—she wanted to be. She did not want to give up Thayer. Already she watched for his return or for some word from him. No matter how deeply he had hurt her, she remained his, heart and soul. Time was needed to ease the hurt enough for her to love him as freely, as openly, as she had before. He had taught her wariness. She wanted him home so that she could let him know she was far from grateful.

On the eve of his forty-first day at court, Thayer told the king he would be leaving for Riverfall come dawn. The king was reluctant to let him go, but Thayer reminded his liege that his debt was paid. He also referred to troubles at home that had been left untended for

221

too long. Since Gytha's abrupt absence from court had been much gossiped about, King Edward did not press. Thayer hurried to leave before the king reconsidered his generosity.

As he settled into bed for the last night at court, he thanked God for it. The nights spent alone in the bed he had shared with Gytha had been the hardest to bear. To force sleep, he had often drunk too much. There had been far too many nights when Roger had struggled to get him undressed and into bed.

Often he had ached for Gytha, yet at times he had cursed her. She had become all important to him. Everything seemed to stir thoughts of her. Sometimes he savored those. Other times he wanted to scream at her to leave him in peace. He began to fear for his sanity.

Lady Elizabeth had continued to plague him, to try to restir the bewitchment he had felt for her years ago. He was eager to get away from her. She had been tedious at times, yet tempting at others. He was a virile man left too long alone, his body aching for a woman who had put herself out of his reach. Yet, when he had found himself but a breath away from accepting Lady Elizabeth's freely offered favors, he had balked, casting aside all semblence of courtesy to send her away. It mattered little to him that, after so many years of savoring the vision, he had fully repaid his youthful humiliation at her hands. What he promised himself he would try to recall was that, in doing so, he had probably made an enemy who would bear watching.

While awaiting the dawn, he tried to build his courage. He was not skilled with words nor with women. Waiting at Riverfall was a woman he had deeply hurt. To mend things would require just the right words, exactly the right approach. He had absolutely no confidence that he could accomplish either.

Chapter Ten

Shouts of welcome echoed through Riverfall. There was a sudden surge of frantic activity. Gytha needed none of that to tell her Thayer had returned. Standing at the tower window she had wasted too many hours at, she had seen his approach. Slowly, she made her way down to the hall to greet him. With every step she struggled for the strength to greet him with a cool, remote dignity.

She had missed him far more than she had wanted to. Each night had seemed unending. Her days had needed to be filled with work or they dragged by. She did not want Thayer to know any of that. At least—not yet. Such knowledge would give him an advantage she was sure he would swiftly recognize and utilize.

He had hurt her. She intended to make him offer some amends for that. Gytha could not allow him to think he could treat her so, then act as if nothing had changed. If she let that happen, she faced a future of hurts inflicted then ignored with impunity. She doubted Thayer wanted a wife who would tolerate that, a wife so weak and lacking in all pride.

In truth, time had eased the depth of the hurt. She had even gained some understanding. Lady Elizabeth had left the man with a deep scar. Gytha suspected other women had picked at that scar over the years. She was deeply insulted that he would think her anything like Lady Elizabeth, but she was willing to understand. However, even if she granted forgiveness for that slur, she had to find a way to change his thinking.

Having relived the incident in her mind so often, she could now see more clearly. She could see how Thayer had looked when he had found her sprawled beneath Dennis. He had been deep in shock. She was certain he had briefly mixed past with present, seeing Elizabeth and ridicule, not her and rape. However, that had been neither the time nor the place for such confusion.

There was also their time apart to be accounted for. How had he spent it? Had he succumbed to Elizabeth yet again? In leaving, had she handed him over to that viper? She wanted to believe he was too wise to fall victim again, but she was haunted by the knowledge that he had never said he had ceased to love Elizabeth. His cure for the obsession had been absence. Alone at court, that cure could not be practiced. Gytha sincerely doubted it was any sort of cure at all.

"Thayer has returned, Gytha."

Smiling crookedly at Margaret, who stood at the bottom of the stairs with an equally worried Edna at her back, Gytha drawled, "I did suspect something of the sort."

"So? What do you plan to do?"

"Go and greet my husband as any dutiful wife would."

"Oh, Gytha."

"Margaret, I know you preach forgiveness. S'truth, you have done so day in, day out. Well, I am willing. Howbeit, I will not meekly lay it at his feet. 'Tis no simple matter, no small quarrel. He stood there while I was nearly raped. Oh, I can see the reasons for it all now, but that soothes the insult and feeling of betrayal only a little.

"Think. If I act as if naught has happened, I make his crime less than it was. Also, if he makes no attempt at amends, that will eat away at me even if it is my meekness that causes it. Nay, Margaret, he must at least apologize or this union is surely doomed." She finished descending the stairs. "I should also like an explanation, although I will understand if he gives me none. He may not understand it all himself."

Pausing at a suitable distance from the door,

she added, "I will not falter in my duties as his wife. I would never shame myself nor my family so. Howbeit, if Thayer wishes more than duty from this union, he must make amends for that incident." She fought the temptation to ease her stance, to relieve the worry in her friend's eyes.

"I was just thinking of something, Margaret."

"Dare I ask what?"

"Well, mayhap the best cure for this wound to my marriage is a good bloodletting." She smiled wryly when her words clearly added to Margaret's worry.

"What do you mean?" Margaret asked with a distinct hint of suspicion.

There was no time to answer, for Thayer and Roger entered. Gytha felt her heart leap with welcome and inwardly groaned as she moved to greet her husband. Her thoughts were already, rapidly, turning carnal. Things could not possibly go as she wished if she was so easily affected by the man. Her desire for him was going to have to be sternly quelled. Thayer would sense it as he always had. That would never do.

Stepping up to Thayer, she presented her cheek as he bent to kiss her. "Greetings, husband. And you, Sir Roger. Your arrival is somewhat of a surprise, but I am sure things are readied for you in your chambers. When you are done, there will be a meal prepared for you." She inwardly congratulated herself on her dignified, courteous air.

"Thank you, m'lady," Roger murmured when Thayer simply stood, struck speechless.

"Ah, Bek," she called when the boy suddenly appeared in the hall, "would you be so kind as to help your father and Sir Roger? Their baths have been prepared in Sir Roger's chambers. I will see how the meal fares." She hurried away, although she tried to hide it, before she was pressed too hard and her guise shattered.

"Hello, Bek," Thayer finally managed to say as he followed his son up the stairs.

"Hello, Papa. Are you angry that I left?" Bek glanced timidly at his father.

"Nay. There were pages aplenty with the royal entourage. I made use of them."

"That is good. She needed me to stay with her."

Thayer could think of no reply to that. He said nothing more until they entered Roger's chambers, where two baths had been set side by side before a strong fire. Curtly, he dismissed the maids. After Bek helped him and Roger out of their armor, he more gently dismissed his son.

"There is a decided chill to the air," he muttered as he eased himself into the steaming bathwater.

"Aye, I felt it." Roger climbed into his bath, sinking into the water with a sigh of pleasure.

"And I stood there like some dumb ox. Not one cursed sound could I utter."

"She is still here, Thayer. She could well have gone to her family."

"Aye, though 'tis difficult to be sure how much that signifies. So stiff. So polite. She has never been like that."

"At least she still keeps your home."

"That means something?"

Roger shrugged. "Many a wife shows her displeasure with cold bathwater and poor meals."

"We have not eaten yet," Thayer jested a little weakly.

"True, yet I cannot see her using that trick." Roger sighed then looked at Thayer with honest sympathy. "Where your real trouble may come is in the bedchamber."

Groaning, Thayer sank into the bathwater up to his shoulders. "Aye, so I fear. She will be as polite and dutiful there as she was when she greeted us. God's teeth, but that will be more than I can bear," he whispered, the mere thought of it twisting his heart.

"Then speak up, man. Tell her all of it."

"Even though 'tis enough to make me look a raging ass?"

"Aye. Even though it does that. I can see no other way."

"Nay, neither can I." Thayer sighed heavily, dreading it.

Nevertheless, he clung to the hope that another way might be found. What happened in the garden had made him feel a complete fool. He knew he had hurt Gytha, but he still hoped she would think it over, understand what happened, and let it rest. While he knew he had to make some amends, he hoped to do so without reviewing the whole shameful event.

The thought that Gytha would bring no more to their bed than a sense of duty was an agony. He flinched from it, not wanting to believe the insult he had dealt could kill her passion. He needed it too much. It had become as necessary to him as breathing.

"Come, my friend," Roger urged in a gentle voice as he dried off, "best climb out or you shall be sorely wrinkled."

"I feel as if I face the scaffold," Thayer muttered as he stepped from his bath to dry off.

"At times, trying to make amends with a lady can feel akin to that."

"There are too many ways I can step wrong."

"That is sadly true." Dressed, Roger started out of the room. "I will be at your side when the meal is served, but now I hope to gain a moment alone with Margaret."

Catching Roger by the arm, Thayer warned, "Do not play your games with that maid."

" 'Tis no game I play," Roger answered, smiling faintly.

Reading the truth of his friend's words in his face Thayer released him. "Then I wish you much good luck."

Thayer sighed as he watched Roger leave. He was pleased for Roger, hoping he would find the rewards his heart sought. Yet, it seemed unfair that fate should place a budding love before his eyes while his marriage stumbled, failure looming on the horizon. As Gytha grew colder towards him, he would have to watch Roger and Margaret grow warmer towards each other. It was a punishment he was not sure he had the strength to endure. Shaking away such thoughts, he prepared himself to face Gytha.

Finally dressed for the coming meal, Gytha sat down so that Edna could arrange her hair. "Have you seen Margaret?" When Edna said nothing, Gytha pressed, "Well?"

"She is with Sir Roger, m'lady," Edna replied, reluctance clear to hear in her voice.

Smiling crookedly, Gytha asked, "Did you fear to speak of it because of my own troubles?" When Edna flushed, Gytha sighed. "Well, do not. I am happy for Margaret. Tell me, do you think Sir Roger's attentions are honourable ones?"

"Aye, I do. 'Tis there to read in his eyes."

"Good. He is a fine man. Our Margaret deserves the best. I suppose she has said little of this to me because of my own difficulties, feeling it might be unkind. 'Tis true I feel the pinch of envy, but I have to let her know she does not need to creep about or hide her happiness. Margaret is like my sister. I can only share her joy."

"As she shares your hurt, m'lady." Meeting Gytha's gaze in the looking-glass Edna said, "I am thinking of being impertinent."

Smiling at the girl who put the finishing

touches on her hair, Gytha teased, "Are you ever otherwise?"

"Well, very impertinent. I wish to speak about you and your husband."

"Speak then. I am not such a fool to think I know all and you nothing. In a matter as grave as this, only a fool would ignore any advice offered."

"Men are strange creatures."

"That is no great revelation, Edna."

"Hush, m'lady. I was not done. Men can know they have erred, but apology comes hard. The prouder a man is, the more the words can choke him. He can know in his heart and mind that the words should be said, but they stick in his throat."

"I must have an apology, Edna," she said with quiet finality, not willing to let any amount of persuasion change her mind.

"I understand. Aye, and agree. You are right on the why of it. Let a man think he will do nary a penance for a slight, and he will run fair wild, ne'er thinking on word nor deed. But that apology may not come as straight or as pretty as you might like. Some men have no skill with fine words. If you do not listen closely and carefully, you may even miss it. To explain why they did what they did? Well, that day may never come. They may not understand themselves."

"I had wondered about that, about whether or not Thayer understood," Gytha murmured.

"Men do not seem to look too close at the

why of things. If what was done makes the man look a fool, no man would want to look at it too closely. That will also make that apology come harder. A man wants that sort of thing banished from mind and memory. If they do apologize, t'will be done quick and blunt. No man likes to beggar his pride."

"And Thayer is a proud man."

"Aye, m'lady. A very proud man in his way. And none too fine with words, if I might be saying so."

"You may. 'Tis naught but the truth."

"But his heart is true. If he has erred, he knows it well. I feel sure he will try to make some recompense, m'lady, but methinks t'will take a sharp ear to catch it."

"A very sharp ear," agreed Gytha. "Unless, of course, my lord is prompted to a modest eloquence."

Edna frowned in confusion. "How do you mean?"

"There is one thing I have learned about men. Some need the heat of anger to free their tongues. What they can find hard to say in a calm, quiet moment, they can bellow and roar with ease." When Edna began to grin, Gytha grinned back. "One must simply put spark to tinder."

"Just beware. You do not wish to get too hot a flame."

"Oh, Thayer would never harm me. He knows his own strength too well. Aye, he may smash all about me, but he would never strike me."

"Most like afraid he would take your head from your shoulders."

"Aye, just so. No matter how fierce his range, 'tis ever in his mind that I am small and light of build." Gytha stood and took a last thorough check of her appearance. "So, Edna, if you hear a storm thundering through these halls, pay it no heed. 'Tis planned. I will have the words I seek even if I am deafened by them," she vowed, then shared a laugh with Edna.

Gytha wished she felt as brave as she sounded. She honestly felt that stirring Thayer's impressive anger was the best way to make him tell her everything. Nor did she have any doubts about her stated conviction that he would never harm her. It was what he might tell her that she worried over. He had been within Lady Elizabeth's grasp for nearly a month.

"M'lady?" Edna called as Gytha started out of the room.

"More advice?" Gytha asked with a little smile.

"Aye. Do not let him shake you or push you about in his fury. 'Tis unwise in your condition."

"My condition?" Gytha spoke calmly, certain that Edna was about to confirm something she had begun to strongly suspect herself.

"The babe you carry. Surely you knew?"

"I suspected. But are you sure?" she whispered, placing her hand over her stomach.

"Aye. Your woman's time has failed to come thrice, nearly four times. You have been sick, though only a little in the morns. Aye, and your shape changes. I have little doubt that you carry his lordship's child."

"Do you know much about this?"

"Well . . . some."

"Are there things I should not do?" It was impossible to stop the blush that darkened her cheeks, and it served better than any words could to tell Edna what 'things' she referred to.

Blushing a little herself, Edna replied, "Nay. Just do not let yourself grow too weary or get knocked about. 'Tis a bad time for this?"

" 'Tis not the best, Edna." Gytha sighed as she headed towards the great hall.

Knowing she was with child left Gytha with an odd mixture of emotions. She loved Thayer, loved him so much it could frighten her at times, so she was elated to be carrying his child. But for now, she had to hide that emotion. First she had to clear away what lay between them. She feared how matters could turn if that was not accomplished. Her hurt would harden. The coolness she now showed him could grow real, no longer simply a tool to prod him into a revealing confrontation. That would be dreadful for a child.

"Gytha."

Startled out of her dark thoughts, Gytha

gasped, then saw Margaret. "Oh, you surprised me. Why are you lurking there?" she asked as Margaret stepped out of the shadowed niches beneath the stairs.

"I wanted to speak with you before we join the men."

" 'Tis astounding how marital troubles free people's tongues," murmured Gytha.

Margaret ignored that. "I know what you plan. Must you anger him?"

"Aye—I must."

"Oh, Gytha, I cannot like it."

"T'will make him speak up. That is all important."

"But are you certain you want to hear all he might say?"

"Not at all, but I will hear it. I know what you worry about, for I share that concern. I left my man unguarded, within reach of a viper who made no secret of wanting him. He could easily have slipped beneath her spell again. I think I can forgive that."

"Are you certain?"

"Aye. I knew what could happen even as I left him there."

"Then why did you leave him?"

"Do you really think we could have settled our problems at court? Amongst the spite, the ploys, the treachery?"

Sighing, Margaret shook her head. "Nay, of course not."

"Also, the wound was too fresh. I really needed time to heal a little. In my pain, I would

237

have driven him from me. Then I may well have seen him turn to another. That would surely have added to our troubles."

"I cannot believe he would break vows. He is an honorable man."

"Very honorable. He once told me he would never take a lover as long as I never took one or threw him from my bed." She nodded when Margaret grimaced. "Aye, he could well have seen my leaving as throwing him from my bed."

Moving to stand next to Gytha, Margaret took her cousin's hands in hers. "That does not mean he did anything."

"True. Yet he is a man of much need." She smiled faintly when Margaret blushed. "After a battle, he is very ardent and I doubt the king let Thayer's sword go rusty. He seeks to prove he has survived, and I guess a man can think of no better way to do so than to bed a woman, something that pleases all a man's senses. Thayer had many a night with an empty bed."

"So did you," Margaret interrupted, then dimmed her bluntness by blushing again.

"Aye, so I would like to think he will not turn to another each time we are apart for any length. Or have had a fight. Still, I believe I can understand—at least this time. We are not talking about some small tiff." She sighed. "I just pray that it was not with Lady Elizabeth."

"Because of what was between them?"

"Because of what may still be between them.

He has never said he does not love her—only that he avoids her."

Margaret vigorously shook her head. "Nay, he could not love a woman like that, not when he has you."

"Now you know the heart cannot be led. It will go where it will."

"Then he is a fool." Margaret crossed her arms under her breasts and nodded.

"That is as may be." She briefly exchanged a grin with Margaret, then grew serious again. "I should certainly like to know if he does still love her, although it could sorely grieve me."

"Aye, but you would know where you stand, know what must be fought."

Gytha nodded and held out her hands in a gesture revealing the helplessness she felt. "For now, I do not know if she stands between us or if I let my fears guide me."

"Well, I am still not sure I agree with your methods, but I do see that something must be done. Marriage is a bond that cannot be broken, and yours held such promise. Aye, 'tis worth a fight."

"There is that. There is yet another reason to mend this breach and quickly—I am with child."

Margaret gasped, her eyes widening as she fixed her gaze upon Gytha's abdomen. "Are you sure?"

"I suspected it, and Edna just gave me her learned opinion that it is so."

Briefly, Margaret hugged Gytha then

stepped back, her expression changing rapidly from joy to concern. "Oh, Gytha, then you must not get him angry with you."

" 'Tis a fearful sight to behold, but he will not hurt me. Unlike some men, he knows what strength lies in his arm, so he is careful where he swings it. Aye, I may get a bruise or two, but I know he will never strike me. I have said this before, Margaret. You must trust me to know." She could see that Margaret was still not confident of it.

"I do not know where you find the courage to even think of such a thing." Margaret sighed as they started towards the great hall. "Mayhap he will feel sorry enough that he will not be spurred to anger."

Laughing softly, Gytha hooked her arm through Margaret's. "Guilt or no, Thayer can always be stirred to fury if prodded enough."

Watching Gytha enter the hall with Margaret, Thayer braced himself for what he knew could prove a very trying time. He swore he would control his ready temper. It was he who deserved to be raged at, not Gytha. Yet, when she greeted him in the same polite tone she used on Roger as she joined them at the head table, he realized that keeping his temper was going to take more strength than he might have.

He suddenly recognized that she was talking to him as she had the fawning courtiers—with courteous indifference. It made him clench his teeth. There was no hint of a tone of wifely intimacy. He had not really noticed it before, but now that it was gone, he sorely missed it. Watching her warily as they took their seats and were served, he saw little hope of regaining it.

After a few moments of heavy silence, the soft sounds of eating all that disturbed it, he ventured, "You have accomplished a lot."

"Aye, but there is still a great deal to do." She took a long drink of wine.

"I have finished my forty days of service to my liege. Now I may stay here to lend a hand."

"As you wish." She was not really surprised to see his hand curl into a fist where it rested upon the table.

Thinking he might divert himself so as to cool his already rising temper, Thayer turned to Margaret. " 'Tis good to see you are recovered from your illness." He wondered idly why Margaret looked so nervous.

"Thank you, m'lord. I had a skillful nurse in Janet."

Using his ignorance of who Janet was, he managed to keep Margaret talking for a few moments. His temper did cool slightly, even though his thoughts stayed centered upon his aloof wife. He grasped for another subject to speak to Gytha about. It had never been so hard before, and he realized that it had always been Gytha who had kept the conversation going, gently freeing him of his usual reticence. Now he was left to fumble along on his own. It was proving to be extremely difficult.

"There has been no trouble?" he asked, inwardly cursing this as a poor gambit.

"Not a murmur. More wine, husband?"

He nodded curtly, then watched her signal a page over to refill his goblet. She was doing it on purpose. He was sure of it. Even when being merely courteous, she had always done better at the art of conversation than he had. She was knowingly letting him flounder. Annoyance gnawed at him, but he struggled to ignore it.

Whenever she could do so covertly, Gytha studied Thayer. She could easily see the rising anger he valiantly fought to control. It was the other emotions she could read in his expression that really interested her. There was the hint of fear in his fine dark eyes. She wondered if he shared her fear that the wound he had dealt would never heal, thus destroying something that had held so much hope. There was also a look of guilt. That pleased her, although she prayed it was only for what had happened in the garden and not for something he had done after she had left court.

A quick glance was all that was needed to tell her that Roger had guessed her ploy. His obvious amusement did not deter her. She felt it could even aid her. Thayer would hate it; it would strain his temper even more.

Looking back at Thayer she knew she was going to push him, push him hard. She wished their troubles to be resolved as quickly as possible. Sitting close to him as she was made her body uncomfortably recall how long they had been apart. She ached for him. She wanted him to take her to bed and make love to her until they were both too exhausted to move. That, she was sure, would help to ease some of her pain.

Worried that her wanton thoughts might reveal themselves in her face, she concentrated on the sweet being served. Thayer knew her too well. He would be able to read her desire in her eyes. It was far too soon for him to know how much she still wanted him. Perhaps, she mused, if he feared the coolness she displayed could seep into their bed, the confrontation they needed would come sooner. It was a fear that could easily strain his swift, hot temper.

Striving for an idleness he did not feel, Thayer said, "We were sent on forays against rebels and thieves."

"There are many about." She forced herself not to think on the danger he would have faced.

Gritting his teeth, Thayer continued, "I was wounded on one foray."

Gytha felt as if her heart had leapt into her throat and lodged there. She fought to calm herself. It was with an extreme effort that she stopped herself from immediately searching him for any sign of injury. It was just as hard to speak in a cool, unperturbed voice, but she felt she had succeeded when she was finally able to speak.

"It appears to have healed well."

Recalling how she had reacted the last time

he was wounded, Thayer found her noncha-lance painfully disappointing. "Aye."

Thinking that he looked remarkably like a sulky little boy, Gytha struggled to hide her amusement. "Would you like Janet to take a look at it? She possesses some skill at healing."

"Nay, I would not like Janet to look at it," he grumbled.

"As you wish, husband."

"The name is Thayer," he snapped, then hastily drank some wine in a vain attempt to regain his rapidly slipping composure.

Adopting a look of wide-eyed innocence mixed with a hint of fear for his sanity, she murmured, "Aye, I know."

"Then why not use it?"

"As you wish, Thayer. Some fruit?" She held out a bowl filled with an assortment of fruit.

Barely restraining a nervous jump as he vi-ciously snatched up an apple, Gytha set the bowl back upon the table. She was sure he growled as he bit into the apple. Laughter bub-bled up inside her, but she hastily smothered it.

Never had she tried so hard, so calculatingly, to rouse someone to fury. And never, in her opinion, had Thayer struggled so mightily to hold on to his temper. She feared he might burst from the effort. He was, she decided, looking rather flushed and wild-eyed. She hoped he would lose his grip before too much longer—and not only for his sake. It was get-ting harder to think of ways to goad him. Biting back another urge to laugh, she mused that holding in all that anger had to be torture on his digestion.

Each cool, polite word Gytha uttered rubbed Thayer raw. They stirred memories of how things had been before the debacle in the garden. It was like slow poison dripping into him, rotting out his insides. He had little doubt that his meal would trouble him later.

Drumming his fingers on the arm of his chair, he finished his apple. He noted crossly that Gytha talked fulsomely with Roger and Margaret. That was like salt rubbed into an open wound. Thayer began to feel like a guest in his own home, not a particularly welcome one either. Even telling himself that Roger and Margaret had done no wrong to Gytha while he had did not still his ever increasing anger. It was not really Gytha he inwardly raged at either. His fury was stirred by the situation he found himself in and the painful knowledge that he had brought it all upon himself.

Determined to make one last concerted effort, he asked, "What other plans have you made for Riverfall?"

"I go day by day."

"Do you. What do you plan for the morrow then?"

"I thought to see to the herbs."

"What herbs?"

"The usual."

"But of course. Do you plan a garden like your father's?"

245

"If you would like one, m'lord."

"I thought you might wish one."

"It would be pleasant."

"Then plant one."

"As you wish, husband. Would you like some more wine?"

"Do you plan to make me drink myself insensible?"

"Whatever pleases you, m'lord."

Gytha wondered if it was wise for Thayer to grind his teeth that way. She took a moment to smile gently at Margaret, whose eyes were wide with a growing fear and concern. Roger's gaze, she idly noted, brimmed with barely suppressed laughter. She hurriedly looked away when the rogue winked at her.

The roar of fury building in Thayer was almost tangible. Gytha was hard pressed not to smile over her coming victory. It sorely tried her wit to keep her answers short, no more than polite remarks. Thayer grew more clever in the questions he asked, spitting ones at her that demanded fuller replies, cried out for elaboration. She knew each terse, cool reply she gave was another breeze to fan the flame growing in him. The game she played exhilarated her. She supposed it was because she courted danger in a small way. As others saw what was happening, the hall grew quiet, all gazes fixed upon her. It confirmed her opinion that few others would purposely goad the Red Devil as she was.

"Bek was a help to you?" Thayer felt short

of breath, so filled with anger he had trouble breathing.

"Aye. Would you like another piece of fruit?"

"Nay," he ground out.

"As you wish, husband." She then braced herself, instinct telling her that she had snapped the last thread of his frayed control.

Chapter Eleven

"Enough!"

Gytha blinked, rather surprised that she was still seated. It would not have surprised her to have found herself blown from her seat. As it was, her ears rang from the huge sound that had erupted from her husband's powerful lungs. She hoped her hearing would clear enough to catch whatever he would say once they were alone.

"Does something trouble you, m'lord?" she asked in a voice so calm half the people in the hall stared at her as if she were utterly mad.

"Thayer!" he bellowed as he surged to his feet, slamming his fist down on the table hard enough to upset many of the dishes.

"As you wish—Thayer." She bit her lip

against a startled cry when he suddenly yanked her from her seat.

Shoving his face close to hers, he hissed, "If you say 'as you wish' once more, I swear I shall strangle you. Come with me."

Since he started dragging her along after him, she had little choice but to obey. "We are done with our meal?"

"Aye, we are done with that."

Just before Thayer yanked her through the door, Gytha managed a reassuring wink for Margaret. It was hard not to giggle over the mix of surprise and concern she briefly read on all the faces in the hall save for Roger's. That man was clearly struggling to hold back his laughter until Thayer was gone. She heard that laughter break free, loud and clear, the moment Thayer slammed the door behind them. The vicious curse Thayer growled told her he had heard it too. She hoped the route to their chambers was not long enough to dim any of Thayer's glorious anger.

Even as he cursed, dragging Gytha along behind him, Thayer fought to gain some control of his raging temper. However, full control seemed to be far beyond his grasp.

When he reached their chambers, he hurled Gytha inside. Slamming the door behind him, he strode to where some wine had been set out for them. Anger always made him feel violent, but he knew she did not deserve it, nor could he deal it to her. Pouring some wine and gulping it down, he wrestled to suppress that feeling. When he finished his drink, he hurled his tankard against the wall in a meager attempt to alleviate the emotions raging inside him. Slowly, he turned to face Gytha, ill-pleased to find her seated calmly on their bed watching him.

"As you please," he snarled as he stalked over to the bed. "If it pleases you. Am I but a guest here?"

"Of course not. You are my husband. I am your dutiful wife."

"Oh, aye. Very dutiful. And cold. Is this how you mean to punish me?"

"I am punishing you, am I?"

"I know I failed in protecting you—"

"Oh, aye, you did that right enough." She stood on the bed to glare at him. "You also insulted me. You have ever compared me to that whore." She could see his anger start to fade but did not care, for her own was now unleashed. "I came to our marriage bed chaste, yet you have ever felt whoring lurked in my blood. You waited like some carrion beast over a corpse, waited for me to act like the fair Lady Elizabeth."

"And why not?" He gripped the bedpost so tightly he could feel the ridges of the carvings imprint themselves on his palm. "Wherever men were, they flocked to you. Like bees to sweet clover. Always plying you with flattery and love words."

"Aye, they did—and more often than not, you left me to them."

"You did not seem anxious for rescue."

"Then you never looked, husband."

"Thayer! Curse your eyes, call me by my name. Cease with all this m'lording."

"As you wish," she bit out, purposely goading him, then had to catch her balance when he punched the bedpost, causing the bed to shake.

"All right," he roared. "I did think what you accuse me of. Such has been my experience with beautiful, well-bred ladies. They mouth sweet words, make promises with their bodies, then scorn you at the next turn. They give their fickle hearts and bodies to another, then another. There lies the reason I was struck with horror to find you as my bride. God's tears, I could forsee years of tripping over fawning courtiers, years of ousting men from your bed. I waited for the laughter, the scorn."

He briefly closed his eyes, shaking his head in a vain attempt to put some order into the maelstrom of emotion battering away at him. Anger, hurt, and a gut-wrenching fear all tore at him. He did not know how to mend matters.

"In the garden that eve," he continued, "I was caught betwixt past and present. My shock was all the stronger, for I had just discovered that I was free of Lady Elizabeth, free of that choking hold she has had on me for so long. You had broken it. Then, there you were ..." He faltered, then took a deep breath. "I know not if t'was but a moment or an hour that I stood there before my muddled brain cleared.

Then I knew that I had seen what was not there. But it was too late. By then you had freed yourself. I have never felt so shamed. Why did you go with him?" he asked in a near whisper.

"Still looking for a sin that never was?" she snapped as she hopped off of the bed. "I went with that cur because I was not thinking. I was easily swayed to his will."

"That cur is dead."

She was a little shocked by that cold pronouncement, but quickly returned to the matter at hand. "I was easily led for, you see, I had just watched my husband leave with his arm about another."

Idly, she began to ready herself for bed. Thayer had said most of what she needed to hear. She also knew how her disrobing always affected him. The need it would arouse could easily stir him to a greater loquacity. There were a few things she would still like to know.

"The sly bitch claimed a faintness, a need for air." He inwardly groaned when he realized what she was about to do.

"An old trick."

"I knew that, but I wished to test myself with her."

Undressed to her chemise, she began to unpin her hair. "You could have chosen a better time for such a test. Then her game would have failed. She knew that, if you saw me in an embrace with another man, you would condemn first and reason later."

"T'was all a plot?" he croaked, shock roughening his voice. "Are you certain?"

"Bek told me so himself. He heard her speak of it with that man before they fled."

"But why? For what purpose? She seeks a husband and I am already wed."

"A rich, generous lover would ease her somewhat impoverished state until a husband was found. He would also fill her bed. She was most precise on how filling you are. If I turned you away, she was certain you would turn to her."

"Yet, knowing her plans, you left me."

She met his gaze in her looking-glass as she finished brushing her hair. "I cared little at that moment how you filled your bed or what mire you chose to roll in. As the beast goes to its lair when hurt, I sought to go home to lick my wounds."

"I did not lie with her, though she tempted me."

"Of that I have little doubt."

"I did not lie with any woman. Nay, I spent my nights—many of them soaked in wine—in an empty bed trying to still the fear that it would always be so." He edged closer to her, taking a lock of her hair between his fingers. "I took no other. Not even when I returned from some foray, my blood still running hot. Aye, and t'was one of those times that Lady Elizabeth sorely tempted me. My refusal was curt, even rude."

Thrilled by those words, Gytha glanced up at him. He looked very much like a child who reaches carefully for a sweet while fearing his knuckles will be rapped. She was not quite sure how to tell him such timidity was unnecessary.

"You must be very hungry, then," she whispered, blushing over her wanton thoughts.

"Gytha?" He carefully eased her into his arms, groaning when he found no reluctance in her. "Gytha," he murmured as he kissed her.

Still intimately entwined with Thayer, Gytha smiled half with pleasure, half with surprise. She marveled at the speed with which Thayer had shed his clothes. For such a large man, he could move with dizzying speed. His clothes were strewn all over the room. Their lovemaking had been as frantic as his disrobing. They had both been too starved for each other to go slowly. She was feeling slightly battered but was too sated, too content, to care.

Thayer finally eased the intimacy of their embrace. Rolling onto his side, he held her tightly against him, nuzzling his face in her hair. The fire within her could still burn for him. Even in his frenzy he had felt it. All had not died as he had feared it would.

"Ah, Gytha," he murmured, his voice not quite steady, "I feared that you would turn cold here as well."

"Nay." She idly threaded her fingers through the red curls on his chest. "Though if all that needed to be said had not been, I might have grown so. All the time we were apart, I thought on the matter. I felt I understood, but

255

I needed it to be said or the wound could fester as I feared. We had to speak out on this before it could all be set aside."

"Aye. I had hoped to simply set it all behind us, then never look at it again."

"So I feared." She blushed a little, assailed by a touch of guilt over her ploys.

Studying her high color, he wondered if the thought taking shape in his mind was too wild, then murmured, "But anger freed my tongue."

"I have noticed that it can do that."

Slowly, he moved so that she lay beneath him, narrowing his eyes as he recognized the touch of guilt in her lovely eyes. "You sought to put me into a rage."

"Now, Thayer..." she began and faltered, seeking to deny all yet unable to lie.

"You did." He shook his head. "Did you not consider that I might grow too angry?"

"I knew you would never strike me."

The confidence behind her words touched him deeply. "T'was very near."

"Near does not hurt."

"Can a man never be free of women and their ploys?" He sighed as he rested his head upon her breasts.

"Wretched man." She smiled a little at his teasing. "We needed to speak on the matter."

"Aye, we did." He circled the tip of her breast with his finger, his gaze fixed upon the hardening nipple.

"Where were you wounded? I found naught

but what was there before, yet I may have missed it."

"I was not wounded." Turning his head, he repeated his finger play upon her other breast.

"Not wounded?" She stared at him for a moment in speechless surprise. "And you dare to complain of women's ploys?"

"Ah, well, I recalled how you were when I was cut that time. I had hoped to stir a little response. I meant to break through that wall you had built between us—or leastwise, to put a chink in it."

"T'was but a little wall, not built to last. Ah, Thayer." She sighed with pleasure as he slid his tongue over the tip of her breast.

"I spent each night recalling the taste of you. Sweet. Silken honey against my tongue."

Burying her fingers in his hair, she tightened her grip as he toyed with the hardened tips of her breasts with his tongue. "Again? So soon?"

"Aye, but slowly this time. I mean to savor you as one does a fine wine."

She cried out, arching against him, when he took the point of her breast into his mouth, drawing upon it slowly. He grazed her tender skin with his teeth as he nibbled her gently, then soothed that pleasurable sting with curling strokes of his tongue. When he began to suckle lazily, she gasped. He savored first one, then the other breast, stroking her body with his hands to further stoke her desire.

"A wine, am I?"

"The finest I have ever sipped. None can compare."

"Such flattery."

He frowned a little when he encircled her waist with his hands. "You have gained some weight, it would seem."

"It would seem so because I have."

"Too lazy at night," he teased, then pressed a kiss to her stomach only to pause, noticing that it was not quite as flat as before.

Gytha's passion began to ebb as she prepared to inform Thayer of his impending fatherhood. "I think the true problem may be that I am too busy at night."

"What do you mean?" He gently pressed his fingers against her stomach finding it oddly hard.

Smiling crookedly, Gytha decided there was nothing romantic about a man prodding at your body while he tried to sort out exactly what was different about it. "Careful," she drawled. "You would not want to bruise him. Or her."

"Him? Or her?" Thayer sat up slowly, his gaze fixed upon her stomach. "There is a babe in there."

"Aye." She tried and failed to hide all her amusement over his reaction to the news.

"I am to be a father."

"You are one."

"Aye but I was not there when Bek was born."

"Where are you going?" she asked when he

leapt from the bed to throw on his robe.

"God's beard, woman, I must tell someone," he cried even as he bolted out of the room.

"I do hope poor Roger is awake." She giggled when the door slammed behind Thayer. Then she slipped out of bed. She could hear Thayer's footsteps echoing down the hallway.

Bursting into Roger's chambers Thayer shook the man awake. " 'Tis no time for you to be sleeping."

Roger sat up with a start. "Trouble?"

"Nay." In his exuberance, Thayer shook his confused friend some more. "I am to be a father."

"You are one." Roger eyed his friend a little warily.

"I mean with Gytha. Gytha is to have my child." Thayer was astounded that his body could contain the wealth of emotion that surged through him at the thought of sharing a child with Gytha.

"Congratulations." Roger grinned, understanding Thayer's odd behavior now and finding it amusing. "When?"

Blinking, Thayer stared at Roger a little blankly. "When?"

"Aye. When is the child due?"

"God's teeth." Thayer slapped the palm of his hand against his forehead. "I forgot to ask." He dashed out of the room paying little heed to Roger's laughter.

Having used the brief moment of privacy to visit the garderobe and then to wash, Gytha slipped on her chemise. Just as she poured herself a glass of wine, Thayer burst into the room. Although she was highly amused by his distraction, she tried to hide it.

"When?" Thayer wondered if she ought to be out of bed, then lost track of his thought.

"When what, Thayer?"

"When is our baby due?"

"Ah—in five months' time." She laughed as he raced out of the room again.

Slamming into Roger's room, Thayer announced, "Five months." Then he groaned, sitting down heavily on Roger's bed. "God's toenails. Five months. I will be an old man for the waiting."

"Most men need wait nine full months." Roger laughed at the look of horror on Thayer's face.

"Sweet Jesu, do you think she has her time amiss?"

"Nay, nay. She is but four months along already, that is all. Near half your waiting is past and gone. Be thankful for it."

"Aye, of course." Recalling how she had been standing when he had last seen her, he leapt to his feet. "She should be resting."

"Women are stronger than they look, my friend. They need not be cosseted as much as we might think—even when with child."

"Mayhap." Thayer was not sure he agreed as he headed out of the room. "I must find out more."

"Is all settled between you and Gytha then?"

Roger asked just before the door shut behind Thayer.

"Aye. 'Tis as it was. Good sleep to you, Roger. Names," he muttered as he shut the door and hurried back to his own chambers. "I must think of some names."

Meeting Thayer's abrupt entrance with a little smile, Gytha sipped her wine as she watched him pace the room muttering to himself. She had envisioned some tender scene when she told him of the coming child. His distracted excitement had pleased her as much. Now she wondered if she had misread that distraction. A strong dismay could have stirred an equal distraction. He certainly did not look happy at the moment.

"You find the news upsetting?" she was finally prompted to ask.

"Upsetting?" He whirled to stare at her. "Nay, nay, of course not. You should be sitting." He scooped her up in his arms then moved to sit on the bed.

Smiling with relief and pleasure, she murmured, "I am quite hale and strong, Thayer. Why, even the sickness fades."

"Sickness?" He stared at her in horror. "You were sick?"

She kissed his cheek. "In the beginning every woman suffers a nausea. It passes. Mine has and it was only slight."

"Ah, of course. I am not thinking clearly. But you feel well now?"

"Very well. You need not cosset me."

"T'will be hard to resist. Can you feel our child?" he whispered, gently placing his hand upon her stomach.

"Only a little. I doubt you will be able to feel the child yet. 'Tis but a quickening."

"Where do you mean to go?" he asked when she started to get up.

"To set my goblet aside. I have finished my wine."

Setting her on the bed, he took the goblet from her. "I will do it. You are to lie down."

She barely had the chance to slip beneath the covers before he was there, tucking her in. When he eased into bed then, ever so gently tucking her up against him, Gytha began to get a very uneasy feeling about how the next five months could go. It was increasingly apparent, as the moments crept by and he did not move, that abstinence was one way he meant to cosset her. She frantically tried to think of a way to rid him of the notion.

Thayer glanced down at her and asked, "How do you feel about this child?"

"Delighted, though that seems a pallid word. I was only sure of it today. Edna confirmed what I had begun to suspect."

"A father." He laughed softly. "By God, 'tis hard to believe, yet 'tis wondrous."

"You are a father already. Bek is your son."

Smoothing his hand over her hair, he pressed a kiss to her forehead. "You worry that I will turn from him. You need not. He is my

262

son. I can never forget that, never wish to forget it.

"This is different. Bek's mother brought me more misery than pleasure. She would have rid her body of him. She tried to murder him when he had barely savored his first breath. I knew nothing of his growth in her womb or of his birth. This child is one I will share in. I will not be tossed the babe and told to do as I like by a woman who could spit poison even on her birthing bed.

"I love Bek. He knows that. He knows I will do all I can to ensure that he has some future, some fortune. So too will I claim him as my son to all and any. Aye, as I have done. He knows he can never inherit from me. Though young, he fully understands all that can weigh against a bastard. He has seen that few are openly recognized even by the man who seeded them. Knowing all the bad of it, he sees how good it is for him. The only bitterness he may ever feel might be towards his mother. Yet, I think that already wanes. You ease that by caring for him."

"I would like to think some affection has grown up between us."

"Oh, aye, it has. He has never left my side. Not once since the day his mother handed him to me."

"Yet, he left with me," Gytha whispered, suddenly realizing what that meant.

"Aye, he did and never once asked me if he could. 'Tis good. I did my best not to sour his mind against his mother, yet I did want him to know what she was, not to think of her too well, for he would be hurt. That he has taken so firmly to you shows me he does not cling to her.

"He had heard things said about her. Aye, and he will. That cannot be avoided. But he is a fair boy. At court, he thought to see for himself."

"Oh? Did he speak to her?"

"Not really. He watched her. Followed her. 'Tis how he knew what game she played with me."

Thayer sighed, filled with sympathy for his son. "A hard lesson for a boy to learn. Boys do not have much to do with their mothers from an early age, but no boy wishes to discover ill about her."

"I do not believe his heart was set upon her either way. He holds no bitterness that I can see, although he has not spoken much about it."

"Well, mayhap I should speak to him."

"It cannot hurt."

"Nay. Mayhap I should have spoken earlier. Gytha, do we have a midwife about?"

"Aye, Janet. Edna, for all she is young, is not without some knowledge." She gently moved against him in what she hoped was an arousing, sensual manner. "Janet is very good at healing and has become a stern practitioner of the art of cleanliness."

He nodded, gritting his teeth against the

urge to take her more fully into his arms. "That eases my mind some. You had best get some sleep."

She peeked up at him and saw that he had closed his eyes. Evidently, subtlety was not good enough. Rubbing her cheek against the fiery pelt on his strong chest, she moved her hand over his smooth hip.

"We can think of some names in the morning," he said, wincing at the telltale hoarseness in his voice. He placed his hand over hers to stop her enticing caress.

Gytha swirled her tongue over his flat, brown nipple, bringing it to a hard nub and causing him to tremble faintly.

Thayer had no doubts left about what she was after, but he struggled to ignore it. "Daughter's names as well."

Biting back a smile over the way he fought the passion she could feel building inside him, Gytha teased his other nipple to hardness. Ever so gently, she drew it into her mouth. The soft groan of pleasure that pulled from him delighted her.

Tangling his fingers in her hair, Thayer tried to hold her still. It only worked to urge her on in her seductive play. "I but pray that, whichever we have bred, boy or girl, takes more from you."

Edging down his body, she kissed her way to his taut midriff. She could not fully suppress a soft, husky laugh when his sentence ended on a high, strained note. Seducing her husband was proving to be great fun indeed.

"Gytha," he ground out as she slid her hand from his lax grip to stroke his thighs. "You are with child."

"I know. Was it not I who told you?" She used her tongue to draw idle designs on his inner thighs.

"Sweet heaven." He groaned, unable to keep his mind clear, his thoughts in order. "You are so small and I am so big."

"Mmmmm. So magnificently big." Feeling increasingly wanton and bold she slid her hand all the way up the inside of his thigh.

"I could hurt the baby." He closed his eyes, shifting with pleasure beneath her intimate stroking.

"While I have much to learn about child-bearing, there is one thing I do know. 'Tis the first three months in which the chances of losing the baby are the highest. Your child has rested within me for four months now."

"Four months," he repeated, telling himself that he would halt her play in a moment.

"Aye. Now, what were we doing a month ago, Thayer?"

"A month ago?" He fought to think, to remember, but it was difficult when her kisses and the warm strokes of her tongue drew ever nearer to his manhood. "Ah, making love. Jesu, 'tis hard to think when I can feel your sweet breath upon my staff," he muttered in a thick voice. "Aye, aye, we were making love. God's blood, I could have hurt you."

"But you did not. So what do you think that means, my large, sometimes stupid husband?"

"That making love to you cannot hurt you or the baby?" he replied a little groggily, wondering if he really had just heard her call him stupid.

"Very good." She laughed, a soft sound thickened and made husky by her own soaring passions.

"Pardee," he cried out when her lips, then her tongue usurped the delightful stroking she had begun with her hand. "Aye, little one, 'tis a sweet torture." He forgot all his fine plans for considerate abstinence, fixing his gaze upon the fair head between his thighs. " 'Tis nearly as intoxicating to watch you pleasure me so as it is to feel your sweet lips upon me."

"I like to pleasure you, Thayer, yet 'tis hard for you tell me naught."

"You are a high-born lady."

"And thus must be denied the joy of pleasuring her husband?"

"It brings you joy to pleasure me?"

Briefly she returned her caresses to his inner thighs. "Does not my pleasure strengthen yours?"

"Aye, tenfold. Do you truly wish to learn what pleasures me?"

"Have I not just said so? Aye"—she kissed the stout proof of his arousal—"and shown you as best I can?"

"Then sheath me, dearling," he whispered, braced to withdraw the request if she revealed any shock or distaste.

"Like so?" She obeyed his almost timid request without hesitation.

"Aye," he cried out in a shaky voice, "just so. You have the way of it. 'Tis glorious. Glorious," he whispered before falling into a passionate incoherency as he struggled to hold back and enjoy her attentions for as long as possible. "Ah, God help me, enough," he finally moaned, grasping her beneath her arms and pulling her up his body to neatly join them.

"Ah, 'tis this again," she managed to gasp out as she gripped his shoulders.

"Aye. Ride your man, my sweet wife. Aye, loving, aye. You do it so well 'tis like to drive me mad."

She lost the control she had clung to in order to seduce him. That he had none as well added to her delight. When her release tore through her body, she felt Thayer buck upwards with the force of his own, and his cry of passion blended with hers. She collapsed into his arms, feeling him wrap them around her tightly. It was a while before she regained either her sanity or control over her breathing. She nestled against him as he made no move to end their union.

Thayer pressed a kiss to the top of her head. "I can see I erred—aye, even deprived myself by bowing to your delicate nature. Well, such as I thought it was."

"Is that what you were about then?" She leisurely kissed his throat.

"Aye, or mayhap I feared to offend your innocence. 'Tis often said a lady must be sheltered from acts that feed the baser passions. Since there is none alive who would call you other than a lady, the ones who say that must be wrong."

"Very wrong, I think. And I like to think that what besets us is more than a baser passion."

"Oh, aye, much more than that, little one." He nuzzled her thick hair. "Are you sure I have not hurt you?"

"Very sure."

"You are so tiny," he murmured.

"So was my mother, but she bore healthy babes with little trouble. You must not fret over me."

Finally easing the rich intimacy of their embrace, he muttered, " 'Tis a thing easier said than done."

She unsuccessfully smothered a yawn. "When I am not so tired, I shall give you a stern lecture on such foolishness."

"Will you now?" He chuckled when she gave a firm if sleepy nod. "I await the event all atremble."

"I have no doubt of that," she murmured as she closed her eyes.

"And shall you call me stupid again?"

Slowly opening one eye, she peeked at him. "Thayer, I would never call you stupid. Why, that would be very disrespectful."

"Aye, it would be." He grinned at her. "So I must have dreamt it."

"That must be it." She closed her eyes again. "I will be fine, Thayer. We shall have a strong, lovely baby."

"Go to sleep, Gytha. Whatever else you tell me, I know it cannot be good for you to grow too tired."

"I have one more question." She hated to touch upon the subject of all that had happened at court, but she needed to know just one more thing. "You said Dennis is dead?"

"Aye. The fool returned to court just before I left. Since I had not chased him immediately, he thought himself safe. I challenged him. T'was a fair fight and he lost. Belated though it was, I avenged the insult to your honor. Does that trouble you?"

She sighed. "What troubles me is how stained honor requires blood shed to cleanse it." She shrugged, "But 'tis the way of it." She also thought Elizabeth the one most at fault, but suspected Thayer knew that also, so she said nothing.

"Enough talk. Go to sleep. You need your rest."

Although she wanted to ease the fear she knew he held, she was too sleepy to do it right. "Do not fret about me."

"Sleep. I will not fret," he lied, hoping he could hide the fears that had replaced his joy over the coming child.

He stroked her hair as she fell asleep in his

arms. It had been too long since she had been there, far too many days of wondering if she would ever be there again. For a little while, he kept his mind clear of all thought save for how good it felt.

Try as he would, though, he could not long hold back all thoughts of what could happen. The worry she urged him not to feel crept up on him and finally demanded to be recognized, refusing to be shoved aside any longer.

Emotions filled him at the thought of the child she carried. They contradicted each other, some more intense than others. He was enthralled, delighted, yet terrified. On the one hand, he thanked God for such a gift. On the other, he bemoaned the fruitfulness of their union. He could not wait to hold their child, yet wished it had never been conceived.

Death hung over the childbed. It was impossible to ignore that. The words 'died in childbed' were chiseled on too many crosses and tombs. It stole the life of too many women, loved and unloved, plain and beautiful. Even the strong and healthy could be taken. Even Gytha, he thought with a shudder, tightening his hold on her, then smiling faintly when she murmured his name in her sleep.

He wrapped his arms around her, cradling her against his body. It was as if he sought to protect her from the threat no sword could vanquish by the sheer force of his will, but he knew that was foolish. Yet, if the depth of a man's want and need accounted for anything, then nothing existed strong enough to take her from him. That too was foolish, he told himself crossly. Rage and plead as he might, there was no changing God's will. All he could do was wait to see what that will would be. However, the thought of a future without Gytha was one he knew would rob him of many a night's sleep.

Chapter Twelve

"I feel as if I lead a procession," Gytha muttered, glancing over her shoulder at the four heavily armed men at her heels.

Margaret laughed and winked at Bek, who was grinning widely. "Thayer says you will be protected."

"And guarded I am. About the only place I am not followed is to the garderobe, and I would not be at all surprised to find one of them posted at the door soon." Glancing around the village they walked through, Gytha sighed. "I think we frighten them with this show of force."

"Nay. Make them wary, mayhap, but not truly frighten them."

"They keep a goodly distance from us."

"Well, they see you are well guarded and

rightly feel there is some reason for it. I suspect they do not wish to make any move the men might see as dangerous. Making no move is safer than making the wrong one."

"I know. I find fault because I grow tired of the whole matter. We have had no further trouble from Pickney."

"So you think he has given up his schemes?"

"Who can say."

"Until someone can for certain, you will be guarded." Margaret tucked her arm through Gytha's, then briefly hugged it to her side. "I doubt your lord would let you stroll about unguarded even if Pickney was no longer a threat."

"And," Bek added as he lightly swung his and Gytha's clasped hands, "Papa says there are now two of you to protect."

Smoothing her hand over her rounding abdomen, Gytha drawled, "I am not that large yet."

Bek giggled, then stared at her stomach for a moment. "Do you think I shall have a brother?"

"Carrying this child has soured my nature some so, aye, I expect it will be a male child." She winked at a giggling Margaret and smiled down at Bek. "You want a brother, do you?"

"Aye, but Papa said my prayers should be for a fine, healthy babe—boy or girl. So . . ." He frowned at a plump young woman who stood in front of the inn waving at them. "Who is that?"

"I have little idea," Gytha murmured, then glanced at Merlion, who had suddenly moved in front of them as they had halted. "Do you or one of the men know the woman, Sir Merlion? She may be waving at one of you."

"Nay, she is naught to do with us. I will see what she wants." He strode towards the woman, who took a nervous step back.

Gytha frowned as she watched the woman talk with Merlion as Merlion's expression turned slowly darker. There was something very familiar about the maid. For a moment, Gytha thought she had seen her at court, but she could not be sure. Not only had there been too many new faces there to remember all of them, but the woman had little about her that stood out. Gytha's curiosity was high when Merlion walked back, yet she also felt an inexplicable uneasiness.

"What does she want?" Gytha asked as a heavily frowning Merlion stopped in front of her.

"She is Lady Elizabeth's handmaiden."

"Lady Elizabeth? What would that woman be doing here?"

"It seems she has come to speak to you. She had intended to ride up to Riverfall on the morrow, but saw you approaching and thought the meeting might be arranged immediately. She would like to see Bek as well."

"Did she say why?"

"To make amends."

There was a strong tone of disbelief in Merlion's voice, and Gytha shared his feeling. Apology was not in Lady Elizabeth. Gytha was sure of it. But then, concern for her own safety could be. Thayer had said he had been terse in pushing the woman away, and Lady Elizabeth had to fear that Thayer now knew of her part in the near-rape in the garden. Dennis had been killed for his part in it. Lady Elizabeth very likely expected some retribution on herself.

For a moment Gytha savored the thought of refusing to see the woman, of leaving Lady Elizabeth to fret herself sick over what, if anything, Thayer might do to her. Then she glanced down at Bek. She had to think of the boy, remember that Lady Elizabeth was his mother. While she doubted there would ever be a relationship between the two, Gytha did not want to be the one who did anything to keep it from forming. Even if the apology was not a heartfelt one and was inspired by self-interest instead of true regret, it would be good for the boy to hear his mother utter it.

"She has a room at the inn?" she asked, looking back at Merlion.

"Aye, the maid says she will take you to her. I cannot like it, m'lady."

"Well, I have no real wish to see the woman again either but"—she tipped her head slightly towards Bek—"it might be best to hear her out." The way Merlion briefly glanced at Bek, then looked back at her with a hint of resignation mixed with annoyance, told her that he understood. "Come, what harm can there be in meeting her?"

"She does not want to see anyone but you and the boy."

"That does not surprise me. I am not sure I would want such a big, well-armed audience if I had to make an apology." She smiled faintly. "Nor do I think you would all fit into one of the inn's rooms."

"I would prefer it if she came to Riverfall to say her piece."

"Actually, I would just as soon put all of this behind me. And," she added with a frown towards the inn, "I certainly prefer to see her far away from Riverfall as soon as possible." She met Bek's gaze. "I am sorry for that, Bek. 'Tis how I feel."

"Aye, I understand. She was mean to you." He looked at Merlion. "I will be with Gytha, sir, if there is trouble."

Merlion smiled. "True. Well, go on then, m'lady. The men and I shall wait below. We will not wait long."

"I do not mean to linger. Let the men have an ale, Sir Merlion." She smiled briefly. "It might soothe some of the—er, discomfort they have endured by being made to walk." Her smile grew a little when he laughed softly.

After squeezing Margaret's hand in a brief, reassuring gesture, Gytha started towards the waiting maid. She could hear the men a step behind her. Although they would not be right at her side, their presence in the inn would be a comfort. While she doubted Lady Elizabeth could be so stupid as to try and hurt her again, Gytha did not trust the woman. Feeling Bek's hand in hers, she hoped he would not have to see the evil side of his mother yet again.

Falling into step behind the nervous maid, Gytha entered the inn. Partway up the stairs, she paused to look back and felt reassured by the sight of the men who eagerly called for ale. She might not see how Lady Elizabeth could accomplish anything very wrong, but it was comforting to know that Merlion and his men were near enough to help if help was needed. Pausing as the maid opened the door to Lady Elizabeth's chambers, Gytha felt Bek's grip on her hand tighten and shared his nervousness.

With a deep breath to steady her uneasiness, Gytha entered the room. Lady Elizabeth looked as beautiful as she had at court. She also looked as haughty, not like a woman ready to seek amends. The sound of the door shutting behind her made Gytha very uncomfortable.

"Oh my," Lady Elizabeth said coldly as she briefly looked at Gytha's stomach, "I can see the man is still fruitful."

Sure now that an apology was not the woman's intention, Gytha asked, "Just what do you want, Lady Elizabeth?"

"Ah—well now, you see I do not want anything."

Alarmed by the look of near delight on the woman's face, Gytha turned to leave when she heard a thudding noise. Bek suddenly became a weight pulling on her arm. She looked to see him sprawled upon the floor, blood trickling down the side of his face even as his limp hand slid free of her grasp. As she opened her mouth to scream, a filthy hand covered it. She started to struggle, but a blinding pain in her head sapped her strength. A soft laugh from Lady Elizabeth was the last sound she heard as blackness swept her into its fold.

"Hurry and get her out of here," Lady Elizabeth snapped as she grabbed her cloak, waving her maid over to help her put it on.

"What about the boy?" asked the man, tossing Gytha over his shoulder.

"Leave him. Those men of hers will be up here before long. We had best be far away by then." Pushing her stunned maid ahead of her, Lady Elizabeth stepped over Bek's body and opened the door for the two men to leave.

Stepping out of the privy, Merlion paused to assure himself that he was presentable. He started back in to the inn determined to end the meeting between Lady Gytha and Lady Elizabeth. It had gone on long enough. Too long. Meeting Roger and Thayer at the door to the inn made him think he had been a fool to allow the meeting at all.

"Where is Gytha?" Thayer asked as he stepped inside of the inn and looked around.

"Up in one of the rooms," Merlion answered.

"Is she ill?"

"Nay. She meets with the Lady Elizabeth."

The look on Thayer's face told Merlion he had seriously erred.

"You let her go to that viper?"

"The woman claimed she wished to make amends."

"Her? Apologize?"

"It seemed possible. She could easily fear that you would seek retribution and means to turn it away."

The reasonableness of that soothed Thayer only slightly. "Mayhap, but to let her meet that scheming vixen alone..."

"Bek was with her. The boy—Oh, sweet Jesu."

Whirling about to see what had widened Merlion's eyes and stolen all the color from his face, Thayer swore. Bek, his face a sickly white and blood-stained, staggered down the stairs that led to the inn's rooms. Thayer raced towards the boy, reaching him in time to catch Bek as he stumbled. Sitting down on a rough-hewn bench, he cradled Bek on his lap. Someone stuffed a dampened rag into his hand. He noticed how unsteady his hands were as he bathed the child's face. Bek's state meant only one thing—someone had taken Gytha.

Crouching beside Bek and Thayer, Roger helped the groggy boy sip some mead. "Felt his head, Thayer. A bad knock, skin broken, but no more. There, lad. Think you can tell us what happened now?"

"I am not sure," Bek whispered, tears

prompted by pain and fear trickling down his cheeks.

"You went to meet your mother," Thayer reminded him, fighting back an anxiousness that had him as taut as a drawn bowstring.

"Aye. She said she wanted to say she was sorry for being mean to Gytha." At Roger's urging, Bek took another drink and his voice was a little less unsteady when he continued, "She lied. Gytha is gone."

Although he had known it, Thayer felt his heart skip with alarm, and a chill seeped through his veins. He had not gone up to the room because he had known she would not be there. Yet, hearing it said aloud hit him hard. It was an effort to glance up at Merlion, who had gone to check. He did not want more confirmation. Merlion shook his head, and Thayer briefly closed his eyes as he fought down his fears. He needed to be strong and clear-headed.

"Did you see who took her?" he asked Bek.

"Nay. Mother said she wanted nothing. Then Gytha looked very worried. Then someone hit me. When I woke up, everyone was gone." Bek took a deep, sniffling breath. "I could not protect her."

"Son, you were attacked from behind. 'Tis a thing that could easily fell me or Roger."

"Aye, Bek," Roger agreed. "They dealt in treachery and that has felled kings."

Margaret edged over to Thayer. "Let me take the boy, m'lord. He should have that cut seen to."

"Thank you, Margaret."

As soon as Bek had gone off with Margaret, Merlion said, "The men have already set out to see if they can find anything or anyone. Do you think Lady Elizabeth allied herself with Pickney?"

"What else could it be?" Thayer frowned. "Pickney is the only one who has been seeking Gytha."

Running a hand through his thick black hair, Merlion looked at Thayer with abject regret. "I did not like to allow the meeting." He sighed. "But I never thought t'would come to this."

"And why should you? As far as I know, Pickney and Elizabeth have never met. I neglected to tell anyone that Elizabeth could bear watching. By the time I had left court, I knew I had made an enemy of the woman. Somehow she found out what Pickney sought. She saw a chance to avenge what she felt was her humiliation at my hands. Why would Gytha go to the woman?"

"Lady Elizabeth said she wished to make amends...." Merlion began.

"I cannot believe Gytha would trust that."

"Well, I think she did it for the boy. I doubt she believed any apology would be heartfelt, but she did not want to keep the boy from hearing it. Bek was shamed by his mother's actions at court. I think your lady sought to ease that if she could."

"Aye, Gytha would." Thayer leapt to his feet. "I have to look for her."

With Merlion's help, Roger halted Thayer's rush to the door. "Wait for the men to report to you. It does no good to strike out blindly," Roger pressed. "Pickney wants her to wed Robert. Her life is not yet in danger."

"Nay? She carries my heir, Roger. If the child lives, Robert cannot gain Saitun Manor. And that is what Pickney wants." The brief looks of horrified realization on his friends' faces brought a grim smile to Thayer's mouth.

"I think," Roger said after a short, heavy silence, " 'tis time to send word to her family."

"Aye, as soon as we know a little more," Thayer agreed, then tensed, listening carefully. "The men return."

Thayer had to clench his fists to remain where he was, waiting. His first sight of the person the men dragged in with them spurred him into immediate action. It was a moment or two before Roger and Merlion could halt his deadly advance on a terrified Lady Elizabeth. He ached to kill the woman but, as his rage eased, he knew that would gain him little. Once he calmed, however, Lady Elizabeth's terror faded. With a simmering fury, he watched the haughty, cool look reappear.

"What did you find?" he demanded of Torr, who had led the men.

"Little, I fear, save these two." Torr nodded at Lady Elizabeth and her weeping, trembling maid.

Hannah Howell

"I demand you release me at once." Lady Elizabeth tried to put some order into her tossled clothing.

"You are in no position to demand anything," Thayer snapped. "What are you doing on my lands?"

"I was traveling to my family."

"Alone? No men-at-arms? You used to be more skilled at lying. Where is Gytha?"

"Your little wife? How should I know her whereabouts?"

"You met with her. Now Bek nurses a sore head and Gytha has disappeared. Mind, Elizabeth, I am not in the humor to tolerate your games." He noticed a flicker of fear briefly touch her expression and knew he had a weapon—he could frighten her. "Answer. Where is Gytha?"

"I tell you, I do not know. We were attacked in the room as we talked. Robbed. My maid and I escaped to flee. Clearly, the rogues have taken your wife. They will probably ask a ransom soon." She gave a high, small screech of panic as Thayer lunged at her, slamming her up against the wall, the hand he had around her throat pinning her there.

"Now you will tell me the truth."

"Thayer, how can you treat me so? I am the mother of your son."

"Mother? You are no mother to Bek. No true mother would let someone bludgeon her own child. No mother would leave him bleeding upon the floor, untended. Now—who has taken Gytha?"

"Pickney. Charles Pickney and your cousin, Robert. Two of their men have fled with her."

"To where?"

"Saitun Manor."

Knowing he would now get the truth from her, he released her. She slid to the floor, gasping for breath, and her distraught maid rushed over to help her to her feet. As soon as she was standing, Lady Elizabeth waved the woman away. Thayer saw that Elizabeth was regaining her haughtiness as well as her breath. The woman did not have the sense to see the danger she was in.

"How can he go to Saitun Manor? I hold the place."

"Not after they use your wife to open the gates and disarm the guard. When the people there see who Charles holds, they will hand the place to him. He need only secure it from you."

"How did you come to be entangled with the man?"

"I met with him as I traveled home from the court. He told me his plans, and I saw a way to help him, a way to make you pay for the ridicule you brought upon me. I shall also gain me a fine purse. Charles promised me a share of what he extracts from you."

"So you think this but some game for ransom? Clearly, Charles is a greater deceiver than you. He has drawn you into a murder plot, woman. The price he means to ask of me is my life."

"Well, we must all go to God at some time."

She sounded calm, but Thayer knew it for another lie. The truth was reflected in her eyes, in the touch of fear there. This was a far deeper game than she wished to play. Even her high birth and the added weight of her married name could not save her from her punishment if a death resulted from her ploys.

"You may make the journey far sooner than you had planned," he drawled.

"What do you mean?" Lady Elizabeth cast a wary glance around at all the well-armed men.

"Take her to Riverfall, Torr, and secure her well," Thayer ordered, watching coldly as Torr roughly grabbed hold of the woman.

Struggling futilely against Torr's firm hold, Elizabeth looked at Thayer. "You cannot do this to me. You cannot hold me like some common felon. Do you forget who I am?"

"Never, m'lady. You will stay at Riverfall until all of this is settled. If I return with my wife, we will return you safely to your family. If Gytha dies, I will have you hanged." He smiled coldly when she went white, all color leaving her face. "If I do not survive to do it by my own hand, I doubt there will be any lack of others eager to tend to it."

"You cannot. I am the mother of your son."

"That will not save you if Gytha dies. And if she lives and your family is called to come and fetch you, I think it would be a good time to speak to them of Bek."

"Tell them? You promised! No one was ever to know. Nay," she cried when he signaled to Torr and the man began to drag her away. "You must listen to me."

"Do I return here, m'lord?" Torr asked.

"Nay, wait for me at Riverfall."

He turned his back on Lady Elizabeth, ignoring her screaming bids for his attention. Glancing around, he met Bek's gaze. The boy looked sad but little else. It reminded Thayer, however, that it might not be as simple as he would like to extract even a just punishment from Lady Elizabeth. Inwardly shaking his head, he decided he would review the problem later. Now the only thing that mattered was Gytha and getting her back safely to Riverfall and to him.

"Here—drink this." Roger placed a tankard of strong ale in Thayer's hand.

After downing nearly half the drink, Thayer wiped his mouth with the back of his hand and sighed. "Do we wait for word or go after her?" he asked Roger and Merlion, who watched him carefully.

"He took her to bring you to him," Roger answered. "He has to know you will seek to get her back."

"Aye." Thayer nodded slowly, accepting that reasoning. "He would expect me to come clamoring for her return."

"So, do you do it or do you sit back and let him call for you?"

"I go, armed and ready for battle, although he seeks no fair fight."

"That is certain, but is it wise to do as he wants you to?"

"What choice do I have? He holds my wife."

"He means to wed her to Robert. That means he will not harm her. At least, not until he benefits from the marriage."

"Can we be so sure of that now, Roger? In her womb rests my heir, and that could destroy all his plans. He gains only a little legitimacy to his claims through the marriage. That my heir could be born and live might seem too great a risk for him to take. There are three solutions to the problem that babe presents him with—he can wait until the child is born, then kill it. He can try to tear it from Gytha's body, which could kill her as well. Or he could kill both mother and child at one stroke."

Simply listing the possibilities he could not ignore had Thayer trembling inside. He took a long drink of ale but found little comfort there. His fear ran too deep. Pickney held all that was dear to him.

Reminding himself that he still had Bek helped little. He loved the boy. They had been through a lot together. Nothing could replace Bek in his heart. Neither could Bek fill the hole that would be left if he lost Gytha and their child.

"I believe," Roger said, breaking the tense

silence, "Pickney will go with the first of those grim choices."

"Do you?" Thayer asked him. "Why?"

"Because he has shown that he is set on gain with little thought to anything else. To get the land and coin you hold has been his only prod. He disregards everything else, even the consequences that must come of his actions. Gytha can add to his gain. For that she will be worth something for a while. She is needed now to get you to come to him and to stop us from going to battle with him. If he kills you, as he intends, she will be his only shield, all he can hold before us to keep us from killing him."

The sound reasoning behind Roger's words gave Thayer a flicker of hope. It also gave him time, which could give him a chance to save Gytha and end Pickney's threats forever. No immediate plan came to mind, but Thayer was not surprised. Still reeling from it all, he was in no state to come up with clever strategy.

"Come, we will return to Riverfall. For now we act as if we head to battle." Thayer started towards the door of the inn, his people quickly falling in behind him. "If naught else,'tis what that dog expects. So we will do as he wants. We will ride to Saitun Manor and clamor before the walls—in force and ready to tear the place down about his ears."

"And our real plan?" Roger asked.

"Our real plan?" Thayer gave a short, bitter laugh. "That does not exist yet. I pray we can devise one ere we set up camp on the fields before Saitun Manor.''

The moment Thayer rode into the bailey of Riverfall, he knew Torr had forewarned the men. Curtly, he gave the order to arm that they all waited for. Without wasting another moment, he made his way to his chambers to prepare himself.

In the privacy of his chambers, he found no haven, no safe place to think clearly. Gytha was everywhere in spirit. Her special scent lingered in the air. He rushed to prepare himself for battle so that he could flee the room, escape the memories. They stirred the fears he sought to control.

Once ready, he hurried to Margaret's chambers, not surprised to find Roger there. The two had become an accepted pair at Riverfall, everyone wondering when the marriage would take place. His interest was not in the couple completing the farewells all lovers indulged in when the man rode off to battle, but in Bek, whom Margaret had settled in her room. The boy was curled up in Margaret's bed fast asleep.

"How does he fare?" he asked Margaret in a low voice as he moved to stand beside the bed.

"Better, m'lord." Margaret, with Roger at her side and his arm draped about her shoulders, moved to stand next to Thayer. "I gave him a gentle potion to ease the ache in his head." She sighed. "But little will ease the hurt in the poor child's heart."

"I know. Instead of seeing some good in his mother, false as it might have been, he saw only the evil yet again. And he has lost Gytha. I know she was becoming important to him."

"Aye, my cousin has a way with children. They all love her, and she loves all of them. Gytha seems to know how they see things."

"I saw how he could speak to her freely."

"You will bring her home safely, m'lord. I know it."

A quick look at Margaret's face told him she did not really believe her words, not enough to still all her worry, but she sorely wanted to. "I pray you are right. Will you tend to sending word of this trouble to Gytha's family?"

"I will, m'lord. I will try to word it—well, gently."

"That would serve. My thanks. Roger, we had best set out." Thayer smiled coldly. "We would not want to keep Charles Pickney waiting."

"Nay, of course not." Lifting Margaret's hand to his lips, Roger pressed a kiss to the back of it. "When I return, my heart." He started towards the door behind Thayer.

"Papa."

Bek's soft call brought Thayer back to his bedside. "I thought you were asleep, son." He gently brushed the hair back from Bek's forehead. "How do you feel?"

"Better. Mistress Margaret gave me something. Are you going to get Gytha?"

"Aye, son. We mean to try. I will make no promises. You know I will do all I am able to."

"I know that, Papa. Why is my mother so mean to Gytha? She never did anything bad to my mother."

"That is a question I have no answer for. Your mother wanted to strike at me, Bek, and she found my weakest point. I will say this— I believe she did not know Pickney meant murder. She thought only of ransom and coin."

"You need not defend her to me, Papa. Where is she now?"

"Torr set her in the dungeons. If naught else, we cannot risk her trying to further aid Pickney."

"Should I visit her?"

"Only if that is what you wish to do. I have to leave now, Bek."

"I know. God go with you, Papa. And with Gytha."

As he strode out of the room, Roger right behind him, Thayer muttered, "We shall sorely need God's help." He hurried towards the great hall, where his leading men-at-arms would be waiting to make final plans before heading out.

"You have no plan yet?"

"Nay, nothing. My wits have gone abegging. I can only think of Gytha, of what harm might come to her."

Stepping ahead of Thayer, Roger opened the

heavy door to the great hall. "That will surprise no one."

Nodding to his men as he went to the head table, Thayer grumbled, "I am expected to lead. A man with addled wits and not even the simplest of cursed plans cannot lead other men."

"We shall think it up as we go along, old friend. We have done it before."

Thayer sat down even as the servants finished laying out food for the men, hearty if plain fare to enjoy as they conferred and to give them strength for what might lie ahead. Roger's words had been intended to be uplifting, but his food still tasted like ashes in his mouth. A plan made in the saddle did not seem good enough when so much was at stake.

"Mayhap we should have run them down," he murmured, pushing aside his half-full trencher.

"In what direction, friend?" Roger asked. "The trail was unclear. They could have gone in ten different directions. We would have wasted time and worn out men and horses. Better to prepare well and go straight to Saitun Manor. You know that."

"Aye, I think I but wanted my decision agreed with. Fear for Gytha eats at my confidence. I doubt myself and wonder if I have already stepped wrong and should have done something else."

"You are a man of battle. Go with what that part of you says. Listen to what gained you the

293

name Red Devil. He has kept us alive. He will help keep Gytha alive. Have faith in him, Thayer."

"If I can find him," Thayer muttered silently. The man who had led and lived through so many battles had apparently deserted him, pushed aside by worry and fear. Love, he thought furiously, could make a man a coward.

He stared blankly at his men as that last thought pounded through his mind. Despite his efforts to keep it at bay, he loved Gytha. That was the emotion that stirred up so much fear now that she was in danger. It was why he was filled with a desperate need to get her back safely, why he saw failure as his death when it did not have to be that way. That he loved her explained a lot of things—things he had done, said, or felt. He had found what a man needs to be fully alive. It was no wonder his wits were scattered when faced with the chance of losing that.

Having some explanation helped him regain a little composure, icy and forced though it was. He concentrated on the plans now being suggested by his men. That composure wavered a little as each plan proved faulty. Torr's was the one that held the most hope. It was one he had briefly thought of and cast aside in one of his few sane moments since Gytha's abduction. Sadly, Torr had no solution for its one glaring weakness. How did they get into Saitun Manor unseen? None of them who had spent any length of time at the manor could recall any entrance one could use yet remain unseen. If Saitun Manor had a bolt hole, only the immediate family had known of it and William had taken the secret to his grave.

Regretfully agreeing that a plan would have to be devised on the spot, Thayer ordered their departure for Saitun Manor. He paused a moment when, with Merlion and Roger flanking him, he prepared to mount. His pride winced at revealing a weakness, yet he knew he owed it to the two men.

"Roger, keep a close watch on me," he said in a low voice as he checked the cinch on his saddle.

"Have I not always watched your back?"

"I do not speak of my back but *me*. Watch me closely. You too, Merlion."

Roger frowned, looking intently at Thayer. "I am not sure I understand."

"I am but a breath away from recklessness, from madness."

"You seem calm enough," murmured Merlion as he mounted. "And you have reason enough to be of a strange humor."

"Reason enough or not, watch me. What churns inside of me is what can get men killed. What little calm I hold is tenuous. 'Tis no time to be led by emotion, but that is so strong within me it could easily take command. I give you leave to wrest command from me if I act with disregard to the lives I take into the field. Swear to me you will not blindly go where I lead, for God alone knows where that might be this time. A man needs cool blood and a clear head to lead others in battle. I possess neither this time. Swear," he urged them as he mounted.

"I swear it," said Roger as he mounted, and Merlion did the same. "But I pray it does not come to that."

"So do I, my friends." Thayer took a deep breath, then smiled grimly. "There is one more thing you can do for me."

"Aye?" Roger and Merlion spoke as one.

"As we ride to Saitun Manor, search your memories for a way to slip inside the cursed place. I believe there lies our best chance of coming away from this true victors."

Chapter Thirteen

Gytha fought conciousness, for with it came pain. A sharp throbbing tore at her head, inside and out. Voices, deep and rough, intruded upon the haze she tried to cling to. She grew aware of movement, each sway and bump bringing more pain.

Cautiously she opened her eyes, finally accepting the unwelcome fact that sweet oblivion would not return. At first, the light only added to the pain in her head, clouding her vision. When she could see clearly, she glanced around and found herself tied hand and foot. She was in a wagon amongst an odd selection of sacks and barrels. There was no need to see how the sky flew by over her head to know the wagon was going at a fast pace. The jolts she was suffering told her that.

Forcing herself not to think too much on her pain, she wriggled about until she was wedged more securely amongst the sacks, which helped protect her body from some of the jolting. The rough movement was not, she believed, good for her child. It was said that once a child was well secured in the womb, as hers was, it took a lot to shake it free. No one had said exactly what constituted a lot, however, and she was not about to take any chances.

The lessening of the roughness of the ride also helped ease some of the throbbing in her head. She viciously cursed Lady Elizabeth. It had all been a trap, and she had walked into it like a blind fool. Consigning the devious Lady Elizabeth to the deepest, fieriest pits of hell did not seem punishment enough. She wished she could think of something worse. She also wished there could be some result from all her curses.

As a clear, complete memory of that brief moment in the inn overcame the aching in her head, Gytha remembered Bek. Worry and horror swept over her as she recalled the boy's state just before she too had been clubbed from behind. Lady Elizabeth had let someone strike her own child so hard that it brought blood and unconciousness. Knowing that, Gytha doubted the woman did anything to help the child afterwards. Elizabeth would have fled the inn as quickly as possible to avoid being caught.

Twisting her head, she looked to the front of

the wagon. Staring at the broad backs of the two men driving the wagon, she wondered if she should ask them about Bek. Then one glanced over his shoulder at her.

"So, you have awakened," he murmured.

"The boy?" she asked, finding her throat so dry it hurt a little to speak.

"Left him behind. Had no need of him."

"How was he?" she pressed.

The man shrugged. "Who can know? I had no time to look. Neither did that fine lady. Stepped right over him and fled as fast as could be. Why stay? She did what she said she would."

"Aye—handed me over to Pickney."

"You will be seeing him soon."

Turning away from the chuckling men, she settled back into her niche amongst the sacks. She had guessed that Charles Pickney was behind it all. Nevertheless, having it confirmed by his men badly sank what little spirit she had left.

Increasing her dismay was the lack of any knowledge of what had happened to Bek. She had wanted some assurance that the boy was at least alive or that Lady Elizabeth had found some scrap of maternal feelings and tended to his injuries before running away. Instead she was left with only her last sight of the boy, a vision suited only to give her torment.

Since there was no way to get an answer to ease her worry, she turned her thoughts to her own precarious position. Taking a closer look

299

at the sky dimmed her brief hope of a swift rescue. The day was nearly at an end. Rescue would clearly not come until she was in Pickney's hold. For now, her safety was in her own hands.

That she would be in Pickney's grasp meant Thayer's life was in danger, she realized with a thrill of alarm. She would be used as the bait to bring her husband to his own murder. It was a thought too horrible to contemplate, but she knew she could not ignore it. For Thayer's sake, it was important that she fully face the danger. If there was any chance of thwarting Pickney's scheme, however small, she had to be alert for it, ready to grasp it quickly.

Closing her eyes, she decided she could well be in an untenable position. A sense of defeat swept over her, and for a moment she gave into it. She was tired, her head hurt, her body felt bruised all over, and she was in increasingly desperate need to relieve herself. Defeat seemed a thoroughly proper thing to be feeling.

The wagon slowing to a stop pulled her from her self-pity. It was as she shifted around to see where they were that she became fully aware of a new discomfort. Looking down at her bound wrists, she saw that they had become swollen. She did not bother to look at her ankles, knowing they would be the same.

She gave a startled cry when one of the men—the shorter, bulkier of the pair—picked her up to lift her out of the wagon. When he set her on her feet, she began to collapse. With her bound-together arms, she managed to use the back of the wagon to stop herself from falling to the ground. She glared at the two men who, oblivious to her plight, began to set up a campsite.

"I need some assistance," she said, using a haughty, imperious tone to ease the sting of having to ask them for help.

"My, my, Henry, heed her ladyship," said the man who had lifted her from the wagon. "Help yourself, m'lady."

"If I did not need help, I would not even lower myself to speak to you. Your bonds have caused some swelling, and it hinders me. If I attempt to move without aid I shall fall, which could hurt the child I carry."

Henry shrugged. "So crawl. Me and John have work to do."

"And Pickney will probably be pleased," said John, "if you did lose that babe."

"He may be, but my husband, the Red Devil, would be sent into a murderous rage."

"Let him rage. He will be dead ere he can do anything. John and me need not fear him."

"Nay? Who is to say he will die?"

"Well, Pickney plans—" began John.

"Plans do not always go as a man wants them to." She almost smiled when she saw the worry that crept into their expressions. "A smart man would weigh his moves carefully."

"What do you mean?" demanded Henry.

"I mean he would think what he could do to

301

please both sides—or, at least, placate them."

"No one can do that." John snorted with nervous scorn.

"Nay? Pickney wishes me brought to him alive. The Red Devil wants me alive and still carrying his child. I cannot see that both would really be so hard to accomplish. It just means a little more care. Recall that the Red Devil is well known to win his battles. What battles has Charles Pickney won?"

"Go help her, John."

"Why listen to her?" grumbled John even as he hurried over to aid Gytha.

"Because she shows some wit for a mere woman."

As she was nearly carried to a spot near the fire, Gytha bit back a sharp response to that slur. She forced her thoughts to something far more important as she sat down. They had to bind her differently. The swelling the bonds caused was not only painful but, she was very sure, could prove bad for her health. Since they clearly feared Thayer, she intended to use that to as full an extent as possible.

"You believe what she says?" John asked his comrade as he squatted by the fire.

"Aye. Pickney has got some fine plans, but we were forgetting what he is up against. The Red Devil has faced better men than Pickney and lived. He has also stayed alive until now, though Pickney has been trying to kill him for years."

"Well, if you thought all this, why have we

set ourselves on Pickney's side?" snapped John.

"The coin is good, fool. That other heir proved no problem despite his fine name and reputation as a warrior."

"He was nothing to what they claim the Red Devil is."

"True, but the Red Devil fights fair. Pickney deals in backstabbing and treachery. I thought that gave him a chance." Henry frowned at their prisoner. "Now, I wonder. He has overcome Pickney's treachery 'til now. The Red Devil could prove a warrior great enough to win despite all Pickney puts against him. The man could even know a treacherous trick or two himself, using them when he is driven to it."

"So, do we leave? Flee this trap ere it closes shut on us?"

"Nay, we cannot do that. Pickney would see us dead for it. We have set forth on this path and must walk it now. What we can do is make sure the Red Devil's lady comes to no harm at our hands."

"But we stole her!" John nearly screamed the words, his fear gaining a tight grip on him.

"Pickney ordered us to. We are but serfs, men-at-arms. That might save us. He will strike at Pickney and that fool boy, Robert, not at their minions. So it will stay if we are careful with his lady. Now, cease being such a coward. We must eat and rest. Pickney expects us early on the morrow. Best we be there."

When John sullenly obeyed Henry, Gytha inwardly cursed. For a brief moment she had let herself hope that John's rising fear would cause the man to flee, run from both Thayer and Pickney. Sadly, Henry had not only more wit but the sort of calm, considering nature that held men like John in place. She had hoped to lessen the number of her opponents by one or, even better, have John's fears infect Henry so that both men ran. Luck, however, was clearly not with her—not yet.

"So," she mused silently, "I will get as much ease as I can." Holding out her bound hands she called, "I must be untied."

Henry looked at her, then whooped with laughter. "Do you think us witless, woman?"

Biting her lip, Gytha refrained from answering that. She wanted to frighten them into making her journey as easy as possible. Responding to that remark with the vicious words on the tip of her tongue would only anger them and would gain her nothing at all.

"Do you see what these bindings have done?" After both men frowned at her swollen wrists, she tugged up her skirts just a little to reveal that her ankles were in as bad a condition.

" 'Tis not enough to fret over, woman."

"Nay? 'tis little surprise that you cannot discern what trouble might result. I doubt either of you have children." She hastily swallowed yet another insult which had nearly followed those words. "Such swelling can be very bad for a woman with child."

"Whether it can or cannot matters little." Despite his growled words, Henry moved to stand over her and frowned down at her wrists. "How can we watch you, keep you at our side, if we unbind you? Silly wench."

"I am sure such clever men as you can think of some way." She knew she had not been able to hide all the contempt in her voice but felt they would attribute it to aristocratic arrogance. "You can think of it whilst I indulge in a moment of privacy"—she held out her bound wrists—"as soon as you untie me." When he hesitated, she pressed, "There is another thing a woman carrying a child has a great, and I fear constant, need for—moments of privacy. If you hesitate much longer, you will know I speak the truth and we shall both suffer some embarrassment."

As he finally untied her wrists and ankles, Henry muttered, "I catch your meaning, but you are not going off alone."

"Going off alone is what a moment of privacy means." She needed his help to stand, much to her chagrin.

"Well, yours will be me turning my back. Come on."

Stumbling, Gytha kept pace with him as he strode towards some bushes. Her need was so desperate that she made no attempt to argue with the man. She doubted there was any argument that would sway him anyway. Despite

knowing all of that, she cringed in embarrassment as he stood close by, his back to her,
while she crouched in the bushes. It was hu-
miliating. Adding to that was her need to use
his burly strength to return to the campsite.
She was stiff and, although the swelling in her
wrists and ankles had lessened it did so painfully.

Once seated by the fire, John thrust a bowl
of thick gruel at her then a crooked wooden
spoon. The mess looked lumpy and far from
inviting, but she was too hungry to quibble.
There was little taste to it, and the texture was
barely tolerable, but she ate it all and drank
the somewhat sour wine handed to her. Her
body, needing sustenance for the child it nur-
tured, helped her ignore all the inadequacies
of the cuisine.

When Henry approached her with the rope,
she backed away. Only now had the pain and
swelling fully eased. She did not think she
could bear its return. To avoid it, she very
nearly swore that she would not try to escape.

"Now, I will not be tying you up as before,
woman," Henry said in a gruff voice.

"You have to tie her," protested John. "She
would run otherwise."

"I mean to tie her to me—waist to waist.
Your choice, woman."

Covering her rounded stomach with her
hands, she frowned slightly. "You cannot bind
my waist. The child . . ."

"I will tie it above the rounding. Well?"

After a brief hesitation she nodded. Anything had to be better. If some discomfort came from the arrangement, she would mention it after the very first twinge.

The way he tied them, the rope encircling her just below her breasts and him around the waist, forced a certain amount of proximity. She pushed away her distaste. Even when she was made to share a blanket with the man as they settled down for the night, she kept quiet. Putting as much distance between them as possible, she closed her eyes, seeking the comforting oblivion of sleep.

"There they be."

At Henry's gruff announcement, Gytha turned to look where they were headed. Her only restraint was a rope around her tying her firmly to the wagon. Since the knotted end of that rope was right next to Henry, she had no chance to untie herself, but she doubted she would even have tried. Jumping from a rapidly moving wagon would be more risk to her child than she was willing to take. However, when she caught sight of Charles Pickney, she briefly contemplated just such an action, thinking it might well be the lesser of two evils.

The wagon pulled to a stop just outside Pickney's campsite. She took quick note of the fact that the man had barely two dozen armed men to help him. As Robert and Pickney walked to the side of the wagon to stare at her, she turned her full attention back to them. The way Pickney glared at her stomach frightened her, but she fought to hide that. Robert, she swiftly noted, looked stricken. She shrugged that away. Pickney was the one she had to watch. He was the leader.

"You are with child." Pickney clenched his hands into fists, fighting the sharp urge to beat Gytha.

"How keen your eye is. 'Tis something that often happens when a woman has a husband."

"Enough of your impertinence. Curse that man and curse you," he hissed, slamming his fist into the palm of his other hand. "Well, that shall have to be dealt with."

Pickney's cold words sent icy tremors of fear through her. She caught a look of horror briefly come and go on Robert's face. There *was* a limit to what Robert could condone. What she needed to find out was whether Robert could gain the courage to stop what so clearly horrified him—or, she thought before she turned her full attention back to Pickney, if she could give him that needed courage.

"I should not make too many plans," she told Pickney in a cold voice, not even trying to hide her hate for the man.

"Are you fool enough to think your great Red Devil can win this time?"

"Are you fool enough to think that he cannot?"

"Woman, I hold you, and through you I will soon hold Saitun Manor. I have that red bastard now."

"Not yet."

Leaning over the side of the wagon, Pickney jabbed his pointing finger at her. "I should be careful, m'lady. I *do* hold you *now*."

"Best you hold me securely and safely, sir. I may be all that stands between you and a well-deserved death at the hands of my husband. You stand there gloating as if you have won, but you best not gloat too soon, for the battle has yet to be fought."

Seeing how Gytha's words were enraging his uncle, Robert dared to murmur, " 'Ware, Gytha."

"Aye, heed my fool of a nephew. 'Tis not wise to taunt me. Enough of this. 'Tis time to ride for Saitun Manor," he bellowed as he strode towards his men.

For a moment it looked as if Robert was going to speak to her, but then he scurried after Pickney. They started on their way too quickly for Gytha's liking. Pickney clearly did not want to chance a pursuing Thayer catching him in the open. Looking away from the men riding ahead of them, Gytha caught Henry staring at her. She was a little surprised to detect a shadow of concern in his dark eyes.

"That fool, Robert, spoke true," Henry said after a moment. "Beware, m'lady. Pickney is given to blind rages. His plan may be to wed you to that weak gosling he calls nephew, but that will not stop him if you stir his fury. He will kill you." He turned away from her, muttering to John to urge the horses to a quicker pace.

Gytha settled against the sacks in the back of the wagon. Her thoughts were not on the warning Henry had given her, but why he had given her one at all. She suddenly realized that she had marked Henry and John as greater rogues than they were. They had not truly treated her poorly. Callously, perhaps, but not cruelly. They did what they were hired to do, no less but no more either. Now it appeared they too had limits to what they could condone. Closing her eyes, she decided to rest and try to think of a way to make use of that.

"She sleeps," Gytha heard Henry say a little while later.

"How can she sleep when the wagon rattles along so?" John muttered.

"I have heard it said a woman with child can sleep most anywheres. 'Tis strange, but I think 'tis true."

"Aye, and something else is true. We have set ourselves in the midst of more than we were told of."

"Curse that bastard, Pickney. To shed an heir, he said. To wed the woman to that suckling Robert, he said. And we believed him. S'truth, all we heeded was the clink of coins, fools that we are. 'Tis much deeper than the ridding of a troublesome heir. Much deeper indeed."

"And we could be pulled down with him. Do you think he means his threat," John whispered, "about the child she carries?"

"Has the man ever uttered a threat he did not mean?"

"Jesu. I felt a bit uneasy over the murder of the two men—but, well, they could fight and 'tis the way of the gentry. Stealing a wife?" John shrugged. "Happens a lot. No real harm. But, he talks of killing a babe. A babe, Henry. And I think he means to kill the woman when her use is past."

"Aye, he means both. Women and babes." Henry shook his head. "I have more sins weighing on my soul than I want to think on, but not that. Not the blood of women and babes. I have no mind to put it there either."

"Then we can flee now? Pull away from this ere it goes any further?"

"And how do we do that? We turn this wagon any way but right behind Pickney there and we are dead men. Pickney will not ask what we do, but will kill us without hesitation."

"So we are trapped."

"Mayhap. But mayhap not. We will see what happens at Saitun Manor."

Gytha waited tensely, but they said no more. Another chance, she thought, but fought against letting her hopes rise too high. John and Henry might have some good in them, but it did not mean they would be persuaded to help her. They could only think of saving their own skins. To escape a part in the crime they now saw in the making, they would simply flee, not exert themselves to stop the crime.

* * *

"Wake up, m'lady. Saitun Manor looms before us."

"Aye, Henry." Gytha blinked sleepily and sat up. "I am awake—more or less."

"I think you have done little else but sleep throughout this journey," grumbled John.

"It passes the time," she murmured, looking towards Saitun Manor.

Their pace had slowed so that their approach would not appear threatening. Gytha was dismayed when they were hailed almost genially by a man on the outer walls. A small part of her had hoped that, somehow, Thayer could have gotten word to the men at the manor, a warning against Pickney. The speed at which they had traveled had dimmed that hope. No messenger could have outridden them. Her brief thought to call out an alarm was halted by Pickney riding up by the wagon's side.

"Not a word, woman. Not one small word." He reached over to tug her cloak over the confining rope about her middle.

She hastily swallowed the warning cry forming on her lips. All she could do was pray, long and hard, that her silence did not cause the deaths of the men guarding the manor. Fear for her child caused her to hold her tongue. She prayed the cost of saving that small life would not be a bloody one.

"Stand up now," Pickney ordered once they were all inside of the walls of the manor.

"Stand up so that they may see that I hold you."

The moment she obeyed him, revealing how she was tied, the sound of swords being drawn echoed through the bailey. Pickney drew his sword and held it on her. The icy tip of his weapon touched her throat. She hardly dared to swallow. Every man posted at the manor suddenly went still.

"I want every fighting and hale man in the bailey. Now! I want all weapons discarded," Pickney continued to yell as, reluctantly, the men of Saitun Manor began to group together. "Make no brave attempt at rescue or I will kill your lady. And with her would go the heir of your master—The Red Devil."

Not one man resisted. To Gytha's great relief, Pickney did not kill the unarmed prisoners he had collected. Instead, he ordered them secured in the dungeons. It was not until he was assured that this had been accomplished that he finally took his sword away from her throat. Weak in the knees, she slowly collapsed onto the sacks in the wagon. She was then left to Henry's and John's care as Pickney saw to the further securing of the manor.

"It seems the key to a secure demesne is a woman," drawled Henry as he edged the wagon towards the stables.

"I doubt it would work with all ladies," murmured John, who then climbed off the wagon to see to putting it and the team away.

Gytha's attention was drawn to the sounds

of weeping women as Henry helped her out of the wagon. She saw Pickney's men rounding up all the women and children within the manor's walls. The way they were being herded into a group surrounded by sword-wielding men made Gytha very nervous. She shared the fear the women and children could not hide, unable to guess what Pickney was going to do with them.

Looking at a frowning Henry, she asked, "What is to happen to them?"

"Pickney means to lock them away as well. He wants none of them trying to help the men or you. Or"—he looked a little nervously towards the closed gates—"the Red Devil, who should be appearing soon. Come along." Holding Gytha by the arm, Henry started towards the manor house. "You are to be put in the west tower room."

Once inside the west tower room, Gytha sat down on the bed. She felt thoroughly worn out and utterly defeated. Soon Thayer would arrive, yet she had discovered no way to aid him or herself, no way to stop Pickney from using her as bait to draw Thayer into a trap. She could only pray that Thayer had some deviousness in him, for it began to look as if trickery or treachery was the only way Pickney would be defeated.

Moving to the window, she stared down into the bailey. Pickney's men busily prepared themselves for Thayer's arrival. She wondered why they worked so hard to prepare for a battle

Pickney had no intention of fighting. He would use her to murder Thayer, then use her to keep Thayer's men from seeking retribution.

For just a moment she wished she was not carrying Thayer's child, resented the life rounding her belly. The baby complicated everything, held her back when she needed to act. Her every move had to be weighed because of the baby. Then she smoothed her hand over her stomach, silently apologizing to the child. Pickney, and he alone, was to blame for the tangle she was in.

Her dismal thoughts were interrupted by the sound of someone unbarring the door. She turned to face Pickney when he and his two closest cohorts, Thomas and Bertrand, entered the room. The look of gloating on Pickney's sly face infuriated her. She ached to beat it out of his features.

"Soon now, Lady Gytha," Pickney's tone of voice turned the title into a slur, "you can watch the Red Devil die."

"Can I? Mayhap, sir, I will soon watch you die. Pray God it will be slowly and agonizingly, but I fear my husband is unable to stoop to the depths you do."

With the back of his hand, he struck her across the face. Gytha barely smothered a cry of pain as she stumbled against the wall. The warm, salty taste of her own blood filled her mouth. Searching with her tongue, she discovered his blow had caused her to badly cut the inside of her cheek. Pushing aside her fury, she

315

forced herself to remember Henry's warnings. Pickney was filled with his own hate and fury—both directed at her. She did not want to prod those too much.

"I have won, but clearly you need more to make you accept my victory." Pickney smiled, a cold flashing of his crooked, yellowed teeth. "You shall have it. Soon, very soon, I shall place the arrogant Red Devil's head in your hands."

Gytha had a sudden, uncomfortable urge to retch at the image his words conjured up, but she struggled against it. She stoutly refused to reveal any weakness to Pickney. "Someday, sir, you shall pay for these crimes you so gleefully commit." Before she could say any more, a man stuck his head around the door.

"A force approaches the walls, sir," the new man announced.

Pickney nodded. "Bertrand, when I signal, you are to hold her ladyship in the window so she may be seen clearly by her man." He laughed softly and took one long look at Gytha before starting out of the room, Thomas and the other man with him. "It seems, m'lady, that your husband is most eager to die."

Chapter Fourteen

"Pickney!"

Thayer glared at the walls of Saitun Manor as his bellow lingered briefly in the air. By the time he had reached the manor, his fear was such that he had needed to be restrained from riding right up to the walls and hurling himself against the barred gate in some mad, futile gesture. When Pickney appeared on the wall encircling the manor, Thayer grasped the hilt of his sword. Never before had he so ached to kill a man.

"Aha, the great Red Devil himself clamors at my gates," Pickney yelled, a heavy tone of ridicule in his voice.

"*My* gates, you bastard. But 'tis not that theft I come about. Where is my wife?"

"Your wife? Now, why should I know the whereabouts of the little whore?"

"When I gain hold of that cur, I shall kill him slowly," Thayer muttered to Roger and Merlion, who flanked him, then raised his voice again as he spoke to Pickney. "Your ally at the inn values her life more than loyalty to you. She told me all of it, Pickney, so cease these games."

"Ah—that wife. Aye, I have her, but there is a price."

"I discuss nothing until I can see that Gytha is alive and well."

"Fair enough."

Watching closely, Thayer saw Pickney wave, clearly signaling someone. The man then pointed towards the west tower. Looking that way, Thayer cursed. Gytha was precariously perched in the narrow window at the top of the tower. His fear for her was eased only slightly when he saw the hands encircling her upper arms. Someone was holding her, keeping her from falling. However, that same someone could also hurl her to her death.

"Gytha," he yelled, not sure his voice would carry so far, "have you been hurt?" She only shook her head slightly, causing him to frown. Then he realized she was undoubtedly terrified. "All right, Pickney, I have seen her. Tell your man to pull her back inside." He relaxed a little when Pickney signaled the man and Gytha was tugged back into the tower.

"So, Red Devil"—Pickney sneered the title—

"you now see that I hold all the reins. You must bow to me."

"That is yet to be seen. What do you want?"

"At the moment, I believe I have all I want. Ah, nay—there is one more thing."

Clenching his teeth so tightly his jaws ached, Thayer took a moment to respond. He could not release the fury that boiled inside of him. Pickney held Gytha. He had to remember exactly what sort of man Pickney was. Thayer knew Pickney would not hesitate to cause Gytha pain. No matter how it tore at him, he had to placate the man, not goad him or anger him. He had to play the game.

"And what is that one more thing, Pickney?"

"You."

"Me, is it? I am to walk into your hold, am I?"

"Aye, unarmed."

"So you may kill me without risk to yourself."

"Your life for the woman's."

"Nay," Roger hissed, afraid Thayer would immediately ride into Pickney's grasp. "Nay, Thayer. Not so quickly."

"He may not give me any time, Roger."

"I think he will, if only to allow himself to savor what he sees as his victory."

"You do not think he has won?"

Roger sighed, then shook his head. "We have just arrived here, just ridden here hard and fast. Gain time for us to survey this place and really think. There must be some solution beside you walking to your death like some ancient sacrifice."

Looking back at the walls, Thayer stared at Pickney. He caught a glimpse of Robert behind his uncle. "Pickney's shadow," he thought with an inner sneer. There would be no help for Gytha from that weak boy.

"It looks to me, Pickney, as if you wish me to give you all with no promise of return or benefit."

"I see no choice for you, Red Devil. But if you feel you cannot meet my demands..."

"I did not say that, Pickney."

"Nay. Well, I am of a generous humor today. I will give you time, let you wriggle about in vain as you try to find a choice, an escape. You have until this time on the morrow to accept that you have lost."

Sharply turning his mount, Thayer rode back to where the rest of his men had made camp. He barely heard Roger and Merlion hurry after him. Pickney's mocking laughter rang in his ears. Abruptly, he reined in, dismounted, and strode to the far end of the camp. He sat down heavily upon a rock and stared blindly off into the distance. For a while, thought was impossible as raging emotion swept over him. He was finally beginning to grasp at a few threads of calm when he heard someone approach. When a hand lightly clasped his shoulder, he knew it was Roger.

"It seems I have failed poor Gytha again, Roger," he murmured.

"Failed her?" Roger sat on the ground in front of Thayer. "Nay."

"Nay? She is captive within those walls and I cannot get her out—not even if I give Pickney my head on a spike. All that will do is keep her alive for a little while longer. You see no failure in that?"

"Nay, I see a well-laid plan. You cannot elude every trap. Pickney set a very secure one. That does not mean it will work."

"You have come up with a way to slip free of it, have you?"

"Not yet, but we have time. As soon as it grows dark, men are ready to thoroughly search the land around Saitun Manor, and the walls of the manor, for some way in—be it a bolthole or a weakly guarded point upon the walls. If any such place exists, they will find it."

Thayer nodded, knowing which men Roger would have chosen, as well as the strength of their skills. "Pickney does not mean to release Gytha, even if I do as he asks."

"I know that. We all know it. 'Tis one reason why the men will search as hard as possible to find what we need. You would lose your life for naught, and they would not even be able to avenge your murder. I have said nothing, but the men also have the wit to know that your child's life is at stake too. If they find no way in, then none exists. And that, I think, is an impossibility. There is always a way in."

Running his hand through his hair, Thayer

looked at the manor. "I pray you are right. If not, tomorrow I walk to my death unsure if it will help Gytha or not. 'Tis a poor way to die."

"Then why do it?"

"Because I could not live with myself if I refused and Pickney killed her. At least I can gain some time for her." He looked back at Roger. "Time in which you might yet free her. If I have to turn myself over to Pickney, I want you to swear to me that you will continue to try and get Gytha away from there."

"I swear it. I also swear to you that, if he hurts her or, God forbid, she dies at his hand, I will not hesitate to kill him. Even if I must tear down the walls of Saitun Manor stone by stone to get at him."

Briefly clasping Roger's hand in gratitude, Thayer found a touch of comfort in that vow. If he had to meet his death on the morrow, he would at least face it knowing that Gytha would still have a protector—knowing that someone would see that Pickney paid for his crimes, no matter how long it might take. He prayed that, before the night was over, his men would give him the comfort he truly craved— that which would come with finding a way to get into Saitun Manor.

Gytha stared out of the window, watching the flicker of the fires from Thayer's camp. She ached to be with him, to hold him and ease his torment.

A noise at the door tore her thoughts from

the dark route they had taken. She watched with disinterest as Henry set some food on a small table while John stood by the door. When they both stared at her, she sighed and moved to sit on the rough stool before the table. A part of her was appalled when, as she stared at the food, her hunger stirred. It somehow felt disloyal to even consider eating when Thayer's life hung in the balance.

"You must eat, m'lady," Henry urged after a moment.

"Why?"

"For the child's sake."

"Ah, I am to fatten him up for the kill, am I?" Out of the corner of her eye, she saw both men flinch.

"So he might have a chance to live."

She gave a brief, scornful laugh even as she broke a piece off of the block of cheese on her tray and ate it. "Do not mouth lies. You know as well as I that Pickney will not let this babe live. If he even lets me bear the child, t'will only be so that he may smash its poor brains out ere it has drawn its first breath. I carry an heir to this place. You know well how Pickney deals with heirs." She ate some more cheese, then spread a little honey on a thick chunk of bread.

"Mayhap you will have a girl."

"And you think that will change the babe's fate, Henry? Do not be such a fool." She ignored his scowl as she continued to eat. "If the king discovers that his knight died leaving a

323

legitimate girl child, he will take her in hand. 'Tis the king's right to do so. He will settle her and all Thayer leaves behind upon the man of his choosing, some lackey he feels a need to reward. Pickney will never take the chance that the king will find out and be of a humor to press his claims."

"Well, we have no part in it all," protested John.

"Nay? Who brought me here? Who snatched me from the safety of Riverfall?"

"We did not know the whole of Pickney's plans."

"A plea of innocence. I see. Well, you are not ignorant now, are you." She briefly looked at both men. "Nay, you know well the full evil of the man, yet you do nothing." She returned to finishing her meal.

"We have no wish to die," Henry snapped. "We are watched very closely. Pickney trusts no one."

"So you will sit here and let yourselves be made part of murder after murder. Simply because you do not wield the sword will not keep your hands free of blood. Standing mutely by does not leave you free of guilt, sirs."

"And to act against Pickney in any way will get us killed, yet we would not have halted his crime." Henry grabbed her empty tray. "I have no wish to die and, curse it, certainly not to die in some fool's attempt to stop that which cannot be stopped."

"You cannot blame us for this," John cried.

Snatching her unfinished tankard of wine from the tray, she said, "Oh, I do not blame you. I know how the pinch of hunger can drive a man to do most anything for coin. I know most men cannot see the wrong in Pickney's grasping what is not his and doing it through murder—nay, nor in the theft of a bride from one man's bed to set her in another. Sadly, such things happen often enough to be accepted. Nor do I blame you for wanting to stay alive. I should like to do the same. So go—go and keep yourselves safe. I will not condemn you for it."

She was not really surprised when they left in an angry mood, the slamming of the door behind them accentuating it. While she had offered forgiveness with one hand, she had slapped them with the other. She did understand what had pulled them into the mess and why they could not extricate themselves. But her life and her child's were also at risk, and she could not help but resent their not aiding her. She did not ask for sacrifice, simply help. Unfortunately, they saw helping her as equal to signing their own death warrants and she doubted she could ever change their minds.

"So I am on my own," she muttered, walking back to the window as she sipped her wine.

Staring out at the fires in Thayer's camp again, she plundered her mind for an idea. What few she came up with did not stand up to any close looks. One failure or weakness after another revealed itself until the plan had to be cast aside. Worse was the constantly recurring need for at least one other person to make it work.

The sound of someone entering her prison made her briefly wonder if fate was sending her that other person. When she saw it was Robert, she decided fate had a cruel sense of humor. Robert gave her a look that was an odd mixture of adoration and terror.

"What do you want, Robert?" she demanded, feeling a strange mix of pity and hate for the man.

"To see that you are not being mistreated."

"Mistreated? Nay. 'Tis quite comfortable in my little tower prison."

" 'Tis more to keep you safe," he stuttered.

"Is it now. Odd, but with the door barred from the outside, I saw it more as a place to hold me in than to keep others out." She leaned against the wall by the window, set her tankard down on the ledge, and crossed her arms beneath her breasts. "You could come in. I have yet been able to get out."

Robert pushed his hand through his fair hair. Gytha looked as beautiful as ever, despite the cool anger in her fine blue eyes, despite the rounding of her belly with Thayer's child. She also looked as inaccessible as ever, far out of his reach. He wanted her so badly it robbed him of sleep at night, but Thayer held her— big, red, plain Thayer. It seemed an injustice.

"You do not want to get caught in the midst of the battle," he said, struggling to keep his nervousness from echoing in his voice.

"Battle?" Gytha gave a short, bitter laugh. "What battle? Your uncle has no stomach to fight Thayer. He uses me to bring Thayer to his death, like a lamb to the slaughter."

The discomfort, even shame, reflected in Robert's sorrowful expression did not really touch Gytha. As far as she was concerned, he should be wallowing in shame. He stood meekly by as his uncle murdered his kin.

"I do not wish to talk about that," muttered Robert.

"Nay, nor look at it. Such blindness will not save your soul, Robert."

Starting to pace the room, Robert murmured, "I will be a good husband to you, Gytha."

"Do you truly believe I would allow you to be anything to me after you aided in the murder of my husband?"

"You will have to marry me. 'Tis part of Uncle's plan."

"Oh, aye, he can probably make me wed you. Between the pair of you, I can probably be forced to share your bed. I cannot be forced to care about you, nor even like you. Considering that your uncle means to kill my child . . ."

"Nay! Nay, 'tis not true. He did not say that."

"He said it. Aye, and you heard and understood. But, 'tis clear you have since convinced yourself otherwise. Well, you will not be able to do that when you stand over the grave of this innocent. T'will be too late then."

She suddenly realized that the door was un-barred and, because of his pacing around, she was now between Robert and the door. It was possible to get out of the room. The question was—what could she do after that? She would still be stuck inside the walls of Saitun Manor, but there was a chance she could slip out, a chance she could hide. Both were very small chances, but, she decided as she bolted for the door, they were better than no chance at all.

"Nay, Gytha! Wait!"

Glancing over her shoulder, she saw Robert finally beginning to move after her. She flung open the door, but her rush to flee the room came to an abrupt halt against a square male body. Her high hopes, so briefly tasted, were shattered. Even before she looked up, she knew whom she had run into. Hands tightly enclosed her upper arms as she was shoved back into the room. Stumbling backwards, she looked up into the hard face of a furious Pickney. Behind him came Thomas and Bertrand.

"What are you doing here, Robert?" Pickney demanded. "Besides nearly losing us our prize." Pushing Gytha towards her bed, he strode over and slapped Robert so hard the younger man staggered backwards.

Gytha frowned as she sat on her bed watching the exchange. Robert had made no move to avoid being struck. He had not even tried to run, let alone defend himself in word or deed. She found it hard to understand how a grown man could allow himself to be treated like that. There was only the smallest hint of rebellion in the sullenness of his expression.

"She had only just begun to run," Robert murmured. "I but sought to ease her worries."

"Ingratiate yourself, you mean." Pickney laughed as he turned to look at Gytha. "I should not trouble myself. You will soon have what you have been mooning after—little Gytha as your wife. Whether she likes it or not matters little."

"And what of how my family feels about it?" Gytha asked. "Or had you forgotten them?"

"Not at all. They will not strike at me for the same reason your hulking brute of a husband holds back—I hold you."

"They can wait to make you pay for your crimes. As my husband's men will wait. The life you plot for yourself will be a very precarious one, sir, with more swords than you can count forever aimed your way. All waiting for the moment they are freed of restraint."

"For a while, mayhap, but they will weary of the game."

"There are those, sir, whose loyalty and need for justice does not wane with the passing of time."

"And you, m'lady, overjudge your worth. Now," he gloated, rubbing his hands together, "for the reason I am here. I mean to allow your husband to see you ere I kill him. Thinking on that, I realized there is yet another way to strike at him, to add further torment to his soul ere he goes to meet his maker."

Fear rippled through her as she saw how he looked at her. "And just what might that be, sir?"

"He is going to see that his little wife has known the thrust of another man's sword." He laughed when Gytha tried to bolt, only to be quickly grabbed by Thomas and Bertrand. "T'will be a pleasurable way to pass the hours until he comes to me. Aye, and I will find out if such a cool, aloof beauty has any warmth at all."

"Uncle, nay," cried Robert, hurrying to the bedside. "You promised her to me."

"And you shall have her. But would you be so selfish as to hold her all to yourself?"

"For God's sweet sake, she is with child. You could make her lose the baby."

"All the better. The brat is of no use to us. In truth, the whelp could prove a real problem."

Gytha struggled furiously against Thomas and Bertrand's hold, but it was in vain. They easily pinned her down on the bed. All she could do was twitch and buck fruitlessly, which amused them. She looked to a pale, trembling Robert but knew there was no help to be found there. Even if he completely rebelled and actively tried to stop Pickney, he lacked the strength needed.

When Pickney reached to tear the bodice of her dress, Robert yanked him away. "Nay, leave her be. I will not allow this."

"*You* will not allow this?" Pickney hissed.

"Nay, I cannot allow you to hurt her like this."

The fight that ensued was brief, furious, and painful to watch. When Thomas moved to aid Pickney, Gytha tried to break free, but the hulking Bertrand easily stopped her. She was not surprised when, in mere moments, a groggy, bleeding Robert was dragged to the door and tossed into the hall. The way Thomas, Bertrand, and Pickney then smiled at her made her feel physically ill. She knew she had no chance of stopping the rape they planned, an assault that could easily rob her child of life, but she began to struggle anyway. Hopeless though it was, she refused to submit without a fight.

From his gracelessly sprawled position on the floor, Robert slowly sat up. He wiped the blood flowing from his split lip on the sleeve of his jupon as he glared at the door to the room where Gytha was being held. A soft cry from within made him shudder, and he struggled to his feet.

"So you finally got the stomach to fight, boy."

Startled, Robert stared at the two men before him, one reaching out to help him to his feet. "Who are you?"

"I be Henry," answered the man who had helped him, "and this is John. We are the fools that brought her here."

"We must stop them." Robert started

towards the door, only to be held back by Henry.

"You go in there and you will only be tossed out again and beaten worse."

"You can help me. There would be three of us then. Three against three."

"I am no swordsman. Neither is John."

"Nor am I." Robert covered his face with his hands. "They are going to hurt her so badly. How can I bear it?"

"Bawling like some unweaned brat will not help either," Henry snapped.

"Then what am I to do?" Robert glared at the man. "Stand here and listen to those animals abuse her?"

"And what would you do if you got her away from them? We would still be captive within these walls."

"Nay, I would get her out. I know how. I would give her back to Thayer," Robert whispered, seeing the last of his dreams of a life with Gytha at his side fade away. "She does not want me anyway."

Grabbing Robert by the arm and shaking him, Henry demanded, "You know a secret way out of this place?"

"Aye. There is a bolthole. William showed it to me long ago."

"Your uncle knows of it?"

"Nay. I held the secret to myself."

"Then there may be a way to right our wrongs." Henry looked at John. "Willing?"

"Aye." John nodded, wincing when there was another cry from Gytha.

"But you just said," Robert protested, frowning at Henry, "that we cannot fight those three."

"So we bring in one who can—the Red Devil." Henry nodded when Robert's bruised eyes widened in understanding. "We slip out that bolthole and bring him back in through it."

"It will be too late to help Gytha. They will have all raped her by then."

"Nay, I will delay that." Henry frowned in thought for a moment, then nodded. "Aye, I can draw their attention elsewhere without rousing their suspicions. I can only give you an hour, mayhap less."

"That should be enough but we may find trouble as we go through the dungeons. There are two men on guard there."

John smiled faintly. "If we cannot slip by them, I do have some skill at knocking heads."

"But . . ." Henry scratched his chin in a gesture of thoughtfulness. "Will the Red Devil let you speak or kill you on the spot?"

"Nay, Thayer will not simply kill us. That is not his nature. He may get in a rage, but his men will halt him from acting whilst gripped so. Thayer is no murderer. He is a fair-minded man." Robert's words dripped with bitterness.

"Fine. Now, you get the guards in the dungeons to keep their eyes on you so John can slip up behind them. Secure them and secure them well. Then run for the Red Devil's camp and bring the brute back here as fast as you can. I can talk a good game, but I cannot promise much time."

As soon as John and Robert were gone, Henry rapped vigorously on the door. A loud curse told him he had interrupted Pickney. He hastily reviewed his ploy and decided it would hold for a while.

"Leave us be," Pickney bellowed.

" 'Tis important, sir. I would ne'er bother you elsewise."

"Have my fool nephew see to it."

"I mean no disrespect to the boy, sir, but I think this problem needs more than he has to give."

"Curse it, and curse these fools," grumbled Pickney as he scrambled off of Gytha. As he relaced his hose, he looked down at her. "It seems you must wait to know the pleasure a true man can give."

A hundred vicious retorts crowded her mind, but Gytha found herself unable to speak. When Bertrand and Thomas eased their hold on her, she tugged her torn clothing back around her exposed body with badly shaking hands. As all three men turned their attention to the door, she edged away, huddling against the wall. It surprised her a little to see Henry at the door when Pickney yanked it open. She had not thought Henry a true part of Pickney's group.

"This had better be as important as you claim," Pickney snapped as he glared at Henry.

"I judge it so, sir." Henry spared barely a glance for Gytha, only enough of a look to tell him that, terrified and bruised as she was, she had not been seriously harmed.

"So? What is it?"

"I believe I have found a weakness in our defenses. 'Tis big enough for a redheaded devil to slip through, I be thinking."

"Then someone is slacking off, for I covered all points. I am sure of it."

"So I thought, sir. That's why I decided to come direct to you. Felt sure you would be wanting to see it and do any needed disciplining yourself. Aye, always best for the leader himself to tend to these matters."

"Aye, so it is. Come along," Pickney said, signaling Bertrand and Thomas to follow him out the door. "It sounds to me as if I will have need of you." He paused to look back at Gytha. "No need to be disappointed, my dear. We will be back soon."

Robert stared at the two trussed-up guards as John rechecked the bindings on the men. He was making a stand against his uncle. The realization both terrified and exhilarated him. He almost laughed. He had hoped Gytha would give him the strength to break free of his uncle's hold. She had done just that, but not in the way he had imagined.

John frowned at Robert, who stared blankly at the two unconcious guards. "Here, you thinking of running out on me?"

"Nay." Robert shook himself free of his introspection. "I but realized that I am free."

"What are you babbling about?"

"Pay no heed to me. We had best hurry. My uncle will do his best to get back to Gytha as quickly as he can."

"Here, what of us? Do you mean to leave us here?"

Turning to look at the men Pickney had locked up, Robert fixed his gaze on the one who had spoken. He recognized him as one called Wee Tom. A huge bull of a man, Wee Tom clutched the iron bars, his homely face pressed hard against them.

"For now," he said, and a murmur of protest began.

"We can fight Pickney."

"Without swords, Wee Tom? Be patient. We will be back." He started towards a small room to the right.

"Wait." John grabbed the keys and went to open the door to the cell. "One of you. Only one of you," he snapped when all the men pressed forward.

"What are you doing?" asked Robert. "What good is letting only one of them out?"

Even as he opened the door, tugged Wee Tom out, and quickly shut the door again, John answered, "He can make sure that anyone who wanders down here does not give out a cry of alarm." After locking the door, he handed Wee Tom the keys. "Do you understand what I mean?"

"Aye. If anyone comes down here, I am to silence him."

"And if you cannot, let the men out. The disturbance that will bring will buy us the time we need."

"Time for what?" demanded Wee Tom.

"To bring back the Red Devil," answered Robert as he grabbed John by the arm and hurried off into the small room he had started towards earlier. "Help me move these chests, John," Robert ordered, even as he started to pull one of four heavy chests away from the wall.

Beneath the chests was a small door. Robert opened it, then crawled into the tunnel behind it, a grumbling John behind him. Rock-lined and damp, it was not quite high enough to walk in but wide enough to accommodate the largest of men. Gritting his teeth against the sound and feel of a multitude of small creatures, Robert groped his way along the tunnel in the dark. He was relieved when it abruptly turned upwards where metal rungs were driven into the rock to aid him to climb. John had to squeeze up next to him when the hatch proved difficult for him to open. The rush of fresh air when the door finally opened almost made up for the small cascade of dead leaves, sticks, and pebbles they had to endure. Robert scrambled out, helping John up after him. The reinforced inside of the huge, hollowed-out tree was cramped for two of them, so Robert quickly stepped out. He stared across the open field to the looming walls of Saitun Manor and prayed Henry's ploy was working.

"Best we hurry," mumbled John as he brushed himself off. "We can stay in the wood until we are near the Red Devil's camp. That way neither side will see us or mistake us for the enemy."

Nodding, Robert started off towards Thayer's camp, John falling into step behind him. They had gone barely ten yards when several men jumped them, getting a firm hold on them before they could even begin to fight. When one stepped close enough for Robert to recognize, Robert felt fear briefly douse his newfound sense of freedom. The cold smile Merlion gave him only added to that fear.

"I want to see Thayer," Robert said, cursing the way fear made his voice shake.

"Oh, aye, you will see him," Merlion drawled. " 'Tis every man's right to face his executioner."

Chapter Fifteen

When Merlion abruptly entered the tent, Thayer leapt to his feet. There was a tense urgency about the man that raised Thayer's hopes.

"Have you found something?" he asked, proud of the calm steadiness of his voice.

"Aye." Merlion signaled to someone behind him, and two men were thrown into the tent, falling gracelessly to the ground. "I know not what game is being played now but"—Merlion ungently nudged Robert with his boot—"we found these two slinking through the wood."

As the men slowly stood up, Thayer recognized his cousin and felt rage grip him tightly. It blinded him to everything but the need to make someone pay dearly for his loss. Growling softly, he lunged for Robert, who gave a high-pitched squeak of terror and tried to hide behind the men gathered at the entrance to the tent.

Roger quickly grabbed Thayer, glad when Merlion rushed to help. For a little while they stumbled around awkwardly as Thayer tried to get a murderous grip on Robert while Roger and Merlion struggled to hold him back. All the while Roger tried to talk to Thayer, pressing for calm. There had to be a reason for Robert to be outside of Saitun Manor, and he wanted Thayer to take the time to see that. He murmured a prayer of thanks when Thayer finally stilled, breathing heavily as he stood lax in their hold.

"I am calm. I will not kill the boy." Thayer glared at Robert, who cowered behind the man who had been captured with him. "Not yet. First he will talk. Stop huddling behind that fellow like some terrified babe," he yelled at Robert, then scowled at the other man. "Who are you?"

"John, sir." John yanked Robert from behind him, forcing the younger man to stand at his side. "We are changing sides."

"Are you now. Sit." He pointed to his cot, watching as John dragged a slowly calming Robert over to sit down. "Why should I believe you?" he asked and moved to pour himself a cup of wine, struggling to stay calm.

"Because why else would two men you have reason to kill come to face you—unarmed?" asked John.

Sipping his wine, Thayer studied both men for a moment. "I need no one to tell me why I should kill Robert." He fixed his gaze upon John. "But why will I want to kill you?"

"I am one of those who brought your wife to Pickney." He leaned back when Thayer took a step towards him. "Me and my friend were told we were just stealing a bride. We were led to believe it was just the usual game the gentry play of stealing land and all from each other. You lot are always killing each other off and taking each other's women."

"Not all of us. What changed your mind?"

" 'Cause it is more—a lot more. You might not be of a mind to believe this, but me and my friend, Henry, do have some sense of what is right."

"I might be persuaded to believe it. Go on."

"Well, Pickney goes too far. He means to hurt women and babes. Me and Henry cannot hold with that. Never had a hand in that sort of thing and never will. We came to see he has no intent of letting your woman live long or the babe live at all."

"And did you but just awaken to that too, Robert?" he demanded of his cousin.

"Aye." Robert finally looked squarely at Thayer. "T'was wrong to let him strike at you and William."

"He killed William?"

"I cannot say for sure, yet when he talks of it, he does not speak of it as an accident." Robert frowned, then shook his head. "It matters little right now. 'Tis Gytha that brings me here. Coward that I am, I sat back while he plotted. I . . . I wanted Gytha, you see."

"That is a confession you did not need to make. T'was clear to all."

"He promised I could have Gytha, but he lied."

"Get on with it, boy," snapped John. "Henry cannot hold those bastards 'til dawn."

"What is happening to Gytha?" Thayer had to struggle hard to restrain himself from vigorously shaking Robert.

"God help me, he means to have her. He and Bertrand and Thomas too. He wants to taunt you with it," Robert replied, unable to stop the tears that streaked down his bruised cheeks.

"And you just left her there?" Thayer bellowed as he tossed his drink aside and strode towards Robert.

"Nay!" Robert stared up at his huge cousin. "That fellow Henry has drawn them away from her for now."

"No need to be too hard on the boy," John spoke up. "See them bruises?"

"He has always had bruises." Thayer took several deep breaths to calm himself a little.

"Aye, no doubt, but he got those for showing a little backbone for once in his wretched life."

Glaring at the man, Robert snapped, "Thank you kindly, sir."

"No need for that. You did well and it ought to be said, even if you did get tossed out on your arse. Now we have to hurry. Like I said, old Henry cannot keep those curs busy for long. We have to get back and stop them from going back to her."

"We have spent half the night looking for a secret way in," Merlion said. "There is none."

"And just how do you think we got out?"

Robert spoke up before Merlion and John began to squabble. "There is a way in. We came here to take you back through it."

"To be murdered once inside?" asked Roger, unable to trust Robert.

Shaking his head, Robert replied, "Why bother with such a trick? On the morrow Pickney gets all he wants. Thayer will simply walk into his grasp. Please, trust me—for Gytha. Henry stopped them this time, but for how long? He cannot stop them a second time. My uncle means to rape her, Thayer, then hand her to Bertrand and Thomas. Do you really believe that even I, coward that I am, could stomach that? You say you could see how I felt about her."

"Aye, I did." Thayer began to buckle on his sword. "Lead on."

"Best you leave some men here," said John as he stood up.

"Aye," agreed Robert. "They cannot see well from the walls, but if there is no sight of a shadow near the fires now and again, that could rouse some suspicion. We do not want anyone alerted."

"Does Pickney know this way out, this bolthole?"

"Nay, Thayer. I never told him. Oh, the men-at-arms are in the dungeons. That is where the entrance to the bolthole lies. They will need weapons. We set Wee Tom there to be sure no one came down and set up an outcry."

Nodding, Thayer strode out of the tent, the rest hurrying after him. He left Roger standing with Robert and John as he issued orders and made preparations. While he felt Robert was sincere in his wish to help, he did not trust his cousin to have the strength to perservere. Robert had grasped a thread of courage for the first time in his life, and Thayer intended to take full advantage of it before Robert lost his grip on it.

Seeing how Robert never took his gaze from Thayer, Roger asked, "Why do you stare at him so?"

"I am not thinking of how to betray him, if that is what you think," Robert snapped.

"It did occur to me. You have been deep in it for a long time."

"What I have been deep in is my uncle's plots and unable to pull myself out. Now that I have taken the first step, I have seen that he forged my chains years ago. He even said as much, but I was too drunk when I heard it to fully grasp it. He had trained me since I was a babe to be just as I am—a weakling. He wanted no argument from me and he never got one.

"Nay, I stare at my cousin bewildered as to why Gytha seems so taken with him. She is, you know."

"Aye, I know."

"She is so beautiful, a woman the troubadours sing of. Yet she holds loyal to Thayer. He is a man of battle, a warrior wild and deadly. Yet Gytha..." He shook his head. "They should not be so firmly mated, yet I feel they are."

"They are, so you had best cast aside all your dreams of her."

"Oh, I have."

"Good, for if you think your cousin is wild in battle, you should see him when caught in the grip of jealousy."

"I should rather not, thank you."

"That is wise of you, boy," muttered John. "Best gird what loins you have, for it looks as if the Red Devil is ready to leave."

"Look, John," Robert began, angry over the not so subtle insults the man kept hurling at him.

Thayer stopped in front of Robert. "You can bicker with him later. We leave now. Show us the way in and, mind you, if a trap awaits, you will die with us." He watched Robert nod, then stride off towards the wood. "Can he have changed?" he asked Roger as they followed Robert and John.

"Aye, I think he can. He adores your wife, Thayer. So much so that, rather than see her hurt, he will give her back to you."

"And find the courage to act against the man he has cowered before for years?"

"Aye, that too. The question is—what do you

do to him, and that fellow John with his friend Henry, after all this is over?"

"Most men would hang them."

"True. Most men would."

"I cannot, I fear—not if they truly help me gain Gytha back safely. How can I punish Robert for being the weak fool his uncle twisted him into? And this John and his friend? He faced me square, spoke honestly. He truly believes stealing brides and murder is the way of the gentry. Yet, he has some sense of right as he put it. No harm to women and babes. I will owe him Gytha's life. How can I punish him even if he did bring her here?"

"Aye, you are presented with a puzzle. I say leave them be. There are two rogues who will surely think twice ere they do anything again that even hints of wrong, no matter what the coin."

"True." He stepped up next to Robert when his cousin halted before a large tree. "Here?"

Cautiously he followed Robert, using a covered lantern Merlion handed him. Thayer cursed in surprise when he saw the hatch door. Although he hesitated a moment, seeing what a perfect trap could be awaiting him, he followed Robert into the dark hole.

Robert's squeak of fright came too late to warn Thayer that his cousin had halted. Looking ahead of Robert, Thayer almost laughed. The faint light from the lantern he still carried revealed it was Wee Tom's bulk which filled the opening at the end. Poor Robert had nearly crawled into the sword Tom held.

"So, you did come back." Wee Tom easily tugged Robert out of the tunnel, stood up, and set the slight young man on his feet. "Began to think you had just run off. M'lord," he greeted Thayer in relief.

Brushing himself off as the others crawled out and filled the room, Thayer said, "We brought weapons for the men."

"Good." Wee Tom nodded and grabbed the keys from where they hung on his belt. "The men have been grumbling to get out."

"Have you heard anything about Gytha?" Robert asked.

"Well, that Henry fellow come down. Nearly silenced him good before I knew he was with you."

"Aye, the brute near snapped my neck," Henry grumbled as he entered the room.

"Henry." Robert grabbed the man by the arm. "How is she?"

"Well, I held Pickney as long as I could. Got a man a good whipping it did. They have just gone back to her. I think you had best hurry to free her."

"Colin, Wee Tom," ordered Thayer, "see to freeing the men down here and arming them. I will take my men to get Gytha. Where has he put her? I saw her in the west tower. There?"

"Aye," answered Henry, "but be careful when you go in there."

"I know," Thayer snapped as he headed out of the room. "They hold her."

Hurrying after him, Henry said, "Not yet. She has found a way to hold them back."

Something in the man's voice made Thayer pause to look at Henry. "What has she done?"

"She is standing in the window, m'lord, and claims she will hurl herself out of it if they touch her. I left but a moment ago, and they were trying to talk her out of that."

"Jesu." Thayer grabbed the man and pushed him ahead of him. "Show me to the room as fast as you can. She may mean it."

Clutching the stone framing of the window, Gytha tried to keep her balance. She was terrified to be standing so unsteadily in the window, but not as terrified as she was of the three men in the room. Although the thought of hurling herself to the ground below, of committing the grave sin of suicide, was abhorrent to her, so was what Pickney and his cohorts planned. Either way, she thought sadly, her child would die.

"Get out of that window, woman," Pickney snapped, his hands clenched into white-knuckled fists.

"Nay. I stay here until you leave."

"You will stain your soul for all eternity if you kill yourself."

"*You* are concerned for my soul? Better that than what you plan. Hell looks a heaven compared to that."

"If you jump, you will also kill your child."

"What you and that filth with you plan will also kill my child. You offer me no choice there."

"All right, all right." Pickney held his hands out, palms up in a conciliatory gesture. "Come down and I swear none of us will touch you. I give you my word. We will leave you be."

"Your word? Ha! That is worth nothing. It has never meant anything. Only a fool would accept your word."

A breeze tugged at her torn skirts, chilling her. It also buffeted her enough to make her wobble. She tightened her grip and tried to still her rapidly beating heart. There was still a large part of her that wanted to live, strongly wanted it. Yet, what would she have to live for if Pickney murdered Thayer and her child? She could not live if what was left of her life was to be spent beneath Pickney's abusive fist.

"Think for a moment, wench," Pickney yelled. "You are no use to me dead. I do not want you dead."

"Not yet," she snapped, then realized that none of the men was listening to her.

She frowned as she realized they were not paying any attention to her at all. Then she heard what they had. Someone—in truth a number of someones—was rapidly clamoring up to the room. Her astonishment was complete when the door was thrown open. There was no mistaking the figure that loomed there.

"Thayer!" Gytha could not believe her eyes.

"Get out of that window before you hurt yourself, you foolish woman," he bellowed even as he prepared to fight Pickney.

"Aye, husband. As you wish."

As carefully as she could, she got down, but before she could savor the feeling of being on firm ground, her legs began to give way beneath her. Slowly, she buckled to the floor. She felt weak and light-headed. Inching along, she got herself in a safe spot against the wall, out of the way of the fight about to begin. Wrapping her arms about herself, she tried to stop the shaking that gripped her.

Assured that Gytha was all right, Thayer turned his full attention to Pickney. The bruises and the torn condition of Gytha's clothes confirmed what Robert had said. Thayer ached to kill Pickney little by little, to prolong the man's pain and obvious fear. He was not surprised when Pickney drew his sword but then pushed his man Thomas in front of him. It was just like Pickney to be too cowardly to face him squarely.

"Cease cowering behind your minions and fight me as a man should," he hissed at Pickney. " 'Tis more than you offered me."

"Kill him!" screamed Pickney, moving further behind Thomas and Bertrand. "Kill him, you fools."

For a moment, Gytha feared Thayer would be facing two, perhaps three, swords. Thayer was a skilled swordsman, but no man could watch all sides at once. Then Roger stepped forward. Merlion edged into the room, ready to act if needed. She briefly closed her eyes in relief, then opened them quickly as she felt someone lightly nudge her. It was hard not to gape when she saw Robert, Henry, and John crouched round her like a shield.

"What are you doing?" she asked, poking Robert in the back.

"Making sure my uncle does not try to use you as his shield."

"Well, at least leave me a space," she hissed as she nudged Robert's and Henry's shoulders apart a little. "I wish to see."

"I am not sure a lady should watch such a thing."

"Do be quiet, Robert." She ignored the way Henry and John snickered, earning a glare from Robert.

Even though the violence horrified her, she felt an odd shiver of excitement in watching her husband skillfully wield his sword. She did, however, briefly turn away from the battle when Thayer slew Thomas. Despite her intense dislike for Pickney's minion, the bloody ending of his life was not something she wished to observe too closely. Knowing Thayer would now face Pickney, she looked back, grimacing when she caught a glimpse of Bertrand's last moments facing Roger.

"Nay, Roger," Thayer said as Roger moved to stand by his side. "He is mine."

" 'T'was all Robert's doing," Pickney cried as Thayer advanced upon him. "T'was his idea.

Tell him, Robert. Tell him how I was but a minion, forced by you to play this game."

Robert's reply was a suggestion so coarse that Gytha stared at him in open-mouthed surprise. Then the clash of swords drew her attention back to Thayer. For all his cowardice, Pickney proved a good fighter. Gytha felt her trembling begin again. She had full confidence in Thayer's skill, and knew he could defeat Pickney in a fair fight. What she had no faith in was Pickney's intention to fight fair.

After a few minutes, she realized that Thayer was playing with Pickney, inflicting small but painful wounds, yet withholding the death blow. Although she knew Pickney deserved whatever punishment was dealt him, she turned away, unable to watch the lingering killing.

Suddenly Pickney cried out, and she knew it was over. Since she had anticipated that the swordplay would continue for quite a while longer, she was almost surprised into looking. She held firm, however, feeling she had seen as much death as she could bear.

Her three guardians moved away. Thayer crouched beside her even as she turned to see why she had been left alone. When he pulled her into his arms, she sagged against him. It was a little hard to believe that their ordeal was over, that they were safe.

"Are you hurt, Gytha?" he asked in a soft voice, afraid he had indeed been too late.

"Nay. Bruised, my clothes torn, but naught else."

"Thank God. I am sorry you had to see such cruelty."

She shook her head. "You were not cruel. Considering the punishment you could have dealt out for his crimes, you were most merciful."

"Merciful? Aye, mayhap, after I recalled that you were watching. Only then did I end it cleanly and quickly. What I wished to do, was trying to do, was to cut him into little pieces."

"You cannot be blamed for that. I had some most bloodthirsty thoughts on how to end his miserable life myself."

"Are you sure you are not hurt? You are trembling."

" 'Tis weariness, I think. 'Tis very tiring to act brave when one is terrified. Oh, sweet Jesu." She clutched at Thayer's arms and looked up at him. "Bek. How is Bek? The last I saw of him—"

He lightly kissed her. "He is fine. He's got a bad crack on the head, but nothing serious. I believe those two men eased the strength of the blow. If they had struck Bek hard enough to fell a grown man, they would have killed the boy."

She briefly closed her eyes in relief, then smiled weakly. "Henry and John told me they know how to knock heads. Thayer, about Henry and John—aye, and Robert too . . ."

"Hush. First we will have one of the women

look at you to be sure you are not hurt. Then you shall be bathed and dressed in a fresh gown. After that we can talk." Even as he stood up, picking her up in his arms, Thayer began to bark out orders.

Gytha wanted to say something in favor of Henry, John, and Robert. She wanted to hear how Thayer had arrived in time to save her. All she was able to do was answer continuous inquiries as to how she felt.

The room was quickly cleared of all signs of the deaths that had occurred there. All sounds of fighting had ceased by the time two women arrived to help her. She was thoroughly looked over, her small injuries tended to, bathed, dressed, and settled back on her bed with a multitude of pillows. Then a huge tray, heavily laden with every delicacy available in Saitun Manor was set before her. She did manage to gain some details of how Thayer had come to rescue her, but she was relieved when Thayer returned from inspecting the manor and shooed the women out of the room.

"They began to make me feel like some royal invalid," she grumbled as he sat on the small bed.

Thayer laughed softly as he nibbled some of the cheese on the tray. "Soon I will take you down to our chambers. Pickney made free use of them. I felt you would prefer them thoroughly scrubbed first."

"Aye. Thank you."

He watched her as she ate one of the small

cakes on the tray. She looked better, but she was still a little pale, a little bruised. He ached to hold her tightly, to make fierce love to her to prove that she was truly safe and returned to him. Inwardly he smiled as he wondered what she would think if she knew how he had spent the last hour—on his knees in the chapel effusively thanking God for sparing her and their child.

A part of him begged to pour out his heart to her, to say everything he felt, but he stayed silent. Although he had needed help to do it, he had just saved her life, saved her from rape at the hands of Pickney and his slaveys. To confess his love now could bring a response born of her gratitude towards him. That was the last thing he wanted. There would come a better time to speak of such things.

"I have sent word to your family that the danger has passed. Aye, and to those waiting at Riverfall," he added.

Pausing in eating a thick piece of bread, she looked at him. "I am sorry for this trouble. If I had not gone to Lady Elizabeth . . ."

"You have naught to ask forgiveness for. I told no one that she bore watching closely, that I had made an enemy of her. When I left court, I reminded myself to speak out on the matter, but then I forgot all about the woman."

"What have you done with her? Did she escape?"

"Nay. She sits in the dungeons of Riverfall. When I return, I shall call her family to come and take her in hand. Ere they leave, I will tell them a few truths about the Lady Elizabeth. Aye, even the truth about the son she left lying in his own blood."

"Oh, poor Bek. Nothing she could have done or said could have better shown the boy how little she cares for him."

"If that hurt him, he hides it well. Truth is, I think he knew that about his mother a long time ago. What truly bothered him was that, yet again, his mother had a hand in hurting you. 'Tis something he cannot understand. I am not sure I helped him do so either. There was no time. I was able to say, in full honesty, that his mother did not know murder was part of the scheme."

"Are you sure of that?"

"Aye. She saw only a scheme for ransom, a way to put some coin in her always empty purse."

Gytha leaned back against the pillows and sipped her wine as she watched Thayer eat what remained on her tray. She reached out to toy with his thick hair, drawing a half-smile from him. Except for that first emotion-laden embrace after Pickney was killed, they had returned to what they had been—close but not too close, comfortable but rarely emotional. It made her sad, but what made her even sadder was her part in it. She said nothing about her own feelings, cowardice tying her tongue every time she contemplated it.

"Thayer? Do you really think you should tell

Lady Elizabeth's family about Bek?"

"Why not?" He got up to move the emptied tray away from the bed.

"Well, what if they want as little to do with the boy as she does?" When he sat next to her on the bed and slipped his arm around her shoulders, she leaned against him. "He would see that he had family besides you, only to have them turn away."

"There is that chance, aye." He frowned as he mulled the problem over. "I must tell them. 'Tis far past time. Mayhap the solution is to not speak to Bek of it until I know how Elizabeth's family feels about him. I do not want to cause him any more hurt."

"Nay. Mayhap when he is older you could tell him the whole truth—that is, if the family will not recognize him."

"Aye, mayhap. We will settle that when the right time comes. Now to another matter. You wished to talk to me of Henry, John, and Robert?"

"What do you mean to do with them?" She mused that it was probably mad to ask for mercy for the disreputable trio.

"I have not given it much thought. What do you think should be done? 'Tis you who suffered most at their hands."

"Nay, at Pickney's hands. I know Henry and John brought me to him, but they are only petty rogues, not truly evil. Despite thumping me over the head, they treated me well. Once they were aware of Pickney's true plans, they were appalled. Unfortunately"—she smiled faintly—"they are not the bravest of men."

"Oh, I am not so sure of that. John looked me straight in the eye and told me he was one of the men who had taken you from Riverfall. Said it whilst sitting there unarmed."

"Well, there is a wonder," Gytha murmured. "He and Henry were not just a little afraid of you."

"Me?" Thayer gave her a look of surprised innocence.

"As I was saying, I think there is some good in them."

"And it will come forth if they are kept well-fed and have a coin or two to spend," Thayer drawled.

Gytha laughed, then lightly punched him in the arm. "You have already decided to spare them."

"Aye, but I wished to be sure you felt the same. And Robert?"

"Poor Robert. Pickney made him what he is. Who knows what sort of man he could have been had Pickney not twisted him into such a weakling. But for a moment, Robert fought his uncle. Of course, he lacked the strength and the skill. Pickney saw to that."

Brushing a kiss over her forehead, he murmured, "I know that. In the end, when it mattered, Robert did what was right. I have no stomach for killing one of my own blood. Also, Robert did not truly know that William was murdered."

She frowned. "But he knew you were to be murdered."

"That he ignored for a reason many men would consider a good one—he wanted you. I believe he has fully given up that dream. Do you know, I begin to think John and Henry have taken him under their wings. Mayhap the best thing to do is to find something the three can do together that will bring them some measure of profit and keep them out of trouble."

Quickly putting a hand over her mouth, she yawned. "And what of Pickney's men?"

"All dead."

"All of them?"

"Aye. The men we set free from the dungeons suffered a hard blow to their honor. They were mayhap a little too eager to avenge that." Standing up, he urged her to lie down and tucked her in. "You need to rest. You have suffered a long ordeal and need to treat yourself gently for a while."

After he slowly, softly kissed her, he started to pull away, but Gytha grasped his hand, holding him at her bedside. She did not want to be left alone. Even though she knew she was now safe, her fear lingered. She knew it would be a while before the fear Pickney had bred in her fully disappeared.

"I know I sound a foolish child, but will you stay with me? At least until I fall asleep?"

"Aye, and you do not sound foolish." Still holding her hand, he sat on the edge of the bed.

"You were badly frightened. That does not always fade simply because the danger has passed. The memory of it must dim a little too."

She smiled faintly in gratitude for his understanding. Slowly, she closed her eyes, feeling the weight of sleep already creeping over her. His nearness not only eased her lingering fears, but reassured her that he was indeed alive, that Pickney's murderous plan had really failed.

"Gytha?" Thayer called in a soft voice after several moments.

"Mmmm?"

"Would you really have jumped from that window?"

So close to sleep, it was hard to answer clearly, but she tried. "I do not know. Part of me saw no reason not to, yet part of me recoiled from the mere thought of it. If Pickney had stepped any closer, mayhap. I was more terrified of him and what he meant to do to me than of dying or God's punishment." She felt his grip on her hand tighten almost painfully as she gave into the pull of sleep.

Long after she fell asleep, Thayer stayed at her side, holding her hand in his. He had come too close to losing her, her and their child. It was going to be very hard not to lock her away from the world, from any other possible danger. He wondered if he was doomed to spend the rest of his days in fear for her life.

Chapter Sixteen

Thayer grunted and slapped at the hand gripping his shoulder. The last thing he wished to do was wake up. He still felt a little drunk. The celebration of Roger's and Margaret's wedding had been a hearty one. If one of the guests needed him, he could go away and wait until a more reasonable hour. In an effort to get away from that irritating presence, he curled up closer to Gytha, carefully slipping his arms around her in a way that would put no weight on her rather large belly. The way she shifted in his hold told him she was already awake. He grew even more annoyed at the intruder, who shook him again.

"If I were some enemy, I could have slit your throat from ear to ear by now."

There was something very familiar about

that deep, rich voice, but Thayer fought to ignore it, to return to sleeping peacefully.

"Jesu," cried Fulke.

Good, Thayer thought with satisfaction. The intruder had managed to rouse Gytha's brothers, who slept on pallets in their chambers. The three Raouilles would soon show the man out.

"We were told you were dead," John muttered. "How is it you are here?"

"Because I am not dead?" came the softly amused reply. "Wake up, you redheaded sot."

Impertinent too, Thayer grumbled to himself. He broke from his cozy place by Gytha long enough to swing a fist at the intruder. That drew a soft "oof," then a laugh—a laugh that was disturbingly familiar. An incredible thought entered Thayer's head. He swore, then shook it away. The drink was still muddling his thinking. He wondered sleepily why Gytha felt so tense.

Gytha felt torn between screaming and fainting. She wanted to pummel her groggy husband awake *and* let him sleep through what had to be some strange, unreal vision. William Saitun was supposed to be dead. He was not supposed to be standing by their bed in Riverfall looking hale and handsome, grinning beatifically.

"From the drunken bodies I have seen, there must have been some wild revel here last eve."

"Roger married my cousin Margaret," she answered, wondering wildly if one was supposed to be able to converse with a vision.

"Ah, so that is what that fool, Robert, was babbling about."

"You spoke to Robert?"

"Well, he stuttered out a few confusing half-sentences before he swooned. That scheming uncle of his is dead?"

"Aye. Thayer killed him. At Saitun Manor."

"A shame. I had wished to kill him myself. 'Tis clear a great deal has happened in the months I have been away." William roughly shook Thayer again. "Wake up, you big fool. We need to talk. Where is your welcome for one arisen from the dead?"

Deciding that William had to be alive since his image had not faded, Gytha gently nudged Thayer. Her brothers had clearly decided the same, for they were scrambling to wash and get dressed, muttering amongst themselves about how to tell her parents. She wondered if Thayer was in any condition to take this shock.

"Thayer, I think you ought to wake and see this man," she said, nudging him again.

"Dearling, I doubt I can see much of anything," he murmured as he finally opened his eyes to look at her.

Seeing the bleary look in his reddened eyes, she suspected he was right. "Well, perhaps this will be enough to clear your head." She watched him slowly ease himself into a sitting position. "Look to your right, Thayer."

Reluctantly obeying, Thayer turned, then gaped. He rubbed his eyes but what he saw did not change. Glancing at Gytha and her brothers, he knew they awaited some reaction. Looking back at the man standing by the bed, he felt too confused to do much more than stare. When William laughed, hugged him, and slapped him on the back, Thayer came out of his stupor enough to return the embrace. Then, as William stepped back, he began to think of the consequences of his cousin's return from the grave.

" 'Tis truly you, William," he mumbled as he sat up straighter, leaning against the pillows Gytha quickly plumped up behind him. "Why were we told you were dead? Aye, and left to believe it for so long."

Sitting on the edge of the bed, William murmured his thanks for the wine Fulke hurriedly served him. "I was very nearly dead. The fall from my horse left me sorely injured. Cortland, my squire, felt it best if all thought me dead. He knew the fall was no accident and that I was in no condition to fight off any further attempt to murder me. Also, we could not be fully certain whence the attack came. I am not without enemies."

"Few of us are. Where have you been?"

"Not so far away, in truth. At an inn. At first I did not realize what Cortland had done. When I was well enough to think clearly, I had to agree. We then tried to find out who had tried to murder me. When we discovered it was Pickney, I did think to warn you, but Cortland assured me that you knew."

"I did. He had had me declared dead as well. It did not take much time to piece it all together. I had experienced a few unusual accidents myself, though I fared better than you. You look hale now."

"Aye, but I have many a new scar. My right leg can grow very stiff at times as well. 'Tis a miracle I am not lame." William smiled faintly at Thayer. "I am sorry for one thing."

"What is that?"

"I fear my return means you shall lose all you gained. Why, it could almost make me wish I was dead. For a fleeting moment at least." He briefly grinned at Thayer.

Thayer managed a thin smile in return. *Lose all you gained*: The words pounded in his mind, causing unbearable agony as he realized their true meaning. Nothing he held was his. That included his wife. The marriage contract had been for Gytha to wed the heir to Saitun Manor. Since William had never been dead, that meant he had never been heir, never had the legal right to wed Gytha. William had the right to be Gytha's husband, not him.

"Well," he looked at William, "I began with naught. T'will be no real hardship to return to the same." *And never have I told a greater lie*, he thought, sure he was about to lose Gytha as well.

"Naught?" Gytha frowned at Thayer. "I know Riverfall is not as rich and fine as Saitun Manor, but 'tis more than nothing."

"Aye, but Riverfall is your dowry land."

365

"I know that, and my dowry went to you when we were married." She decided it might be best to try and keep Thayer from drinking too heavily too often for it made him very slow-witted on the morning after.

"Gytha, we were married because it was thought William was dead."

"So?" Gytha got the sinking feeling that she was not going to like the turn the conversation was about to take.

"So, by the terms of the marriage contract, you were to be wed to the heir to Saitun Manor. I am no longer that heir. William is." He wondered why she was taking so long to understand.

"So?" she said, grinding the word out between clenched teeth.

"You are not usually so slow of wit. The contract was for you to marry the heir, William. Since he is alive, you must be returned to him." He was diverted from her by the need to pat William on the back as the man had choked on his wine.

For a moment Gytha felt as dumbstruck as her brothers looked. Where did Thayer get such reasoning? They had been man and wife for months. The marriage had been consummated a hundredfold and was about to produce fruit. He could not possibly think that he could simply nullify all that and hand her over to William just because the man had turned up alive. However, it certainly looked as if Thayer thought exactly that.

Then she grew angry. She had done everything she could to make Thayer believe she was
happy with him and wanted only him. Obviously, she had failed miserably. He felt she
would be willing to walk from his bed straight
into William's.

A deep sense of insult added to her fury. He
saw her as no more than part of an inheritance,
no more than one of the stones in Saitun
Manor. William had returned to claim the
manor; therefore Thayer felt his cousin should
claim her as well. It made her feel little better
than worthless to him.

She hit Thayer as hard as she could. When
he cursed and turned to look at her in surprise,
she hit him again. Then she scrambled out of
bed, oblivious for once to how awkward her
swollen belly made her.

Turning to glare at Thayer, she found William staring at her in open-mouthed surprise.
His gaze was fixed upon her large stomach,
shown clearly by her nightrail which was almost too tight now. Somehow he had failed to
notice her condition before. She supposed
Thayer's bulk had hidden it. Gytha could not
help but wonder furiously if Thayer had forgotten that she carried his child or if he
planned to hand the babe over to William as
well.

"You mean to toss me back like scraps to the
dogs? Is that it?" she snapped. "Offer me on a
salver to the returning heir? Well, William,

367

since you have the manor and title back, why not take the wife too?"

"You misunderstand," Thayer said, wishing he was dressed, for he felt a little foolish sitting naked in bed while trying to have a serious discussion with an obviously enraged Gytha. "The marriage contract—"

"A plague on the contract! Curse you, what am I? Some piece of goods to be toted along with the land? And what of this?" She patted her stomach. "Does the child stay with you or get tossed in the pile with the manor, discarded with his mother?"

"I am not discarding you!" he bellowed. "Why do you twist my words?"

"Twist them? Twist them? They were twisted when they came out of your fool mouth. What do you plan to do? Annul our marriage? This"—she pointed to her stomach—"might make that difficult. 'Tis clear to all who have eyes in their heads that this marriage has been well consummated. Do you think you can wave your hand and make me virgin again?"

"Now you are being silly." He decided he could not continue the argument in bed, so roughly nudging William out of the way, he got up and put on his braies. "William understands the reasons for what has happened."

"William has not yet been asked what he thinks," William murmured but was ignored.

The gripping pain came and went again, and Gytha frowned. That one really hurt. Suddenly, she knew what was happening, knew why she had slept so poorly through the night. She glared at Thayer and decided to ignore the signs of impending birth. Berating her husband was far more important at the moment.

" 'Tis fine that William is so understanding, but I fear I am not. How can you toss me about so callously, without a thought to how I might feel? Or what I might want? You just start ordering people about."

"Calm down and listen. I but mentioned the contract. 'Tis legal, binding, approved by the king. Your parents wed you to me because they thought me the heir. 'Tis as if they have been deceived, though it was not meant so. This has to be discussed. You are a lady of gentle birth who was to have been wed to title and manor. I now have neither."

"How odd. I had thought I was wed to a man."

"You are being purposely difficult." Although he was pleased beyond words to have her protest so vociferously, he also found it painful, wishing she would let matters go quietly along the course he felt honor demanded.

"I am being difficult?" She glared at her brothers. "Have you got nothing to say about this?"

Fulke nervously cleared his throat before replying. "Fact is, I have not had a clear thought since I saw William arisen from his grave." He ran a hand through his hair. "Mad as it sounds, there may be some weight to Thayer's words."

The rich insult she was about to make concerning the state of her brother's wits turned into a moan of pain. Gytha grabbed the bedpost with one hand, wrapped her arm around her swollen abdomen, and bent over slightly as a painful contraction tore through her. When she was able to think of more than that, she glanced at the men. They stood staring at her in dawning and horrified understanding.

"Well?" she snapped. "Do you mean to just stand there and gawk until the poor thing drops to the floor?"

Thayer took a hesitant step towards her. "Gytha? 'Tis the baby?"

"What do you think?" She decided, in what she recognized was probably a total lack of reason, that she was in no humor to have her childbirth start now. "Fetch Janet and my mother," she ordered, and her brothers obeyed with alacrity. Even though another contraction gripped her, she tried to pull away when Thayer reached for her. "What are you doing?"

"Putting you back into bed," he muttered as he picked her up and settled her back in the bed. "You should have stayed there."

"I would have, if you had not been such a wooden-headed fool."

Ignoring her, Thayer turned to William, saying, "Help me dress ere the women arrive."

Even as he moved to do so, William asked, "Where is Bek, then? He is no longer your page?"

"Aye, he is, but he went to spend time with his mother's people."

Seeing the shock on William's face, Thayer quickly told him about most everything that had happened in his absence. He was glad when William shared his opinion that it could only help Bek to be so gladly accepted by his mother's powerful family, acknowledged as kin even as Elizabeth was very nearly disowned. It was hard to keep his mind on explanations, however, for his attention was fixed solely on Gytha. As soon as he was dressed, he hurried to her side, frowning when William moved to stand on the opposite side of the bed. He was relieved, though, when he took Gytha's hand in his and she did not yank it free, only giving him a cross look. She quickly made it clear that her temper had not eased at all.

"You mean you do not intend to hand this chore over to William as well?"

Before Thayer could respond, William took Gytha's other hand in his, ignoring the scowl Thayer gave him. "Gytha, do not be so harsh on my poor cousin. A marriage contract is a bond of honor. And if there is a man who values honor as high as it can be valued, 'tis Thayer." He shrugged. "Mad as it may seem, there is a question of what is legal here."

He winced when, as a contraction gripped Gytha, she squeezed his hand. "You are stronger than you look," he told her admiringly.

Relieved when she eased her grip on his hand, Thayer asked a panting Gytha, "Are you in much pain?"

"You are asking a great many stupid questions this morning," she grumbled, trying to catch her breath before the next contraction gripped her.

As Thayer opened his mouth to respond, William continued, "Now, about this marital—er, dilemma."

" 'Tis only a dilemma," Gytha snapped, "to people who wish to throw away their wives." She glared at Thayer.

"I did not say I wished to throw you away," Thayer snapped back.

"Hold," William yelled, drawing their attention. "Allow me to have my say. Ere I left you the last time, Gytha, I was more than content with the arrangement. Howbeit, matters have changed, and 'tis not merely because you lie here bearing Thayer's child. Not at all. Now I feel it best if you stay with Thayer. I relinquish all claim."

Gytha stared at him as she struggled through another contraction. William had just solved whatever conflict there might have been. She was still furious with Thayer for his apparent willingness to hand her to William, but she no longer needed to fear that some strange twist of law might take her from him. However, the ease with which William handed her back was hardly flattering.

" 'Tis odd," she murmured, "since I do not

wish to change husbands, but I feel insulted."

Although he kept silent, Thayer knew exactly what she meant. After the shock had begun to wear off, he knew he would fight giving her up with every ounce of will he possessed. William had neatly ended all possibility of conflict. Even so, he found himself wondering, a little angrily, why William was turning down the offered sacrifice. It had torn his heart in two to even suggest giving Gytha up, and William did not seem appropriately appreciative.

William laughed softly and lightly kissed Gytha's cheek. "I was, at first, sorely disappointed to lose such a lovely bride to my cousin. But, being free, I soon found my heart held in other hands. I married the girl three months past."

Before she had a chance to ask about that, Gytha found her mother and Janet at her bedside. Thayer and William were quickly shooed out of the room. She felt a twinge of disappointment over not being able to immediately satisfy her curiosity, but then the birth of her child took all her attention.

"Cease that cursed pacing," Thayer bellowed and threw his tankard at Henry and John, who paused only briefly before starting to pace the hall again. "What is taking so long?" he grumbled to William, who sat next to him at the head table.

"Birthing is a slow affair." William signaled

a page to get Thayer another tankard of wine. "Do not worry so."

"Not worry?" Thayer snatched up the tankard and downed half its contents. "Gytha is such a small, dainty woman, and you saw how large she had grown."

"Aye, she was well rounded." William glanced at Robert, who sat on the other side of Thayer. "Cousin, more wine?"

"Nay, I try to lessen my need for drink. I should not wish to drink up the profits at the inn. I swore to Henry and John that I would cease being such a sot. I will see if I can get them to settle somewhere," he murmured as he stood and walked towards his two new friends.

Half smiling, William turned his attention back to Thayer. "I am glad you were not forced to kill him. It had been my thought to take him back to Saitun with me, but I doubt he should wish to do that."

Trying desperately to keep his thoughts from clinging to what was happening to Gytha or from turning too dark, Thayer attempted to concentrate on discussing Robert. "Nay, he would rather stay here, if only because too many at Saitun recall the Robert that was Pickney's whipping-boy for so many years. Keeping an inn may not be what a man of his birth should settle to, but he has taken to it. He mostly attends the accounts while those two rogues"—he nodded towards John and Henry—"see to the labor. I believe Robert may even have found a young woman winsome enough to turn his devotion from my wife. 'Tis good, for I may have need to leave her alone for a long while, even ask him to keep an eye on her."

"Why? You are due to do your forty days' service? The king has called upon you again?"

"Nay, but I am landless and titleless now."

"Well, not landless. This is a fine keep."

"But 'tis what Gytha brought to our union. I have now brought nothing. I must work to get what is due her. She was to have wed a lord with a fine manor. That is what she accepted. I must seek that, give her back what she needs and has lost."

"Cousin, I always thought you a man of the keenest wits, yet it seems any thought of your fair wife scatters them."

Before Thayer could respond to that, Lady Bertha entered the hall. He watched her approach with an intense stare, momentarily robbed of speech. The woman looked weary, but happy, yet he remained fearful, not daring to believe Gytha had escaped the ordeal of childbirth unscathed.

"You have a fine son, Thayer," she announced, then sank into a seat next to her husband.

Thayer absently accepted and responded to the rounds of hearty congratulations. He wished them quickly done, however, for he needed to ask Lady Bertha something. She had not yet told him what was, at that moment, most important.

"And how is Gytha?" he was finally able to ask after several long moments.

"Fine. Tired but hale. She will give you many children with ease. Go on, she is waiting for you."

He needed no further encouragement. Despite the eagerness to see her that sent him hurrying towards their chambers, he hesitated for a moment outside the door. He could not help but recall the last time he had gone to the birthing bed of a woman who had given him a son. Sternly reminding himself that Gytha was nothing like the cold, amoral Elizabeth, he entered. Nodding to Janet, who quickly left, he strode to Gytha's bedside. She looked bruised with weariness, yet radiant, their swaddled child held in her arms.

"Are you well?" he asked, needing to hear the assurances from her own lips.

"Aye." She loosened the swaddling on their child. "Look at your son."

"Bek will be pleased," he murmured, smiling faintly when she gave a soft laugh.

Gytha watched him as he bent to examine their child, his big, calloused hands gentle as he lovingly touched the baby. As he silently assured himself that the boy had all he should have, she found it strangely moving to watch him. There was no need to ask him if he was pleased. The answer shone in his face.

Lurking beneath her delight, however, was

a lingering anger and hurt. She had told her mother about the argument preceding the birth. Her mother had been a little shocked, but had tried to make her see that there was good reason for Thayer to have thought as he did. Gytha realized that good reasoning was not enough to soothe her. She wanted some indication from Thayer that he would have been at least reluctant to hand her over to William. He had seemed painfully complacent.

"He is a fine, handsome son, Gytha." Thayer kissed her, wishing he could find a more satisfactory way to express the depth of the feelings assailing him. "The name is still to be Everard? After my father?"

"Aye, I have not changed my mind on that. 'Tis a fine name. I but wondered if you had thought to hand that duty to William as well."

Inwardly sighing, Thayer sat down on the stool someone had placed by the bed. He ran a hand through his hair as he warily eyed Gytha. While he had forgotten their confrontation, it was clear she had not. He wished she had, for he was not sure he would better his cause by trying to explain himself.

"Gytha, you must understand about such contracts," he began, thinking it a poor start even as he spoke.

"Oh, that has been explained. It seems mad to me, but then I have noticed how such bonds and legalities often do not seem to be concerned with the people they affect."

"Then why are you still angry? When William came back, I was honor-bound to at least offer to return all I had gained through his reported death—Saitun Manor, the title, and you."

She almost swore. There she was listed with the manor again, as if she were part of the furnishings. It infuriated her. She suspected it was that anger that kept her from giving in to the exhaustion weighting her body.

"I see. What if, when William appeared, I had turned to you and said, 'well, Thayer, my true husband has returned, so I will leave you now?' Would that have been acceptable to you?"

He blinked. The sense of having a revelation came over him. She said she understood about the marriage contract and about how William's being alive had to raise a question about which man she should be married to. However, Gytha was feeling, not thinking. She saw that he was ready to give her to William, but she could not know the turmoil that had caused him. She had seen callousness instead of fiercely enforced calm. He had unintentionally inflicted hurt, even insult. Sighing, he leaned forward to take her hand into his.

"Gytha, dearling, if I led you to believe I wanted to give you to William, I beg your pardon."

Frowning, she wondered if, in trying to explain himself, he was going to say things that might inadvertantly hurt her. She knew he did not mean to be cruel; that was not his way.

Unfortunately, loving him as she did, a simple lack of emotion or mention of such on his part was enough to hurt her.

"It sounded very much as if you did," she murmured.

"I can see that now, loving." He brushed a kiss over the back of her hand. "You are right. At times, I can be a wooden-headed fool. I could claim the shock of finding William was alive dulled my wits, and there was indeed a little of that."

"I can understand that. Seeing him certainly scattered my wits for a moment."

"When he reminded me that I must give back all I had gained, I naturally included you. I found myself torn between what honor demanded of me and what I wished to do. Saitun Manor and the title mattered little. If, by putting you together with those, I made you feel you mattered little, I can only say I never intended to. Even as I spoke the words, I knew I could never hand you back to William as I did the land and the title. And the babe. Did I fail somehow in showing you my pleasure over the child you carried? Failed so that you could think I could so easily give him up?"

"Nay. I did know—do know—that you are very pleased with our child."

"No man could have been as relieved as I felt when William said he had wed another. It meant I did not need to stand against him."

"You would have done that?"

"Aye. Once my head cleared I knew I could

not return you to what should have been. The contract did not matter. You are *my* wife. This is *our* son. All else I would return to William willingly, but not you. There was one other thing."

"What other thing?" she pressed when he fell silent, staring at her hand.

"I wished to allow you the chance to choose. Since there was a chance for you to go with William, I did not wish to hold you where you might not wish to be." He grimaced when she gave him a look heavily tainted with disgust.

It was just as she had suspected. Though not surprised, she was hurt, something she struggled to hide. She also felt deeply discouraged. Nothing she had said or done had really reached him. How could she tell such a man she loved him? He would never believe it. Not when he could even consider her leaving him for another man, following where the title and land led her. While he did believe she would not cuckold him, he clearly did not trust in the strength of their marriage. A part of him still thought she could not want him as her husband forever. She did not know how to overcome that.

"Thayer, have I not always been honest with you?" She ignored the little voice in her head that reminded her she still held a secret, still kept one truth from him.

"Aye. Painfully so at times."

"Well, then, if I had wanted to go with William, would I not have simply let it happen?

Perhaps said so, plain and clean? I probably would have mentioned the marriage contract myself." With the lessening of her anger, her weariness came to the fore and she yawned, unable to hide it from Thayer.

"How could you have mentioned it when you considered it mad, did not understand what we were talking of? Here, let me put Everard in his cradle." He carefully took the sleeping child up in his arms.

Watching her large, strong husband handle their child so well, so tenderly, made Gytha feel weak inside. He was going to be such a good father. She had seen it in how he treated Bek. He was the best man she could have found to entrust her children to. As she forced her mind back to the matter at hand, she hoped that knowledge would give her the strength to keep trying to prove to him that he was all she could ever want.

"If I had thought such idiocy would serve me, I would have thought of it."

Sitting on the edge of the bed, he took her hand in his again and half-smiled at her cross reply. She was right. When it concerned something necessary or wanted, Gytha showed more wit than any woman he knew. It had simply never occurred to her to go to William. She held firm to her vows, vows spoken to him, not to William. He brought her hand to his lips and kissed her palm, touched by the soft look in her eyes.

"Am I forgiven then, wife?"

"For being so stupid?" She decided that one secret she would never tell him was what he could do to her with those magnificent dark eyes of his.

"You should not call your husband stupid." He bit back a smile, knowing by her tone of voice that all was forgiven.

"Of course."

"Very disrespectful."

"I know."

"Am I forgiven then?"

"Aye, I forgive you for being so dim-witted."

He laughed and brushed a kiss over her mouth. "Get some rest. I will have Janet place our son in the next chamber. That way those who wish to see him will not disturb you. You need to sleep. Do not try to tell me otherwise. I can see the weariness in your face."

"I told you I would be fine, that you did not need to worry over me. T'was not as hard as I had thought it would be."

"You shall not make me believe it was easy."

"Oh, nay, not easy. Simply not as hard as I had thought." She yawned again, then smiled at Thayer. "Mayhap it was because I was so angry at you I forgot to worry about it. My thoughts were crowded with what I wished to say to you. You shall have to make me furious with you each time I give birth."

"Each time?" He laughed with a hint of surprise. "I should think another child would be far from your mind right now."

"Well, 'tis not too near. That is true enough.

But this has not frightened me into wishing to have no more. I do not mean to have so many children that I am old before my time, but I do hope God and"—she winked at Thayer—"my husband will allow me more than one child." She briefly squeezed his hand. "Which should tell you that I mean to linger with you, so mayhap you will cease to think I am about to walk away at every turn."

"And nothing could please me more, except mayhap," he murmured, pausing briefly to signal Janet to come in when she peeked into the room, "to give you back all that has been lost, all you deserve and should, by right, have."

Something about those last words struck Gytha as ominous. She had no chance to press him on the matter, however. He kissed her, gently ordering her to sleep, then saw to moving the baby to the next chamber. She promised herself that she would get an explanation the first chance she had. Instinct told her Thayer was getting some strange male idea in his head, one she would not like at all.

Thayer crouched by his new son's cradle and watched the baby sleep. Gytha had given him the greatest of gifts, yet he had nothing to offer her. But hours before she had borne his son, he had been returned to his landless, titleless state. It was no longer a tolerable one. Not only did Gytha deserve more, but so did his sons— so did whatever other children she blessed him with. Recently the king had hinted that some

reward other than honor was long overdue for
his service. Thayer decided it was past time to
stop murmuring thanks for such hints and
press for what they promised.

Chapter Seventeen

"You are leaving. Do not try to deny it again."

Gytha glared at her husband over her nursing son's head. She had seen the preparations despite his obvious attempts to hide them and to keep her confined to their chambers. Shifting slightly against the pillows he had set behind her back, she watched him closely, silently daring him to lie to her. He had neatly avoided the subject, sometimes even avoided her, but she could tolerate that no longer.

Thayer sighed and sat down on the side of the bed. Cowardly though it was, he had hoped to keep her ignorant of his plans until just before he rode off. He did not want to lie to her, but instinct told him not to tell her exactly why he was leaving. When he returned victorious with the rewards he sought would be time enough.

"I had hoped to keep you from worrying for as long as possible."

"And you did not think all this stealth would set me to thinking *and* worrying?"

"My hope had been that you would fail to notice."

"I began to notice something soon after my family and William left. 'Tis hard not to notice something when so many men ready themselves to ride off to battle. That is what they are doing, is it not? You leave soon to fight somewhere."

"Aye, to Scotland. Well, the north at least. The Scots are sorely troubling the area again."

"But you have already given the king your forty days' service. A year has not quite passed since then." Seeing that Everard was done feeding, she held him up to her shoulder and lightly rubbed his back.

"One cannot easily refuse a king's request." *Especially*, he mused silently, *when one has asked him to make it*.

"Well, mayhap not easily, but it has been done. A knight who has fought as often and as well for him as you have ought to be able to beg leave."

She knew, even as she spoke, that he was not one who would do that. If the king had claimed a need of Thayer's services, Thayer would dutifully provide them. She suspected the king knew that all too well.

"Nay, I cannot. Fighting men are too sorely needed. The Scots seem to think us their larder. They cannot be allowed to plunder our land freely and unpunished. That would leave us appearing weak and tempt them to act even more brazenly."

"I have not seen that punishing them does much to deter their brazen activities."

Neither had he, but he was not about to say so. To invoke the need of king and country was the only way he knew of to get her to accept his leaving, reluctant though that acceptance might be. She would never ask him to shirk his duty to his liege and England. He felt guilty about using such an underhanded method of ensuring her compliance but, for the moment, he deemed it a necessary subterfuge.

"The raids do not just bring the quick death dealt by a sword or arrow. They steal needed food and cause the slow, sad death of hunger. The North cannot afford to lose supplies."

"I know, I know." She sighed and eased Everard off her shoulder. "Your glutton of a son has fallen asleep. Would you set him in his cradle for me? Edna will not return until she sees you leave."

He obeyed her request without hesitation, gently taking the sleeping babe from her arms. She sagged against her pillows as she watched him settle Everard in his cradle, then return to sit on the edge of the bed. There were no more arguments she could offer to make him stay. To try would be to compromise his honor and sense of duty. That was not something she could do to Thayer.

When he took her hand in his and met her gaze, she studied him. There was not even the hint of reluctance in him, which disappointed but did not surprise her. She had married a warrior, a man who had spent most of his life wielding a sword. Presented with a chance to fight a just battle, he could not refuse.

It was the call of battle he harkened to. A part of her had hoped to dull the lure of that call, but clearly she had failed. He was known as a wild and glorious warior. She had foolishly wished to tame that part of him, to bring forth the gentle side he showed her and the children. Thayer was a man whose blood stirred now and again with the need for the dangerous thrill of battle. If the need was strong enough, she would only push him away from her by trying to hold him back. She had to hide her fear and worry and send him off without tears or condemnation.

"You want to go and show the Scots the fury of the Red Devil, aye?" She managed a faint smile.

"Well, as Roger says, we meet enough of their fierce, flame-haired warriors. Never hurts to show them we have one or two of our own."

"When do you leave?"

"In two days' time," he replied, inwardly grimacing over the cowardice that had kept him from telling her sooner.

"Two days?" she whispered, shock robbing

her voice of all strength. "But . . . so soon? Can you not delay it a few more days? A week?"

She could not believe he was going so soon. Worse, she could not think of how to explain why that troubled her as much as it did. In a week she would be considered healed enough from the birth to make love, something she ached for. Despite being his wife for over a year, she found it hard to say that clearly.

Thayer inwardly groaned. He knew exactly what she could not say. Little else had been on his mind. After three months of not being able to make love to her, it was torture to even think of leaving her before he could love her just once more. Knowing he could face death made it all the harder. He would do it, however, and not simply because the battle he rode for would not wait for him.

In Gytha's slim arms he could lose the strength to do what he had to do. She would never use the pleasure they shared to turn him to her will, but she could do so all unwittingly. To make love to her again would make him too painfully aware of all he risked losing. He did not dare take that chance.

"The Scots will not wait on me, dearling," he said in a quiet voice, making no effort to hide his honest regret.

"Curse the Scots."

"Many do." It was a weak attempt at teasing, but he was pleased to see it pull a faint smile from her. "I will not be gone very long." He lightly kissed her.

"How can you be certain of that?"

"These are raiders, not a war foray. They are coming to steal, not to fight. Oh, they will not shy from a battle, but 'tis not truly what they seek. Their main concern will be to get as much of their plunder back home as they can. Ours will be to reclaim all we can. Such things never take as long as a war."

Although she did not wholly agree, she did not argue. There was some comfort to be found in seeing the confrontation as he did. If all the Scots wanted was plunder, they would be less dangerous, more interested in escaping than fighting. She promised herself that, until Thayer returned, she would pray that the Scots he met were the most cowardly reivers who had ever lived.

"There is a chill in the wind. That babe should be inside. So should you."

Gytha spared a brief glance for a grumbling Edna before returning her full attention to Thayer. When she had stepped out of the keep, even Thayer had argued against it, but no one would deter her. She would watch Thayer ride off, as would his new son. Only briefly did she let herself think that it could be her last sight of him alive. He would come back to her. She had to believe that.

When Bek came over to kiss his new brother's cheek in farewell, then hers, she forced herself to smile and return his kiss. She wanted to keep him from going. He was just a boy. She kept that wish to herself. Bek was Thayer's page. It was all part of the boy's training to be a knight. She would only mortify the poor boy if she tried to keep him safe at Riverfall. As she watched him stride away, she mused a little sadly that it was good practice for her. Some day she would need the same restraint with Everard and whatever other sons God might bless her with.

Watching Thayer approach her, she prayed for the same strength she had shown in bidding Bek farewell.

"You should not remain out here too long, dearling," Thayer murmured as he stepped up beside her, slipping his arm about her shoulders.

"Humph." Edna shook her head. "There is no talking sense to her."

Ignoring her maid, Gytha managed a smile for Thayer. "We are well swaddled against the cold. Your son and I wish to bid you God's protection and a good journey. Especially," she added with some force, "a quick and safe return."

"Something I want too, sweet Gytha." He gave her a gentle kiss. "We shall send these Scots scurrying like frightened rabbits and return ere you can miss us."

"I doubt that. You shall not even reach Berwick ere that starts," she muttered, then frowned when he grinned at her. "I shall have to resort to putting heated rocks in the bed for warmth."

"As long as that is all you put in the bed," he teased, then kissed his wide-eyed child's forehead.

"And they would have to be very large rocks so that I could get the right sense of bulk," she continued.

"Bulk?" He tried to look offended and lightly poked his hard, flat stomach.

"Aye, bulk." She rested her cheek against his chest, slipping her arm around his waist, and edged closer to him. "You will take care, will you not?" It sounded weak, but she swore to herself it would be her only show of doubt or reluctance.

Careful not to press the baby too tightly between them, he briefly held her closer. It was pleasing to see that she was not as calm about his leaving as she had acted. For a moment he had thought she accepted his riding off to battle a little too well. While he did not want copious tears and wailing, teasing and smiles were a little unsettling as well.

When she glanced up at him, he studied her for a moment. As ever, looking at her brought an odd tightness in his chest. She was more beautiful than he knew how to describe, a few curls of her sun-kissed hair escaping her headdress, and her huge, lovely blue eyes soft with worry for him. Only a fool would leave her, he mused, and silently promised that he would do so as little as possible after this. He touched a soft kiss to her mouth, then stepped away.

"I will be as careful as any man can be, Gytha. You take care as well." He winked. "I expect you to be hale and well rested when I return."

She managed a smile, then stood quietly as she watched him leave. She kept her gaze fixed upon him until the heavy gates of Riverfall shut behind him. As she turned to go back inside, Margaret brushed by, hurrying up to her chambers. Gytha called to her cousin but was ignored. She sighed, realizing that Margaret was clearly as upset as she felt. As she returned to her own chambers, Gytha hoped Margaret shook her sorrow before too long. They would need to help each other keep up their spirits as they waited for their men to return.

"Where is Margaret?" Gytha demanded of Edna when the maid arrived in her chambers to take over the care of Everard.

"She has gone up on the walls again."

"This has gone on long enough. Where is my cloak?"

Hurrying to help Gytha wrap up against the chill night air, Edna murmured, "She is a new bride."

"I am hardly an old one. Edna, I do not mean to scold her. Well, not badly. But she wed a knight. She has to learn to accept these absences. She risks not only making herself ill but shaming Roger with her weakness."

"Aye, you are right. Just do not stay out in that cold, damp air too long."

Gytha nodded as she left the chambers, but

her thoughts were concentrated on Margaret. Thayer and Roger had been gone over a week now. She began to wonder if Roger's going off to battle was the only thing troubling her cousin. In the last day or two, she had begun to think Margaret was angry with her, was purposely avoiding her. No matter how often she told herself she was being foolish and that there was no reason for such a thing, Gytha could not shake the feeling.

She found Margaret on the wall staring off in the direction Roger had ridden. It was something she had done a time or two herself and would likely do again until Thayer came home. Margaret did it an unsettling number of times. She put her hand on Margaret's arm in a gesture of sympathetic understanding, only to have Margaret glance at her and edge away.

"Margaret, I know how you must miss Roger. I miss Thayer."

"Do you?"

Frowning not only at the question but at the angry tone of Margaret's voice, Gytha replied, "Of course I do. How can you ask such a thing?"

"It seems strange to me that you would claim to miss Thayer when you sent him off to battle."

"I sent him?" Gytha wondered if she had played the part of the brave wife a little too well.

"Aye. I would never have thought it of you, Gytha. I did not think you one to care about such things as titles and lands. After all, you have Riverfall and you appeared content. Neither did I think you one to care if your husband was a mere knight instead of a lord. Mayhap when one has always had such things, 'tis more sorely felt when they are taken away.

"But did you give no thought to me when you asked this of Thayer? You had to know Roger would ride at Thayer's side as he always does. 'Tis one thing to send your own husband into danger to gain you a title and demesne. But to send the man I love as well?" Margaret shook her head. "I never would have thought you so cruel, Gytha. So thoughtless."

Turning to look squarely at Gytha, Margaret frowned. Even in the dim light of a waning moon and the scattered torches, she could see the utter shock on Gytha's face. Margaret began to think she might have misunderstood something or misjudged her cousin badly. It was the possibility of the latter that truly troubled her.

It was a moment before Gytha could speak, then she whispered in a hoarse voice, "What are you saying?"

"Mayhap I was wrong. I should not worry on it."

Grasping her cousin by the arms, Gytha shook Margaret. "Repeat what you said, Margaret. Very clearly. Thayer said he went to fight the Scots because the king asked him to."

"Only after Thayer asked the king if there was anything that needed to be done."

"Thayer asked to be sent to fight?" Gytha spoke the words in a flat voice, trying to fully understand what she was being told.

"Aye. The king has long hinted that Thayer was past due some reward more than accolades and honor. Thayer asked to fight for that reward, for title and land. He had to get it for you, to give back what had to be returned to William."

"And he said I asked him to do this? He told Roger I had asked for it?"

"Well, nay, no one said that exactly." Margaret sighed, slumping against the parapets. "No one said it. 'Tis the way Roger told me. I could not believe Thayer would ride off to battle, put himself and all the rest at risk, for a reward he did not need. He had the land he had once sought. So I could only think that you had asked him for it or led him to believe you wanted it. Gytha, if I was wrong..."

"Of course you were wrong. Margaret," Gytha suddenly realized she was nearly screaming, drawing the curious interest of the guards, and lowered her voice. "Margaret, you know how I feel about Thayer. No matter what the prize, do you think I would risk him to gain it?"

"Nay, yet it seemed the only answer. He returned land and title to William without any sign of rancor. And if you did not press him for this, why should he go?"

"I have no idea, but I shall be sure to ask the fool, if I do not kill him first."

Seeing how furious Gytha was, Margaret sought to calm her. "He does it for you."

"I did not ask it, nor do I want it."

"Pride may push him. He may feel he needs to have such things or it will look as if he wed you for gain."

"That is the reason most marriages are arranged." She waved her hand to halt what Margaret was about to say. "Aye, pride may be a part of it." A sense of defeat stole some of the strength from her anger. "There is another reason. I know it. 'Tis what I have fought for months but cannot seem to conquer. I begin to see no hope of changing it."

"What is that?"

"I cannot seem to make him believe he is the man I want."

"But when you did not even try to go with William, he must have seen that."

"You would think so." Gytha shrugged. "Mayhap Thayer thought I but held to my vows."

"How can he doubt it when he knows you love him." Margaret frowned. "You have told him, have you not?"

"Nay, I have not. Do not scold me. I truly feel he would not believe me. I have tried everything I can to make him see that I want him, that I am content with him. Yet, and this nonsense proves it, he still feels that I must suffer some lack, as if I made some sacrifice in wedding him. As regards me and our marriage, he has no faith in his worth, and I do not know how to give it to him."

"Just love him, Gytha. That must reach him soon. He cannot remain blind to it forever."

Gytha had the sinking feeling that he could. "Sweet God, I wish he was home. I pray for it every night."

"As I do."

"Good. Perhaps our combined prayers will bear fruit and he, and Roger too, will ride back to Riverfall hale and whole. Then, I shall walk up to that great, stupid man I am married to and strangle him."

With his hand over his mount's nose to silence the animal, Thayer stared into the darkness. The Scots were out there. He could almost smell them. Some might slip by him or his men, but not all. Any other time he would simply let them run, for a great deal of their plunder had been retrieved. However, the king wanted blood, wanted the Scots to pay a high price for their raiding. Thayer felt enough had died, but his orders were to kill any he found on English soil, to search them out until none remained in England.

So, he thought crossly, he stood in the moist darkness listening for the enemy he could not see. The Scots were swift and stealthy, slipping from one place to another like spirits. He admired that skill even though he hated it. An acre fight, where armies faced each other across an open field in daylight, was much more to his liking.

What would be even more to his liking, he thought with a sigh, would be going home. He missed Gytha so much it was painful. He missed little Everard, watching him change daily as small babies did. It amused him a little, but he also missed Riverfall. What other men found mundane, tedious, in the day-to-day managing of a demesne he found interesting and comforting. He knew his days as a man who lived from battle to battle were over.

Deciding he had skulked in the dark long enough, he turned to mount. At that instant, a man charged from the shadows. Thayer barely managed to raise his sword in time to block the man's lethal strike. He staggered under the unanticipated force of the blow. Recovering slightly, he struck back.

As he fought, he cursed the noise they made. Every crash of swords, every grunt, every softly hissed curse echoed like some clarion call in the night. It marked his position to anyone who cared to listen. In an area creeping with foes, that was the last thing he wanted.

Killing the man brought him no real sense of victory. What little there was faded quickly when he heard a sound from behind. Even as he turned to meet what he knew was a second threat, an agonizing pain in the back of his left leg sent him tumbling to the ground. As swiftly as he could, he turned to meet his enemy even though he could not stand. His sword did not immediately respond to his pull on it so he was forced to meet the man's dagger attack with his left hand. Another swift shock of pain tore through him as the dagger blade cut into his fingers. He was, however, able to swing his sword up in time to stop the man's sword thrust, killing him with one clean strike.

Shoving the body aside was difficult. Thayer knew he was fast losing his strength. One attempt to stand was all it took to tell him his wounded leg was useless. He tried to crawl towards his mount but barely got halfway to the nervous animal before he could go no farther. He thought of Gytha as unconsciousness swept over him.

Roger cursed as he stumbled through the bracken, Merlion and Torr behind him. "I tell you, I heard the sounds of a battle over here."

"How can you tell which direction they came from in the dark?" grumbled Torr.

"Listen," hissed Merlion. "Hear that?"

"A horse," whispered Roger. "Just ahead." He continued with greater caution until he recognized Thayer's mount. " 'Tis his horse for certain." Two more steps brought Thayer's prone body into view. "Jesu." He hurried over and knelt by his friend, quickly searching for some sign of life as Torr and Merlion joined him.

"Is he still alive?" Merlion asked after a long moment of tense silence.

"Aye, but he will not be for long if we do not bind these wounds." With his companions's swift help, Roger moved to do that even as he spoke. "God's beard, he is a bit shorter of fingers now," he muttered as he used a strip of Torr's hastily torn shirt to roughly bandage Thayer's wounded hand.

"We had best get him to the leech in town," muttered Merlion as he and Torr struggled to securely bind the gash in Thayer's leg.

"The man has lost too much blood. He needs no more drawn out," Roger snapped. "That old woman that tended some of the men yester eve would be better."

The three of them managed to get Thayer on his horse, holding him in the saddle as they led the mount towards town. It was a long, slow journey, and Roger feared it cost Thayer dearly in strength and lost blood. By the time they reached the cottage they used as their quarters, Roger doubted his friend would live to see Riverfall again.

Thayer was aware of only pain for a long while. Then he heard a soft snoring. His eyes still closed, he moved his hands in a blind exploration of his immediate surroundings. He was on a bed. Someone had found him. Hazy memories assailed him. Roger's voice, cool cloths against his skin, a priest muttering and—he frowned—the king. Curiosity as to how much was dream, how much real, gave him the strength to open his eyes. It took a moment for him to conquer the adverse effects of the sudden light, but he was not surprised when his first clear sight showed him Roger sprawled on a pallet by his bed.

"Roger." His voice was a weak hoarse whisper, and it hurt his throat but he forced himself to call out louder. "Roger." He almost smiled at the way Roger groggily staggered to his feet, sword in hand, looking blindly around until his gaze fixed upon him. "You wake up poorly for a soldier."

Hearing the painful dryness in Thayer's voice, Roger quickly got his friend some mead. Slipping his arm beneath Thayer's shoulders, Roger helped him raise his head enough to drink without choking. He could feel the weakness afflicting Thayer as he eased the man back down on the bed and it troubled him. The wounds and resultant fever had badly sapped Thayer's strength.

"That was very welcome," Thayer murmured as Roger fetched a stool and sat at his bedside. "God's beard, I feel so weak. How long have I been lying here?"

"Near to a week. You were nearly bled dry when we found you. I had that old woman tend you."

"Aye, aye. I remember her. Better her than some leech. That ugly crone has thrice any leech's healing skills." He frowned down at his bandage-swathed left hand. "How bad is this?"

"Well, two of your fingers are a bit shorter. The tops were severed."

"And my leg?"

Sighing, Roger shrugged. "You still have it. The wound was deep. The man tried to hobble you."

"And he succeeded."

"Mayhap. There is no way to tell until you try walking. T'will be stiff for certain, but none can guess if that stiffness will linger or ease away as you walk again. As I have said, you still have it. There is that to be thankful for."

Thayer was not so sure of that, but pushed the concern aside for a moment. "Any further injuries?"

"A few new scars, but no more than you usually gain from a battle."

Not wanting to think too much on his injuries, Thayer decided to confirm some of the broken, indistinct memories that assailed him. "And, you, my friend, have had the sorry duty of tending me? You loom large in what few memories I have."

"T'was not a sorry chore. You have done the same for me. Do not forget that time in France."

"A time I doubt I shall ever fully forget. The king? Did the king come to see me or do I muddle a dream with a memory?"

"Aye, the king was here. For a moment, I thought you had shaken free of the fever and delirium. You spoke clearly to our liege, but 'tis good he left when he did. He was but a moment gone before I knew you were not as clearheaded as you sounded. What you said next told me your thoughts were locked in the past, a time three years ago when he came to our tent. You spoke to a ghost born of a feverish memory. No matter. Our liege did not see it. He gave you the reward you sought, and you responded as was expected."

"I got what I came here for?"

"Aye, you are now Baron of Riverfall, m'lord." Roger smiled faintly and half-bowed. "You are also the holder of a small demesne but three days' ride south of Riverfall. I can tell you more when you are stronger. This is the first time in too long that you have not been wracked with fever. Do not tire yourself and use up what little strength you have. You will sorely need it in the days to come. The fighting has ended, you have all you sought, and now you must work to get well enough to return to Riverfall and Gytha."

"Ah, Gytha." Thayer sighed and stared at his bandaged hand. "I was no fair knight before but at least I was whole. Now I bring her a cripple. Mayhap it would be best if—"

Cursing softly but viciously, Robert stood up so abruptly he sent the stool skittering across the dirt floor. "If you say it would be best to stay away from her now, I shall add to your wounds. By God's sweet grace, half your fevered ramblings were cries for Gytha. She is such a part of you, you could not even shed her in your pain. Do you truly believe you could turn away from her, set her from your life now when you have all you think she wants?"

"I may now have what her good birth demands, but look at me. My hand is mutilated and I shall limp. The one thing I had to offer of myself was a strong, whole body. No longer. The rest of me is now as lacking in beauty as my face."

Leaning over Thayer, Roger snapped, "At times, my friend, you are the greatest of fools. You belabor your lack of fine looks but do not look to see how others may view you. You seem to think Gytha is troubled by your lack of beauty, but have you ever looked closely enough at her to judge the truth of that belief? I think, if you did, you would see how wrong you are."

"Do you try to tell me a beauty like Gytha could love a huge, red, and well-scarred man?"

Straightening up, Roger shrugged. "I do not know how deep her feelings run. What I am sure of is that she does not see you as you persist in thinking she does. Have you ever seen a look of disappointment or dislike in her gaze when she looks at you? I wager not, not even when she was first presented with you as her husband. Has she ever shied from letting all know you are her wedded man? Nay. The woman has stood firm at your side with no show of reluctance."

"Aye, she has," Thayer murmured, realizing all Roger said was true and feeling a strong lifting of his spirits. "You are right. I never looked closely at how she was looking at me. Well do I know the look you mean, for I have seen it often enough, especially in the eyes of women."

"But never in your wife's."

"Nay, never in Gytha's." He started to smile, but a glance at his marred hand made him frown. "Of course, that was before I suffered these wounds. This might be more than she can endure."

"You had some startling scars before this. I would be most surprised if she was repulsed."

Thayer considered that for a moment, then half-smiled. Roger was right again. It was an exhilarating revelation. He had been unfair to Gytha, insulted her in a way. Search his mind as he would, he could find no time when she had shown any disappointment or dislike of his appearance. It simply did not matter to her. Then he recalled the time she had flattered him for his eyes and his form and had no doubts left that Roger spoke the full truth.

"Nay, she will not be repulsed." He then thought of why he was there and grimaced. "Howbeit, when she discovers why I came here, what I did this for, she will probably be furious with me."

"Ah, well, for once, my friend, I believe you judge your fair wife exactly right."

Chapter Eighteen

"They are back! The men have returned!"

Gytha barely spared a glance for Edna when the young maid burst into her room shouting the news. It was somthing she already knew. She had seen the approach of Thayer and his men from the walls of Riverfall. It did not surprise her that Thayer had sent no one ahead to announce his arrival. He probably thought the brief message he had sent nearly a month ago enough, even though it left the date of his return extremely vague.

She suspected guilt played some part in his manner of return. He might think she already knew of the real reasons he had gone to fight the Scots. If not, he would be contemplating the need to tell her or the possibility that she would guess it. Either situation could be eased for him, if only slightly, by the tactic of surprise. She had every intention of taking that tactic from him and using it against him.

Edna edged closer to where Gytha sat calmly brushing her hair. "M'lady, I said your husband has returned."

"I heard you."

"Are you not going to greet him?"

"Oh, aye, soon. Have baths readied for the men. You may place Thayer's in with Roger's, in Roger's chambers. Nay, wait. Margaret will be there. Set Thayer's bath here. I will move to the ladies' bower to ready myself for the welcome feast."

"But they will soon be riding into the bailey...."

"Aye, so you had best hurry. You need to help with preparing Thayer's bath and getting my things to the ladies' bower."

Ignoring Edna's muttering, Gytha collected what she would need to prepare herself for the feast the servants were rushing to prepare. Not greeting Thayer in the bailey or in their chambers would tell him more clearly than words that she was furious with him. He could easily guess why, even if Margaret did not tell him. The surprise would be in when she would confront him and how. She hoped he did a lot of squirming.

Thayer sighed heavily as he watched Margaret and Roger embrace while he stood with his arms empty, Gytha nowhere in sight. A sudden thrill of alarm went through him. While

it could be that she was angry, it could also be
that she was not at Riverfall at all. The moment Roger eased his hold on Margaret,
Thayer grasped the time to speak to her.

"Where is Gytha?" He did not feel very com-
forted by the nervous, reluctant look on Margaret's face.

"Inside," Margaret answered in a weak voice
as she got a good look at Thayer and the result
of his now healed wounds.

"She is still here?" Margaret nodded. "She
is not ill?" Margaret shook her head. "Nor is
my son?" She shook her head again. "So that
leaves angry. Little else could say it clearer.
She must have found out the truth," he muttered and saw Margaret blush, confirming that
guess. "Do not look so guilty. I did mean to
tell her the truth."

"Oh. Well, that should soothe her."

The lack of conviction in Margaret's voice
nearly made him laugh. He slung his arm
about Bek's shoulders and headed for his
chambers. It did not surprise him to find Gytha
gone from there as well, although a hot bath
awaited him. She was choosing her time. He
could not help but worry about just how angry
she was.

As a silent Bek helped him prepare for his
bath, Thayer briefly considered exerting his
authority as her husband and ordering Gytha
to face him—now. He quickly discarded that
idea. Gytha did not get angry that often, but
although he was not yet sure how to approach

her when she was, he knew that ordering her about was not the way.

"Have you made Gytha mad again?" Bek asked as his father stepped into his bath.

"Aye, I fear so."

"But you went to win rewards for her."

"True, but I neglected to ask if she wanted those rewards. Can you scrub my back, son?"

Moving to do so, Bek frowned in thought. "Is a wife not supposed to be pleased at all her husband does?"

It was not easy, but Thayer swallowed his impulse to laugh. "Bek, I will tell you two things about women. Heed me well, now, for you had best remember them. The first is—never do as I do. I fear your poor father knows very little. If I handled a sword as I do women, I should have been killed in my first battle." He smiled faintly when Bek giggled. "Second—few men are true masters over their women. In truth, I would eye with suspicion any woman who acts as if that is the truth. Either she lies, or she is so dull-witted or weak-spirited that she will make you a tedious wife."

"So you do not really mind that Gytha is angry with you."

"I did not say that." He grimaced. "T'will depend upon how angry she is and if there is any soothing her."

He was still wondering about that as he entered the great hall. There was no sign of Gytha there either. It was beginning to embarrass him. He did not need to look at those gathered in the hall to know they were all trying to covertly watch him or catch some sight of his missing wife. Even as he sat down at the head table, he gave serious thought to finding her and dragging her down to the great hall. She could be as angry as she wished, but she should not make him look foolish before his people. He was just standing up to go and find her when she walked in. Thayer suddenly wished he was sitting down.

Gytha walked towards the head table, her step slowing as she looked closely at her husband. There was something not quite right about his stance. It took her a moment to understand what was different. She stopped by his seat and stared at his legs. He was holding the left one in a very stiff manner. It was now clear to her that he had received some serious wound.

Slowly, she looked him over, moving her gaze up from his leg. She felt her eyes widen with the shock she suffered when she saw his left hand. The tips were gone from two of his fingers. Clenching her hands into fists, she forced her gaze to continue upwards. She felt a brief flare of relief when she found no other signs of serious injury, but her relief did little to stem her rising anger.

He had sent her no word at all. She knew he had been seriously hurt, but no one had told her how seriously. For all she knew, he could have been near death. All her worries had been justified. When she met his gaze, she was not really surprised to find him eyeing her warily. She suspected she looked as furious as she felt, for she had no will to hide it.

"So, did you gain all you sought in battling these Scottish reivers?" she hissed.

"Aye. I am now a baron, Lord of Riverfall." He did feel some pride in his title, but he could see it would be a while before Gytha shared that.

"What? No land?"

"A small demesne a few days' ride south of here."

"How fortuitous. You need not ride far and long to play the great liege."

"Now, Gytha, I felt it necessary to do this for you."

He knew that was the wrong thing to say the moment the words were out of his mouth but decided to stay with that argument. It was, in part, true. During his time of healing, he had come to realize that he had gone after those rewards for himself more than for her. Pride had spurred him. It was not something he felt inclined to admit before all those so avidly listening.

"For me? I did not ask for these things. I did not ask you to ride off and get yourself all cut up."

"Nay, you did not ask it of me. I chose to do that. Howbeit, a woman of your high birth should be wed to better than a knight. So I went to gain a title."

"Did you. And what happens when you decide that what you have now is not enough? To become a baron you gave your fingers. What shall you give for a—an earldom? An arm? Aye, mayhap you shall take it into your head to gain a long trail of titles as some men have. I may have to tow what is left of you about in a wee cart, but I can proudly say you are the lord of this, and the baron of that, and the earl of somewhere else. There will be a comfort for me."

She was working herself into a fine state, Thayer mused. It did not surprise him to see his men staring at her in open-mouthed wonder. He felt inclined to do the same. She was far angrier than he could have imagined. He wanted to calm her, to soothe her, but he was not sure how. It was hard when he was not sure why she was as angry as she was.

Gytha felt as if she were being torn apart. She wished to weep over his wounds and scream at him for marring his fine body for what she felt were useless trappings. Although she wished to rail at him for his stupidity, she also wished to flee, to go somewhere to try and sort out her tormented feelings.

"Why do you do these things to me?" she asked him in a softer tone, helplessness tinging her voice. "What have I done to make you think I care about such things as titles and lands? What have I done to make you think I should value such things above your life? Everything I have done or said should have told you otherwise, but you are blind to it all.

"I do not care if you are a baron or a black-smith. I do not care if you hold the finest de-mesne in all of England or live in a hovel. I want you—not riches."

Thayer was deeply moved. There was a great deal of emotion behind her words. He wanted to see just how deep and rich those emotions were, but that was something better done in private. That there were so many listening av-idly to this exchange made him all too aware of how personal it was becoming. He began to feel a little awkward.

"Well, that is very nice, Gytha."

"Very nice?" She could not believe he would greet words that had spilled from her very soul so blandly. "Nice." Briefly looking up as if to seek divine help, she held her hands out to her sides in a gesture displaying her confusion. "I may as well speak to the moon. T'will under-stand me as well as you do. My wits certainly have gone a-begging. 'Tis the only explanation for why I should love you more than my very life when you are the stupidest man in all of England."

The astounded look on his face ended her tirade. She cursed, then lifting her skirts slightly, hurried out of the hall. Her emotions were in such a sad tangle that she was close to tears. The very last thing she wished to do was start weeping before Thayer and the oth-ers. As she raced towards the shelter of her chambers, she briefly wondered if he would follow her, but she was mostly concerned with

Beauty & The Beast

getting out of sight before all the emotion boiling inside of her broke free in a display she had no wish to show anyone.

For a long moment, Thayer simply gaped after Gytha. Then he became aware of a low murmur of voices and realized that everyone in the crowded hall was watching him and discussing what they had witnessed. His lovely wife had just confessed to loving him before everyone at Riverfall. He could only partly suppress a wide grin. Such words should be private, but he could feel no regret over her rather loud confession before so many. If he ever doubted what he had heard there would be a great many witnesses he could ask for reassuring confirmation. Pride also made it hard to regret having so many know that he—plain, red Thayer Saitun—had won the heart of such a beautiful woman.

"Well?" pressed Roger, who sprawled comfortably in the seat at Thayer's side.

Looking at Roger and briefly noticing the wide-eyed Margaret at his friend's side, Thayer murmured, "Well what?"

"Are you not going to go after her?"

Glancing down at the food on the table, Thayer said, "Can I not eat first?" He grinned when Margaret gasped and Roger laughed. "I suppose I should go and scold her once again for being so disrespectful as to call her lawful husband stupid."

"Oh, aye, that is important. If you do not get going, there are one or two here who may start to agree with her appallingly impertinent remark."

Since Margaret was beginning to look as if she wanted to strike one or both of them, Thayer started on his way. Going up the stairs showed him, yet again, that his left leg was awkwardly stiff, but for once he did not care. His Gytha had given him far too much to feel joyous about.

As he opened the door to their chambers, he heard her weeping. She wept as if her heart would break and it very nearly had him weeping as well. Closing the door, he moved towards the bed where she lay sprawled on her stomach, her face pressed into the pillow. Sitting on the edge of the bed, he pried open the fingers of her clenched hand and pressed his handkerchief into it. He wanted to take her into his arms, but after so many months of deprivation, he suspected he would not long think of simply consoling her.

"Gytha . . ." He smoothed his hand over her hair. "Please do not weep so. I cannot bear it. Better that you rail at me or treat me as some guest as you did before. For all I hate that, it tears at me far less than this does."

She could hear the truth of those soft words in his voice. Rolling onto her back, she used his handkerchief to clean her face, vainly struggling to stop her tears. Although it had tired her, her weeping had eased the turmoil within her a little. She just wished she was not left with such a feeling of loss, of failure.

Sighing, Thayer ran a hand through his hair. "Gytha, I say I went after those rewards for you, but 'tis because *I* wanted to. *I* wanted these things for you. The reason I did not tell you the full truth was because I knew you would not want me to fight for such things and would try and stop me."

"Aye, I would have. I did not because I thought t'was a matter of honor and loyalty."

"Instead, t'was pride. Little else. I wished to have what was returned to William. In my heart I knew you did not care, but *I* did. I did not want you to have lost anything by remaining wed to me. That had more importance to me than I wished to admit. I faced the truth of it as I was healing from my wounds."

"Which you told me nothing of. You should have sent for me."

Reaching out, he gently brushed a few stray wisps of hair from her face. "Nay. The journey there was long and dangerous. The town and all about it was also dangerous. There was a very skilled old woman who tended me, as did Roger. He and I have had many years of tending each other's wounds. We are not without some skill ourselves." He realized he was now stroking her face.

Gytha felt the need in his touch, read it in his dark eyes, and responded to it. "Just how badly were you wounded? You could have been near death, and I would have known nothing of it until too late."

"Oh, nay, I was not near death." He found

it impossible to keep his gaze from her breasts or her slim legs, revealed up to the knee by her tangled skirts.

"You are a poor liar." When he slid his hand up her leg to her thigh, she shuddered and knew that they would have to feed the hunger that gnawed at them before they could have any real, sensible discussion.

"Tsk. First you call me stupid, now a liar," he murmured and bent to place a kiss upon the rapid pulse in her throat. "Gytha."

She sighed as her whole being responded to the aching want in his voice. "I know." She consoled the part of her that felt she was giving in too easily by telling herself that he had adequately explained his reasons for going to fight the Scots.

His whole body taut with need, even though he had barely touched her, he sat up and gave her a crooked smile. "How fast can you remove that gown?"

"I shall be ready ere you are."

It did not really surprise her to lose that challenge. If there was anything Thayer could do with greater speed than any other, it was shed his clothes, she mused happily as her now naked husband turned to help her discard her chemise and hose. He then fell upon her with a hunger she welcomed, clearing all thought from her mind save that of giving and getting pleasure. Their loving was fierce and swift, leaving them both weak with satisfaction and short of breath.

It took Gytha a moment before she realized that Thayer had held on to enough sanity to press her to speak during the height of their somewhat frantic coupling. Another moment or two passed as she fought to recall what he had been saying and, more important, what she had replied. When the memory became clear, she nearly struck him.

He had pried a declaration of love from her. Clearly, her admission in the hall had not gone unnoticed as she had hoped it would. Catching her at a weak moment, he had gotten her to admit it again yet had offered no declaration of his own. That both hurt and annoyed her. If he thought to have her repeat it at his convenience to stroke his vanity, he would have to think again. She briefly thought of pushing him off her but told herself she was too tired. She ignored the inner voice that whispered she was a liar, that she held him close because she craved the unity of their bodies, needed it badly after being so long apart from him.

When Thayer finally found the strength to ease the intimacy of their embrace, he cursed the stiffness in his leg which caused his movements to be slightly awkward. He quickly moved to pull the coverlet over them but was not quick enough. Gytha grasped his wrist to stop him, her gaze fixed upon the ragged new scar on his leg. He sighed when she slowly grew very pale.

"I know, 'tis an ugly thing...." he began.

"That is not what pains me, though aye, 'tis

not pretty." She stared at him, fighting to shake the fear-soaked horror that gripped her so tightly. "God's beard, Thayer, the man nearly cut your leg clean off at the knee."

" 'Tis not quite that bad," he murmured as he tugged her into his arms and pulled the coverlet over them. "T'was a deep cut, but not enough to make me lose my leg unless infection set in. Which," he said, kissing her frowning mouth, "it did not. I had a fever for a while but fought it off. It took me a long time to return here, for I was stubborn. I wished to be fully returned to health, to walk without aid or too much awkwardness."

"You have done that well enough." She knew he smoothed over the truth of his illness, but decided not to press him on the matter.

"Have I?" He grimaced. " 'Tis still very stiff."

"Aye, but there is little awkwardness. I should have been there to help you."

"Nay, you would have simply worried yourself ill." He smiled faintly. "Seeing as you care for me so much."

He glanced down to catch her eyeing him warily and with a hint of annoyance. It was a little mean to keep pulling the words from her, but he could not help himself. They were words he doubted he would ever hear often enough to satisfy his need for them. In them rested not only all his happiness but comfort and a feeling of security. She was his, all his.

"You believe me." She was a little surprised

at how quickly he had accepted her declaration.

"Aye. Should I not?"

"I doubted you would. Why do you believe me?" When he frowned at her, making no secret of his puzzlement, she sighed. "I need to know. I must have done something right for you to heed that declaration when you have so stubbornly refused to heed most everything else I have said."

"Well, you screamed it at me."

"I did not scream," she muttered, knowing full well that she had.

Ignoring that, he continued, "You were furious. The words just tumbled out of you. Such a thing, a confession made without prodding and so impulsively, holds the strength of truth. And you are not one to lie or use such words for gain. Have you held back the words because you thought I would not believe you?"

"And would you have before now?"

"Aye." He frowned, then sighed. "Nay, mayhap not."

"I thought not. Little else I have tried to show you or tell you seemed to have been heeded."

"Gytha," he kissed her forehead and held her close, "you are so beautiful and perfect."

"Perfect?" She peeked up at him in disbelief. "Perfect? Hah! Does a perfect wife refuse to greet her husband when he arrives home after months away at some battle? Does she leave him to seek his meal alone? I did that out of angry spite, you know. 'Tis hardly how a good wife should act. I wanted you to worry over how angry I was and maybe sting your pride some."

"I know. You did that," he said with perfect calm.

"You are most forgiving."

"Nay, not truly. I gave serious thought to coming after you and dragging you down to the hall, but I felt that would only make you angrier at me."

"Aye." she smiled and cuddled up to him. "It would have."

"Then 'tis good you came down to the hall when you did, for I was standing up to do just that." He smiled when she laughed softly, then combed his fingers through her thick hair, pleasured by the feel of it. "So, you are not perfect except in my eyes. Nay, truly," he added when she made a soft scoffing noise. "Faults and all. That is what makes you perfect to me, for me. You are Gytha—no shadows, no lies, no deceiving twists and turns. You *do* have a lot of twists and turns, but they are just part of you."

"Are you trying to say 'tis my fault I have been unable to make you understand anything I have tried to tell you, silently or elsewise?"

"Nay, dearling. I did not trust myself to judge correctly. What I feared was deceiving myself by hearing what I wished to or seeing what was not there. I made myself accept only what could not be questioned, what did not need to be considered or guessed at. Like the passion we share. I could clearly see the truth of that, could feel it. Surprise me though it did, I knew it for a fact." He grimaced as he glanced at her. "Am I being clear or is this all coming out as a muddle?"

"Very clear." She brushed a quick kiss over his cheek. "I understand. You were wary. You had learned to be."

"True, but it was unfair to treat you so warily."

"Mayhap. But, 'tis also not wise to ignore a lesson well learned."

He shrugged and idly moved his hand up and down her side. "You are so beautiful." He heard her cluck her tongue in annoyance and smiled at her. "You cannot tell me you are not beautiful."

"To say I am sounds vain."

"You are not vain simply because you recognize the truth."

Leaning away from him, she studied his face. "The truth as others see it. Since the day I first understood words, I have heard that I am beautiful. All I met seem to think it, so I must be. I see only me, only Gytha. I see flesh, bone, and hair that God has seen fit to arrange in a manner pleasing to the eye—for now. Age can steal it away. Sickness can mar it. So much can end it. T'would be a sorry thing to put all my faith and hope in. There are many more important and lasting things to reach for and hold on to—although I am glad for it in that it pleases you."

"Pleases me? Aye, though at first it terrified me. When I first set eyes upon you, I felt as if a hand had reached inside me to curl around my heart and squeeze it. I feel that grip each time I look at you."

He gently traced the delicate lines of her face with his fingers. "Ah, Gytha, can you blame this poor man for wondering how he could hold on to such a prize? Every morning I wake up to find you curled up in my arms, I wonder if I am but dreaming. 'Tis the same feeling I have when you warm to my touch. I feel as if, somehow, some great mistake has been made and that at any moment someone will come to rectify it, to take you away."

Touched by all he was telling her, she nevertheless remained fixed upon one thing he had said that had startled her. "You were terrified of me?" She sat up to stare at him in disbelief.

"Aye." Lying fully on his back, he kept one arm tucked around her waist.

"But I am just a woman. A tiny woman."

"Gytha, you could wound me more deeply with a word than could any man with sword, arrow, or mace."

Thayer was a little surprised to find her staring at him in astonishment. He had not said anything particularly shocking or revealing. His weakness there was painfully clear to all. He was certain of it. Pickney had definitely seen it.

"You love me." Even as she blurted out the words, Gytha felt a shiver of fear that she was wrong.

"Of course I do." He caught her when she flung herself into his arms, then frowned as he felt a slight dampness where her face pressed against his chest. "God's sweet grace, Gytha, do not cry."

"I am not crying," she lied as she tried to hug him using her whole body. "So I did finally reach your heart. I was feeling so defeated because it appeared as if I never would and I had no more ideas on how to do it."

"Surely you knew." He suddenly realized that she had been suffering the same uncertainty he had and wrapped his arms more tightly around her.

"And would you have known how I felt if I had not told you?"

"Nay. I needed the words. You know," he murmured, "the ones you screamed at me in the hall?"

"Oh? That you are the stupidest man in all of England?" When he laughed, she smiled at him and slipped her arms around his neck. "I love you, Thayer Bek Saitun. I love you, m'lord, my husband, my life." She decided she would have to say it often, for it made his fine eyes darken and soften in a way that warmed her as no fire ever could.

"And I love you," he murmured, cupping her face in his hands and tugging her mouth to his.

Even after the kiss ended, it was a long while

before Gytha could speak. She felt choked with emotion. The truth of his declaration had been fully conveyed by that tender kiss. She decided that this moment was worth every minute of doubt, fear, and defeat she had suffered through. Curled up in his arms, her head resting upon his hard chest, she listened to the steady beat of his heart and knew she had never felt so content, so at peace.

"When did you know?" she asked as curiosity crept through her sense of quiet contentment.

"I think I saw my fate the moment I set eyes upon you."

"But when did you *know*?" she pressed, moving slightly so that she could comfortably watch him as he answered.

"When Pickney took you. I was like a madman. I could not even do what I had always done so well before—fight my enemy. Never have I felt so afraid. Oh, I knew you were vital to me before that, but I stoutly refused to see why." He brushed a kiss over her forehead. "After that I was forever trying to decide if or when I should tell you. When you gave me our son . . ." He frowned, lifted his head a little, and looked around the room. "Where *is* Everard?"

"With the women in the ladies' bower. You shall see him soon. This is our time. He has more than enough of my time each and every day."

"Aye." He settled back down. "Having been away, I forgot how much he can demand of you. I can recall feeling jealous at times. And, tell me, sweet wife, when did you know you loved me?"

"I knew from the very start that this was right."

"Right?"

"Aye. Right. When you were presented as the Saitun I was to wed, I felt only a sense of rightness, that this was how it must be."

"You did not feel right with William or Robert?"

"Nay. With William I accepted. He was handsome and amiable. With Robert? Well, I fear I was disappointed, for the only real feeling I had was the urge to cuff him as everyone else did." She smiled faintly when he chuckled. "But with you, I had no qualms, felt no hesitation.

"As for when I actually *knew* I loved you? Well, that was when you were wounded on our journey here. I had given a lot of thought to how I felt, but that was when I was really sure. That was when I began to wonder how to make you believe in me and get at least some feeling from you." Laughing softly as she settled herself in his arms, she murmured, "Feelings aside from passion that is. I had no trouble getting that from you or giving it."

"Mayhap we both tried too hard not to put too much faith in what that passion signified. I begin to think," he whispered as he nibbled her ear, "that the sudden, strong desire we felt for each other was a sign we should have read with much more care."

"Mmmmm." She closed her eyes, enjoying the feel of desire's warmth stealing through her veins as he covered her throat with soft, warm kisses. Sliding her hand down his leg, she brushed the edge of his new, ragged scar with her fingertips and frowned slightly. "Thayer? Will this injury add more danger when you go off to battle?"

"This injury will probably allow me to elude most battles in the future." He rolled so that she was beneath him and kissed the tip of her nose.

Although delighted, she wondered if she was foolish to feel so. Thayer was a warrior. It could soon eat at him to know he could no longer freely answer any call to battle. He could well find it bitter to become a man of property only.

"But you could fight well if you felt the need to go? If the lure of battle tugged at you again?"

"Well enough, but battle holds no lure for me now."

"You need not say that just to please me or still my fears."

"I do not say it to please you, though I am glad it does. When I faced the Scots, there was no thrill, no desire for it any longer. All I wanted was to be done with it and come back to Riverfall. It was a just cause with the chance of a fine reward, yet I did not even feel a sense of victory when it was done."

Twining her arms about his neck, she smiled with a relief she could not hide. "Has being a man of property tamed the Red Devil then?"

"Nay, a tiny angel with huge blue eyes has. The Red Devil is no more."

"Well, I should not wish him to disappear from all places. Nor do I wish him to become too tame."

"Oh? And where should you like this wild Red Devil to remain?"

"Here. In our bed. Mayhap one or two other places I have yet to think of. Right here—loving me."

"I think I can pull him forth for that. Even a wild devil like him could not tire of loving and being loved by such an angel."

"Even if he must do so forever? For that is what she demands."

"Forever, my heart, just might not be long enough."

Special Sneak Preview!

By Shirl Henke

**Winner of *Romantic Times* Reviewers' Choice Award
for Best Indian Romance**

**Shirl Henke writes "historical romance at its best!"
—*Romantic Times***

**Enjoy a selection from Shirl Henke's fabulous new
bestseller, the historical romance that's bursting with
love and adventure!**

*On Sale In October
At Booksellers Everywhere*

Kyle grinned cryptically. "Jist cool down. Yew'll find out soon 'nough."

Pueblo

Cass crumpled the telegram in a ball and threw it in a corner. She let out a volley of oaths damning Bennett Ames by several rather ingenious methods. Two more shipments of expensive mining supplies lost over the side of a mountain. Sabotage! It was costing her money to sit here in Pueblo waiting for Kyle. He'd been gone nearly a month. Every chance of breaking the will had been exhausted, and she was running out of time. "Please let him bring me a man," she murmured to herself.

Hearing hoofbeats outside, Cass thought it was Chris Alders, back from his latest stock purchasing trip in Arizona. The Pueblo place, located at a convenient midway point in the territory, was their main road ranch, or livestock supply center. Clayton Freighting owned over one hundred thousand oxen and mules to pull its wagons from the heights of the western mountains all the way south to the Arizona army posts. From the San Luis Valley's agricultural centers to the Wyoming border where the Union Pacific Railroad needed supplies, Cass ran her wagons. Denver housed her main business office, but Pueblo was where the livestock was wintered over and new mules and oxen were broken and trained.

Pueblo was also isolated and small, a good place for meeting her doubtlessly reluctant bridegroom. When she opened the front door and stepped onto the porch, she recognized Kyle riding in with a stranger. Her heart began to pound, and she gritted her teeth in self-loathing at the fear knotting her belly. She must let him get a child on her, but only if he passed muster, she resolutely assured herself.

Setting her mind to put on a show of bravado, she stepped down from the porch to meet her fate. "You've handled barrooms full of drunken mule-skinners. You can handle one man," she gritted out beneath her breath.

Steve was baffled by his introduction to Miss Cassandra Clayton. She had inspected him like he was one of the Loring racing stable's most expensive studs, then dismissed him as if he were a down-on-his-luck drifter riding the grub line. Even as Hunnicut untied his hands, Steve suspected his deliverance into this nest of unreconstructed rebels might not be such a blessing after all. He decided to get the lay of the land as quickly as possible.

As they walked toward the long log building at the far side of the maze of corrals, Steve looked over the road ranch. Clayton Freighting was one hell of a big operation. That much was clear, even to his untrained Easterner's eyes. Cassandra Clayton must be one rich young woman, he mused.

Anxious to defuse the tense confrontation between Cass and Loring, Kyle began to explain the operations of her Rocky Mountains freight empire and how she had made it prosper since her father's untimely stroke and subsequent death.

Steve shook his head as he considered the foul-mouthed, hard-drinking teamsters he'd met in his travels west. Hard, dirty, and dangerous were the kindest terms that could be used to describe them, and she worked side by side with such men on the road. They respected her as their boss!

He considered his own appearance, then grinned. He no doubt looked as bad as the worst of them. It might be interesting to take Cass Clayton's measure. He decided to play the role of desperado to the hilt. Treat him like some damn gelding, would she!

While Steve soaked away his prison grime in a tub of hot water and shaved three weeks' worth of beard off his face, Kyle posted guards from among his own hand-picked men to watch the prospective bridegroom. Lober, one of his men, was roughly Steve's size and agreed to lend a pair of dress pants and boots to the mysterious stranger, as well as a clean shirt. Besides Kyle, only two of his men had seen Loring brought in tied up for the first meeting with Cass. The inspection in Pueblo was planned so there would be no gossip when they arrived at Denver City for a very public wedding.

As Kyle walked up to the big house for a talk with Cass, he wondered if she was happy with his choice. "What a son-of-a-bitchin' pickle," he muttered.

He found Cass in the parlor, a plain, functional room with rough-hewn masculine furniture and bright Mexican rugs spread across the plank floor. She had changed into a dress and had her hair swept up in some sort of fancy concoction. He could smell the fragrance of Rosario's home cooking wafting from the kitchen.

He smiled to himself as he realized she planned to soften Loring up with feminine wiles. "Shore smells better 'n Sour Mash's sonofabitch stew," he said, sniffing deeply.

Cass's fingers whitened as she gripped the back

of a big oak chair. "After days on the trail, the least I can do is feed him before I present my deal to him."

" 'N ta make it more appealin', yew decided ta dress th' part." His face was guileless. "Good idee, Cass." Maybe this would work out after all. If Loring cleaned up half as well as he suspected the Yankee would, he and Cass would make a striking couple.

Cass dismissed the Texan's remarks and began briskly ticking off a list of details. "We should reach an agreement this evening. If so, I'll ride to Denver tomorrow early and notify that wretched Attorney Smith. He'll need to witness the ceremony. I'll contact Father Evans at the Episcopal church. The marriage will be private and small. This has to be legal, but I don't want any more publicity or questions than absolutely necessary. Oh, yes, another thing. He'll need a complete wardrobe. I'll send the tailor from Denver with a selection of clothes to be altered. We received a shipment of men's suits and accessories recently. Loring's 'trousseau' will be ready before he arrives." She smiled with sardonic humor.

Damned if she hadn't given this a lot of thought! "Whut yew gonna tell folks 'bout how yew met yore bridegroom?"

Cass shrugged. "I'll just tell Attorney Smith and Father Evans that we met back East when I was making that wagon deal last year. I'll concoct a few more details with Loring tonight." She hated the nervous edge to her voice.

Sensing her tension in spite of her veneer of control, Kyle hesitated, then said, "Yew shore yew don't wanna wait a few days? Sorta git ta know one another a mite first?"

"No. I've wasted too much time as it is."

"Whut if he says no?" Sensing the stubborn toughness in the Yankee, Kyle feared the possible consequences.

Cass's face looked pale and strained, but her expression was hard. "Then he'll hang."

Still under guard, Steve was escorted to the big house. *Damn, this is an armed camp!* He looked around the corrals full of mules and horses. Plenty of stock to steal, but too many armed men guarding them—and him. He was as much a prisoner in Colorado as he'd been in the Nations. "At least I'm clean," he muttered under his breath as he was ushered into the house by Lober. The two gunmen then withdrew, leaving him standing like a dunce in the big open room that served as a parlor of sorts. The smell of food wafting from the kitchen made his mouth water. He wondered how many people were here in the house with Cass Clayton.

His thought was interrupted by a soft swish as she entered the room from a side door. Cass was dressed in a simple yellow muslin gown, plainly cut, yet revealing an ample amount of creamy skin and outlining the softly swelling curves of her willowy body. Bright masses of coppery curls were piled high on her head, adding to her already considerable height. Dressed in the outlandish shirt and pants she had been attractive. Dressed as a woman, she was breathtaking.

Cass steeled herself for his perusal. Men had always found her physically attractive, but all the simpering dandies and leering miners in the territory had never upset her as this man did. She countered his inspection by giving one of her own.

Bathed and shaven, he was much more than passable looking. The crisp white shirt stretched tautly across broad shoulders. Plain dark wool pants outlined his long, rangy legs. If she didn't know him to be a dude, she'd envision him as a horseman. His every move was lithe and graceful. That chiseled face, with the grizzled beard removed, was arrestingly handsome.

Not liking the train of her own thoughts, she addressed him brusquely, "We might as well have dinner before we discuss business. I assume you're hungry?"

Puzzled, he let her mention of "business" pass by and admitted, "I'm starved. Neither Hunnicut nor I have had anything but charred jackrabbit and beans for a week."

"Rosario is a good cook," she said as she preceded him into the dining room. A long table was set with only two places at one end. It looked embarrassingly intimate to Cass as she sat down. As if by habit, Steve pulled out her chair and assisted her, then seated himself across from her. His unconscious manners were not lost on Cass. He was obviously a man of some refinement.

The short, plump Mexican woman named Rosario served them roasted pork with candied yams and crisp green beans. The meal was delicious, and Steve found himself voraciously hungry. Not knowing what lay ahead, but glad of a reprieve from prison and its meager fare, he decided to enjoy the meal before they discussed whatever her business was. He noted as he took a second helping that she ate sparingly, methodically cutting the tender meat, then chewing and swallowing it slowly, as if forcing herself to do so. *What the hell's going on here?*

Cass watched him eat. In spite of his obvious hunger, his manners were impeccable. She asked him about his trip through Colorado with Kyle and again noted the educated quality of his voice. Back East he would have been a master of small talk, a real charmer with the ladies. She prayed her nervousness didn't show as she prodded him with a barrage of simple questions. Some he answered, some he evaded.

"I've given you an Easterner's impression of the barren waste of the Great American Desert. Now you tell me about your life in the West," he said with a frankly disarming smile.

"I run a freight line—the biggest in the territory. We ship everything from calico to dynamite—up in the farthest reaches of the Rockies, all the way down to the Arizona desert." The pride in her voice and glow in her eyes as she described the freighting business made her even more beautiful. She became so animated in describing her freight lines that the cold, calculating facade of earlier vanished. Steve began to feel he could genuinely like a woman who possessed such a passion for her work, unorthodox as it was for a female.

Lord knew, Cass Clayton was nothing like Amelia or Marcia. Still, she was holding something back, and a warning prickled his spine when she nodded for Rosario to clear the table and asked him to follow her back to the parlor.

"Now, I think it's time to discuss some important matters," she said as she turned to face him in the middle of the big, comfortable room. "Have a seat, Mr. Loring. I promise not to eat you," she added tartly, indicating the sofa and seating herself briskly in a chair across from it.

He grinned lazily and took the proffered seat,

noting how she had chosen to distance herself from him. "But I haven't said a word about not eating you."

Her head jerked up from fussing with her skirts and her eyes flashed. "After the dinner you just polished off, I should think you'd have had your fill. Besides, if I snap my fingers, three rifle barrels will be leveled on you before you can blink," she replied sweetly.

Steve's grin faded, but his voice betrayed no emotion. "You obviously take pleasure in brutalizing people you have at a disadvantage, Miss Clayton." Cass's cheeks appeared scorched, as if they had been touched by a torch.

He leaned forward, placed his arms on his knees, and stared witheringly at her. "Why don't we end this little charade right now? Your hired gun paid three hundred dollars and change to get me out of a tumbleweed wagon. He escorted me at gunpoint across the most godforsaken wilderness west of the Sahara, just to deliver me to you. Why, Miss Clayton?"

His eyes bore into her like posthole spades into soft mud. She swallowed and forced herself to return the hard stare. Facing down mean drunks, even armed bandits, had never been this difficult!

She willed herself to answer his question with one of her own. "Are you married, Mr. Loring?" Her voice was cool and steady. Good.

He quirked an elegant brow until it almost met the straight, thick lock of hair falling across his forehead. "Odd. Hunnicut asked me the same question. I wasn't desperate enough to marry him. In your case, Miss Clayton, I don't think I'm desperate enough either. Care to elaborate a bit further?"

She stood up, fury flashing across her face. "Just answer my question, damn you!"

He smiled coldly. "No."

"As to being desperate enough, Mr. Loring, I think you'd better reevaluate your options." She paced swiftly across the floor to the fireplace. Gripping the mantel with one slim hand she stated, "You'll marry me or you'll hang. Kyle rescued you. Kyle can return you, right to Judge Parker's waiting gallows."

Again that chilly smile slashed across his hard, handsome face. "Don't you think, under the circumstances, we might at least be on a first name basis, Cass? Call me Steve. It isn't every day I get proposed to. Why me?"

She didn't move, but did avert her eyes from his harsh, questioning glare. Ignoring his attempt at familiarity, she said, "That should be pretty obvious, Mr. Loring. You're completely in my power."

A look of honest bewilderment crossed his face as he watched the beautiful woman's profile. He could see her swallow painfully. There was a great deal more going on here than she was telling him. "I still don't understand, Cass. Why would a wealthy, beautiful young woman force a wanted man to marry her?"

Now it was her turn to smile coldly. "Precisely because you *are* a wanted man. I could marry any one of hundreds of men in the territory—and they'd get everything—everything I've slaved to build! Clayton Freighting is my birthright, and I won't give it over to any man." She bit off each word as if it was wrenched from deep inside her.

Dawning comprehension spread across his face.

"To keep your 'empire' you have to marry. Your parents' decision?"

"My father's decision. His will was quite explicit. My brothers would have inherited, but they died in childhood. A mere female was all he had left. Of course, I was deemed unworthy."

"So he wanted a son-in-law to take over—and you want to keep control yourself. Neat. I'm under your thumb but the will's fulfilled. A docile husband. Very neat!" He stood up and walked over to a side table where he saw a decanter and glasses. He needed a drink. Maybe the ice princess with the incongruously volcanic temper could use one, too.

"There's more," she said softly, still unable to look at him. Suddenly he was standing much too close to her, handing her a glass of sherry. She took it and sipped, then coughed.

He swallowed the amber liquid in one clean gulp. Leaning against the mantel, he let the empty glass dangle casually in his hand. "How long must this marriage of convenience go on? Is it a life sentence?"

She stiffened and took another fortifying swallow. "No. Only a year, maybe less . . ." She hesitated and then steeled herself, "It won't be a 'marriage of convenience,' Mr. Loring. My father's will was not only unbreakable, but very thorough. I have to produce a male child to inherit. I . . . we have only a year left in which to accomplish it." She forced herself to look at him.

At first his dark gold cougar's eyes widened in amazement. Then, to her utter mortification, he threw back his head and roared with laughter. If she'd been carrying her blacksnake, she'd have peeled off his lips!

"I used to work on a stud farm in Kentucky before the war. How ironic!"

"Now you'll learn how the stallion must feel," she shot back coldly.

He stopped laughing and reached out to touch her cheek in a soft caress. As she flinched back instinctively, he said, "And you, my dear Cass, will learn how a mare feels."

She sensed the color stealing into her face and swore aloud. She hadn't blushed since she was twelve! "Don't think you can threaten me, Mr. Loring, or think you can escape. Kyle Hunnicut can track fly sign over cracked pepper. If you do anything to hurt me, I'll have you hunted down and killed—and believe me, out West you'll find hanging is one of the pleasanter ways to die!"

He strode over to the decanter and poured another glass of sherry. Tossing it down with a mock salute, he said, "To our wedding day, Cass . . . and night." His lips smiled, but his eyes were glacial.

She returned the cold stare. "We have an understanding, I assume. Good. As soon as you've . . . fulfilled your marital responsibilities, you'll be allowed to leave. I'll even see to it you receive ample compensation and safe passage back East—wherever you want to go to escape hanging," she added with a hint of spite to cover her humiliation. Discussing the subject of producing offspring with this hateful stranger was unhinging her usually unshakable nerve.

"How much?" His question was a flat, bold insult and he knew it, but if he was reduced to being a stud, he would damn well receive a decent fee for services rendered.

Cass flinched, but recovered quickly. "I hadn't considered the amount. You say you worked on a breeding farm. The irony doesn't escape me, either, I can assure you. What did your employer receive for the services of one of his thoroughbred stallions?''

He saluted her with his empty glass. "I'll give you your due, lady. You've got plenty of nerve. At least as long as I don't get too close."

With that he set the glass down, strode over to the mantel, and swept an arm around her waist pulling her against him. She didn't back down or struggle as he studied her strong, beautiful face. Her cold, level stare indicated she was damn sure of her power to control him.

As he bent down and savaged her mouth, he could feel the soft pressure of her breasts against his chest. Her long, slim legs pressed to his thighs as he pulled her tighter into his embrace. God, she fit so well, felt so good, smelled so sweet! It had been months since he'd had a woman, and the beautiful, infuriating one in his arms inflamed his senses with a sudden rush of passion. His tongue teased her tightly clamped lips. He pulled her hair loose from it pins and buried one hand against her scalp. She gasped in outrage and he took advantage, plunging his tongue inside to taste her mouth. His ardor was rewarded with a sharp bite. Simultaneously, she dug a wickedly pointed heel into his instep, forcing him to release her.

Cass backed off, panting and shivering with loathing as he touched his bloody tongue with one hand and cursed fluently.

"I might have known your stupid Yankee army couldn't even teach a man how to swear," she said contemptuously. "Now, if you have the brains of a piss ant and the discipline of a half-broke jackass, you'll keep your filthy hands to yourself, you misbegotten son-of-a-bitch dog in the heat of hell's lowest level!"

The whole diatribe of epithets was delivered so fast and effortlessly that Steve realized it had to be a reflex action born of much practice. He smiled nastily. "I never heard a woman cuss that well ... too bad your voice isn't deep enough!"

Cass's triumphant sneer turned to fury. "You damn Yankee," she said with loathing.

He shrugged dismissively. "I'm getting no lady wife in this bargain, am I?"

"No gentleman paws a woman the way you did, so we're even!" After retreating a pace, she stood her ground defiantly.

"One thousand," he said quietly. "That's my stud fee. And if you want to fulfill your father's will, you'll not only have to pay me, you'll have to suffer my *pawing* you a lot more after we're married. I assume a woman with your colorful vocabulary understands barnyard facts of life?"

She hated him, standing in front of her so calm, so overbearing, daring her! Cass was caught in her own trap and she knew it, but she would never let him know how badly frightened she was.

Her mother's face, wan and listless, flashed before her eyes, then her father's scowling, harsh countenance. She forced the images to recede, then clenched her fists and said, "One thousand it is, but I'll tell you when you may 'be of service,' Mr. Loring. Try touching me at any other time and I'll show you how well I wield a blacksnake!"

Winner of 6 *Romantic Times* Awards!

Cassandra Clayton could run her father's freighting empire without the help of any man, but without one she could never produce a male child who would inherit it all. When Cass saved Steve Loring from a hangman's noose, he seemed to be just what she needed—a stud who would perform on command. But from the first, Steve made it clear that he wanted Cass's heart and soul in the bargain. Although his sarcastic taunts made her dread the nights she must give him her body, his exquisite lovemaking made her long to give him all that he asked—and more!

_3345-3 $4.99 US/$5.99 CAN